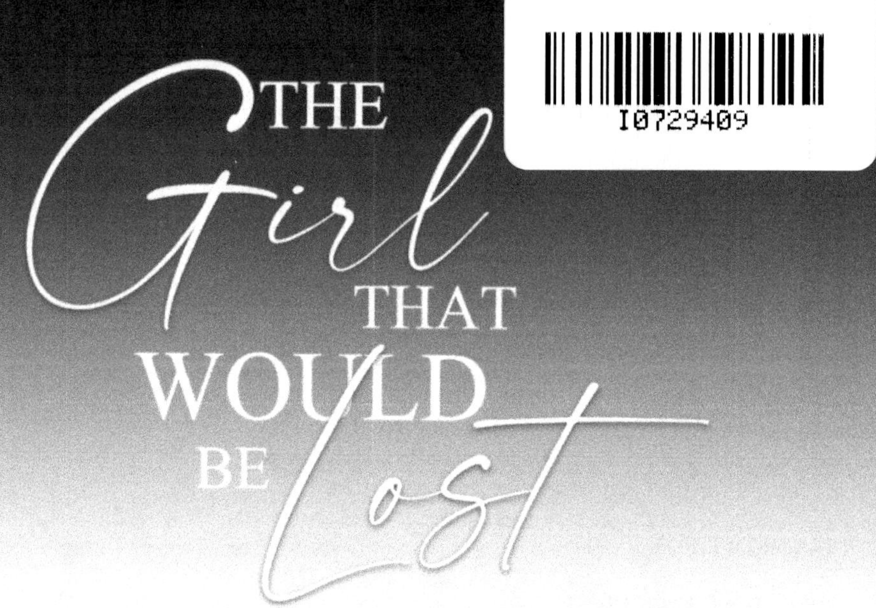

BROOKLYN CROSS

The author Brooklyn Cross acknowledges the trademarked status and trademark owners of familiar wordmarks, products, actors' names, television shows, books, characters, video games, and films mentioned in this fiction work.

❀ Created with Vellum

Warning

This is a Dramatic Romance novel and
is intended for mature audiences only.
This book is for sale to adults ONLY, as defined
by the country's laws in which you made
your purchase.
This book may contain violence,
graphic scences that include
non-consensual
and dubious consensual sexual scenes,
alcohol, tobacco drug use, strong language,
real life and fictional depicted scenes
that some readers may find disturbing
or hard to read.
Like most other content rating systems this is
only used as a guide.

The Battered Souls World

The collection of stories in, The Battered Souls World
is dedicated to everyone who has felt the
harsh touch of this world and bent but did not break.

Autumn Winds doth what blow,
Scattering my soul too and fro.
I reach for your hand from the sky, but
You don't see me...I float on by.
Tossed and turned I tumble on,
Winds of autumn ravage this lowly pawn.
But, then one day wings do grow,
So I no longer simply blow.
The sky is now my domain,
And I can weather any rain.
~ Brooklyn Cross

Playlist

Right Through You - Alanis Morissette

Strawberry Wine - Deana Carter

Love Yourself - Justin Bieber

Fingers Crossed - Lauren Spencer Smith

I Hope - Gabby Barrett

SNAP - Rosa Linn

Wagon Wheel - Darius Rucker

Leave A Light On - Tom Walker

Numb - Marshmello & Khalid

House of Memories - Panic! At the Disco

Flowers Need Rain - Preston Pablo & Banx

Slow Hands - Niall Horan

Rescue Me - Unions & Half Light

Back in Time - Daughtry

You Don't Own Me - SAYGRACE

You Are The Reason - Calum Scott

A Woman Like You - Johnny Reid

Home - Michael Buble

Amazing Grace - Annie Villeneuve

(Standalone Books Shared World Romance- Dark 2-3 Spice 2-3)

The Girl That Would Be Lost

The Boy That Learned To Swim (Coming Soon)

The Girl That Would Not Break (Coming Soon)

The Brothers of Shadow and Death Series

(Dystopian/Cult/Occult/Poly MMF Romance - Dark 3-4 Spice 3-4)

Anywhere (Coming Soon)

Seven Sin Series

(Multi Author/PNR/Angel and Demons/Redemption - Dark 2-5 Spice 3-5)

Greed by Brooklyn Cross

Lust by Drethi Anis

Envy by Dylan Page

Gluttony by Marissa Honeycutt

Wrath by Billie Blue

Sloth by Talli Wyndham

Pride by T.L. Hodel

BEST
FRIENDS

KAT

THE ARGUMENT WAS LOUD, *louder than any I'd ever heard them have before. As it went on and on, rising and falling in violence, I sat with my legs curled up under me on the bed and leaned into Jake, who mirrored my position. We didn't need to say anything—we knew what this argument meant. Words like 'divorce' and 'I hate you' and the sound of pots crashing screamed out that we would be shipped off to another home.*

It would be yet another place where we couldn't trust anyone—another place where monsters came in the form of other people and not some harmless blue, furry creatures that snuck out of the closet at night like in the stories my mom used to tell me. Jake laid his hand on the bed between us, palm upward and fingers spread, and I took the invite, laying my hand on top of his.

"Do you think they'll send us to separate homes?" I asked, not really wanting an answer and fearing that he would confirm my suspicions.

Lifting my head from his shoulder, I stared into the green eyes that always reminded me of spring grass. They were so bright, standing out against his dark hair and fair skin. He was the cutest boy I'd ever seen, but he was my best friend. He was my only friend.

Jake was the only person I trusted in this entire world, and I didn't want to be forced to leave him.

Jake stared into my eyes and didn't say anything for the longest time. His hand gently squeezed mine before he lifted a shoulder and let it drop.

"It don't matter. I'll look for you, and everything will still be like normal, just with two homes to choose from to hang out."

"I think you're trying to make me feel better," I mumbled before laying my cheek on my knees. "I don't have that kind of luck."

"We don't need luck. We will make a pact right now that we will always look for one another. No matter what happens, we will find one another again," he said. I could hear the quiet sincerity in his voice.

Jake straightened his legs, which were way longer than my own even though he was only a year and a half older. Following his lead, I did the same, giggling as I wiggled my brightly colored toenails in front of me. The nail polish had been my birthday gift from Jake. I was pretty sure he'd stolen it, but I didn't ask because I didn't want to know. It was the nicest gift anyone had gotten me since before my parents died, and asking would've felt like ruining it.

"You really like that polish, huh?"

My smile as I looked over at him couldn't have been any wider. His answering smirk clued me in that I'd been staring at the dimple in his cheek, and I blushed, ducking my head to look back at my toes.

"I love it. Now, wherever I am, I'll have a rainbow with me."

"I kinda got you something else, too," Jake said, running his hand through his hair.

Slam!

We both jumped, the little bubble we'd cocooned ourselves in popping with the loud noise. The following vibrations shook the walls, rattling the lone picture hanging on the other side of the room.

"I fucking hate you, you mother fucking asshole!"

My eyes went wide as I heard Mrs. Jones scream the house down. More doors slammed, and Jake's arm went around my shoulders, pulling me into his side as I shook. I hated the sound of shouting, and I couldn't stop the tears from filling my eyes as the fight seemed to go on and on with no sign of stopping. Embarrassed, I looked away from Jake, but if he saw them, he didn't say anything.

When the sounds of the house being torn apart finally stopped, Jake jumped off the bed and went to his side of the room. I'd always thought it was strange that they'd put him and me in the same room together and had even argued against it when I'd first arrived. I mean, who ever heard of a foster brother and sister who weren't little kids anymore sharing a room? It was weird, and my experience with guys up to that point hadn't been good, either.

The thing was, now I couldn't picture living any other way.

"What are you doing?" I asked.

"I told you I got you something else," he said, glancing over his shoulder at me as he opened the nightstand drawer. He stood and turned, his face glowing with mischief as he smiled widely. His fist was clenched tightly, so I couldn't tell what it held.

"What is it?" I bounced to the end of the bed, my eyes glued to his hand.

"Kat, I want you to always feel like I'm with you, even when, you know...shit goes sideways." He nodded toward the door. We both knew that no home you were sent to was safe and that at any moment, your

entire world could be blown up. This wasn't the first foster home for either of us. We were both products of a broken system that no one cared enough to fix.

Stepping forward, Jake came to a stop in front of me. After a moment of silently staring, he blushed, and I could feel my own face heating up.

"Just...here." He held out his hand, and I cupped mine underneath it to catch whatever he was giving me. A sudden thought had me pulling them back.

"Wait, it's not a spider or something gross, is it?"

"No, it's not a spider or something gross. I promised that I'd never do that again," he said, rolling his eyes.

Laughing at his exasperation, I nodded, sticking a hand back out.

"Okay."

"Close your eyes. Please," Jake pouted, and even though I thought he was being ridiculous, I closed them anyway. As soon as my eyes were shut, I felt something softly fall into my hand. It was light and cool to the touch. "Okay. You can look now."

I opened my eyes, and as soon as they fell on the necklace now nestled in my palm, I wanted to cry.

"Jake, it's beautiful." I held up the necklace, a gold-colored chain with a tiny rainbow pendant hanging from the end, and had to cover my mouth to choke back a sob.

"Hey, don't cry. It was supposed to make you happy."

"I am happy, and sad, and I don't want to be separated." The tears finally fell—there was no holding them back anymore.

Jake sat down on the edge of the bed and tucked back a piece of hair from my face.

"I know, Kit Kat, but if we are, you'll have this to remind you that one day, we will find our end of the rainbow together."

I'd fallen in love with my best friend that day. I might only have been thirteen, but that love was as real and as strong as any that an adult might feel, and the feeling had never left. Over the years, there had always been a hole inside me that never healed, an emptiness that I couldn't explain, that had formed on the day Jake was taken from my life.

Only a week after Jake gave me the necklace, a pair of social workers had come and torn us apart, just like I'd feared. Even though Jake and I cried and screamed that we wanted to go to the same home, nothing we said mattered. The social workers had their orders, and those orders outlined exactly how much they cared about what we wanted—which was not at all. Tired of trying to reason with us, the social workers had just grabbed ahold of whatever arm or clothing they could reach to tug us toward the cars waiting to take us away.

In a rush of strength fueled by desperation from watching Jake get pulled farther and farther away, I'd broken out of the hold my social worker had on me to run to him. Throwing our arms around each other, we'd clung together as hard as we could until we were physically ripped apart. At that point, the social workers had given up on being gentle and half-drug, half-carried us where they wanted us to go.

Still struggling, I'd watched him disappear into one car while I was shoved in the back seat of another. As the cars drove off in opposite directions, the only thing we could do was stare into each other's terrified eyes through the rear windows. Even when I couldn't see him any longer, I hadn't taken my eyes off that window. I'd felt like if I didn't, then maybe, by some magic, he would appear again if I just kept looking long enough.

But of course, he hadn't, and that was the problem.

Jake was *the one*. He wasn't just a boy I shared a room with, not just my friend, and not just the one I trusted when shit went bad. No, he was my heart person, the other half of my soul, and I'd never felt complete ever since. Not many can say they met their soulmate at the age of ten or was forced to leave them at thirteen, and every day it hurt like hell that I'd never see mine again. Like a desert starving for the rain, I longed for him.

All of it—the years of abuse and heartache and never belonging —had led me to where I was now: in the back of a bus riding away from the trash fire that was my life.

I aimlessly rubbed at the little rainbow pendant in my hand. It was tarnished, the color long gone, but I always did my best to keep it on me. I'd had more than one panic attack stemming from not being able to find it, and I'd always had to keep it hidden from Richard. If he'd seen it, he would've thrown it out.

As the bus finally slowed, I lifted my head from where it lay against the glass and wiped away the tear trailing down my chin. Stuffing the pendant into the little velvet bag I kept it in, I put it in my purse and stood up to grab my suitcase.

In a long list of terrifying things that had happened to me in my life, this move felt like the most frightening. Here I was, thirty years old with no job experience and in the middle of a messy divorce, moving to a new city to start my life over once again. A fresh start, they called it—a clean slate. I didn't really care what they called it. I just wanted a chance to be normal, and maybe even to be happy, if either of those things were even possible. I hoped to find them here.

As I stepped off the bus and looked around, I drew in a deep breath of the seaside air, the cool breeze lifting my spirits the same as it lifted the hair from my shoulders.

From this moment on, I could no longer be Kat. I needed to be someone who could stand on their own, and I couldn't let Richard find me. Something I'd realized as I'd planned my escape was that I wasn't entirely sure that he wouldn't try to kill me if he did. I wasn't taking the risk, not again.

Katelin Andrews was officially dead, and Alexis Dupree was born.

BEST
FRIENDS

KAT

WALKING down the sidewalk along the main street of my new home, a little spark of hope came alive inside me as people I'd never met before smiled at me and said hello as they walked past. Continuing down the street, I looked around, taking everything in with eager eyes. The little town I'd decided to call home was lined with old shops that looked out toward the water. A white church sat on the hill like a bright beacon among the spattering of pretty homes. I loved that some were painted bright colors and had docks that led down to the water.

Taking a deep breath I sighed. This place felt like where I was always supposed to be. A vibrant red leaf fluttered to the ground in front of me, and as I bent to pick it up, I smiled. It was beautiful here.

"Hi ya, dear. You look a little lost. Do you need some help?" I gave a start and lurched forward at the sudden sound of a voice right behind me. "Oh, my dear, I'm so sorry. I didn't mean to startle you," it continued, and I turned around to find an older woman standing there.

I couldn't help the pounding in my chest, but I tried to hide my nervousness as I held out a hand.

"Sorry about that. I was lost in thought. Hi, I'm K...Alexis, but everyone calls me Lexi."

"Nice to meet you K...Alexis, otherwise known as Lexi," the older woman teased, the corner of her mouth turning up and showing off a dimple.

I flushed hotly at the epic fail that was my first try with the new name.

"It's Alexis." I shook my head. "Not sure what I was about to answer."

"Just teasing you, dear. I'm Marie." She held out her hand in return, and I was surprised by the firmness of her grip. She had a perfectly styled haircut full of lush curls that were pure white. I'd never seen hair so naturally white. It looked stunning with her blue eyes and bright pink vest. On closer inspection, it looked like she was in the middle of working out. She had on hot pink yoga pants and sneakers, and instead of standing still, she bounced slightly back and forth from foot to foot.

"Nice to meet you, Marie."

"So, did you want help to find your way?"

The question was so simple, yet in my world, it seemed so much bigger.

"Yes, I'd love it, thank you. I'm trying to find this address." I held out the small paper I had clutched in my hand. Marie took the paper and inspected it before smiling.

"Well, well, well. So you're the new girl that has moved in next door to me. Us meeting like this was kismet. Come on, follow me." Marie paused. "Do you need me to go get a car for your suitcases?"

I looked at the plain gray suitcase on wheels next to me and shook my head.

"No, this is all I brought."

Although I smiled widely, trying to deflect, Marie gave me a look that had me shifting uncomfortably. I didn't want to share my past. This move was supposed to be a step forward. Marie pursed her lips and made a humming noise, like she was going to press for answers, but decided to hold her tongue.

"Well, alright, then. Follow me." With that, Marie was off. For someone who looked retired, she was *fast*.

"Have you lived here your whole life?" I asked as I practically had to sprint to keep up with the older woman, who was busy power walking like a machine up the incline toward the white church.

"Yup. Third generation in the same house. My daughter Olivia lives with me." Marie looked over at me. "You two will probably hit it off. She's about your age."

"Oh, that's great," I said, but internally I groaned. The last thing I needed right now was a new friend.

"Olivia owns the local bookstore, and if you want a good deal, you tell her that I sent you in." Marie gave me a wink.

As we moved higher up the slope, the area was even prettier than in the pictures of the town I'd looked up. The place was so different from Vegas's bright lights, yet it already felt more like home than Vegas ever had.

Whenever you talked to someone who didn't live in the city, they talked about it like it was this magical and mystical place full of endless parties, colorful lights, and limitless possibilities. That was all true—if you owned a casino or were a doctor, politician, or someone famous. Once you panned away from the bright lights and lies of fortune, there was a lot of poverty and violence that television liked to sweep under the rug hiding just out of sight.

"How long do you think you'll be staying?" Marie asked.

"I don't know. I've leased the house for six months, and I have to let the property owner know if I want to continue on at the five-month mark." I gave a little shrug. "I already love the look of it here, but I will have to wait and see if we're a good match," I said jokingly, gesturing around to show I meant the town and me.

"Good idea. Never want to marry too quickly," she teased back. I managed to keep the smile on my face, but the comment scraped at the scar in my chest that was my heart. That was advice I could've used ten years ago.

"Hi, Marie," a gentleman across the road called out and waved. He was busy watering his flowers, but he smiled widely at Marie as she got closer. He looked like he'd stepped right out of a small-town movie, with a thick mustache, sweater vest, khaki pants, and, to complete the look, glasses and a tweed golf cap.

"Hi, Douglas," Marie called, waving back. She lowered her voice and whispered, "He has been hitting on me for years. He just won't give up."

I took in the soft blush on her cheeks. It could've been caused by the brisk walk, sure, but I had a feeling it had everything to do with Douglas despite what she said.

"Here you go, my dear. This is the spot. And, of course, I live right there." Marie pointed to a pretty yellow home with white shutters and, despite the changing season, large flower baskets filled with a wide array of species, all surrounded by immaculately bright green grass. It was gorgeous.

It was also in stark contrast to the little home I'd just rented next to it. The green walls were in desperate need of a sanding and a new coat of paint, while the decorative trim along the roof was half missing, the parts left were gray and weathered. The lawn was both uneven and overgrown, with patches that hadn't filled in at all making it look more like the back of a mangy coyote than a proper yard.

"I know she's not much to look at, but the home has been kept up inside, and you can't find a prettier view," Marie assured.

I turned around and took a deep breath as I stared out over the wide expanse of water that stretched out to border more homes along the far bank. They dotted the swath of land with bright pops of salmon and blue interspersed with the colors of the trees standing tall around them. I loved the look of the trees. I'd never seen the changing of leaf colors in person, and the cool air mixed with the fiery reds and vibrant oranges filled me with more warmth than a record-high summer day in Vegas. It was truly the prettiest site I'd ever seen.

I wiped away the lone tear that had escaped my eye as I turned back to give the woman standing next to me a smile.

"Thank you, Marie."

"No problem, dear. Are you okay?" she asked. At her concerned look, I nodded, actually meaning it.

"I am now."

Marie patted my shoulder before giving it a gentle shove.

"The key is under the flowerpot closest to the door."

"Oh yeah, I hadn't thought about that," I replied, startled. Everything had ended up moving so fast right at the end that some of the little details hadn't gotten worked out before I had to leave...like how to get into my house.

Marie laughed, and the sound somehow made me feel like the world was made of fresh apple pie.

"Well then, I guess it's a good thing I'm your landlord and knew about that great hiding spot."

"You're my landlord?"

"Don't look so surprised, dear. Even us old birds can be business savvy."

It was my turn to blush, my face heating up instantly.

"Of course, I wasn't insinuating, it's just...oh, never mind." I stuck out my hand. "Nice to meet you, Marie-my-landlord, and thank you for showing me the way." She gripped my hand in return, the smile never fading from her face.

"I'll have to have you over for dinner one night. I make a mean lasagna. Let me know if you need anything," Marie said, waving as she wandered away toward her own home. With her departure, a little of my optimism seemed to leave as well.

Now that I was finally here and this was real, the apprehension over all the what-ifs was settling in. What if he didn't sign the divorce papers? What if I couldn't find a job here? What if I hated it here? What if he found me?

No matter what, I couldn't go back. It had taken ten years to cut the ropes Richard had mentally, and at times, physically, tied around my throat.

"You're not going to know if you don't like it here unless you give it a try," I whispered to myself before taking the first step toward my new home and the new life it represented. My eyes roamed over everything that needed fixing, and instead of seeing the home as run down, I saw it as if I were looking at my own heart.

It was worn, battered and abused by the world around it, but there was potential.

3

JAKE

MY HEAD FUCKING HURT. Blinking a couple of times in the piercing morning light, I reached blearily for my sunglasses before realizing that I didn't even remember where they were. I didn't know where *I* was, for that matter.

"Mmm, you're awake," a female voice said as a hand landed on my chest and rubbed all over it. Laying one arm over my eyes to block out the intense light, I turned my head to stare at the brunette in bed next to me. She was cute, with her hair a tousled mess and her blue eyes sparkling with sexual mischief, but they weren't the blue eyes I longed to see.

It had been seventeen years since I'd last spoke to Kat, and no matter what I did, who I fucked, or where I traveled, I couldn't get her out of my mind.

"Did you want to stay for breakfast? I can order something in," the girl asked.

"I'm sorry...." I paused as I wracked my brain trying to remember her name.

"Lisa," she prompted.

"Yes, of course, Lisa, but I need to get going." Swinging my legs over the side of the bed, I looked around and found my clothes lying in a pile on the floor. A pad of paper on the nightstand obnoxiously stated the name of the hotel, and as I reached out to grab it, I tried to remember how in the hell I'd gotten to Miami. I'd been in New York. Where the fuck was my motorcycle?

Lisa's hands rubbed at my shoulders before sliding down my chest, her tits pressing into my back as she pressed close.

"Are you sure you don't want to stay?" she purred into my ear, and though my dick twitched, I shook my head.

"Thanks, but I've got to go." Standing, I grabbed my clothes and stumbled across the room before closing the bathroom door behind me. I made sure to lock it—Lisa seemed like the type that would try for a third time.

The lights were too bright for the small space, and my head violently swam from all of the movement. Grabbing the counter, I closed my eyes and spent a few moments focusing on keeping my stomach from flipping inside out before reaching to turn on the tap. I splashed some cool water on my face before daring to actually look at myself.

"Yup, I look as bad as I feel," I mumbled to my reflection. If my eyes were any more bloodshot, people would think I had pinkeye, and the redness was only accentuated by the dark circles ringing my eyes like I was some kind of raccoon.

Pinching the bridge of my nose, I tried to piece together what had happened, but all I could come up with was a party at some swanky joint in the Big Apple that was thrown in honor of reaching twenty million followers.

The door handle rattled, and I stared at it like a grizzly was trying to break in.

"Jake, are you sure you don't want me to join you?"

What the fuck was it with this girl?

"No, I'm good." I shoved my hand into the pocket of the black jeans I was still clutching and pulled out my phone. It was almost dead, but it informed me that it had been an entire day since the party. Unlocking the phone, I thumbed through my call log, texts, and photos trying to get a timeline together of the shit I'd gotten into since then.

"Are you sure? I don't want to head home yet. My husband isn't as much fun."

Great, she was fucking married. I hated having run-ins with pissed-off husbands or boyfriends.

"Where are you from, Lisa?" I asked, assuming she was still panting like a dog in heat on the other side of the door.

"From here in Miami. We met at the Dark Rose Club, don't you remember?"

I didn't, but I wasn't letting her know that.

"Yeah, just couldn't remember if you were from here. You might as well go home, Lisa. I need to have a business meeting shortly."

"I could wait and—."

"No. The answer is no. Now take a hint and get the fuck out," I barked out before immediately rubbing at my aching forehead. I hadn't meant to be that rude, but all I wanted was for her to go.

"Wow, rude. No wonder you don't have a girlfriend." I could hear her stomp around the large suite, presumably gathering her things, before the door to the hallway unceremoniously slammed shut.

Sighing, I unlocked the bathroom door and peeked my head out to make sure that Lisa wasn't actually still in the bedroom waiting to spring a sneak attack. She wasn't. Wandering over to the hallway door, I grabbed the 'do not disturb' sign and hung it outside on the doorknob before closing the door and flipping the bar lock. I'd learned the hard way that you couldn't be too careful.

The next destination was the mini bar, where I grabbed as many of the miniature bottles as I could before making my way over to the bed to dump my haul onto the rumpled sheets. Sitting, I stared down at the bottles surrounding me and groaned. What the fuck was I doing?

Flopping back on the bed, I spotted a half-empty bottle of water on the nightstand and managed to push myself far enough up the bed to grab it instead. The room was fancy enough to have little charging stations built into the nightstands. I took the opportunity to plug the phone into one of the charging docks before I chugged the water and rolled over to stare at the generic landscape picture hanging on the wall.

You'd think that being adored by millions would make you feel less lonely, but the opposite was true. It seemed like with each new follower gained, each new hit video put out, the more people only wanted to be around me for my money and a spot in the nonstop party that seemed to follow me around wherever I went. Sure, women threw themselves at me, but all they really wanted was the fancy meals, the selfies for their own social media feeds, and of course, the wild parties. They didn't actually give two fucks about me.

I should really go home and get my head right.

It had been over six months since I'd seen my parents, and each day that passed, it got harder and harder to think about facing them after all the shit I'd been doing. They had to know what I was up to —they weren't oblivious even though they tried to stay away from all the gossip.

The phone buzzed, pulling me out of the whirlpool of depression I'd fallen into, and I rolled over to see Miles's face on the screen.

"Oh shit," I mumbled, reaching for the damn thing before it vibrated right off the stand. After a deep breath, I swiped to accept the call. "Hey," I said, playing it casual. Miles was the closest thing I had to a friend on the road, but he also happened to be my manager, so he wasn't exactly fond of my habitual disappearing acts.

"Where the fuck are you? I've been looking for you everywhere," Miles said. The sound of a car door closing loudly echoed through the speaker and into my ear, making me wince.

"I told you, just use that 'find me' app thing."

"That's not the point, man. You fucking disappeared from the party that I arranged and didn't even have the decency to let me know where the fuck you were going, or if you were even still alive."

"Okay, mom," I teased, and a loud streak of swearing came through the phone in response. Someone was pissy.

"You're an asshole. How did you get to *Miami*, anyway?"

"So you knew where I was this whole time?" As my stomach flipped, my mouth filled with sour saliva, and I decided to lay my head down and put the phone on speaker before I threw up all over everything. I swallowed a couple of times to keep the contents of my stomach in place.

"I did, and I've already arranged a yacht cruise with a few girls for you to head back up here where you're supposed to be. At least the only place you can run off to on a boat is overboard."

My stomach did another flip at the idea of being on a moving boat.

"I don't want to," I groaned. I even sounded whiny to myself. Most people would be waving their hands in the air and yelling 'sign me up' if someone started handing out surprise cruises. The problem was, I was burnt out, and although the party life was great in short spurts, I couldn't remember the last time I had been sober for more than a week at a time. Even I could admit I was heading for a problem.

"I have a new potential sponsor from a hip clothing line and cologne brand that wants to meet you. I have it all arranged for you to show them a good time on the yacht. You'll have a week to convince them that you're the man they should be using for all their promotions. I'll take over from there."

"Did you not hear what I said?" I asked, getting annoyed.

"Oh, I heard you, but I'm choosing to ignore you. This is big, Jake. Like 'set for life' big."

"I don't think I can, man. I'm just not in the right headspace." I sighed, and from the other end of the line, I was greeted by silence, which was a change. "My liver, if nothing else, needs a break."

"How about this? You meet them for the meeting on the yacht. You show them a good time. Convince them to use you, and I won't book anything for you to attend for at least two weeks after," Jake said. He was starting to sound a little pissed himself.

"Two months," I countered.

"What?"

"You heard me. I want two months off to go home and just…I don't know, but I need the time off."

"Two months without posting or singing or appearances? Are you crazy? That is a lifetime in social media land. You'll be replaced."

A sudden wave of nausea made it clear my luck had run out. I rolled out of bed and grabbed blindly for the phone as I sprinted for the bathroom, making it to the toilet just in time before my stomach finally revolted. The smell of the puke was enough to make me do it again until I was reduced to dry heaving. Grabbing the handle, I flushed the toilet before flopping bonelessly back onto the tiled floor.

"I don't care," I panted into the phone. "It's either two months off or I end up in rehab and never do anything again. It's your choice." I hit the end call button before Miles could say anything more.

The phone buzzed a few moments later with the yacht information, which was apparently shoving off in about sixteen hours. That meant I had time to fucking sleep. The bed seemed too far away, though, so I simply closed my eyes.

BEST
FRIENDS

KAT

YAWNING, I stretched and wandered out of my new, very nice bedroom to find the coffee maker. The night before, I hadn't taken much time to figure out my surroundings, other than locating the bathroom, before crashing. Once I was in and the door was locked, all I'd wanted to do was sleep. The queen-sized bed was extremely comfortable, luckily, but the room was on the side of the house that faced the rising sun. No sleeping in was likely in my future, not with the sun pouring in the window and yelling at me to get up and get going.

The only other thing I'd done yesterday was text Eve to let her know I'd arrived alive. She'd texted back 'good' with a smiley face, and that was it. We'd agreed that we wouldn't communicate much until it was safe.

Part of me felt like I was being paranoid, yet the other part of my mind was yelling that I wasn't doing enough—that I should be moving to the other side of the world and hiring bodyguards. If I *could* hire any, that is. Other than the money I'd managed to hide away and the small sum that Eve was able to give me, I was essentially penniless. Every cent had to be used wisely. It sucked, but I'd choose poverty any day over what I'd left behind.

Almost everyone who'd listened to my story acted like I was crazy. The first thing anyone wanted to know was if he hit me. I almost walked out on the lawyer the only time I met him in person when he asked me that. All I could think was, "Oh great, here we go again—another man who thinks I'm overreacting."

Richard had threatened me, screamed at me, belittled me, and sexually assaulted me. Did he have to actually punch me to make it matter or to make the trauma more valid? It was such bullshit.

Pulling the housecoat someone had left behind in the closet around myself, I tied the sash in place and made my way around the small kitchen as I tried to find coffee to go with the coffee maker sitting on the counter. I was just standing up triumphantly with the coffee tin in my arms when a knock sounded through the house. My heart pounded hard as I stared at the wooden door, and the room shrunk in on me as I clung tightly to the tin.

Knock, knock.

"Kate, we need to get going," Richard said through the door.

"Just a second."

I smoothed down the golden dress that I'd spent hours trying to find, going from one boutique to the next in search of the perfect dress that would make me worthy of being on Richard's arm. I always felt like the ugly duckling next to my husband. He was tall, with perfect sun-kissed skin from spending hours a day on the golf course. His blond hair had just a smattering of salt and pepper at the sides, making him look even more handsome than he did the day I met him.

I'd met Richard during my Junior year of high school. I mean, I'd seen him around school before that, but I'd always been too shy to speak to the popular quarterback. Even though I'd managed to make the cheerleading squad, I never really fit in with the girls, or at the parties they would go to, because I didn't have the bank account that the rest of them had. The only girl on the team that I clicked with was a girl named Evelynn, though she only liked to be called Eve.

Eve was one of the most popular girls in school, yet she didn't have the typical self-absorbed air about her that the rest of the popular girls had. In fact, until I met Eve, I'd always felt like everyone was looking down on me, and honestly, I couldn't blame them—and that was with them not even knowing that I slept in a storage room in the back of an ice cream shop. With Eve, though, I never felt lesser. Her very presence somehow helped build up those around her.

As for Richard, he was the shining golden boy at the school, and when he asked me out on a date one day out of the blue, I almost fainted. I said yes, of course, even though I had no idea then what he saw in me—much like how I wasn't always sure what he saw in me now.

Primping once more in the mirror while staring critically at the updo I had done for the benefit tonight, I decided it was as good as it was going to get. Opening the door, I smiled widely as I watched my husband button his cufflink.

"So, what do you think?" I asked, twirling in a slow circle.

Richard looked over at me, and as his eyes roamed over my body in the dress, I was sure he was about to say something sweet. Instead, he shook his head.

"You can't go in that."

"What? Why?" I looked down at the stunning dress. He always said I looked amazing and that I could wear a paper bag and still make it look good. How was this dress not okay?

"I don't understand you, Kate. This is a doctor's benefit, not a whore parade. I'm not taking my wife out wearing that piece of classless trash."

"But...."

"Is that what you spent all my money on? That thing? Really, Kate?" He looked down at his watch before grabbing his suit jacket off the bed. "I don't have time to wait for you to change. Don't bother waiting up. I might just get a hotel room near the benefit." Without another look, Richard marched past me.

"But Richard, I can be quick," I said, chasing him out of the room.

He spun on his heel and glared at me.

"I'm too angry right now to take you anywhere. I swear you did this on purpose just to embarrass me in front of my friends and co-workers. You'd think you'd be a little more grateful for what I've done for you since I pulled you out of that rat-infested storage room and offered you the stars."

"But I am grateful," I said, voice barely above a whisper.

As Richard sneered in response, his eyes showed nothing but disgust.

"You have a funny way of showing it. No one else would put up with the shit you pull. I can't even be bothered listing all the things you've done lately. Like I said, don't wait up." Richard stormed out, taking all of the anger but none of the confusion or pain with him.

Tears pricked my eyes and slowly fell as I looked at myself in the large mirror in the hallway. The graceful line of the dress showed off my figure, while the scoop neck accentuated my chest without it being inappropriate for the event. The dress was long but stopped high enough to show off the cute golden heels I'd purchased to match.

It was a black-tie affair and the theme was glitter and gold. I didn't think I could have looked any more the part. What was wrong with the way I looked? In my mind, the words 'whore parade' replayed over and over again.

The knock sounded through the house again, and I gulped in a large mouthful of air as I forced myself to breathe as the present snapped back into being around me.

He doesn't know where you are. He doesn't know where you are. He doesn't know where you are.

Chanting the mantra in my head, I made my way to the door. Peeking out the window, the only thing I saw was a pretty blonde woman, and I felt relief wash through my body. Unlocking the door, I opened it to the smiling woman.

"Hi, I'm Olivia. My mom, Marie, said you'd be expecting me. You can call me Olly. My mom said you just moved in and that I should introduce myself on my way to work." As she held out a cookie tin for me to take, her eyes smiled just like her mother's.

"Hi, Olly. I'm Alexis, but everyone calls me Lexi," I said, taking the tin from her hands. "Did you want to come in? I'm just about to put some coffee on." I smiled back at her a little shakily but genuinely.

"I'd love to, but I have to get to the store and open up. Those rowdy romance readers are ravenous when I get my latest romance books in." She giggled, and even though it would have sounded silly coming from most adults, for some reason, it only made her seem more adorable. It made her nose wrinkle up like a bunny's. "You should totally come by once you're up to it. If you can come around lunchtime, I'll show you around. Pete's has the best sandwiches and homemade pizza, and the Maverick and Musket is *the* place to go for a burger and beer, but don't eat any of the desserts." Olly made a face like she was remembering something terrible, and I laughed.

"I'll keep that in mind. I'm just beginning the process of unpacking, but if I can get myself motivated, I'll come meet you for lunch."

"Perfect. See you later." Olly turned and made her way back to Marie's house. She waved as she slipped into a silver Volkswagen, and I waved back. Closing the door after stepping back inside, I opened the tin to find a mouthwatering assortment of cookies. They all looked homemade, too.

Picking out a sugar cookie, I took a big bite. I paused as I wondered what Richard would think of me eating cookies out of a tin for breakfast. There was no question—he would totally hate it. A smile spread across my face as I marched into the kitchen and grabbed a handful of goodness from the tin just because I could.

It was a small victory, but it felt momentous. He'd never make me feel bad ever again. I put on the pot of coffee and then turned on the radio sitting on the counter, which was tuned to some top hits station. I didn't even care what song was playing and just sang along at the top of my lungs, making up words when I didn't know them.

I'd never been allowed to hum or sing when Richard was around, just like I wasn't allowed to go out with any of my friends who he felt tarnished his image, which was basically all of them, or eat chocolate or anything sweet because I could put on weight. I wasn't allowed to wear anything revealing, but I also couldn't look like trailer park trash. I had to have dinner ready and waiting for when he got home, but I never knew what time he'd arrive—and I most certainly wasn't allowed to question the lipstick stains or smell of perfume on his clothes.

I was finally free, but did I even really know what that word meant anymore? It had been so long since I'd been able to make choices for myself that it was exciting yet completely terrifying to think about the limitless possibilities in front of me.

With a spring in my step, I wandered down to Main Street a couple of hours later. This, too, was also new. The ability to leave the house for something as frivolous as a walk had been absurd in my world. The only acceptable places I was ever allowed to go to were gyms, spas, or clothing shops, which Richard had seemed to think would appease my need to feel like a real person and not a pampered *thing* he controlled.

I'd been so young and dumb when I married him, but this fresh start was my do-over, and this time, I was doing things for *me*.

Shaking off my thoughts, I took in everything the quaint town had to offer. It seemed so perfect and idyllic. At a flower shop, I had to pause to stare in the window because the display was decorated so prettily. The woman behind the counter waved, and I smiled and waved back. Was this real? Could a place like this really exist? The more I saw, the more it looked like it did.

Douglas had been out sweeping the sidewalk in front of his home when I'd passed by, and there was something about the simple act that had made me want to cry.

Olly's bookstore, when I found it, was by far the busiest spot I'd seen in town. As the door opened, loud chatter and laughter drifted out along with the scent of fresh coffee. A cinnamon and spice scent was also strong in the air, like someone had just made fresh apple pie, and I sighed happily. The energy as I stepped into the store was truly infectious. I watched with amusement as women of all ages clung to books with half-naked guys on the front who would make anyone want to fan themselves. Olly hadn't been kidding about this being her best day or these her most ravenous of shoppers.

A hand raised above the crowd, and when I followed it down, I could see Olly's smiling face as she waved me over. Trying not to bump into anyone, I worked my way through a packed seating area where women lounging in large, plush chairs were already digging into their new purchases as they sipped hot drinks. Around the seating area, even more women perused the store while talking together about their favorite authors and book boyfriends.

"Hi there. You weren't kidding about being busy," I said as I glanced back at the packed store.

"Honestly, the romance books of all tropes are my biggest sellers. I'm thinking of downsizing some of the other areas to make room for more authors. I'd really like to create a whole indie author section over there to support them." Olly pointed to a section of shelves along the wall that was conspicuously free of book browsers. "I just need to figure out how to expand. Unfortunately, this spot really isn't big enough anymore for the store's needs."

"That seems like a great idea, and you know, I just might have to do some shopping of my own after lunch."

Olly held up a book with a steamy cover. A very steamy cover.

"I'm setting this one aside for you, then. I've been keeping it hidden for myself, but if you like things a little dark and spicy, this is the book for you."

"I don't know if I do. I haven't done much reading, but this is a great time to catch up and try new things," I answered, intrigued.

"Trust me. You're going to love it." Olly turned to look at the girl who was working the cash register. "Sam, this book is on hold, and I'm heading to Pete's for lunch. Are you okay here?"

"For sure. The rush has already died down a lot. See you after," Sam answered with a grin and a wink. She didn't look much older than nineteen, and as I stared at her youthful smile and her wireframe glasses and bright pink hair, a ripple of sadness spread through my chest.

I'd been young and full of life like that once, years ago. I'd had so many hopes and dreams, and a rush of bad decisions had turned everything upside down.

"You ready?" Olly touched my arm suddenly, and I jerked at the touch.

"Yeah," I smiled, hoping that it reached my eyes.

The walk to Pete's was brief, but the breeze off the water was cool enough to have me shivering despite the bright sun and the heavy sweater and jeans that I was wearing. Olly waved to everyone in the bistro as we entered, and I promptly wanted to drop down and crawl out the door as she called for everyone's attention. Every eye in the place turned to look at us.

"Hey, this is Lexi, everyone. She has just leased my mom's place, so if you see her around town, she is now one of us."

"Hi, Lexi," the group said, and although my cheeks warmed in embarrassment, I couldn't stop a grin from pulling at the corners of my mouth.

"Hi, everyone," I said quietly in response, tentatively raising my hand for a short wave.

"Don't worry. None of them bite, but they do love to call the Sheriff whenever they see someone new hanging around. It's like they think anyone new stopping in the town must automatically be a criminal." Olly rolled her eyes and stepped up to the counter.

There was comfort in knowing that about the town—it meant that if Richard did find me and showed up, I'd have that layer of protection. I suddenly felt a little calmer.

"What would you like? It's my treat," Olly asked, turning to look back at me.

"Oh, you don't have to do that."

"I know, but I want to. Now don't waste time arguing. I always get my way." The way she leaned on the counter and stared me down made me believe that wholeheartedly. Olly reminded me of Eve. People always gave in to her eventually.

Thinking of Eve sent a pang of sadness through me. I missed my friend, but I understood why it was too dangerous to talk. I wanted to tell her about the sights and how nice everyone was and then bug her to come visit.

"Alright, but only if I can treat you next," I said, crossing my arms over my chest.

Olly tapped her chin thoughtfully.

"You drive a hard bargain, but I'm in."

Laughing, I nodded in acceptance.

"What do you recommend?" I asked, looking over the menu board.

"Everything is good, but the pizza is to die for. Just heed the warning that it will become an obsession."

Olly turned to order her food while I stared dumbfounded at all the choices. The fact that I didn't know there were this many pizza choices available practically screamed out how locked up I'd been. Olly stepped aside, and then it was my turn. Casting my eyes around the board, I made a snap decision.

"Can I get the personal-size Mediterranean chicken pizza?" I asked the guy behind the counter.

Olly made a face, and I thought she was going to say my choice was terrible, but instead, she turned back to the guy.

"Pete, Lexi here would like a large Mediterranean with a take-home Caesar salad."

"Olly, I can't eat all that," I whispered.

"Of course you can't. It's for you to take home so you'll have lunch tomorrow or a midnight snack. Trust me. A personal size will just leave you hankering for more."

The guy, Pete, repeated back the order, and after paying, Olly guided us to a table near the window. As I sat down and stared at the woman across from me, I realized just how relaxed I felt around her. Up until that moment, every woman I met, aside from Eve, seemed like a threat—a threat to my marriage, a threat to my mental health, and a threat to my entire life, or at least, what I *thought* was my entire life. Richard's eyes, and other parts, liked to wander.

They were also a constant reminder of what I wished I had—the ability to be my own woman, not forced into the shadows by a man who was supposed to want the best for me, a man who spouted well-timed, pretty words when it suited him but showed time and time again that all of those words were hollow. I wondered over and over again, for years, why he'd even asked me to marry him. He made it abundantly clear that I was far from what he wanted in a wife. Then again maybe I was exactly what he wanted. Someone he could control because I was desperate.

It had taken a lot of time and self-growth to realize the other women weren't the issue, the man who I'd chosen to marry was. The issue was completely with the man who routinely tore my soul apart yet knew exactly how to keep me hanging on for more of the same while he made me question my own value in the world.

"So, where are you from?" Olly asked, breaking me out of my thoughts.

The question startled me, as I hadn't anticipated needing to bust out any real background details this soon after arriving in town. I fumbled over how to answer in my head as I debated whether I should be lying about anything other than my name. Across the table, Olly was still staring at me expectantly, and I tried to play off the delay by laughing and shaking my head.

"Sorry. Apparently, I need more coffee. I'm from Vegas."

"Oh, wow." Olly leaned on the table. "Is it like in the movies? All bright lights and excitement and everything is always open? Is it as glamorous as it seems?"

That was what everyone thought about the desert city founded by the mafia. I felt like saying that the city was much like my ex-husband—all shiny from the outside looking in, but once you lived there, you saw the darkness that hid under all that glitz. But I couldn't say that.

"It has its moments, but it's a lot different when you live there. You don't tend to spend time on the Strip unless you're working in a casino, and outside of that area, things are pretty much like in any other city."

Olly sat back and sighed, disappointment clear on her face.

"That's a shame, but that seems to be the way of it. Nothing's really how it looks. I went on a trip a couple of years ago to this resort I'd only ever heard great things about. When I arrived, I wondered why I hadn't just stayed home and saved the money. Total letdown."

I grinned, but I couldn't comment on that. When Richard took me places, it was always to be his trophy wife showpiece. That meant I was dressed in fancy clothes and told to sit pretty in the room or on the boat like some kind of expensive, purebred family dog. Most of all, I was supposed to shut up and not say a word unless I was asked a direct question. I never saw the cities we visited, never got to experience the amazing and tantalizing cuisine, and certainly never got to socialize with anyone, not even the room staff.

"Have you lived here your whole life?" I asked, eager to shift the focus off of me.

"I have, and if you'd asked my younger self, I would've said that the first thing I was going to do once I reached eighteen was wave goodbye and not look back at this sleepy little town." Olly looked out the window toward the sea, where the sun reflecting off of the water created a hypnotic feel to the gentle waves. Small boats of all styles and colors bobbed along on the dark, glistening water. "Now, I couldn't picture ever leaving. This place has a warmth I didn't appreciate back then but have grown to love."

Olly looked like she was getting geared up to ask another question, and I was shamefully thankful when the food chose that very moment to arrive. Talking about myself was still very uncomfortable, and I needed a moment to catch my mental breath.

The pizza smelled amazing, and my mouth instantly began to water. However, as I looked at the overly large pizza, a thread of fear snaked its way up through my system. Old guilt about eating something I shouldn't had my hands shaking in moments.

"Are you okay?" Olly asked. Her hand reached across the table and found mine. I drew my hand back as a fresh wave of shame over my reaction to a simple pizza made me want to run and hide. "Hey, why don't I get the food to go, and you can eat the pizza for dinner or have a slice on our walk?"

I couldn't get myself to breathe normally or do anything but take short, shallow gasps—my chest had constricted with the overwhelming emotions running through me. Without waiting for an answer, Olly picked up the food and walked over to where the server was doing something behind the counter. Listening in, I could hear her telling him that the store had called and we had to get going. Even through my panic, I appreciated her quick thinking. I appreciated even more that she was trying to protect me from becoming a public spectacle—I knew how fast gossip could spread.

The server took the food to the back to box it, and I used those precious minutes to try to gather myself. When he came back out, I took a deep breath and stood, forcing myself to go over to the counter. Glancing over, Olly grabbed the boxes of food before putting her arm through mine and guiding me out of the restaurant. As soon as I was outside, I had to stifle a sob.

"Come on. Let's head to the park over there." Olly pointed, and all I could do was nod. Nothing like having your first real impression of the new girl involve a complete emotional breakdown in a bistro over a pizza. I bet she'd be just dying to hang out again after this.

After a few minutes of walking, we reached a small picnic area. We sat down at one of the picnic tables, and I had to grip my hands together under the table to keep the shaking from worsening.

"How long?" Olly asked.

"I don't know what you mean," I answered, looking into her eyes blankly as she tentatively laid a hand on my shoulder.

"How long were you in an abusive relationship?"

Anger and embarrassment flared in my chest at the question. I stood abruptly and moved away from the table.

"That's a big assumption. I barely know you, and you're questioning me like this?"

"Lexi, that's not what I'm doing, and your reaction tells me that I've hit a nerve," she said softly, her eyes pleading with me. I didn't want to hear it, and I certainly didn't want to be seen as the damaged-goods girl who'd run away from her life. The whole point of coming here had been to start fresh, and I was already letting the shadows of the past ruin things on day two.

The fact that Olly saw through my act so easily bothered me more than her actually knowing about the abuse did. It meant that every person I passed on the street could probably see the train wreck that I'd become just as clearly, and they'd pity the girl who'd been stupid enough to fall for the rich man's charm. I wanted no one's pity.

"Thank you for inviting me to lunch, but I have to go," I said, back straight and jaw tight. As Olly went to stand, I swiftly turned and walked away. It felt like every pair of eyes was staring at me from the shops I passed.

By the time I got back to my little home, I was barely able to get through the front door before the tears started. Slamming the door closed, I leaned against it and sunk to the ground as I wrapped my arms around my legs and cried. I cried for the little girl who'd lost her innocence so young and for the woman who'd had her soul crushed by a man who claimed he loved her.

JAKE

IF I'D EVER WONDERED what it would be like to be stuck on a boat in the middle of the Atlantic Ocean with three egotistical males, a slew of alcohol, party drugs, and more women than the boat could feasibly hold, I no longer needed to wonder. It was a special type of mass chaos that my horny twenty-year-old self would have been all over. However, my thirty-one-year-old self just wanted to lie quietly on the deck and nurse the still-pounding migraine from my last party-induced hangover.

The yacht had turned into a floating orgy session full of drunk or high people, and I was doing everything possible to avoid it like the plague. I'd managed to get one sensible meeting in before the craziness had taken over—I'd decided that I'd had enough of the action when I spotted the Captain of the yacht fucking a girl while driving.

I was currently walking the hallways and planning my escape route to one of the small lifeboats on board for when the yacht crashed like the Titanic, because at this rate, that was exactly what was going to happen. I was not going down with the ship.

Three of the party girls and one of the yacht's waitstaff wandered toward me, completely naked, as one of the girls idly stroked the dick standing tall between the guy's legs. So much for the girlfriend he'd been showing around pictures of earlier.

"You want to join us?" one of the women asked as she peeled away from the small entourage to come closer.

Shit. I'd made the rookie mistake of standing still in the hall to let them pass, and now I was in their sights. I felt uncomfortably like a gazelle being stalked by hungry predators, which was ironic, as I'd only come down to the underbelly of the yacht in the first place to try to get some food for myself since the waitstaff was apparently busy doing other things.

"I'm sure we can have a lot of fun," the woman continued. She ran her hand down my arm and bit her lip in that seductive way that women seemed to be able to do instinctually, but I had no interest.

"Thanks, but I have plans," I lied, giving her my best 'get lost' look. The girls who signed up for these parties were not my friends. It was something I'd learned the hard way too many times already. I'd lost count of how many passed-out images of me, or videos of me partying, had ended up on a social media site or in a tell-all tabloid. At this point, it had become second nature to look up and see my name in lights, but not in a good way.

She rolled her eyes at me, losing all of the seduction and gaining a hefty dose of attitude.

"Suit yourself," she said, wandering back to the other three.

Shaking my head, I made it back to my cabin without any further interactions, and without any food, and promptly locked the door.

Miles would be pissed that I wasn't top side rubbing myself up against all of the willing bodies at the party for the photo ops, but I just couldn't bring myself to do it anymore.

The wonder and the thrill was gone. The feeling of being someone special had dissipated. It was all a lie, a mask put on to show the world a different face for a short while, and I was done letting myself get lost behind it.

What had started out as a great way to see the world on my motorcycle and sing a few of the songs I'd written to a larger audience had turned into a constant three-ring circus—no, a madhouse. Sitting on the edge of the bed, I stared out the window at the bright blue water and sunny sky outside.

I wasn't a victim. I could admit that. I'd gone along with the flow for a long time, happy to be swept up in the current of excitement in order to feel…what exactly had I been after?

Reaching into the nightstand drawer, I pulled out the notebook that I didn't go anywhere without and opened the cover to look at the picture tucked inside. It had become slightly faded over time, but the memory of the moment it preserved was still as vivid in my mind as on the day the picture had been taken.

I ran my thumb over the image of the two of us, little Kat and Jake, standing outside our foster home. My arm was wrapped around Kat's shoulders as we held up little American flags for the Fourth of July party the neighborhood was throwing. The T-shirts we were wearing were cheesy—remembering the look on Kat's face when Mrs. Jones had pulled them out of the bag for us made me laugh even now. They really were ugly, but we couldn't say no. Instead, we'd laughed hard and teased one another all day until we were able to run off together to watch the fireworks.

"What do you wish for?" Kat asked, her eyes trained on the colorful fireworks that lit up the sky in every direction.

"You mean on fireworks? I don't think you make wishes on fireworks," I said, frowning as the corner of her smile fell just a little. "But I don't see why we can't make our own rules." At that, her face lit up brighter than any of the fireworks going off in the sky. I was glad—I hated to see her sad.

"Really? I love that idea." She turned on the wooden ledge of the treehouse we were sitting in so she could face me, and I found I couldn't take my eyes off of her or the way her eyes reflected the fireworks in the distance. She was so pretty. When she'd first arrived at the house, I was already angry that I was going to have to share a room with anyone, let alone some strange girl, but she'd won me over with one smile and a flick of the long braid draped down her back.

"Yeah, why not? Grownups are boring. They always do the same things on the same days because a calendar tells them to. Let's never be boring. We can make an ice cream day in July or a funny face-off day in September," I said before making a crazy face at her.

She laughed so hard I thought she was going to fall out of the old treehouse.

"In that case, I want us to make a wish every July fourth. It can be for anything, and we have to make it at...," Kat looked at her watch, "eight-thirty at night. That way, no matter where we are on that day and at that time, we will always know what the other is doing. Unless *you think that's lame," she said, looking down to play with the end of the T-shirt where she'd tied it into a knot.*

"I don't think it's lame."

Kat lifted her eyes to meet mine, and I suddenly knew that I wanted to marry her when we turned eighteen. We would be adults, free of needing to listen to anyone else, and I could tell her that I liked her not just because we'd bonded over being a pair of foster kids with terrible secrets in our pasts who'd been shoved into the same room in the same house, but because she was the one for me.

Taking me by surprise, she leaned in and wrapped her arms around my neck to grip me in a hug. I could feel her heart beating against mine.

"Thank you for being my friend," she said so, so softly.

"Okay, enough of that. What do you want to wish for?" I asked, pulling away, not sure what to do with the sudden affection. Kat didn't like to be touched and shied away anytime anyone went to lay a hand on her. I knew that something really bad had happened to her, but she didn't like to talk about it.

"I can't tell you what I'm going to wish for. That's not how wishes work." Kat rolled her eyes at me before turning to look back toward the fireworks as a new set started with a large bang.

"Fine. It's your holiday ritual, so it's your rule, but we're following my rules when I create the next one."

"Deal." She held out her hand to shake.

I spat on my hand before holding it out, and she made a disgusted face as she stared at it. Her nose crinkled up as she glared at me looking faintly betrayed.

"Why did you do that?"

I shrugged.

"They do it all the time in the movies when they are making a pact. It means that we really promise, or something."

"That's dumb," she stated. I smiled as she spat on her hand anyway, and we clasped our hands together. The pact was sealed.

I stood and went to gaze out the window, the loud thumping from the music of the party going on above me becoming inconsequential background noise as images of Kat danced through my mind. Her gentle smile, which spoke to her sweet nature. Her eyes, always sparkling with mischievous humor.

I'd never broken my promise. Even when I was drunk and couldn't walk straight, I'd made sure to make that wish. Mine was always the same—for Kat and me to reconnect and finally have the chance we'd lost—but it had been seventeen years since that night, and my wish had gone unanswered. Well, that wasn't entirely true. I'd found her once, but I couldn't bring myself to talk to her.

Nothing like finding the soulmate you'd been searching for through a wedding announcement.

I felt nothing but shame as I sat in the coffee shop across the street from the bridal store I'd followed Kat to—I'd never thought 'stalker' would

ever be a term I'd fit, but here I was. Having to watch her walk inside to pick out her wedding dress had almost killed me despite how amazing it felt to finally see her in the flesh again, not just in pictures in news blurbs. The guy she'd chosen to marry came from a rich family, and her face was plastered all over the 'who's who' sites as a result.

I could tell just by looking at his picture that the guy was a dick wad who would break her heart. That's the only thing that men like that ever did. They destroyed and they devoured. Kat was like a precious gem, and he was going to chip away at her slowly until only dust remained.

Kat now lived in a dream home, a fancy mansion nestled in a gated community in one of the posh sections of the city. It was one of those spots where you could end up saying good morning to someone famous at every turn when you walked your dog. He was too young to have afforded all of that on his own, so it had to be family money.

At the thought, a sliver of bitterness brewed in my gut. Why did those with money always get everything? There was more to life than the green shit everyone seemed to worship, but there was no denying that if you had it, you had more options.

I took a gulp from the cup of black coffee in my hand as I tried to work up the courage to walk across the street and talk to her. I wanted to tell her not to marry some money-bags prick who wasn't good enough for her and to marry me instead. The problem was, I wasn't any better as a choice.

I looked down at my leather jacket, torn jeans, and T-shirt, which had all seen better days. They were so far removed from the glamor of the sparkling life she'd found. Glancing up, I saw Kat come out of the store. She was radiant and smiling, her dark hair shining in the bright midday sun. She had another girl with her, and they giggled as they wandered down the sidewalk arm in arm.

A sharp pain stabbed me through the heart. She was happy, truly happy.

I couldn't do it. I couldn't go over there and potentially complicate or ruin her life when I had nothing to offer her except the clothes on my back and my pathetic, shoebox apartment. Nothing I'd tried to get ahead had worked. I'd been pounding down every door and going to every audition that I could to try and make it as an actor, but the callbacks never came. I'd started singing in clubs, putting every last cent I had into making a demo to hand out, but no one had gotten in touch. My photographs fetched a whopping ten dollars a pop.

All I could offer her was poverty, but Kat deserved the world. Sighing, I watched Kat and her friend until they disappeared around a corner. I knew in my heart, in my soul, that I couldn't talk to her until I had something more to offer.

I peeled myself off the stool I'd been sitting on and slipped on my black shades. I'd make something of myself, and after I did, I'd find Kat again.

I'd regretted it every single day since that I hadn't taken the leap—that I hadn't pushed my own fears aside and talked to her that day. As I looked around the large, luxurious cabin and all the fancy things filling it, none of it made me feel even an ounce of happiness. 'Making it' was a joke.

Balling my hands into fists, I let out a yell and then proceeded to smash or break everything that I could get my hands on into pieces like I was the Hulk on a rampage. Nothing was safe. Soon, I heard frantic knocking at my door.

"Fuck off." I screamed through the door as I panted to catch my breath. Wading through the debris littering the floor, I flopped face-first on the bed. I couldn't do it. I couldn't come back to this life. Even if the two months did rejuvenate me, I couldn't continue on like this.

When you found your mind contemplating jumping off a yacht into the ocean to take your chances with drowning or sharks over having to live another day of your own life, you knew it was time for a change. Reaching over to the nightstand, which had miraculously stayed intact, I grabbed my phone and earbuds. Putting on the playlist I'd created of all the old songs that Kat and I had loved, I closed my eyes and prayed that when I woke up, the yacht would either be docked or have sunk. At the moment, I didn't really care which.

BEST
FRIENDS

KAT

THE SHOWER HAD FELT GOOD. I'd managed to scrub away the tears while I felt terrible all over again for the way I'd stormed off on Olly. My stomach was screaming at me since I'd missed lunch, so I decided to pad my way out to the kitchen to make some food. A knock on the door had me freezing in place.

I knew I had to stop freaking myself out, but even as I told my brain that, I still made my way over to the door while watching it like it was going to bust inward at any moment and a monster was going to storm into the room.

"Lexi, it's me, Olly."

Sighing with relief, I opened the door.

"Hey," I said. Not sure what to do with my hands, I stuffed them into the pockets of the knit sweater I was wearing.

"I come with a peace offering." Olly held out the box of pizza and salad I'd left behind and two bottles of wine.

I gave her a smile, before stepping back to let her in.

"I'm the one who should be apologizing. I never should've stormed off like that."

"Nope. This one is my fault. You barely know me, and I could see you were upset and not ready to talk, but I pushed anyway. I'm sorry, but I wanted you to know why I asked what I did. If you'll hear me out, that is?"

"Of course. Come on in. I hope you like Mediterranean pizza—I just had some delivered," I teased as I took the containers of food and bottles from her hands.

"I'm all for that, but I'm definitely going to need the wine," Olly said as she followed me into the kitchen. Pausing by the table, she looked around with a grin. "I'd forgotten how much I loved this house. And you'll find the bottle opener in the drawer by the oven, not there." Olly pointed to the drawer in question, stopping my noisy search through the utensils drawer.

"Thanks." I quickly opened the wine with a deft hand. The cork pulled free with a pop, and I took a moment to sniff the little vapors and the dark contents of the bottle. "Oh, that's nice."

My mouth could almost taste the ripe fruit and hints of spice. Good wine was one of the few perks I'd enjoyed from being married to Richard. The house was always stocked with a wide assortment of vintages, and sometimes, it had been a little too tempting to drink more than a glass with a massive cellar brimming with the world's finest right under my feet. I poured out two glasses and took a slow sip, rewarded with a bold flavor that carried a touch of sweetness and undertones of cinnamon, something nutty and apple.

"What do you think?" Olly asked as she watched me closely.

"That's phenomenal. Where did you get this?" I checked the label, styled simply in purple, gold, and white with a cluster of grapes, for the logo. Not that I'd consider myself a connoisseur or anything, but I'd tried enough to know I didn't recognize the company.

Olly smiled widely in response, a hint of mischief in her eyes.

"It's mine. You really like it?"

"You made this?" I asked, unable to keep the shock from my voice, then felt myself blush when Olly laughed.

"Don't look so surprised. I have many hidden talents."

"Bookstore owner, good Samaritan, and now winemaker? Is there anything you can't do?" I asked as I turned on the oven and put some of the pizza on a pan to warm it up.

The smile slowly faded from Olly's face, and her eyes fixed on the dark liquid as she swirled the wine around in her glass.

"I always wanted to own my own business, and when I graduated high school, I immediately started to look around for something that fit my talents. I'd just turned twenty-two when I started dating this woman who was a little older, by a few years, and we really hit it off...."

She paused, as if checking to see how I was going to react to the news she dated women, and when I didn't jump up and kick her out or exclaim something stupid like 'oh my gosh,' she continued.

"We started dating after an entrepreneur's conference, where we met at the meet and greet reception. Anyway, we got this crazy idea to get into winemaking. I can't even remember how the thought came about, but I'm sure it had something to do with a lot of the liquid in question being consumed. At first, everything was *glamourous.*"

She ended her sentence in a very put-on English accent, hand lifted in an extravagant wave. It made me grin. Olly apparently had quite the dramatic personality.

"We got the company conceptualized and off the ground, and in a short time, we'd grown too big for the small space we'd been renting. The business was starting to make money to the point we had to look at expanding and reinvesting, and of course, that's when things changed between us. We had this amazing business that was taking off, we were in the middle of buying our first farm property to start growing our own grapes, and we were living together—to me, it couldn't have been any better." As she paused again, her eyes lost a bit of their spark.

"I guess this is where things took a turn? Was it due to the money?" I asked. Remembering the forgotten pizza, I put the pan in the oven to warm everything up and then poured the rest of the first wine bottle into our glasses.

"The money may have been the catalyst, but it wasn't what started the issues. To be honest, I don't know when exactly they started—it was so subtle. Could've been during our first year together, or maybe the second. Heck, they could've been there the entire time, and I was just too blind to see them. But it was little things, like something she would casually sprinkle into a conversation that seemed like an offhand comment, but then it would blow up into a bigger argument on a weekly basis, and then on a daily basis. You get the idea."

I nodded with a grimace.

"Oh, do I ever. It sneaks up on you. Like, you don't see it coming at all, and then one day, you wake up and second guess everything you've ever done—everything you've ever said or worn or eaten. Every moment turns into looking for approval out of fear you'd been doing everything wrong to begin with," I said. Olly nodded solemnly in agreement.

"Exactly. She told me I was getting pudgy—me, five foot four and a whopping one hundred and twenty pounds—right before we went out to dinner to celebrate our third anniversary. Then she proceeded to ruin a perfectly wonderful dinner because I dared to order a dessert after she'd already told me I was putting on weight. Claimed I never listened to her or cared about her feelings and created this entire scene."

Olly paused and cleared her throat, obviously getting choked up as she recounted the painful memory.

"Then, she stood up and yelled loudly enough for the entire place to hear her that if I kept it up, she'd no longer find me desirable. She just said that and stormed right out. I'd never been more mortified or felt so low. I was in this strange common law-like marriage with a woman who ripped another strip off my last remaining bits of self-worth almost hourly, yet I stayed, and I couldn't even understand why," Olly said. The wetness in her eyes made it clear how deeply the hurt still ran.

"Oh my god, Olly! I'm so sorry." I rushed around the small island we'd been leaning against and wrapped her in a tight hug. I knew exactly how she felt. I'd lost count of how many times Richard had embarrassed me in public. I'd felt torn down and unable to breathe properly for fear of inviting ridicule. Olly hugged me back just as tightly, and when I pulled away to give her a little space, she quickly wiped at the tears now flowing down her cheeks.

"Oh no, don't cry. You'll make me cry," I said, laughing, and sure enough, I realized I had my own little stream of remorse to wipe away when I reached up to check my own cheeks. Grabbing the box of tissues, I offered them to Olly before taking a few for myself.

"It gets worse. I caught her cheating. I mean, I pretty much knew she'd moved on, but I kept lying to myself about it until I actually walked in on them in the living room. She had the audacity to say that it was my fault since I couldn't satisfy her anymore," Olly added after a moment.

"Wow!"

"Right? Would you believe I almost apologized? Like, I stood there for a moment and thought to myself that I should say sorry for not pleasuring her better even though it was her choice not to have sex for months. That was the moment I knew I'd lost my ever-loving mind and needed to get out."

"Good for you," I said, meaning it with all my heart. Judging enough time had passed, I pulled the pizza out of the oven and dished it out onto two plates before walking with Olly to the table to sit down.

"The legalities of separating out the business—holy sweet baby Jesus, I don't wish that kind of a fight on my worst enemy. If it weren't for my mother, I would've just given up and handed over the keys. It was that painful and emotionally traumatizing."

"What happened? Did you get to keep the business and your sanity?"

"With the help of my mom, a good lawyer, and my special batch of wine, I got to keep my sanity, my dignity, and half of the company. We divided the business up, and while this might be unholy of me to say, the fact that my business is doing better than hers always makes me smile. So much for me being the problem with the business and why it wasn't growing."

I laughed at the look on her face and then moaned as I took the first bite of pizza. It was an explosion of goodness in my mouth.

"You were right. This is amazing."

"I told you. You'll end up an addict like me," Olly said before taking her own big bite.

We ate in silence for a bit, and I knew Olly wanted to know what had happened to me. Which was fair—she'd just shared this painful, intimate story about her life. But I couldn't return the favor. Not yet. The wounds were too raw.

"I'm not ready to share my story yet." I looked down at my plate and picked off a piece of tender chicken to toss into my mouth, avoiding her eyes. "I'm sorry."

"It's okay. That's not why I told you. I just wanted you to know that I wasn't being snoopy earlier—though I can be very pushy at times," she said right as I took a sip of my wine, and I almost choked on it. We burst out laughing, the tension broken. As we settled down again, Olly fixed me with a look.

"I just wanted you to know you're not alone. I recognized the look in your eyes, and I needed you to know that if you want to talk, or simply get out of the house, I'm here."

"Thanks, Olly. It means a lot that you'd do that, or even care at all. I mean, like you said, we barely know one another, yet both you and your mom have been so kind and welcoming." It was my turn to pause as I cleared the emotion from my throat. I looked around the small house. "You mentioned that you liked this house. Did you live in it before?" I asked, wanting to change the topic.

"Sure did. My mom and dad were one of those Hallmark romance stories." She smiled, and the warm look on her face told me she'd had a storybook childhood. I'd had that up until my parents were killed—things went on a fast trip downhill from there.

"They grew up as kids next door to one another," Olly continued, visibly getting into the story. "Both were only children, and they got married at eighteen. My dad bought this house from my nana and papa when they wanted to move into an apartment. Then they decided to purchase my granny and grandpa's house when I was in my Junior year of high school, and after they moved into that house, I lived here until I moved in with Alisha. Sorry, that's the ex's name."

Olly paused to take a drink. I understood. Sometimes, just saying the name could be difficult.

"Anyway, by the time I saw the light, my mom had this house rented out because she couldn't bear the thought of selling it to some stranger. When the last tenant left to move into a bigger home, I could've moved in, but my mom is getting up there in age and it's nice having someone to come home to, even if it's my mom." She lifted her shoulder in a shrug.

"I can understand why your mom has kept the houses," I said. "There would be too many memories lost otherwise. If you don't mind me asking, when did your dad pass?"

"Just after my high school graduation. He'd been sick for a while, but he said he refused to die until he got to see his baby girl graduate. What about you? Are you close with your family?"

I stood and took my empty plate to the sink to buy myself a moment.

"I think that's a story for another time." I turned and leaned against the counter. That was another landmine that only led to more landmines.

Olly followed to hand over her plate, but she held on to it until I looked at her.

"I hope you know that I already think of you as a friend. I know it's probably very hard for you to trust anyone—I really know, I was there, too—but I hope one day you'll see me as your friend."

"I already do. I'm just...." All the sharing had strung out my nerves. There was only so much talking about all the crappy things that had happened to me that I could take in one sitting before I wanted to pull my hair out and scream at the top of my lungs.

"It's okay, Lexi. You don't have to try and explain. If you need anything, just ask." Olly let go of the plate and gave my arm a gentle squeeze. "I'm going to take off. Have a good night, girl, and don't stress. This is a good place. We take care of those who live here."

After walking Olly to the door, I waved goodnight as she turned onto the sidewalk and then closed the door, making sure it locked. Then I checked again. And again.

I hated that I felt like I needed to check every lock three times like I was under some kind of compulsion.

"Damn you, Richard," I mumbled as I made my way to the sink to start cleaning the dishes.

I walked into the kitchen to put my leftovers from dinner in the fridge, freezing as I spotted Richard standing at the counter. He was glaring at me, and I didn't know what I'd done.

"Where were you?" he gritted out.

"I was out with Eve. I told you I was going to dinner last week and put it on your calendar," I said, making my way swiftly to the large stainless, shiny contraption that was meant more for a five-star restaurant than a residence. It was massive and half empty most of the time —way too much space for just the two of us. I had no idea why Richard wanted the insanely large appliance.

"Bullshit!"

Richard's sudden outburst split the silence, making me jump. Spinning around, I stared at his glowering expression. It clearly screamed that he didn't believe me. I had no idea why he'd think I was lying.

"What do you mean?"

He took a threatening step closer as he slammed the glass of scotch he held down on the counter. The remaining contents sloshed out and splashed onto his hand, soaking both it and the countertop.

"Look what you made me do." He shook his hand like a wet dog would shake out its coat, sending little droplets of alcohol sailing all over the place.

"Here, let me help," I offered, jumping into action to grab a hand towel.

"Don't touch me." Richard jerked his hand away before I could touch it, and my heart raced as I wracked my brain trying to figure out what I'd done to make him so angry.

"After everything I've done for you, given you, you go and fuck someone else?" Richard sneered.

I took a step back, eyes wide.

"What? I wouldn't...I've never—," I stammered, completely confused.

Richard was up in my face in an instant, and I took a step back, flinching, thinking he was going to hit me.

"Don't you lie to me, you slut. I should never have pulled you out of the trash. That was where you deserved to stay."

"Richard, I didn't cheat. I swear. Why would I?"

His fist slammed down on the island, and I jumped back this time.

"Because that's who you are! You're a bottom-feeding, soul-sucking leech, and I should divorce you. I should leave you penniless to match your worthlessness."

He stormed past me and stomped out of the room. Panic clawing at my throat that he might actually follow through on his threat, I ran after him. I didn't understand where this was coming from, but I didn't want him to divorce me. I loved him. I reached out and grabbed his arm.

"Richard, please stop and talk to me. I just don't understand why you'd think I was cheating. I can prove that I wasn't. I promise I wouldn't do that to you," I said, desperation tightening my throat and making it hard to speak. He yanked his arm away so hard that I stumbled back and tripped over the hallway runner, landing hard on my ass.

Richard glared down at me.

"I said don't touch me. You made this bed, so now you can lay in it. From now on, if you want to stay married, you don't leave this house unless I know where you're going, and with whom."

"But you knew who I was with. You know Eve and I always get together every two weeks for dinner. I swear, it's in your calendar." I tried to reason with Richard, but as it became obvious he didn't care what I had to say, the panic turned into flat-out cold fear. Who would I even be without Richard?

"I don't want you to see her anymore. She's a bad influence. She's probably why you decided to betray me."

"I didn't," I said with as much earnestness as I could.

"Shut up! I don't want to hear one more lie out of your mouth."

I sat there, dumbfounded over how a night that had been going so well had turned into this huge argument over something I'd never done. Down the hall, Richard grabbed his coat from the front hall closet before wrenching open the front door. Pausing in the doorway, he turned his glare on me again.

"I'm going out. Maybe I should cheat on you so you know what it feels like." Richard slammed the door behind him, the sound echoing through the large house.

I sucked in a sharp breath and grabbed at my heart as the panic attack tried to grip me. Lifting my eyes to the dark window behind the sink, I stared at my reflection. Tears I hadn't felt falling were streaming down my cheeks. I'd promised myself that I'd never be a victim again after the life I'd lived in foster care, yet I'd walked right into a marriage full of abuse that wore a different mask.

The worst part was that I stayed. For ten years, I stayed and let him slowly beat me down until it was an effort to get out of bed. I second-guessed everything I said or did for fear that I'd anger him.

I turned away from my reflection, unable to stand the look on my face. I didn't recognize who I was anymore. Grabbing my cell off the counter, I walked over to the couch and sat down, settling in to do what I'd done almost every night for the last seven years.

My fake social media account had started out innocently enough

—it was a way to stay in touch with the outside world. And then, seven years ago, a video came across the screen and sent my heart tumbling through the floor as I stared at Jake's smiling face. In the video, he sang only one verse of a song as he sat on a motorcycle at sunset, and I must have cried a million tears over it since that first time seeing it.

I was officially stalker status, an addict who couldn't stop even though every time I opened up the app and looked at his pictures, it felt like a thousand fresh cuts to my heart. I longed to have even one of those smiling sunset days with him, to travel the world carefree like in all of his posts, and I became obsessed with pretending I was with him and the videos and pictures were from our adventures together.

The first image to appear was a new post of him at some strip club in Miami dancing with one of the strippers. Then the image changed, now showing him on a yacht with a beer in his hand as he toasted a man I didn't recognize. They were surrounded by so many women that you could barely see the boat.

As always, my heart skipped and pounded hard at seeing his smiling face—those green eyes and that midnight hair were still the sexiest things I'd ever seen. How many times had I debated about reaching out to him but hadn't done it? My thumb would hover over the little message button, but no words ever came to me. Would he even remember me? Would he laugh in my face and ask why I thought he would care?

Here he was, living the life of a celebrity, and I was an emotionally damaged housewife who didn't have anything other than trouble to offer anyone. Bitterly, I scrolled down to my favorite picture. It was an image of him sitting alone on a black motorcycle with a farm in the background. In the image, he looked like the happy, jokester Jake I remembered— he looked like the boy my heart still pined for.

Pulling the blanket off the back of the couch, I curled up and laid the phone down on the couch next to me. It was sad and it was pathetic, but even as the tears silently trailed down my cheeks, I knew I wouldn't turn off the phone. If this were the only way for us to be together, I'd take it. Of all the major regrets in my life, not trying to find Jake was always at the top of my list. He was the one, and I'd let him get away.

JAKE

"MOM, I'M HOME," I called out as I stepped into the front hall of my family's large farmhouse. In moments, I could hear her feet running down the hall, and my heart swelled as she rounded the corner like she always did—with a smile that could warm the coldest of hearts and covered in flour from her latest kitchen adventure. Over the years, I'd eaten more than one mysterious offering that she'd created, and for most of them, I was pretty sure I never wanted to know the ingredients.

"Is that my baby?" My mom squealed, and I braced myself for impact as she ran at me. With a distinct 'oomph,' I caught her as she slammed into me with all the force of a miniature freight train.

"I think I'm too old for you to still be calling me baby," I teased as I gripped her in a hard hug and picked her up to swing her around like a rag doll.

"Put me down. You're crazy," she said, laughing hard. After giving her cheek a loud kiss, I put her back on her feet, and she immediately swatted my arm. "You darn well know that you'll always be my baby no matter how old you get. You look great, Jake."

She smiled, and I had to look away from her happy face because I didn't feel like I looked great. I felt like I was a walking billboard for how to lie to yourself and the world around you. If I offered master-classes, they'd probably sell out.

She sniffed, blinking back a little mistiness in the corners of her eyes, but carried on with being the bright beacon of happiness that she always was.

"Come on in. I've got a new batch of cookies coming out of the oven to have after dinner, and your father will be in from checking the fields shortly." She linked arms with me, practically dragging me deeper into the house.

When Joy and Mark Russell, my incredible mom and dad, first took me in, I tried to make their lives a living hell. At the time, I wanted nothing more than to run away and find Kat, and they stopped every attempt. Once I accepted that running wouldn't work, I switched tactics, instead begging them to take in Kat, too. As long as we were together, I didn't really care how it happened.

The two of them talked together seriously about trying to find Kat, but in the end, they decided they couldn't take in any more children—they were just too tapped out with the three boys already under their roof.

Subsequently, I acted out in all the worst ways. The thing was, I'd never met people like the Russells before. I didn't even know they existed. No matter what buttons I pushed or what I did, I was only met with kindness. Once I finally learned to appreciate it, I didn't know how I'd gotten so lucky—to this day, I still didn't.

"How are the grapes doing this year?" I asked, picking one of the bright red ones out of the bowl of grapes on the kitchen counter and popping it into my mouth. The juice ran down my throat, amazingly flavorful.

"Great, actually. It will be our best crop since we started."

A delicious smell caught my attention. I sniffed the air, and the scent of fresh cookies made my mouth water. Nothing beat the smell of Mom's baking, especially when it was her pirate cookies. They were her signature creation, and they always disappeared faster than she could keep them stocked.

"Do you need any help with dinner?" I asked, forcefully pulling my attention away from the cookies—my mom was way too good at thwarting my sticky fingers to go for one. I looked out the large window that faced the vineyard and smiled as I watched all the people in the distance working. It was amazing to see how lively the place had become.

After spending their entire lives working soul-sucking corporate jobs that they hated, my parents had decided to move across to this country property and start a vineyard. They now had a number of contracts with local wineries. My mom told everyone who asked that their grapes were the best because they were grown with love, and she wasn't exaggerating.

"Did you want to barbeque the steaks?" she asked, already back to mixing something in a bowl.

"Bring it on."

"Are you sure now? You haven't gotten too soft from having everyone serve all your meals to you?" My mom lifted her brow at me, and I swallowed hard. It was her subtle way of telling me she'd been keeping an eye on me and wasn't too impressed with my behavior. Well, she would have to get in line. No one could be more disappointed in me right now than myself. The direction my life had taken was not what I'd envisioned when I first set out to chase my dreams.

"You've seen the stories?" I looked down at the floor, afraid to meet her gaze. Even though I was standing in front of her as a man of thirty-one, I still felt like I was the fourteen-year-old version of myself who couldn't handle seeing her disappointment.

"I'm not going to berate you, Jake, if that's what you're waiting for. You're a grown man and can make your own decisions. But I will say that I'm disappointed. I know you're a better man than the one I see on the covers of those trashy magazines."

My mom reached out and gripped my arm, making me lift my eyes up to meet her soft gray ones.

"I love you. I'll always love you. I'll even bury a body for you," she said, making me smirk. "But, you must know that you're better than this and you deserve to be happy, and I don't see my happy boy when I look at those photos. I see the same boy who first came to us focused on lashing out at the world—you just have the money to do it in a loud and expensive way now."

Pushing away from the counter, I wrapped my arms around her.

"How do you always know exactly what to say to make me feel better and worse all at the same time?"

"It's a gift you receive when you have a child. You'll understand when you have your own family."

"I don't know about that. I haven't even found someone I could spend more than a few nights with, let alone a lifetime," I said. My mom narrowed her eyes at me. Shit. I knew I was in for round two with that comment. I'd spent more than one night whining to my mom about Kat, and she'd encouraged me more than once to find her again.

Again and again, I'd stubbornly refused to do so. It had been a procession of excuses, really. First, I was too young. Then, I didn't know where she was. Once I did find her, she was happily engaged to a very rich man, and now...well, now I was a mess and a fuck up, and who the hell was I to storm into her wonderful life and try to steal her away from it? She could have kids by now or be happily celebrating an anniversary, and while I was many things, when it came to my Kat, I'd never intentionally hurt her like that.

The oven chose that moment to buzz and announce that the cookies were done. I was literally saved by the bell, and I took the opportunity to run.

"I'll go get the steaks started," I said, already halfway to the door. I was being a total chicken, but I had two months of being dragged over the proverbial coals and back again to look forward to—once for today was good enough.

Stepping out the back door onto the deck, I could see my dad in the fields driving around on the old tractor he refused to get rid of. I'd even purchased him a brand new one that had air conditioning and heating, but he said there was nothing wrong with the old one, that the two of them had a lot in common, and to my knowledge, he'd never used it.

The corner of my mouth turned up as he looked over, and I waved as he spotted me by the barbecue. He quickly stood up and waved back, and my heart seized in my chest as he almost fell off the moving tractor from his overzealous launch out of the seat.

"Jesus Christ. That man is going to give me heart failure," I mumbled. Kneeling, I fiddled around with the barbecue for a few minutes until I got the flame to catch. The fire built quickly, and when I looked up from watching the flames lick against the grill, I wasn't surprised to see my dad already making his way across the large lawn.

"Sport!"

"Dad, I'm thirty-one. Please stop calling me Sport," I groaned as I moved to meet him on the green grass. He instantly wrapped me in a tight embrace, and I returned it, sighing into the familiarity. I'd had to learn to get over my aversion to bear hugs when I'd arrived at this home. The entire family was big on both hugs and loud, boisterous parties with lots of laughs. Those first few months, those first few *years*, it had all seemed so completely alien to me.

My home life before foster care had been one of constant worry. Warm and affectionate it was not, and once in foster care, it had been a whirlwind of hopping from one home after another until I'd landed at the Joneses with Kat. That was the longest I'd stayed in any one location until the Russells came into my life.

Standing at six foot four, my dad was a big man, and after he stepped back to clasp my upper arms in his large hands, we easily stood eye to eye. He'd seemed like such a mountain of a man when I first met him. I'd been secretly terrified of him, and of what he might do to me, until I realized that he was nothing but a giant, gooey cinnamon roll on the inside.

"You look good, Son...I'll try to remember about the 'Sport' thing, but no promises." He moved to wrap his arm around my shoulders instead, and we headed back over to the barbecue—and just in the nick of time.

"Jasper, don't you dare," my father yelled at our St. Bernard. Jasper whipped his head in our direction with a look that clearly said, *Who, me?*, like his nose hadn't been leading him directly to the delicious-smelling meat laid out on the platter a few inches away from his greedy face.

As soon as the dog spotted me, he came running, and I prepared myself for another round of impact. Kneeling, I got as low as I could right before the huge animal, who hit like a small car, leaped into my arms and knocked me flat on my back.

"Jasper, no," I tried to say, but I was laughing too hard to get it out as I got assaulted with doggie kisses. "Oh man," I groaned as things got increasingly slobbery.

The only choice left was defense. Holding my hands over my face kept me from getting a tongue in the mouth, but I got one in the ear instead—still the better deal. All I could hear over Jasper's excited barks was my dad's deep barrel-chested laugh. There was no rescue coming from that direction.

"Help," I said to no one in particular, still laughing and trying to hug the furry attacker into submission. "Hey bud, I take it you missed me?" I stared up into Jasper's kind brown eyes, which looked small for the size of his massive head and lolling tongue. He was always the goofiest creature, and I'd wanted so badly to name him that, but at the time, it had been my younger foster brother Jayce's turn to choose the new pup's name.

"We all missed you, Son," my Dad said. I sat up and rubbed absently at Jasper's ears.

"I've missed everyone, too. I had a blast, but it feels good to be home." When I was a kid, I'd never have thought that a farm in what felt like the middle of nowhere could ever end up feeling like home— not that I'd always longed for bright lights and fame, it just wasn't the kind of place I saw myself. Live and learn, right?

"Are Tripp and Jayce going to be here for dinner?"

"Your brothers won't be back until the weekend. We're looking at expanding production, and they're checking out land in a couple of areas farther south. I'd like to have a longer growing season for our grapes, and it will give us some more variety in the types of grapes we can grow."

"Good thinking," I said, nodding. Jasper, taking the shift in attention as a dismissal, trotted off to explore something in the grass, and I stood and dusted myself off from his attack.

"Come on, you two. Dinner isn't goin' to cook itself," my mom yelled, her body half in and half out the back door.

"Oops, we're in trouble," my dad laughed. As we continued toward the house, though, the humor slowly left his face. As we reached the deck, he placed a hand on my arm, stopping me from going farther. "Son...," he said, then peeked in the window and lowered his voice even more. "Are you planning on staying for a while this trip?"

"At least two months, maybe longer. Why?" I could tell by his worried tone that something fishy was up.

"Your mother would skin me alive for telling you this, but I feel you have the right to know."

"Know what?" A cold trickle of fear snaked down my spine as every alarm bell in my body rang out loud and clear.

"We don't know what it is yet, but your mother has been going in for tests on a lump they found in her breast." My dad rubbed the back of his neck. "They're saying that if it's cancer, she'll need a full mastectomy and chemo."

I stumbled back like he'd just punched me in the gut. The pain was worse than if he had. My dad grabbed my shoulder to help steady me as I searched his face.

"How long ago?"

"Since she found out there was an issue?" I nodded at the question. "Almost a year, but you know your mother. She's a tough, stubborn woman who's not big on doctors. It took Jayce resurrecting one of his famous childhood tantrums to get her to finally agree to further testing." He took his hat off and banged the dust off against the jeans he was wearing, somehow looking older than I'd ever seen him look before.

"Why didn't you tell me sooner? I could've come back. I could've helped try and talk her into it. I could've done...something. Anything," I said, a hint of anger creeping into my voice.

"Don't you look at me like that. You damn well know I'm scared of that woman, and I have to sleep beside her at night. I've no doubt she would've suffocated me in my sleep if I'd called you after she told me not to," he teased. I knew he was trying to make the blow less painful, but his eyes held worry that his normally jovial features never showed.

"But, why? Why doesn't she want me to know?"

He looked over his shoulder at the fields, collecting himself, and then back again.

"Because she didn't want you to give up your dreams or make the decision to come home and then regret it. I'm not telling you this to force you to stay longer, Son. I'm telling you because she gets her results next week, and good or bad, I felt it was time you knew what was going on. What you decide to do is up to you, and you know she'd never want you to feel forced into sticking around, so if that's what you have swimming around up in that head of yours, then you can forget it. She will see right through any act."

My dad opened the lid to the barbecue and tossed on the steaks before we could get scolded again while I stood staring off into space trying to process this information. My mom, potentially sick? No, this wasn't happening.

"I need to go for a walk for a minute," I said before turning on my heel and marching away toward the pond. Jasper followed behind like a shadow. Once I was out of sight of the house, I sank to the ground and stared at the water.

My gaze found the pretty dock and gazebo that my mom had wanted to put in as soon as we moved here and she saw the view. It had, of course, been one of the first home improvement projects my dad had finished. It was decorated with flowers and little lights that made the spot *shine* at night. It was a little slice of heaven.

Leaving Kat had been the worst day of my life, yet it had also led me to the Russells and the best mom and dad I could ever have dreamed of having. A choked sob wracked my body as all the emotions twisting inside me bubbled to the surface. It wasn't just that my mom might be sick, it was the fact that I'd wasted so much time on the road taking something so precious for granted.

For a long time after joining the family, I'd been bitter and distrustful of the new happiness. It felt like anytime I ever started to get comfortable somewhere, that was when it would inevitably get taken away. To say the first couple of years I was 'unpleasant' and things were 'tense' would be an understatement. Then I spent the better part of my twenties on the road, rarely coming home or bothering to call, as I chased big dreams. Now that I had achieved the dreams I thought I wanted, I realized they didn't make me happy—the family I'd distanced myself from did.

The guilt was as crushing as the news itself, and they were running a high-speed race through my mind that abruptly, with no warning, hit a wall. It was too much. Dropping my head between my knees, I let all the emotions I'd been bottling up for the last few years out until I couldn't breathe and had to gasp for breath. Jasper whimpered and began licking the tears from my cheek, bringing the smallest of smiles to my face. He was such a good boy. I felt like I was a teen again in all the worst ways—I hadn't cried since the night Kat and I had been torn apart.

"You okay, Son?" my dad asked from behind me, and it wasn't until he spoke that I became aware the sun was starting to set.

"I will be." Rolling out my shoulders, I slowly stood and faced him. "No matter what happens with Mom, I'm not going back to that life."

"But, what about everything you've worked for? The contracts and—."

I shook my head and laid my hand on my dad's shoulder, cutting him off.

"I've never been as happy anywhere as I am when I'm here." I looked over at the farm, which was now quiet and still aside from the odd person still moving about in the vineyard. "I don't know what I was hoping to find out there, but it wasn't there and I'm done searching. It was time to come home, anyway."

A smile slowly crept across his face.

"Well then, we'd better go eat that steak before it gets cold or your mother will have both our heads."

"Indeed, she would."

The elephant-sized weight on my chest that I'd been struggling with lifted like it had never been there with the decision not to go back to the life I'd been living. Honestly, the decision had been made months ago, but I'd been too scared to let go since I'd fought for it so fiercely. Looking around, I took a deep breath and felt like I could truly get air in my lungs for the first time in a long time.

Whatever my mom's diagnosis was, I would be here, and that meant she would have her entire family supporting her. Other than Kat, my mom was the toughest woman I'd ever met. If anyone was going to beat this, it would be her.

JAKE

AS I ROLLED out of bed, the noise and commotion of the day was already impossible to ignore. Outside, tractors drove past the house, and I could hear my mom and dad talking someplace downstairs. I wasn't used to having anyone still in the house with me in the morning unless they were passed out or hungover, but here, you could feel the energy in the air. It was like the sun itself was pushing me to get going because the day was already wasting away.

Fumbling with the few articles of clothing I'd grabbed to change into, I wandered to the bathroom, and it struck me as refreshing that I didn't need to check my path for surprise vomit. It also struck me just how pathetic it was to be pleased by that. You know shit has gone sideways in your life when you need to make sure you don't need to puke before you can take your morning piss. Pushing the disturbing thoughts aside, I quickly finished getting ready and wandered down the stairs, following the scent of bacon like a bloodhound.

My mouth was already watering by the time I walked into the

kitchen to see my mom rolling out some sort of dough even though homemade biscuits and a tray of bacon were already on the table. I loved my mom.

"I totally missed this," I said, making my way over to the woman who never seemed to sleep to give her a kiss on the cheek. "Morning, Mom. How are you today?"

"I'm good. Fresh orange juice is in the fridge, food is on the table, and your father said to head on out as soon as you've eaten." She stopped to hand me a glass as I headed over to the fridge.

"No rest for the wicked. How is the harvest going?" I asked before pouring a tall glass of fresh juice and chugging it down. I sighed and smacked my lips as I pulled the glass away. What was it about homemade stuff that tasted so much better than anything you could buy?

"Late. The weather has been a little uncooperative this year, and everything is now a rush to finish before we get a frost and it ruins the crop." She paused to wipe her floury hands on her apron, and I couldn't stop myself from staring a little closer at everything about her, like the fact she'd lost weight, and the fact she had darker than normal circles under her eyes, and the fact that her hair seemed messier than normal. Most of all, I noticed how she smiled and acted like her normal, chipper self, but it didn't quite reach her eyes.

"He told you, didn't he?"

"What do you mean?" I asked, turning to grab a coffee cup to busy my hands. I was a terrible poker player, and my mom was the worst person for me to play. I hadn't been able to get away with a single lie, even a well-intentioned one, since the moment I first walked in her door.

"Don't even bother trying to hide it. I can tell by the weird way you were looking at me like I was going to disappear before your eyes, and now by your tone. You aren't subtle, you know."

I slowly turned around to face the firing squad and leaned against the counter, dark roast coffee in hand.

"I think you missed your calling. You should've been a detective."

"Ha!" my mom laughed, and the smile was genuine as she used her arm to brush the loose strands of hair away from her face. "Do you really want me licensed to kill?"

"That's a spy, not a detective, but good point."

She looked down at the ground for a moment, and when she looked up again, her soft gray eyes were filled with tears. My heart broke a bit.

"I'm glad that you know," she said, then sniffed. Setting the coffee down, I wrapped her up in a hug and kissed the top of her head.

"It's going to be okay, Mom. No matter what, I know you're going to be okay," I said, rubbing her back gently as she softly cried. I couldn't remember a single time in the last seventeen years that I'd seen my mom cry unless it was happy tears. Her worry pulled at me, and when she stepped back, I grabbed the tissue box from the counter to hand it over.

"Mom, I mean it. You're the strongest person I know, and your whole family is going to be here to help out and take care of you."

"I don't want to have to be taken care of," she said, a stubborn glint in her eyes.

"I know, but sometimes we all need it. I mean, look at me. Here I am, this hot-shot influencer, and I had to come running home to find myself again." I gave her shoulders a gentle squeeze. "You gave me, Tripp, and Jayce a new life, a chance to have a real family, and you and

Dad have been there for us no matter what shit and havoc we have caused. Lean on us for a change."

She nodded, but I didn't believe for one second that she was planning on doing so. If that meant we had to force her to take it easy sometimes, I'd lock her up in her room and pay the consequences later. All that mattered was that she was okay.

"Does this mean you're staying longer than you thought? You'd better not be staying because of me, young man." She gave me her best mom glare.

"Yes, I'll be staying. No, I don't know what that's going to look like yet, but I'm working on it, and no, I'm not staying because you may have cancer. I made the decision to come home for good before I even left New York."

As her eyes searched my face, the corners of her mouth pulled up in a small smile.

"Okay, then. You know you're always welcome here. Now go eat your breakfast and get out there to help before your father comes stomping in here like an old bear looking for you."

Smirking, I did as she asked and filled my mouth with home cooked goodness as I listened to her fill me in on all the latest gossip from the area, like who was dating who and who had married who. There was also who was cheating on who, and of course, the latest developments with her baking and her self-imposed quest to beat all the ladies at the local fairs. She still had one major fair left to enter, and if she won, she'd be crowned Queen of the Jam.

My heart swelled as I listened to her talk and realized just how much I'd missed home.

Walking out of the house half an hour later in my ripped jeans and work boots, I felt like a whole new me. After pausing a moment to stretch out the kinks in my back, I pulled the baseball cap low on my face and made my way toward my dad, who was on his way in from the fields with the tractor. The wagon he was towing was filled with baskets of plump grapes. I jogged the remaining distance and leaped up onto the wagon while it was still moving.

"You know I hate it when you do that," my dad said, tone stern but with a grin. "Good to have you back."

I leaned on the wooden wall along the back of the wagon and waved to the workers I knew as we passed. At last count, the farm employed over twenty people, but a good crop one year meant all the difference moving into the next on what we were able to grow and if we could expand operations, or if we could even afford to employ the same number of people.

Once the wagon made it inside the unloading bay, I grabbed one of the baskets and sat it on the conveyor belt that would take the grapes to the inspection and quality control area.

"I have a meeting later today with a niche winery in the area that's interested in switching suppliers. Do you think you could take the lead on the harvest while I attend the meeting?" my dad asked, coming up beside me.

"It's been a while, but I'm sure I can handle it."

He beamed, and something inside me warmed a little bit more.

"Great, thanks."

"But I'm not using this old tractor," I said, smacking my hand on the old, rusted wheel well, and then laughed as he grumbled about young people not appreciating the finer things and how it wasn't old. I really didn't care which tractor I used, but it was good fun getting under his skin. As he unloaded the last of the baskets, I made my way over to the large equipment garage and smiled at the large green tractor parked inside. No point in it just sitting there.

Climbing up into the driver's seat, I could tell it was as new as the day I'd purchased it for my dad. There was not a speck of dust or dirt in the cab. I turned the key, and the big tractor immediately rumbled to life. Now *this* was a tractor. I pulled the gleaming vehicle out and laughed as my dad shook his head as I made my way over to the wagon storage area.

After hooking up one of the largest wagons, I drove back to the vineyard and went down the next aisle being harvested. It didn't take long to figure out why my dad didn't like using this tractor for this work. They'd added rows to the end of the field, and you couldn't make the turn at the end with the longer, wider tractor and wagon like you could with the old one.

"Well shit," I grumbled as I hopped out to take a look at the narrow turn and then all the way back up the row to where it started, which was so far away that the people working there looked like ants. "So this is how today is going to go, is it?" I asked the world at large as I tried to solve the conundrum. This was what being a smart ass got you.

BEST
FRIENDS

9

KAT

THERE REALLY NEEDED to be a book on how to move on with your life after you ran away from your abusive husband, the for dummies version. It would be very frickin' helpful to have right about now. I'd been going through my phone all morning, cross-legged on the couch with coffee in hand, as I tried to decide what to do with my life. Clarity was being very elusive.

I could only hide out for so long, and I could only last for so long without any income. The money that I'd managed to squirrel away was only going to last for a short while, and then I would be broke. The idea of having to live on the streets again was not something I wanted to think about too closely.

To the outside world looking in on my relationship with Richard, I must have looked incredibly spoiled. After all, I hadn't worked a day since high school. But, that was only because Richard didn't want me to work—that was too much freedom.

When he first suggested that I stay home and look after things there instead of joining the job search, we were in the process of building our own home, and my brain was still fogged by the shine of a new marriage. I thought he was so kind and chivalrous. It wasn't until years later that I saw through the gesture for what it really was—just another way to keep me trapped and tied to him.

I was willing to work any job, but what I really wanted was to do something that was all mine for a change. Something that screamed 'me,' and where I wouldn't have to be ordered around by someone else. There were only two things that I loved doing enough that I could see myself opening up my own place as a business. The first was yoga and the other was baking, so my two choices were either yoga studio or small bakery. Taking a chance, I hit Olly's number.

"Olivia speaking," Olly said, her voice practically singing into the phone.

I smiled at the sound of the upbeat woman's voice.

"Hey, Olly, it's Lexi. I was wondering if you might be free for a couple of hours later?"

"Hey, Lexi. I'm on my way to a meeting with a local grower for my winery, but I'll be free after that. Do you want me to give you a call when I'm back?"

"Sure, that would be great. Thanks, Olly."

"Of course. Do I want to know what you're getting me into?"

Laughing, I shook my head even though she couldn't see it.

"It's not bad. I'm not going to ask you to bury a body with me or anything," I said. I immediately slapped a hand over my mouth, slightly mortified, but at least Olly must have found the dark humor funny because she burst out laughing.

"Girl, I knew I was going to like you from the moment I saw you.

For the record, I'd help you with the body, especially if it's that ass that hurt you."

"Thanks, Olly, that means a lot. I'll talk to you later, and good luck at your meeting." I hung up the phone and couldn't wipe the smile off my face. Jumping up, I ran into the kitchen and pulled out every ingredient I had to begin making a list of what I'd need to purchase. As soon as the list was made, I ran into the bedroom to get changed, more invigorated than I'd felt in a very long time.

I was pulling on my shoes when the phone rang, and when I pulled out the phone and saw who was calling, I smiled widely.

"Hey, bestie!" I said. Eve had given me the number to her new burner phone before I left, and I'd memorized it and burned the paper. It had seemed like I was going to extremes, even to me, but after what Richard put me through, I wasn't taking any chances.

"Lexi, it's so good to hear your voice," Eve said with a sigh. She really sounded relieved.

"I have to tell you, it seems really strange hearing you call me that name." Grabbing my purse, I left the small house and locked the door behind me.

"I know, but it's safer," she whispered, and I realized that her greeting had been very quiet, too.

"Why are you whispering? Is everything okay?" The hair stood up on the back of my neck as I waited for her response.

"Someone broke into my place last night before I got home from work and trashed everything."

"And you think it's Richard, don't you?" The silence that greeted me after the question was all the confirmation I needed. "Why do you think it's him?" I asked as my heart began to pound a little harder. I chewed on the soft inside of my cheek, needing something to do.

"The police are saying it was a random break-in, but I don't think so. I just have a gut feeling it was him sending a message. He knows that you couldn't have left without help."

"God, Eve, I'm so sorry. I never thought he'd resort to something like that to find me." I knew he'd be pissed, but sending someone to destroy her place was a whole different level of anger. He wouldn't have done it himself, of course. Too plebian. He was never one for getting his hands dirty when he could pay to have his wishes fulfilled. Zero effort was his favorite amount to give.

That included with sex. The bitterness and resentment that had been festering inside me threatened to bubble up and break loose, but I took a deep breath of the cool early fall air and kept walking.

"Don't blame yourself, girl. They're just things, and besides, I wanted to remodel. This will give me the excuse." She laughed, but her voice was still a little guarded.

"Is there something else you're not telling me?"

There was a heavy sigh on the other end of the line. My dread grew.

"I could never keep anything from you."

"What is it, Eve?" My eyes darted around the quiet street. There were a few people out for a stroll and a few women sitting in the park, all minding their own business, and the cars driving by held no one I knew, but an eerie feeling was still very much with me. How could I not feel like the boogeyman was around every corner? Despite how hard I was trying not to give that power to Richard, the feeling of being watched lingered.

"The lawyer who took care of all your paperwork, including

creating the divorce papers his office served on your behalf...well—his office was broken into as well. He reassured me that he never keeps files like yours out of the safe for obvious reasons, luckily. But Lexi, if this is Richard, and I think it is, you need to keep an eye open at all times. Don't let your guard down, and it might be wise to get a dog or a slew of attack cats."

Even as the icy dread settled into the pit of my stomach, I couldn't help but giggle at the image of Richard opening the door to a house of attack cats ready to spring.

"I really miss you, Eve," I said, unable to keep the sadness out of my voice.

"I miss you too, girl, but I'm just happy you're away from that asshole. I'll let you know if I hear anything else. Be safe, bestie."

"I will, and you too."

"Oh, don't you worry about me. If I catch his ass anywhere near me or my property, it's him who will have to worry," she said with bravado.

We hung up, and after we did, I stared at the phone for a few seconds. I believed Eve. She was tough, and she didn't take shit from anyone. She was also a black belt in karate. If Richard were smart, he'd keep his distance from that five-foot tall ball of ginger fury. Still, I worried.

My hand trembled slightly as I put the phone back in my pocket. I was tempted to turn around and run back to the house, block the door, and board the windows, but I couldn't do that. I needed to have a life, and that meant I needed to be brave. Before Richard, I used to be brave—I'd had to be brave—and I needed to find that version of myself again. I knew she was in there, and it was time she stepped back out into the light.

I practically jogged across the room to get to the door when the knock came, and after checking through the peephole, I smiled widely as I threw open the door to let Olly inside.

"Well, someone certainly woke up on the right side of the bed this morning," Olly said, eyeing me suspiciously. She suddenly sniffed the air, the smell doing exactly what I'd wanted it to as her head turned toward the island. "Oh my god, it smells divine in here."

Smirking, I closed the door and watched as the scent of fresh baked goods drew Olly over to the island, where she stared down at the assortment of plates I had set up.

"I'm glad you said that because the favor I'm about to ask is two-fold."

"If you're going to ask me to enter a food-eating contest and scarf all this down, then you have a deal. I'm in." She went to reach for one of the German chocolate brownies, but I gently smacked her hand. Before she ate, she needed to understand.

"Ouch, meanie," Olly pouted. I rolled my eyes at her even as I couldn't keep myself from grinning.

"Okay, first thing, I do need you to sample everything that is on the island, and then I'll need your help with bundling up little sample packages to take around town. I'd like to say hi and introduce myself with a sweet little treat. But...there's also the fact that I'd like your help with finding a space I can rent."

Olly sat down on one of the tall stools surrounding the island.

"Rent. What for?"

Leaning on the counter, I puffed out my chest, already feeling a little pride in myself even though nothing had been accomplished yet.

"I'm taking a page from your book. You inspired me with your story, and I've decided I want to carve out my own space and create something that is mine, completely mine, and something that I can be proud of."

"I'm loving this idea. Does this mean you're planning on sticking around?"

I looked around the small house, my home, and smiled.

"Yeah, I think I will stay. I mean, it's not like I had a particular destination in mind to start with, and I kinda like the people I've met so far."

Olly smiled widely before shifting closer to lean over the island and all of its fragrant treasures.

"Okay, so where do you want me to start?"

I poured a glass of water and sat it down beside her as a palate cleanser. It was important to get the best feedback possible.

"Start anywhere. Take a bite and really focus on tasting it, just like how you'd taste one of your wines, and let me know which ones you can't live without having another bite of."

"Pretty dramatic for a treat tasting, but I'm so in." Olly picked up a chocolate chip cookie with caramel and pecans in it. She took a bite and moaned. "Do you have a pen and paper? I'll give them a rating and tell you the pros and cons."

"Super-efficient, I love it." I grabbed some paper from the small printer I'd found in the spare room, making a mental note to buy a notebook for writing down ideas and suggestions. Thank god the house had come pre-furnished and with as many left-behind items as it had.

I tried hard not to look nervous as, one at a time, Olly picked up and tried each treat. She was all business, closing her eyes and sniffing it to take in the aroma before taking a bite and letting it linger in her mouth. With each mouthful, she scribbled down a score out of five and made a few notes on what she loved or thought could be improved.

I felt like an anxious parent waiting for feedback on how my child had done on the first day of school as I waited for Olly to finish with the last of the sweets. Finally, she finished writing and looked up at me. Her face was so serious that I was suddenly scared to hear her response.

"So? You're freaking me out, here. How did you like them?" I asked.

Olly leaned forward over the island and hit me with a hard stare.

"Where the hell have you been hiding my whole life and will you marry me?"

My cheeks flamed red, and I so badly wanted to squeal like a teenage girl. I pushed it down to reply like the grown woman I was. Barely.

"So that means you liked them?"

"Liked? Girl, are you freaking serious? They are delicious! No, they are better than delicious. This is the kind of thing that people flock to purchase. I'm already going to book you to stock the sweets section in my winery's tasting room. We serve wine and snacks right now, and I'm hoping to upgrade to a full-size restaurant sometime soon. I would be honored, and I won't take no for an answer, to have your baked goods be a part of my restaurant."

The feeling inside me was so big that I had to sit down. I rounded the island to flop onto one of the stools, my heart beating worse than on the day I got married.

"You really think they're that good?"

"I do." Olly grabbed my hand and gave it a squeeze. "The way I look at it, there's only one problem."

I stared at the array of items, analyzing.

"There's not enough color, is there? I knew I should've done some pretty macarons," I said, kicking myself a little for not thinking of it. There was a lot of brown.

Olly laughed so hard I thought she was going to fall right off the stool.

"No, I mean I want to eat them all by myself, and that is problematic for my hips."

"Oh." I snickered at my jump to a conclusion. "So, will you help me pack these up?"

"You could just give them all to me. I really wouldn't mind."

Standing, I grabbed the bag of small, colorful tins I'd purchased earlier. It had been stupidly fun picking them out at the store.

"Don't worry. You can request whatever you want, whenever you want, and don't forget that you're my official guinea pig."

"I don't think I've ever been so happy to be called a large rodent before," Olly said, laughing. She was just as organized with packing and balancing out the tins as she'd been about the tasting, and by the time we were done, I could clearly see why she was a business owner and where I needed to improve. It was going to take a lot more than simply coming up with ideas and making the goodies if I wanted to be successful.

"Are you still up for helping out with a little delivery and looking for a space I could rent for the business?" I asked.

"I am, and I think I know the perfect spot for you to rent." Olly stood and gave me a wink as I placed the last of the tins into the waiting canvas bags. "I just have to make sure I'm home before six. I decided to get back on the horse, and I have a date tonight."

"Really? And who is the lucky lady?" I had to resist the urge to elbow her playfully like I might have done with Eve. We were getting there, but I still didn't know Olly that well yet.

"Man, actually."

I lifted the bags, and the confusion I was trying to hide must have been written all across my face because Olly laughed until tears streamed from her eyes. "I like both men and women. It's more about who I hit it off with and have chemistry with than what gender they are."

"I like that a lot. It seems freeing to just like who you like and not let old-fashioned boundaries stop you."

"Exactly. Although, I don't know how this date is going to go. His father is the local goat cheese maker, and I only agreed to the date when I was negotiating for some cheese because his father wouldn't stop telling me how great the two of us would be together. More than anything, I think I said yes simply to shut him up about it."

"How romantic. That will be a story to tell the grandkids," I teased as we made our way outside. It was still early afternoon, and the sun was high in the sky. The brightly glowing ball seemed different today. It felt like there was a splash of hope in the world once again, and I wanted to hang on to every second of this feeling that I could.

By the time we were done delivering the last of the little tins, I was completely talked out. It wasn't a new experience, but it had been a while. I knew how exhausting it could be to socialize this much from the few galas that Richard had taken me to before he deemed me a disgrace and became disgusted by my presence at them. I didn't have proof, but I was pretty sure the real reason he stopped wanting me to go was so he could pick up some woman and fuck her in a hotel room for the night without having to worry about me.

"Hey, you okay?" Olly asked, grabbing my arm. Startled, I jerked and looked at her. "You looked like you might kill someone, and you're shaking."

"I'm sorry. I...." Looking down at my plain black sneakers, I took a deep breath. "Just a bad memory sneaking in. I'm good."

"You sure? We can take a look at the building another day."

Rolling out my shoulders, I shook my head.

"No. I'm done with letting my ex control anything about me or what I do, and that includes looking at this building. This is something for me, and I'm excited about that."

Olly gave my arm a gentle squeeze before letting go.

"Great, because I'm really excited for you to see this spot." We continued along the main street until we reached her bookstore and stopped. "What do you think?"

"About your store? I don't understand."

"You see that spot right there?" She pointed to the much larger unit next door that stretched to the end of the small strip of stores. "I need to expand, but not enough to take up both this unit and that one, which is already twice as big. I've been considering renting that unit for a little while, and I've already spoken to the landlord about potentially breaking my contract for here without penalty to take over the larger unit instead."

"Oh my god." I looked around at the prime location, close to both the park and the coffee shop and right beside what would be Olly's bookstore, and this time, I did squeal like a teenager, making Olly laugh.

"And, since my lease is technically not broken yet, I could sublease to you for what my contract is, and that way, you won't get hit with the higher cost while you're trying to start up."

Tears welled in my eyes. How was it that I'd gotten so lucky and met the sweetest family in the world? Finally, a ray of real hope was starting to shine in my heart. I could picture the sign and the line of people waiting to get in. Turning to Olly, I was at a loss for words as the tears spilled over and trickled down my cheeks. How do you thank someone for that?

"I don't know what to say," I said through the tears of joy.

"How about I get a permanent discount of twenty percent on any orders for my business and we call it fair?"

"Deal," I said, laughing. I held out my hand, but Olly scoffed and pulled me into a hug. It had been so long since I was able to hug someone without fearing that Richard would see and call me a cheater, or that he would see me with Eve and start another huge fight, that I almost started crying all over again.

"Come on. Let's go get some dinner and wine to celebrate."

"What about your date?"

"Oh yeah, shit." Olly tapped her chin. "Oh, screw it. I didn't want to meet this guy anyway. I'll just cancel."

"But...."

"No buts. We are going out for a nice meal and wine in celebration. This is far more important than some date with some random guy." Olly marched up the sidewalk a few feet before looking over her shoulder at me. "Well, come on. We have to look presentable if we're going out."

The only thing that would've made this day better was if I could've shared it with Eve. It was because of her that I even had this opportunity, and it was her who was left taking the brunt of Richard's fury.

I'd make it up to her. I had to.

10

JAKE

I WAS MORE bone tired than I had been in a very long time as my dad and I headed inside for dinner. Unlike when I'd felt exhausted from partying and my late-night, bad boy habits, I actually felt proud of my sore hands, dirty jeans, and heavy eyelids. I'd earned them.

"You two look a mess. Why don't you go shower and freshen up? Dinner will be ready in fifteen minutes," my mom said as my dad and I walked into the house looking like a pair of zombies.

"Good call, Mom," I said, going in for a hug, but she laughed and beat me off with a dish towel.

"Don't you touch me, mister. You're smelly, sweaty, and very dirty," she said as she swatted my arm with the piece of material better than any of the guys in the locker room ever could. Saluting sharply, I turned to go upstairs and savor the wonders of modern plumbing.

The stairs felt like a mountain to climb, and I had to hand it to my dad—despite his age, he was still in great physical condition and was just as fast as I was. As I wandered into my bedroom and was tempted to simply flop down on top of the comforter and pass out without showering or eating dinner, but if I didn't come down to eat and my mom saw my dirty ass on the clean comforter, I would be a dead man.

My phone dinged as I was stripping off my jeans, and I pulled it out to see Miles's name and a message notification. I really didn't want to open it, but if I didn't, I knew he would do nothing but bombard me with texts and calls until I finally answered.

M. *Hey. Mr. Russo wants to go forward with the cologne ads. The filming starts next week in Hawaii.*

I shook my head as I read the message, not even pausing to think before I typed.

J. *No. I'm not going.*

M. *What do you mean you're not going?*

Well, this was about to get fun. Rolling my head back to stare at the ceiling, I groaned. I did not have the energy for this conversation right now, but it looked like it was going to happen anyway.

J. *I'm pretty sure those four words are simple enough to understand. NO. I'm not going. Tell him if he wants me to be in his ads, he'll have to wait until I'm done with my vacation. Or he can film where I am. Only options.*

The phone was silent for so long that I thought Miles either must have disappeared somehow or was choosing to ignore me...again. Finally, a message appeared.

M. *Do you have any idea what this contract could mean for you?*

J. *I do, and I don't care. I told—*

The phone rang in my hand while I was in the middle of typing, displaying Miles's name across the screen. Great, this was about to get ten times worse.

"Dammit," I muttered before hitting the talk button. "Calling me won't make me change my mind."

"What the fuck? I've poured every waking moment into this deal, and you're just going to fuck it up for us?"

"Miles...."

"No. I can't believe you'd do this. We're talking seven figures, Jake, *seven fucking figures* for three ads."

"Miles...."

"Why do I bother? Why did you hire me at all if you're not going to listen to my sound advice? This one contract would set us up for *life*—no more begging and bad parties and everything else you said you don't want anymore. What the fuck is wrong with you?"

By that point, I was fuming. I slammed my hand down on the bathroom counter, needing some outlet for the rage bubbling up inside me.

"Miles, enough!" I barked. When it seemed like he was going to remain quiet, I lowered my voice. "I can't go back, not right now, and if you want me to be honest, maybe not ever. I will do the ads if he sends the film crew here to my parent's farm, or he can wait until my vacation is over. Maybe pitch that it would look more romantic in the middle of a grape harvest surrounded by all the rows of grapes in a vineyard or some shit."

"Woah, what do you mean you might never come back? I thought this was just a break, some time to recharge the batteries?" Miles demanded.

"I still want to do some things, maybe some more commercials, but I'm done with playing up the social media life, Miles. I've realized that I don't want it. I can't live like that anymore, and I want to remain here." I rubbed my eyes. "Look, no matter what, you will get paid for all the work you've already done, and I wouldn't just let you go, but don't book me for anything else for now and let me know what Mr. Russo wants to do."

"You're serious about this?" Miles sounded both surprised and exasperated as he huffed into the phone.

"I've never been more serious about anything. I'm done for now, maybe forever."

"I...I...fuck!" The phone went silent, and when I looked down at it, I realized it was because Miles had hung up on me. I'd never heard him that mad, and I'd heard him plenty mad over the years.

It wasn't like I didn't understand that Miles had my best interests at heart. We'd been friends before he became my manager, and he'd dedicated all his time since to me and not building up any other clients, but still, I just couldn't continue on the way I was. Things needed to change.

Pushing aside the guilt gnawing at me, I quickly hopped into the shower, not caring that the water was still cold. It felt good on my heated skin, and as I scrubbed away in the cold water, it helped wash away not only the grime of the day's work, but also the remnants of the dream I'd had last night.

The dream was always some variation of the same thing. It started out with Kat and me as teens and drifted to how I remembered seeing her from the café window, and then it would sink dangerously into a vivid play-by-play of having her under me while I made love to her. She was like a beautiful curse that I sometimes wished I could rid myself of, yet deep down, I never wanted to let her go. Being stuck in purgatory for eternity with just the ghost of her was still better than any heaven without her could ever be.

I would give up every dime I had for just one more touch, one real kiss—not the awkward, childish one I'd given her the night before our lives were torn in two different directions. My heart ached to find her, but it was selfish to think that way. What good would it do to storm into her life after all this time hellbent on destroying her marriage? And what if she really did have kids? They'd been married long enough to have several. Could I ruin that?

I needed to be honest with myself—I wanted way more than a smile and a kiss. I was asshole enough to want everything, and if I were given the opportunity, I'd take it, and her, and whatever else she'd give me if I could, which was why I had to stay away.

I looked down at my cock, which had stood up at the slightest thought of Kat, and shook my head. As if that would help.

"Sorry, no time for that. Miles took up all your playtime. And now I sound fucking crazy because I'm talking to my dick. Fucking awesome."

Scrubbing down quickly, I jumped out of the shower to get dressed, grateful that the water had still been cool enough not to make getting my little problem to go away any harder. Or not hard. Whatever. For all the expensive clothes I had, which was a pretty significant amount at this point, my selection of simple jeans and T-shirts needed an overhaul.

Dressed and more than ready for dinner, I headed toward the kitchen. As I wandered down the stairs still rubbing at my hair with a towel, I could hear multiple voices speaking. Rounding the corner, I caught sight of my younger brother.

"It's fucking true! You're home, brother," Jayce yelled before running at me.

"Oh, shit," I mumbled right before he hit me like we still played football, grabbing me around the middle and slamming me to the floor. "You ass," I groaned with the impact of the carpeted floor, and then the wrestling match was on. Jayce was only slightly shorter than I was and incredibly fit from rock climbing, making it hard to get him locked into a hold. I didn't remember it hurting as badly when we were younger, but I wasn't going to be the one to surrender.

We rolled around the living room like we were teens again to the sound of laughter from my dad, but at the sound of my mom yelling for us to cut it out and grow up, we quickly broke apart. That was one opponent we could never win against. Jayce flopped onto his back in the middle of the floor, and I followed suit, my chest heaving from the effort of the match.

"You're a dick and worse than Jasper, you bulldozing menace," I said, hitting him in the arm with a smile plastered across my face. Some things just never changed. Jayce's sandy-blond hair still managed to flop over his gray eyes and look like he'd styled it that way even though he was too laid back to ever care about something like using hair products.

"What? I didn't lick your face, but I could." Jayce stuck out his tongue, waving it around like a dog, and I grabbed a pillow off the couch to smack him a couple of times. Satisfied, I stood up to put the pillow back. Not putting things away was a surefire way to get an earful.

"You win, you're still the fucking weird one," I said.

"Language! Use those words outside. I don't care how filthy your mouth gets, but never inside these walls," my mom said before storming back into the kitchen, leaving me to help Jayce up and give him a hug.

I turned to look at my dad and Tripp, who'd just walked in the front door, the old thing squeaking as it banged into place. Tripp definitely didn't look as happy to see me as Jayce.

"Hey, brother," I said, holding out my hand for him to shake. He wasn't much of a hugger. Tripp glared at me in response, his bright blue eyes cutting as coolly as ice would. Those eyes flicked down to my hand and then back up to my face before he crossed his arms over his large chest. No handshake, then.

Tripp had always been the beast of the three of us—a major reason why he'd been a linebacker on the school football team. His midnight black hair looked like it had been shaved down into a buzz cut recently, and he genuinely looked like he'd just stepped off an army base and was about to kick my ass.

"Why are you home this time? Too many drunken nights and whores in your bed? Need to sober up for a week and scrub off the germs before you take off again?" Tripp sneered.

The room fell so silent you could've heard a pin drop. It was as if all the oxygen had been sucked out with his words, and they hurt because, on some level, they were true. It had been my MO since I started doing the whole social media life thing, but I didn't like him calling me out on it. If Mom or Dad wanted to kick me out or tell me off, then they were more than welcome to, but not Tripp. We might have been brothers, but he didn't have that right.

"It's not like that this time. I'm home for good," I said, trying not to hold on to my anger. I dropped my hand as Tripp continued to let it hang between us. He let out a snort and rolled his eyes, pissing me off more.

"Yeah, I'll believe that when I see it," he said.

"What the hell is your problem, Tripp?"

He shook his head, looking me up and down like I was a piece of garbage. My fists curled, and I took a step toward my older brother.

"That's enough, boys," my dad said, his voice ringing out as he stepped in close and placed a hand on each of our shoulders. "No fighting inside these walls. In here, we're family, and while we can disagree with one another's decisions, there will be no real fighting or harsh feelings."

Tripp rolled his eyes, a look of disgust on his face as he looked away from Dad, but he kept his mouth shut and didn't say anything further. I guess, in the grand scheme of things, having everyone except for one person be happy to see me was a win, but it was Tripp, and we'd always been as close as best friends—at least, I thought we'd been.

"Come on, you lot. Dinner is getting cold," Mom called out from the kitchen, and at her words, the testosterone that had been building up finally dissipated.

"Don't mind him. He's been really grumpy lately," Jayce whispered in my ear once Tripp was out of earshot. I raised my eyebrows in question. "Later," Jayce promised, shooting a look toward the kitchen. Apparently, it was not a topic he wanted to be caught talking about with me.

"So what's up? I didn't think you guys were due back until the weekend," I said, letting it go for now.

Jayce wrapped his arm around my shoulders and made an exaggeratedly sad face at me.

"What, are you not happy to see me?"

Reaching the table, we took our usual spots, and it felt both right and strange to be sitting around the table with everyone like this again.

"Of course I am. It's just that Mom said you were going to be a couple more days."

"We decided there was no point spending the time to look at the others. We found two properties that are a perfect fit, so now, it's just going to be a matter of deciding which one to purchase. The rest were not as good for one reason or another."

We all held still and bowed our heads when Mom started grace. I hadn't been much of the church-going type, ever, but she'd insisted on us all attending church every Sunday until we turned eighteen. Even now, you said grace at every meal and thanked the Lord for a good growing season and all of your blessings.

Maybe it was the fact that I was the one who found my birth mother floating in her own pool of blood because she'd been murdered by my father. Maybe it was my father getting sent to prison for life, which had put me smack in the middle of the foster system, or it might even have been bouncing around from home to home, always feeling like I never belonged. Heck, it could've been due to none of that and it was just my nature, but whatever it was, the whole concept of praying to someone you couldn't see or hear had always felt so strange to me.

My whole first year with the Russels, I would sit crossed-armed and silent for every prayer, but as I began to feel safe and see Joy as my mom, well—I decided that if it made her happy, then I should participate.

Around me, the conversation erupted into excitement as Dad asked questions about the properties. Tripp even chilled out and laughed a few times. It helped that Mom had cooked Tripp's favorite, peach-glazed pork chops, but he still barely looked at me. I knew my actions and poor choices wouldn't be well received by anyone in the family, but they didn't hurt him, only me, so I couldn't understand the hostility.

"What do you think, Jake?" my dad asked, breaking my mental wandering.

My head snapped up from where I'd been pushing around my food. I'd been lost in thought and had no idea what the question was.

"What?"

"You've always had an eye for land and crops. Which property do you think would be the better one to purchase?"

"You're asking his opinion?" The room went silent at Tripp's outburst. He stared back and forth between myself and Dad. "I don't fucking believe this."

"Language, Tripp," Mom scolded, but before she could say anything more, he stood from the table and tossed his knife and fork down onto his plate with a clatter, sending pieces of mashed potato flying. The short laugh he let out sounded more like a bark.

"I guess once the favorite, always the favorite. I can't sit here and listen to this. I'm outta here." Tripp stormed away from the table. The back door squeaked open and then slammed shut behind him as he practically ran out of the house.

"I'll go talk to him," Dad said, but I placed my hand on his arm.

"No, I'd better go speak to him. Whatever he's angry about, it's because of me, not you." Standing from the table, I made my own way outside. After taking a moment to adjust, my eyes scanned the darkness for my brother, and I found him stomping his way toward the gazebo. I followed in his wake like a stalker, and with each step, the angrier I got.

"Hey! What the hell is your problem?" I shouted.

Tripp looked over his shoulder but then continued on until he was under the gazebo, which was decorated with a large round table and little glittering lights. I stomped up the two stairs leading to it and leaned against one of the support beams close to where Tripp had leaned over to grip the railing. I folded my arms across my chest when it became clear he wasn't going to be the one to speak first.

"Are you going to tell me what the hell you're pissed at me for?"

"What's the point?" Tripp's blue eyes found mine, and the anger and hurt I saw in them was staggering. "It's not like you care, anyway."

"What the hell is that supposed to mean? Of course I care," I said, dropping my arms as the anger notched a little higher on my rage meter.

"Really? You have a fucking funny way of showing it, bro," Tripp bit out, the sarcasm heavy in his voice. "When was the last time you gave a shit about any of us or this place? Always off traveling the world, doing nothing with your life other than partying, yet it's always the same story when you eventually ride up the driveway on your stupid motorcycle. You always end up back in the fold, no questions asked."

"That's not fair, Tripp. I was working. I was building something that would allow me to—."

"To what?" Tripp cut in before standing straight and taking a small, threatening step in my direction. Even though he was the same height, he had more muscle than I'd ever be able to put on, and I was pretty damn built. "Work at getting drunk and high every night? Go to parties and have your picture taken in situations that Mom has to try to explain away or defend you from whenever she sees anyone she knows?"

He took another step closer, his eyes flashing with anger.

"Or maybe you're working at fucking as many people as you can? Maybe you're vying to pick up some disease so Mom and Dad are forced to look after your sorry ass for the remainder of your short, pathetic life, you ungrateful asshole." Tripp poked me in the chest. "When was the last time you remembered a birthday or an anniversary? Fuck, how about just a call to say hi and see if we're still breathing? You're an ungrateful prick, that's what you are!"

Before I realized what I was doing, my fist flew for Tripp's face. The momentary satisfaction that came from connecting solidly with his chin was gone in the next heartbeat as Tripp glared at me and wiped off the blood at the corner of his mouth. He'd barely moved from the hit.

Oh shit.

Tripp was on me before I could take another breath. Fists flew as we crashed to the gazebo floor, the impact forcing the air from my lungs in a whoosh for the second time tonight. Despite his muscles, we were fairly evenly matched as fighters, and I managed to get him off of me and land a solid blow to his side before he flipped me on my back and landed a hard left across my face. I bucked my body up sharply, dislodging him enough to push him into the wooden spindles on the gazebo railing. Several spindles cracked.

Leaping up, I staggered back from my brother several steps to catch my breath. Catching movement out of the corner of my eye instead, I looked over his shoulder in the direction of the house. All three family members were running toward us, with Jayce in the lead.

"Son of a bitch," Tripp roared as he jumped up from the ground and tackled me around the waist. I stumbled back from the force of his body weight and momentum and, unable to stop, crashed into the railing. The top rail gave way, snapping under our weight with a loud crack.

"Fuck," we yelled together as we splashed into the cold pond. The water was dark, but it luckily wasn't deep, and we both stood there in the water gasping and staring at one another. That was one way to cool off.

"Oh my god, boys, are you okay?" Mom called out.

"Yeah, we're fine," I said. Giving Tripp a once over to make sure he wasn't planning on using a sneak attack to drown me, I sloshed my way toward the edge of the pond.

Jayce was laughing hysterically on the bank, tears rolling down his face as he tried to catch his breath.

"That was the best fucking thing I've ever seen," he roared, holding his stomach. "Can you do it again so I can get that shit on film? The two...of you...." Jayce wheezed, in such hysterics that he ended up falling down onto his ass. It did nothing to stop his laughter.

"Well, at least that was amusing to someone," I muttered before rubbing at my sore jaw. Whipping off my damp T-shirt, I hurled it at Jayce to shut his annoying hyena ass up, but it only made him laugh harder until I had to give up and join in along with him.

Tripp stomped past the both of us, his waterlogged shoes squishing with every stride.

"Tripp, come on," I called out, but he just held up his hand to stop me from saying anything more or following him.

"Just leave me alone, Jake. You're good at that."

The laughter died down, the smile slipping from my face as I watched my brother retreat toward his truck. The lights of the Chevy came on, and he was soon peeling down the driveway and off into the darkness.

"Are you okay?" my mom asked, giving me a motherly once-over.

"Yeah. A few bumps and bruises, nothing more. We weren't out for blood," I said. Tears welled in her eyes, making me feel like a piece of shit for worrying her.

"I'm sorry, Jake. I know he's angry and hurt, but I didn't think it would come to this."

I placed my hands on her shoulders.

"It's not your fault that you have two sons in their thirties who think they are still teens. We will get past this. We always do when we fight."

"Come on, Joy. Let's go back inside and let Jake and Jayce talk," Dad offered, wrapping his arm around her shoulders. They quietly walked back toward the house like that, still tucked together tightly.

As I flopped down onto the grass beside Jayce, a shiver raced along my dampened skin. The nights were getting chilly, but I loved the feel of it and just stared out at the water.

"What's going on with Tripp?" I asked once Mom and Dad were out of earshot.

Jayce looked over at me and sighed, clearly conflicted.

"I don't know if it's my place to say."

"Man, I've never seen him that angry. We've argued and wrestled before, but he was downright pissed off. You would've thought he hated me, the way he was going at it. If you know something, then I'm calling brother code on this."

"Oh, you would pull that out, you dick." Jayce rubbed at his face and then nodded. "Fine, I'll tell you, but if I end up with a black eye for telling you, it's your ass I'm coming for."

"That's fair enough."

A coyote yipped in the distance, and the two of us turned to watch the dark shadow it made run across the field in the moonlight. Goosebumps rose on my arms as I stared.

"Look, there are a few things happening here. The first is that Tripp is pissed that you practically packed up and disappeared years ago only to keep dropping by like the prodigal son before disappearing once again."

I rolled my eyes as I picked up a tiny stone and lobbed it into the pond. It only skipped once.

"Yeah, I got that much out of him before shit went sideways," I said with Sahara levels of dryness. Jayce snickered.

"Don't get me started again. I'll be out here laughing all night." Jayce smiled widely, and it was the same look he always gave the teachers, or the priest, if he was being devious but still wanted to melt your resolve.

"Just get on with it."

"Man, I hate being the one to tell you this." Jayce's fist hit the ground, and he let out a low groan before talking again. "Aside from the stuff with Mom and the lack of you being around to help or whatever with the farm, Tripp's marriage fell apart like four months ago. Lanny filed for divorce and is threatening to move across the country with Syd, Bri and her new guy. He's not taking any of it well, man, like not at all."

My mouth fell open. What the actual fuck? I hadn't heard anything about any of this.

"Oh shit," I muttered. Tripp and Lanny were like the dream

marriage, or so I had thought. They were always together and laughing. When I'd been home last Christmas, they'd seemed as tight as ever, and their kids were smiling little bundles of awesomeness. "What happened?"

Jayce shrugged as he hugged his knees.

"I don't really know. He doesn't talk to any of us about it, but the cops showed up here and asked us all sorts questions about him. It was like they were looking to see if he had anger issues or some shit. It was fucking weird. I asked him what was going on and he announced that they were getting divorced and Lanny had moved on, and then he clammed up after that." Jayce looked over at me, and his eyes said it all. It felt like I'd been sucker punched.

"And I'm the one he's closest to, and he already felt abandoned by me." I rubbed at my face and pinched the bridge of my nose. I really had been so caught up in my own sparkly ball of crap that I hadn't realized until now that it had been at least six months since I'd called either of my brothers and longer still since I'd last been home.

I hadn't even thought about contacting them—not to say hi or shoot the shit, or even to see if their lives were going okay. It was always them reaching out, and I tried to remember the last time Tripp had sent me anything at all. I couldn't.

It was easier to simply assume that their lives were perfect and nothing here would ever change, like it was all stuck in some weird time capsule. I could come and go as I pleased, and everything would always be the same when I got back.

"I really am an asshole," I said, hanging my head.

"Ya kinda are. And I got dumped, too."

I looked at Jayce's sad face and promptly laughed, earning a glare.

"You always deserve it, though," I ribbed, trying to poke a little fun at him, but I stopped when he just shrugged instead of playing along.

"Maybe, but I'm still human, you know? I have feelings." The words were serious, but Jayce said them as if he were joking. Even though his face was filled with amusement, I now had to wonder how much of it was real and how much of Jayce was kept hidden under the comedian.

There was nothing more to say. I was a prick. It was the truth, and now I needed to find a way to make things right with my entire family. As with all things in life, there was a balance to be maintained, and I'd abused that balance and hurt those closest to me.

Sighing, I looked up at the stars and couldn't help thinking about Kat. The same old lonely ache settled in my chest as I thought about how I'd lost her, and we hadn't even been married or had kids. I simply couldn't imagine what Tripp was going through, and because of my selfishness, I'd let him suffer through it alone.

BEST
FRIENDS

11

KAT

OH HOLY HELL my head hurt. I blamed Olly. She had insisted that we do a fancy celebration dinner, during and after which we had proceeded to drink multiple bottles of wine as we hashed out plans for the bakery and bookstore. Olly had said she worried about her waist around my baked goods, but after last night, I was low-key worried about my kidneys. Her wine was just too good.

By the end of the night, I think we'd decided that unicorns would look great as a decorating motif and that I should have them painted on the walls of the bakery prancing through fluffy clouds. Seemed like a great idea at the time—not so much now. Apparently, drunk Olly should never be trusted for decorating advice. Or drunk Lexi.

I peeled one eyelid open and then jolted up as something banged in the kitchen. Immediately, my heart began hammering like a drum until I spied a mop of blonde hair moving around in the kitchen. I grabbed my head as the headache bit harder from the sudden movement.

"Olly, what are you doing?" I asked before leaning my head back onto the couch.

"Making breakfast, what does it look like?" she answered with an abundance of cheer, which annoyed me. How was it that we drank the same amount, yet I looked like I'd been run over by a garbage truck that then proceeded to dump its garbage all over me while she looked perfect? Not only that, but my mouth tasted worse than I felt. "Come on, lazy bones. The day is a-wastin'."

I looked toward the window and saw that it was still dark. What the heck?

"Olly, how old are you? 'Cause you sounded eighty just now, and what freaking time is it, anyway? The sun is not even up," I ground out.

"First rule of being a business owner—it's never too early in the morning to get going. We have contracts to sign, décor to plan, and suppliers to find." She stuffed a piece of bacon in her mouth. "Oh, and I have already sent an email to the landlord explaining what we plan on doing, and I signed that new contract for the larger space, so I hope you haven't changed your mind."

I stared at her in shock. The words were going in, but my brain was too sore and scrambled to make out much of her bubbly rant.

"I need a shower, to brush my teeth, and a coffee before I can unpack anything you just said."

"Well, hurry up. Chop chop. I need to get this grease into you so your head will feel better, and then we have a meeting with a friend of mine to go over how to set up the insides of both locations properly."

"Olly," I said, then gave up and just shook my head.

"I know, I know. I can be overbearing and annoying and pushy and...." She stopped talking and looked down.

"No, I just wanted to say thanks. This is the kick in the ass I needed," I said. Olly smiled widely as I turned and headed to the bedroom. I stared longingly at the bed, but I didn't dare so much as sit down, or I knew I was going to flop right over. In my head, I saw an image of Olly coming in with a pot and a wooden spoon to bang it with like the lead drummer in a band. Hard pass.

Flicking on the water, I stripped and stared at myself in the mirror. A long scar followed the line of my ribs, and I ran a hand over it, wondering if it would ever go away or if it would be a constant reminder of the bad decisions I'd made. Taking a deep breath, I grabbed the Aspirin and tossed a couple in my mouth, washing them down before getting into the shower.

The warm spray felt glorious. I stuck my head under the water, then had to grab for the edge of the shower door as a flash from the car accident hit. I sank to my knees, trying to take a deep breath, but the sounds of screeching tires and crunching metal were loud in my ears.

"Where the fuck do you think you're going?" Richard yelled. He stepped forward aggressively, making a grab for my arm. I pulled it out of his reach before he could get a grip on it.

"Anywhere that isn't here with you. We're done," I yelled back.

His face looked shocked, and I shook my head that he could be so surprised by this. What reason had he given me to stay?

"You can't leave me," he stated.

My eyebrows raised as I took another step toward the front door.

"Oh yeah? Watch me, Richard."

As I grabbed the door handle, I felt his hands grab my arms and haul me back hard. Suddenly, I was being tossed like a doll across the hallway, where I slammed into a decorative table. The impact rattled my teeth, and my side dragged harshly along the pointed corner as I fell. Screaming, I hit the floor.

"Shit, Kate. I'm sorry. I didn't mean to!" Richard said as he knelt down next to me. He lifted my shirt to show a deep gash across my ribs and the blood already streaming to the floor.

I stared at him, fear gripping my heart as he pressed on the wound. Grabbing my hand, he pressed it to my side, making me suck in a sharp breath as I winced.

"I'll be right back. My phone and the first aid are upstairs," he said. It was just a glimmer, but in that moment, it felt like he actually cared. The thing was, I'd seen too many of those glimmers come and go —I knew they never lasted.

As he ran up the stairs, I grabbed my purse and keys and pulled myself up and over to the door. My shaking hand had to try twice to get the door unlocked, but I finally made it outside into the night and stumbled to my car. Pressing unlock on the key fob, I slipped inside and locked the door as I stomped on the brake pedal and pushed the start button.

I'd taken too long—Richard had noticed I wasn't in the hall anymore. He came running out the door, phone in hand, yelling for me to stop. Tears blinded me as much as the fear, making it hard to see what I was doing. As Richard ran for the driver's side door, I threw the car into gear and backed down the driveway.

"Stop, Kate! Stop!"

He chased after the car, and a hysterical bubble of terror clogged my throat, making me gasp as I hit the quiet street and turned the car. I kept driving in reverse to put more distance between the car and Richard, who was running down the street after it.

"Kate!"

I could still hear him screaming my name, but I just pushed the white Mercedes faster, not stopping when it scraped down the side of a vehicle parked on the road. Seeing my chance, I wheeled the car backward into a driveway and slammed it into drive before flooring it. The wheels spun as smoke rose into the air at the sudden burst of power.

A van had just left the gated community, and I pushed the car to its limits as the gates began to close behind it. I screamed like I was in some messed-up action movie as the car crashed through the closing gates, both side mirrors flying off on impact. With a wild screech, I ran the red light outside the gates and flew around the corner onto the main street. I didn't know where I was going—all I knew was that I needed to run. I needed to escape. The fear and adrenaline were making me irrational and even though my brain recognized it, I couldn't stop the reaction.

A few minutes later the adrenaline started to wane, the pain in my side returned with a vengeance, and I cried out as I pressed on the wound. My hand came away bright red with the blood that was steadily seeping from my side. Hospital. I definitely needed a hospital, yet the thought of being trapped in one of those buildings while they called Richard kept me pushing the car blindly forward.

Horns blared as I raced through red light after red light, narrowly missing car after car. I shook my head as a bout of lightheadedness came out of nowhere.

"No, no, you can't pass out." The road and street lights in front of

me seemed to narrow down into a tunnel with fuzzy sides. Then there was a bang and a sudden lurch to a stop. Something slammed into my face, and all was dark.

No. There were bright lights, blue ones and pretty red ones, and people yelling. I couldn't make out any of their faces, and I swatted irritatedly at their hands, not knowing who they were and not wanting them to touch me.

"Strap her hands down," someone said, and panic had me fighting whoever was holding me down.

"No, no, please," I begged. I couldn't go back. I just couldn't go back.

I woke up, and the lights overhead were bright and hurt my eyes. I was lying down and moving fast, which made me feel sick to my stomach. I was so confused. Wasn't I in the car?

"How bad is it?" Richard asked from somewhere to the side. He sounded really close.

No, no, no. I didn't want him there. He grabbed my hand, and even though I wanted to jerk it away, I couldn't get my hand free. I realized I wasn't moving them at all. What was wrong with me?

"She needs emergency surgery or she'll never walk again," someone else said. He looked like a doctor. What the hell was that guy talking about? Of course I was going to walk again.

"Okay. Do whatever you have to do," Richard said. He leaned over me and stared into my eyes. "I love you, Kate. You can't leave me."

I swallowed hard as I stared into eyes I didn't recognize anymore. Eyes that said he would sooner see me buried alive than out of his control. Eyes that said he was going to make sure I was never free again. A tear trickled down my cheek as I was wheeled away before my eyes fluttered closed. The darkness was easier.

"Lexi? Are you okay in there? Lexi?" I could hear knocking and Olly's voice, but I couldn't move and couldn't breathe as the panic attack pressed in on my chest. "I'm coming in." The door opened, and I still couldn't move from where I was on all fours in the shower. "Oh my god, Lexi, what's wrong?"

Olly dashed across the floor and reached in to shut off the water, which had turned ice cold. She grabbed the towel I had set out and wrapped it around my shaking shoulders.

"Can't breathe," I managed to get out as she grabbed a couple more of the large towels and got into the shower with me. Kneeling down, she wrapped two of them around my body and sat down, pulling me hard until I was on my side in her lap.

"Just breathe, Lexi. Whatever it is, whoever it is, is not here. You're going to be fine." She rubbed her hand slowly in a circle on my back and up and down the arm she could reach to try and warm my chilled skin. The tears that had been threatening to fall broke free at her gentle kindness, pouring down my cheeks.

"I'm sorry," I blubbered, completely humiliated as I clutched the towels around me like a shield. This was so much worse than the pizza shop.

"Don't be sorry. Don't you ever be sorry. Try and picture how pretty the bakery is going to be. Smell the warm scents of rich coffee and freshly baked treats. Brownies and cookies and tarts, all made by your hand—each one a work of art that people everywhere are going to enjoy. There will be tables for people to sit at and a beautiful patio area out front for the summer."

The tears slowly subsided as Olly's calm and soothing tone washed over me. My lungs slowly loosened like they were finally remembering how to breathe as the fear eased and sank back into the far reaches of my traumatized mind.

"Thank you, Olly. Thank you for being my friend," I stammered through my chattering teeth.

"Always, girl. I've got you, and whatever has you this scared will never hurt you again as long as I'm around. I might be small, but I'm mighty," she stated, conviction in her eyes.

I laughed and just let Olly hold me until the shaking stopped and it felt like I could stand. She helped me to my feet before grabbing my shoulders to make me look at her.

"Are you sure you're okay?" she asked. Her eyes searched mine quizzically.

"I will be."

"Did you want help getting dressed?"

I shook my head.

"I still need to shower. I'll suffer through the cold. Again, thank you. I promise the worst is over."

"Okay, but I'm leaving the door partially open so I can hear you call if you need me," Olly said.

I nodded and she left the bathroom, so I could turn on the shower again. They say it is a 'one day at a time' process to get over trauma, but I didn't know if I could ever be alright as long as the threat of Richard coming after me hung over my head.

No matter what, I couldn't let him find me.

JAKE

I PULLED up to the pretty country home that overlooked lush rolling hills and a deep stream, which Tripp and I had spent a lot of time swimming in as teens. His truck was in the driveway, and as I put the kickstand down on my motorcycle, Tripp came out of the house with a coffee cup in hand.

Pulling off my helmet, I set it on the seat and made my way toward my brother. He looked as pissed off as he had last night. Apparently, sleeping on it, hadn't put him in any better of a mood. Awesome.

"Come to even up the other side?" Tripp asked.

My eyes scanned over the dark bruise covering a good part of the right side of his face. A curl of guilt twisted in my gut at the sight. Instead of acknowledging it, I stuffed my hands in my pockets and nodded toward his cup.

"No, but I'll take a coffee and a do-over."

"I don't think you're going to want what I have." He tossed back the rest of the drink and turned to walk inside the open front door. I took that as an invitation and stepped inside, closing the door behind me. It seemed strange not to hear any thundering feet or yelling as my nieces stormed around in princess outfits.

The house looked the exact same as the last time I'd visited. The dark teals and bright yellows that Lanny had picked out for the home were scattered throughout every room, from a pillow here to a bit of backsplash there. Pictures of the girls hung on the walls in their normal positions, but the large wedding photo was missing, the hook bare. The place felt empty even with the two of us standing in the house together. If I hadn't known better, I would've said that someone had just died, and a chill ran up my spine at the thought.

Tripp was already pouring two cups of fresh coffee as I walked into the bright, spacious kitchen, but as I watched, he proceeded to grab a bottle of whiskey to top off his cup.

"You want some?" he asked, eyes firmly on his hands.

"No thanks. I'm trying to stay away and dry out."

He made a muffled snorting sound as he placed the open bottle on the counter.

"Suit yourself."

I grabbed the cream and sugar to finish doctoring my coffee before making my way over to one of the large chairs in the living room. It had a stunning view of the large backyard and the swing set sitting empty in the middle of it.

"What happened?" I asked when it became clear that Tripp wasn't going to open up first. He took a sip of his coffee, stalling, before he sighed.

"Let me guess, Jayce," he said, his voice bitter.

"Don't blame him I called on brother code."

"Of course, you would." He took another sip of his coffee. "What does it matter? Gone is gone. The 'why' is irrelevant."

"I don't think I've ever heard such a pile of shit come out of your mouth before, and you've said some pretty stupid crap over the years," I said. Tripp's angry glare shot to me, and I shrugged. "What? It's the truth."

Tripp shook his head, one large hand clenched into a fist, but he just turned to look out at the backyard again.

"She took my babies," he bit out before a tear made an appearance and trailed slowly down his cheek. Tripp scrubbed it away and stood, swiftly going over to the window. I stared at his reflection—he looked like a ghost of his former happy self. I barely recognized the bitter man in the glass. "I'm sorry about last night," He added.

"Don't be. I deserved to be told off. I'm sorry I haven't been around, Tripp. I won't get into it right now, but I've been dealing with my own inner demons, and I guess I buried myself so deep that I forgot that I had this whole other world and people in it that I love."

Tripp nodded, and there was another long silence that I was about to break when Tripp suddenly spoke.

"She met someone else. Said she needed more in her life than to be stuck here in this small country town with two kids and church and that she wanted to explore the world." Turning, he leaned his shoulder against one of the rustic wooden beams that separated the large panes of glass. His gaze was hollow.

"I told her we could take a vacation every year, two if she wanted. That we could still explore the world. That was when she told me that it wasn't good enough, *I* wasn't good enough, and she'd met someone else on a dating app." He laughed, and the sound was bitter.

The dark circles under his eyes were even more distinct in the early morning light shining through the window.

"Shit, Tripp. I'm sorry." I stood and went over to my brother, but he backed away, a hand covering his eyes as he tried to reel in the pain that laced his voice.

"I thought we were forever, you know? I've loved her since I was sixteen, and not once did I ever consider a life without her. She moved out and took the girls, who we are now in a brutal custody battle over, and I haven't spoken to or seen her since. She refuses to take my calls, and when I showed up at her parent's house to see if she was there and if I could see my girls, they had the gall to look me in the eyes while calling the Sheriff. The fucking Sheriff, like I'd hurt them, like I'd *ever* hurt my girls, or even Lanny, no matter what."

He shook his head, and I didn't know what to do as he stumbled back until his ass fell into the chair he'd been occupying originally. What could ever fix something like this?

Tripp leaned forward, elbows on his knees, and started to cry. This was not our thing. We were never afraid to speak our minds or feel our emotions, but Tripp and I were cut from the same cloth. We didn't like people to see us break.

Walking over to the large ottoman, I sat down and grabbed his arm to pull him forward until I could hug my brother. I could feel his pain with every gasp he took. He was breaking—he might already be broken—but that didn't mean he couldn't pull himself out of it.

I let him cry and didn't say a word until he pulled back and grabbed the box of tissue off the side table.

"Do you know where Lanny is?" I asked as he wiped.

"My lawyer says she's shacked up with the new guy a few hours from here, but I'm not allowed to go to the house. She told her lawyer that if I just showed up, she'd file for a restraining order." He held open his hands and looked at his palms like they might hold all the answers.

"I don't understand, Jake. She had the cops come and talk to me, had them interview Mom and Dad and Jayce and all our friends, to see if I have any history of abuse. I'm supposed to go through the lawyer for everything, and if we happen to show up at the same place, like a grocery store, then for now, it would be best if I stayed a hundred meters away from her or the girls." He sucked in a shaky breath. I was stunned, and it was clear he still had more to say.

"My lawyer is fighting all of it, and he says I'll win since there is no proof of any of her vague allegations, but until it's finalized, I can't see the girls. Either way, my name has been dragged through the mud. I see it in everyone's eyes, Jake. No matter where I go, I see the questions they want to ask. 'Is he really an abuser? Did he hurt Lanny or his kids?' They glare at me, and someone even called me a wife beater from their car window while I was getting coffee the other day. I don't even know who it was. Never seen the guy before in my life." He took in another deep breath, and I wished more than anything that I could help make him feel better, take away some of his pain.

"I don't dare go to church. You wouldn't believe what the people there have said to me, and...." Tripp stopped again, looking shell-shocked. I couldn't blame him. I had no idea why Lanny was doing this, but it was killing Tripp.

"Why?" Tripp finally got out. "All I want to know is why she is doing this to me, to us? I gave her everything I had and anything she asked for. I was loving and faithful and a good father. I'd never hurt her, Jake. You have to believe me. I never did anything to warrant this kind of scrutiny." His eyes were desperate as he stared at me, searching for some kind of reassurance.

"I believe you," I said, and I meant it. Tripp noticeably slumped into the chair like he'd been worried I'd believe the rumors and lies. He had always been a big guy—even in our teens, he'd towered over everyone—but he'd always been the cool-headed one, which was why his outburst last night had been so shocking.

I was the one always getting into fights, and he was the one always breaking them up. If any of the guys said something even somewhat offensive about a woman, he would be the first person to jump in and tell the guy to back off. He was one of the best men I knew.

"She tried calling you," Tripp said out of nowhere.

I sat back on the ottoman. What was he talking about?

"Lanny tried to call me? Why?"

"I don't know. It was before everything went crazy. I think it might even have been before she met this new guy. I overheard her leaving a message saying that she wanted to talk to you about your platforms. I don't know what she was talking about, but as soon as I walked into the room, she hung up the phone and pretended the message was for one of her girlfriends. But I heard her say your name."

He lifted his shoulders and let them drop, defeated.

"No idea why she'd lie unless she didn't want me to know. I actually assumed she was arranging a surprise for my birthday since it was a couple weeks away and didn't think anymore of it. What an idiot I am," he said.

"You're not an idiot. You had no reason to mistrust her. It was probably Miles who got the message and, not knowing who she was, deleted it, 'cause I didn't get any messages from her. For a long stretch there, he did all of that for me."

I figured this was as good a time as any to talk to him about what the hell I'd had going on, or at least some of it. He'd spilled his heart to me, and he deserved to see that I trusted him just as much as I always had.

"I'll be honest, man. I haven't been in a good headspace, and now that I know what you were going through, I'm kinda glad I wasn't around," I said. Tripp's eyebrows drew down as he glowered at me. "I mean, because I was no good to anyone. It wasn't until a few weeks ago that I realized just how far I'd slipped. I was too busy dealing with my own messed up head to have been any help, but I'm working on getting the ship righted."

After giving me a long, searching look, Tripp nodded in acceptance. He reached for his coffee cup, pausing when he noticed it was empty.

"I'll get you some more, but no whisky this time," I said.

"Whatever," he sighed. "What exactly happened to you?"

"That's a tough question to answer." I stood, grabbing up my cup as well. I proceeded to refill the mugs before answering, giving myself a moment to think. "I started out wanting to just be authentically me and post fun, cool content. When acting fell through, I decided to travel and sing and take photographs and videos of it all to build my popularity that way." I shrugged. Even I wasn't completely sure when things had started to change—when I'd started to change.

"It got to the point that if I wanted to be noticed, my content had to be more spectacular and exciting then the post before. Soon, the parties and wild posts were gathering thousands of followers in minutes, and it all kind of snowballed from there. Miles was hired to set up parties with celebrities, and...." I rubbed at my face. "I wanted the followers and the money of being a big social media influencer, but I didn't notice how much I was losing of myself until I no longer recognized my own reflection."

I made my way back over to Tripp, who'd managed to pull himself together again, and handed him the hot cup. He sipped it with a grimace, probably because it really was just coffee this time, but nodded his thanks.

"Bri's birthday is next week. My baby is going to be six, and I can't even celebrate her birthday with her."

"I hate to ask this, but is Lanny asking for a lot of money as a settlement or something?"

"What do you think? Traveling the world doesn't come cheap. The thing is, I don't care about the money, but she wants to take the girls with her, and I said no."

I shook my head and stared out the window.

"Ah, so that's when things got nasty." I looked over at Tripp, and he nodded. "Who is this new guy?"

"Dr. Charles. I've yet to meet him, but all I can picture in my head is the bald X-Man." Tripp smirked as I smiled. It was good to see that the Tripp I knew was still in there. "And get this. He's... he's...."

Tripp suddenly stopped and laughed, and then he laughed again even harder until tears were leaking from his eyes once more, though for a very different reason this time. He grabbed at his stomach, not even able to sit up straight. The laughter was contagious, and I found myself laughing at him as he tried to get out what he was trying to say and continued to fail miserably.

"Oh shit, he's a...a gynecologist," Tripp finally blurted out. "She left me for a man who stares at other women's pussies all day." We both continued to laugh until Tripp fell silent again.

"Would you want her back? I mean, after all this, could you forgive her?"

Tripp didn't look at me and just continued to stare out the bay window.

"I love her. I've always loved her. It might make me an idiot or stupid, but yes. I'd want to try and work it out. My girls are my life," he said.

"I'm thinking I should move in here with you."

Tripp scoffed and then barked out a laugh, obviously amused at the thought.

"Oh, you're serious," he said as he took in my annoyed expression.

"Hear me out. This place is too big and too quiet for just you, and besides, Mom will continue doting on me if I stay at the house with them, and depending on her results next week, she is not going to need baggage from either one of us around the house."

Tripp rubbed his eyes.

"They finally told you. That's good. It was bugging me that you didn't know." Tripp's hand dropped to his lap. He stared again into his open palms. "So you're saying misery likes company?" he asked, cracking a grin.

"Something like that. This way, we can keep each other accountable, make sure no one gets too dark, and it might be fun."

Tripp looked at me, and his eyes already looked better from the slight glimmer of hope shining through them.

"We're probably going to kill one another," he said.

"Also a distinct possibility," I agreed.

Rolling his eyes, Tripp shook his head. I could tell I had him.

"I must be crazy, but alright. You should know, though, that I won't put up with having any of that party shit you were doing here." Tripp took a sip of his coffee before stretching out like a cat to bathe in the sun now streaming through the window.

"Deal. And no more moping around the house or snapping at people at work. I'll help you with anything you need with Lanny and the girls, but you need to keep your shit together. People are watching."

Tripp gave me a small smile.

"Deal. Thanks, Jake. I will deny this if anyone asks, but I missed you."

Mimicking his position, I settled down and got comfortable.

"I missed you, too."

13

JAKE

"OHHH, I LIKE HIM," Mr. Russo said, nodding toward Tripp. "Is he taken?"

My mouth fell open as my head swivelled over to stare at my brooding brother. With his large arms crossed in front of him and the dark scowl on his face, he looked like he was one of the site guards—a particularly unhappy site guard.

"He's single, but unfortunately, he only likes women," I said, trying to keep it casual.

Mr. Russo sighed.

"That's too bad. A delicious threesome with a hot blonde would've been on the menu. Mmm. He really is fine, though. What a pity."

I bit my lip to keep from throwing up. The last thing I ever wanted to picture was my brother in a three-way with Mr. Russo and some random girl. Now I knew how my family must have felt seeing my face plastered all over the place with a different girl all the time.

My very disturbing train of thought was broken when Mr. Russo suddenly spun around to the side.

"No, this is not working. There is too much light coming from behind, and I want it to look seductive. I want Jakey here to look dangerous as he drives his motorcycle between the grapes," Mr. Russo shouted. He walked away to go and talk to the film crew, and I tried not to notice how everyone was staring at me.

It was, of course, Jayce who couldn't hold his tongue.

"Wow, Jakey. You're just sooo seductive and dangerous," Jayce said with a shit-eating grin. I rolled my eyes at him as heat crept up my neck before I turned to walk away myself, low-key hoping he might drop it for once. Jayce walked behind me and ran his hand across my shoulder teasingly. No such luck.

"You're just so sexy," he teased as I glared at him. "And that smoldering look, oh my." He fanned his face.

"Shut up, man." I shrugged off his hand, and as he walked away, still laughing, I wondered if this had been a good idea after all. Mom and Dad had said they were excited, but we were losing two whole days of harvest for half of the farm, and I was worried the production crew was going to damage the grapes with all its equipment. Miles had said that Mr. Russo had agreed to pay for any damages in the contract, but that wasn't the point.

We had our own contracts to fulfill, and if we couldn't do that, then we ran the chance of losing them all together or owing money to the wineries that'd been promised the harvest. Either outcome would cause serious problems for the business my parents had put their hearts into, and I didn't want to be responsible for that. I'd already put them through enough.

From the corner of my eye, I saw Miles, ever the professional, strutting over with clipboard in hand. The man was like a peacock on a red carpet at all times. No matter what he did or where he went, he put on a show, and that was part of what made him such an incredible manager. As he came to a halt, his tailored suit looked impeccable as always—he made me feel like a bum in my leather jacket and ripped jeans.

"This was actually a brilliant idea. Makes everything look classy. I hope you don't mind that I told Mr. Russo it was my ingenious suggestion." Miles gave me a little smirk. "I felt I deserved the recognition for all the trouble you insist on putting me through. I've eaten an entire bottle of antacids this week alone."

"You worry way too much, Miles."

"If I don't, who is going to? Certainly not you."

I turned to stare at him, stunned and a little pissed. Looking around at all the crew members, I grabbed his arm to drag him out of earshot.

"What part of 'I can't do it anymore' do you not understand? Look at me." I made a gesture to my body. "I was a wreck—I'm just starting to recover from it all. It's not you out there snorting shit up your nose and drinking until you can't remember your own name, yet you still benefit, don't you? The stress...I can't go back. It's going to kill me. Do you understand that?"

"And people call *me* the dramatic one." Miles waved his hand in my direction. "Fine. I get it, but you're my favorite client. I just don't like hearing that you're hanging up your jacket and guitar. You know I don't want you to die, Jake. I'm sorry that I'm so hard on you sometimes."

"I'm only your favorite because of the boatload of money I make you," I muttered. Crossing my arms, I turned to watch my stunt double race between the rows, the motorcycle roaring as dust rose into the air and blanketed the grapes hanging heavily from the vines. I internally groaned, and my eyes flicked over to Tripp, who looked like he was about ready to faint. Well shit.

"This is true. You do bring in a pretty penny," Miles agreed, nodding. "Do you think you want to do anything else after this?"

I shrugged. I stared at the group of those working on the set, wiped the bike down for my part.

"I don't know. If it doesn't entail what's been the norm, then I'd consider it. Look on the bright side—you always like a good challenge, and this can be a rebranding opportunity."

Miles pulled his sunglasses down and stared at me over the rims like I was being an annoying child. Talk about feeling judged.

"Jake, you've always been a challenge, but yes, I guess it was time for a bit of an image change. A thirty-year-old naked in a dance club doesn't sell as well, anyway."

"Thanks, I think. Or not. Did you just say I'm old?"

Over near the bike cleaners, Mr. Russo looked around before raising his hand in the air to wave me over.

"Showtime, I guess," I said, shooting Miles a wry grin. I made my way toward my bike, which had been positioned at the end of the row like I'd just raced down it and skidded sideways to a stop. One of the crew handed me a bottle of the cologne we were promoting as soon as I got settled on the seat.

The single line I had to say was simple, yet I must have had to say it twenty times before Mr. Russo was happy enough to call it a wrap and pop a bottle of champagne. I shied away from the fizzy drink, instead grabbing two bottles of water and making my way over to Tripp, who still hadn't moved from the spot I'd seen him in earlier.

"You okay?" I asked, holding out a bottle of water as a peace offering.

"This was what she wanted," he said, staring out at all the people hustling around. After a moment, he accepted the water.

"Who, Lanny?" I asked, not quite certain where he was going with that segue.

Tripp looked at me, and his eyes were unbearably sad.

"I asked your manager, Miles, if he remembered a message from her, and he said he keeps copies of all messages just in case someone turns out to be a crazy-ass stalker."

"Good to know, and smart. Sounds like Miles." I shrugged and took a sip of my water.

"He let me listen to the message." Tripp paused, and the look on his face made me want to take a step back. With the way he was glaring, I thought he was going to attack me again. "She asked you to call her back and wanted to know if she could meet up to travel with you."

My eyes went wide. What the absolute fuck?

"Wait. You don't think I had a thing going on with Lanny, do you?"

Tripp just stared at me, his eyes boring holes into mine.

"Don't look at me like that. You fucking well know I'd never sleep with her no matter how many girls I've fucked. I'm bad, man, but I'm not into stealing my brother's wife. *Fuck.*"

Tripp's nose flared, but his eyes finally softened as he turned his head to look at the small party taking place around us. Mr. Russo spared no expense when it came to having a good time. Music was playing, and Mom and Dad were laughing as they danced.

"I'm sorry. I shouldn't have suggested that—but she just sounded like it was so normal. Like she'd met up with you before and missed you. I...I'm sorry," he said, his shoulders slumping. I'd never seen my brother look so dejected. I placed my hand on his shoulder in support, and the sadness wafting off of him in waves was almost palpable.

"Do you think she was cheating on me before this guy? Do you think my girls are even mine? Am I going to end up on some show one day talking about how I love my girls, but their real dad came storming into our lives and claimed parental rights? Is this really what my life has turned into?" he asked, voice hollow.

"Don't say that, Tripp. I have no idea if she was faithful or not, but those girls are the spitting image of you. If they looked any more like you, I'd have to tease them about how unfortunate they are."

He snorted, the corner of his mouth curling up.

"Yeah. Bri really does, doesn't she?"

"Same freaking eyes, and those dimples of hers are killer—and so very you. She's going to be a knockout, and you're going to have to chase away all the boys sniffing around her. Syd has Lanny's eyes, but she has your hair and is a miniature you personality-wise. She's just as stubborn as you are, too. I see her wanting to date at like, ten, and you having a heart attack.

Tripp rubbed his eyes.

"Oh god, don't say that. I'm going to end up arrested, aren't I?" he groaned. We laughed, the tension broken, but in the back of my mind, I couldn't help but wonder if he was right about what Lanny had wanted from me.

Was she really trying to hook up with me, and if she'd gotten ahold of me while I was drunk or high, what the hell would I have said? The thought terrified me, and I suddenly felt a strong need to give Miles a bonus for helping make sure I dodged that bullet.

"Come on. How often do you get a gourmet dinner like that?" I pointed to the large, almost overflowing buffet table that had been set up off to one side. "Let's go get something to eat and then head on out of here. I need to count all those bills I just earned for looking sexy as hell. Do you mind if I put them in the pool and swim around?"

"You're such a fucker. You know that, right?" Tripp asked, but he did so smiling.

"I do, and that's why you love me," I teased, leading him toward the table. Jayce, of course, was already there loading a plate. It was piled obscenely high.

The information about Lanny was interesting, and the more I thought about it, the more I wondered if I could do something to help Tripp with it. What, exactly, that might look like, I didn't know yet, but if fame and excitement were what Lanny wanted, then maybe that was exactly what she should get.

BEST
FRIENDS

14

KAT

IT WAS unbelievable what we'd managed to get accomplished in three weeks. I took a step back to stare up at the sign that proudly read 'Lexi's Sweet Retreat' in curling script. Olly had a moving company come in and move everything from the bookstore to the next unit over, and not only did her new place look fantastic with its large sitting area that looked out toward the water, but my space looked beautiful.

The walls were soft gray with bright accents scattered about in every corner like splashes of a rainbow. From the modern dangling lights to the mural of a sunflower that a friend of Olly's had graciously painted on one wall, every darn thing was perfect. Even the new glass display cases, which I'd managed to pick up for a song at a clearance warehouse to display the bakery items in, looked like they'd been made for the space. The kitchen would eventually need to be upgraded, but for now, the equipment I'd managed to get was working just fine.

I simply couldn't believe this place was mine.

"Sooo, what do you think? Is it everything you wanted?" Olly asked, holding out a cup of coffee as she stepped up beside me.

"Thank you." As I took the paper cup from her hand, I couldn't have wiped the smile off my face if I'd wanted to, and I definitely didn't want to. "It's perfect, Olly. Absolutely perfect."

"Why the rainbow for a logo? Doesn't seem very bakery-like. I mean, it looks great, don't get me wrong. I'm just curious," she said.

My cheeks warmed, and I could feel the necklace I was once again able to wear under my T-shirt. The little rainbow pressed into my skin like it was marking me.

"It's from a fond childhood memory. I don't have many, but the rainbow was a symbol of hope for me, and I thought it was fitting for this new beginning."

"And now I'm going to cry," Olly said. She wasn't completely joking—the corners of her eyes looked decidedly damp.

I laughed, peeling my eyes away from the sign after one last look to face Olly fully.

"Oh, stop. If I'm not crying, then you don't get to cry," I teased.

"Fine, fine...oh, look." Olly nodded down the road. I turned my head to see the delivery truck I'd been waiting for coming down the road and raised my hand to wave. The big white truck pulled over, and as soon as the engine fell silent, two guys hopped out.

"You've got a big delivery here. Where would you like us to put it all?" the driver asked.

"In the kitchen. I'll prop all the doors open for you." As I went to open the first door, Olly was hot on my heels.

"Did you *see* that?" Olly whispered as I locked the door into place.

"What?"

"The second guy, the one in the back, was totally checking you out. Like, hardcore staring at your ass."

Olly was smiling like she thought this would excite me, but I had no interest. I wasn't ready for that next step in my life. Richard was still looking for me. The proof of it was undeniable and terrifying.

Eve now had cameras installed all throughout her home because there had been a second break-in. Her regular phone, the one Richard would have known about, was one of the only things stolen —the cops had located it in a dumpster around the corner from Richard's medical building. Of course, there were no prints on it, but there didn't need to be. The threat was real, the message received. He was still searching, and if he was searching, I wasn't safe.

I didn't understand why he didn't just choose one of the girls he fucked regularly and move on with his life. I'm sure they all thought he was Prince Charming. As far as I was concerned, they all deserved one another. Hell, he could have a big old orgy in the middle of the house now if he wanted, so why did he still want me?

I rubbed my hands up and down my arms as the thought of him finding me flashed through my mind. It wasn't fair that I had to live in hiding while he still got to act like he was this big shot, and a perfect husband. It made me sick to my stomach.

However, because Olly wouldn't be deterred, I looked over my shoulder to where the man in question was currently hauling large bags of flour out of the truck. He was wearing a plain white work T-shirt that showed off the tattoos covering both of his defined arms. He was a good-looking man, but again, there was no interest.

"Thanks, Olly, but I'm not there yet."

"Not even to simply go for a ride?"

"Where would we ride to?" I asked, and Olly burst into a roar of laughter. As I stared at her face, befuddled, she laughed all the harder, practically folding herself over one of the glass display cases to stay upright.

"Oh my god! I can't breathe," she gasped out, then continued to laugh some more. The guy in question walked past with a dolly full of supplies, and as he did, Olly grabbed at her stomach. She was laughing so hard she wasn't even making noise anymore, just releasing a stream of soft, hissy exhales. The poor delivery guy sidled up next to me looking very concerned.

"Is she okay?" he whispered. We stared at the petite blonde, who seemed to be losing her mind. It was anyone's guess.

"Some days, I honestly don't know. I'm Lexi." I offered my hand to shake.

"I'm Xayne. I'll be doing most of the deliveries around here, so I'm sure we'll be seeing lots of each other," he said. Even though he seemed nice, now that Olly had brought up that he was probably flirting, not just being friendly, I felt awkward. I did a stupid head bob, not sure how else to respond.

"Yeah, I guess so."

"Are you new to the area? I can't place your accent."

"Sorry, but I better go make sure she's okay," I said, making my escape to the girls' bathroom, where Olly had just disappeared to have her moment in private. As I reached the door, I turned back, not wanting to just brush him off completely.

"Umm, you can put everything else over there," I said, pointing to a corner. "Thanks."

If I offended him with my abrupt departure, he didn't show it. I pushed open the bathroom door to see Olly splashing cold water on her face.

"Have you lost your mind," I asked.

She snickered and then closed her eyes and covered her mouth. After a moment, she recovered again.

"It's not really that funny, but I couldn't stop laughing," she said. I stepped into the bathroom and crossed my arms over my chest as she steadied herself. "When I mentioned going for a ride, I meant on *him*, like on his...." She pointed one hand down at her jeans.

"Oh!" I was pretty sure I was blushing at least a little.

Olly grabbed a piece of paper towel to dry her hands.

"It was the look on your face that got me. Anyway, how is Mr. Delivery? Did he make a move?" Olly asked, smoothly switching gears.

I shrugged.

"Not really. I'm going to start putting stuff away. If I want to have anything to sell for the grand opening on Saturday, I'd better get started putting these ingredients to use." I pulled open the bathroom door to peek out, and thankfully, the front door was closed and Xayne seemed to be gone.

"So that's it? We're not going to celebrate tonight?" Olly pouted.

Grabbing my apron, I put it on over my head and tied it into place.

"I'm starting to get the impression you like to find any excuse to go out and celebrate," I said as I pulled my hair up into a bun on top of my head.

"Hell yeah, and so should you." Olly leaned up against the doorway as I shook my head in disagreement. "Girl, you are turning this amazing, big page in your life. Look around. You own a bakery. You met me, and I'm a pretty awesome friend. And now, you have a hot delivery guy hitting on you. I'd say that's a win all the way around."

I'd been setting out all the large bins that I was going to put the bulk ingredients in, letting Olly say her piece, but at that, I paused and turned to look at her.

"It's not really mine. I mean, your name is on everything. I can't believe you trust me enough to do this for me, Olly. I can't repay you."

"I can see the desire in your eyes to succeed, and...." She shrugged. "I just have a good feeling about you and this place."

I smiled at her as I rolled out my shoulders.

"You're right. I do have a lot to be thankful for, but right now, all I can think about is having a grand opening for a bakery with no food because I'm the only one making it all and I have less than forty-eight hours to get everything ready. Can we do a rain check on the celebration until my grand opening is over with?" I placed a hand over my stomach as the butterflies that had been afflicting me all week took flight. "I don't think I could even enjoy a meal right now."

"Okay, rain check it is." Olly walked forward and rolled up her sleeves. "Now, what can I do to help?"

"No, no. You just moved as well. Go get your place looking perfect, and I'll take care of this. I think I need to take this step on my own, anyway." I walked over to Olly and gripped her in a tight hug. "Thank you for being my friend and for everything. I don't know what I would do without you, Olly."

"You know I've got your back. Are you sure you don't want me to help?"

Stepping back, I slowly turned in a circle to take in the pretty kitchen and smiled as I caught a glimpse out the window—you could see the water and the boats floating by.

"Yeah, I think I'm going to be fine. I just need this moment for me."

Olly smiled widely and nodded.

"Alright, then. If you change your mind, I'm right next door," she said. I followed her to the front door and locked it behind her, waving her off through the glass.

A well of emotions was bubbling inside of me. Though there was an equal amount of positivity and negativity roiling around together, the unceasing swells of emotion were making me jittery. The only thing that had ever truly helped calm my mind when it got like this was baking, and as I had a lot of that to do, it was time to get to work.

JAKE

"Hey, look at this," Mom said, making me look over at her across the kitchen. She was holding up the local newspaper. "A new bakery is opening today in town." She smiled widely as she waved the paper around like it was the most exciting thing in the world.

"It says here that the owner, Alexis, is new to town and fell in love with the area. It says that she's always had a passion for baking and felt that opening a bakery was the next logical step in her journey. She is going to be featuring mostly baked goods and coffee but will be expanding as time goes on," she recited, sitting down at the table. She kept looking between each of us, and it was obvious what she wanted.

"Okay, Mom, I'll go with you," I said.

She squealed like she'd been told she was going to a concert and not a bakery as she jumped up from the table. Racing around to where I was sitting, she kissed my cheek with an audible smooching sound.

"I need to go get ready. I'm so excited," she said before dashing off.

The three other men at the table all looked at me judgingly, but it was Jayce who broke the silence.

"Tripp's right. You really are the suck-up of the family."

I decided to own it and leaned back in my chair with a wide smile.

"You betcha. And that, gentlemen, is how I always get my favorite dinner cooked, and now I don't have to deal with the shipment going out today, either. I'll also score a box of goodies that I'm not sure I'll want to share."

Jayce gave me a shove, and I had to catch myself from falling backward.

"Jerk," he said with a mock scowl.

"Hey, you had your chance."

Dad, Tripp, and Jayce all got up, grumbling, and made their way out the back door to head to the fields while I snickered. Hearing my mom singing happily as she came back down the stairs, I hurriedly scarfed down the rest of my coffee and toast. She'd gotten ready fast.

"Thank you for taking me, Jake—though I would've asked someone else if you really didn't want to go, you know."

Standing, I grabbed my mom and hugged her tightly.

"I'm happy to go. I've missed too many of these opportunities. Did you want to ride on the back of the motorcycle? Make all those lady friends of yours swoon with jealousy?"

"Oh, stop it, you." She grabbed her purse but then paused to look outside and back at me. "Were you serious? Could we really take the motorcycle?"

I laughed hard at the giddy excitement on her face. My mom was the best.

"Yes, but I thought you were terrified of the thing?"

She chewed her lip, and for a moment, I could picture what she must've looked like in her twenties as a less sure version of herself still feeling out her way in the world. It looked so different than her normal exuberant confidence.

"I have to go for chemo in a few weeks and then hopefully on to surgery to get rid of this thing for good." She looked down at her chest, and my heart hurt for her and for what was to come. No matter how strong my mom was, this was going to be a battle, maybe for her life, and she knew it. The doctors were all optimistic, but there were no guarantees.

"I need to live a little, check a few things off my bucket list, and I've secretly always wanted to ride one. If I'm going to plunk myself on the back of a bike and put my life in someone's hands, I want it to be you."

The fact she even mentioned a bucket list bothered me. It meant she was thinking she might not make it, and I had to clamp down on the fear that was building in my chest.

"That's high praise indeed. Def' don't let Dad, Tripp, or Jayce hear you say that," I joked, but I really did feel honored that she trusted me that much.

"Oh, stop. Come on, let's get going before the line is around the block," Mom said, gripping her purse a little tighter to her chest.

I walked over to the large entryway closet and pushed the jackets around until I found the black leather jacket I remembered leaving in there. It was an old favorite of mine that I didn't have the heart to throw out even though it was way too small now—it would fit my mom decently enough. Shuffling a few more things aside, I pulled down the extra helmet that I'd stored on the top shelf. Turning, I held the items out to her.

"If you're going to ride one, then you need to look the badass part," I said with a smirk.

"Is it sad that this is so exciting to me?"

"No. No, it's not." I gave her a wink as I opened the front door for her to walk out. I couldn't appreciate until I'd gotten older how much my mom had sacrificed in her life—how much she'd endured as a woman and as a person.

Both of her parents had passed away when she was young, and when she and Dad had realized they couldn't have kids, her first thought wasn't to give up on her dreams for a family and be sad. Her first thought was that God was sending her the message that she was to find those who needed her and give them a home like her adoptive parents had done for her.

To say that the three of us had been a handful was like saying rolling around in a mud puddle might make you a little dirty—a vast understatement. She'd given more of herself to Dad and us three pains in the ass than anyone else would, and that wasn't just my bias talking.

My bike was parked right up near the house, and as we walked over to it, it was clear from the way my mom was fidgeting with the helmet in her hands that she was feeling some pre-ride jitters. Understandable, but not how I wanted her first ride to start. It needed to be memorable in all the best ways. Climbing on, I settled into place and shot her a cocky grin.

"Just swing your leg over and hang on." I pushed the motorcycle back until she was standing right beside it. "Have you changed your mind?"

"No. I'm going to do this." Looking determined, she pulled the strap of her purse over her head and slipped on behind me. "Wait, where will we put the goodies?"

I reached back and smacked one of the black saddlebags strapped to the Harley.

"These hold a lot more than they look like they do," I said.

Appeased, my mom nodded and wrapped her arms around my waist. As the motorcycle roared to life and I pulled out of the driveway, she screamed and cheered loudly, making me laugh. It was being able to make memories like this that made the decision to stay here and not go back out on the road so worthwhile. To me, being able to experience these moments in such an uncertain world was priceless.

15

JAKE

AS WE DROVE along Main Street, it was easy to tell where the new bakery was. I'd thought Mom had been joking about the number of people who would turn up for this grand opening, but she most certainly hadn't been. The situation outside the store looked as crazy as one of the few red carpet events I'd attended.

Well, maybe it wasn't *quite* that busy, and there was no photography area set up with bright lights and people decked out in the newest fashions, but it was still crazy to see people lined up clear down the street and wrapping around the end of the building. I pulled the bike into a spot that someone had just finished backing out of and let Mom get off before I pushed the kickstand into place.

Dismounting, I turned around and pulled off my helmet to stare at the front of the building. The logo was a simple rainbow, and my heart warmed at the image. I couldn't look at one without thinking of Kat—it was why I'd spent so much time chasing the prettiest ones with my camera.

"Wow, look at this turnout. I knew it would be busy, but now I'm worried we won't even get a chance to buy anything," Mom said, brow furrowed in worry.

"If they're sold out, we will come back tomorrow, and the next day, and every day until you get to try everything. You might even be able to talk this owner into featuring your pirate cookies."

"She wouldn't want anything I make. I just like to dabble, and to beat that snobby group at the fair, of course," she said as we made our way to the end of the line.

"Enough of that," I said, mimicking the same look she always gave me when I was being ridiculous about something. "You are great, and you need to believe that. You said you wanted to check things off a bucket list. Well, here is the second one for the day. This is your chance to show those ladies at the fair that you really do have the best baking in the area."

Mom laughed as we moved up in line and then nudged my arm as she nodded toward a girl who had been staring at me until she saw us looking back and quickly turned around. Subtle.

"I think you have someone interested," she whispered.

I gave her a little smile and nodded, but there was no enthusiasm. Even the thought of dating anyone was like having a thousand-pound weight around my neck threatening to choke me.

I'd already dated and fucked my way across the world and back again, and honestly, I had no more interest. Trying to deal with all of that again—it would be like the time I'd tried to make myself go back to my favorite fast-food restaurant after eating at it so many times that just seeing the place's logo made me feel a little queasy. I still couldn't eat there.

"Why aren't you doing something? She's cute," Mom urged, poking me again.

"I'm not feeling it. Trust me. When I get back into the saddle, you'll be sick of hearing all the girls complain about my terrible ways."

One elegant eyebrow lifted as my mom made a face that I didn't quite understand.

"I hate to see you alone. With you and Tripp all holed up in his house like you are these days...it's not good for either of you."

Thankfully, the line was moving faster than I'd thought it would, and we took another couple of steps forward as some space opened up.

"What exactly do you think we're doing? Sitting around crying into our beers all night about our pathetic lives and passing out with our heads on the table as our misery drags us down into a whirlpool of despair?" I asked, eyebrow raised.

"You haven't lost your dramatic side, good grief. But, if you're going to go that extreme, then at least be honest in your telling—it would be whiskey in the glass, not beer," Mom teased, and I couldn't help but laugh. The sun was almost directly above us, and the warm golden light shone down on us as I wrapped my arm around her shoulders. Fear clenched tightly in my stomach. I couldn't even picture what this world would look like without her in it. I refused to.

"Are you okay?" she asked, looking up at me.

"Yeah, I'm good." We stepped up to the door as a group of people came out of the shop all raving about how good the brownies were. I held the door open for them before stepping inside behind my mom.

I froze. I sucked in a sharp breath, but it felt like my heart had stopped in my chest. The woman behind the counter was the spitting image of Kat.

It couldn't really be her, but everything about her was the same. Even the sound of her laugh as she handed over a box to a customer and the sweet sound of her voice as she greeted another hummed through my body just as they always had, warming me. She looked up at the next woman in line, and glimpsing those blue eyes of hers, which could always melt the coldest of hearts, had my own beating out of my chest. Her hair was in the most adorable twist on top of her head, though several wild little wisps had fallen down to frame her face.

She was just as beautiful as I remembered. She glowed behind the counter—that was how it felt to me. It was like an angel had been plucked from the clouds of heaven and dropped into this small town in the middle of nowhere. No, not *like*—Kat *was* my angel.

My mom grabbed my arm, making me jump. Her eyes asked what was wrong, but I couldn't find my voice as a sudden panic gripped me. What was she doing here? Was it really her? Was I losing my mind? And if it *was* her, what the hell did I say other than 'you're still the most fucking beautiful woman I've ever seen?'

I wheeled around the person who had stepped in behind us and pushed my way outside. Stepping off to the side, I leaned against the wall to catch my breath. With how hard my heart was beating, it almost felt like it was gearing up for a panic attack.

Why was I so terrified? Realistically, it might not even be her—the chance of her showing up here, in my town, working at the new bakery, was astronomically small. But, what if it was her? What if it was her, but she didn't remember me?

What if it was her, but she didn't want me back? That was what I really wanted—to at least have a chance to have her in my life. My heart wouldn't stop racing, thumping so hard I could almost feel it against the back of my ribs, making it hard to focus.

"Jake, what's wrong?" Mom asked as she followed me outside.

I tried to wave her off so she'd go back inside.

"Don't lose your place in line. I'll be okay," I pushed out through the numbness in my lips.

She crossed her arms over her chest, obviously unimpressed.

"Don't bother trying to deter me. You tell me right this instant what's wrong. You look like you've seen a ghost."

I looked into her worried eyes and swallowed hard.

"That's just it—I think I have. That's Kat—Kate—serving behind the counter, and if it's not, then it's her doppelganger."

My mom's eyes grew wide before a sly smile spread across her face. She fixed the strap of her purse to lay smoothly against the leather jacket, which was a little big but still looked great on her, like she was settling a suit of armor into place.

"Well then, I think it's high time I met the girl who has held your heart all these years."

"What? No. No, no, no." I went to grab her arm to stop her, but she was quick for a woman in her sixties and I completely missed her as she darted through the open door.

I wanted to follow her, but my hands were shaking and I'd broken out in a cold sweat that had me shivering. This was not my best moment. I also didn't think that appearing in front of her out of the blue after all this time, with all those people around, was the right call. If she felt even a quarter of the nervousness I was experiencing after seeing me, then she might not be able to continue working.

I paced around along the sidewalk while waiting for my mom to return, which seemed to take an eternity. Every possible scenario as to why Kat might be here in this small town and on the other side of the country from Nevada was pinging around in my skull like a pinball. My head jerked up as the door jingled again for the millionth time, and I spun around to see my mom finally coming outside.

Her eyes found mine after a moment of searching, and she smiled as she walked over while balancing four pink boxes in her hands. She stopped in front of me, grinning, and I shifted nervously from foot to foot as I waited for her to say something.

"Well?" I finally said when it became obvious she was enjoying torturing me. Had I thought she was the best? She was the worst.

"Well, my boy. If that's your Kate, she's not going by Kate. She's using the name Lexi. Also, if that's your Kate, then she is sweeter than sweet tea on a hot summer night and I love her already."

I swallowed hard, tasting my heartbeat in my throat. I wanted it all to be true so badly.

"But it may not be her. Could just be someone who looks a lot like her," I said, trying to manage my mom's, and my, expectations. I wandered away from her to pace some more. "Why would she be using a different name?" I asked out loud. I didn't expect an answer, but my mom spoke up behind me, interrupting my pacing.

"A woman might change her name for a variety of reasons, but the two most common are because they no longer like their name for whatever reason and because they are hiding from someone or something. When you no longer want to be found, you move and you become someone else. If she has run all the way from Vegas, then whatever she's running from has to be big."

My hands clenched into tight fists at my sides as I pictured someone hurting my Kat. If that piece-of-shit husband had laid even one finger on her, he was going to find out just how protective I could be—and that was not going to end well for him.

"Did you want to go in and talk to her? Maybe you're right and it's not her."

I stared at my mom while dark images of pummeling the shit out of the man Kat had married played like a broken record in my brain. It was the only reason I ever needed to hear to storm into her life and take her from it, and it felt like the barrier of restraint I'd constructed in my mind years ago had just cracked.

I couldn't bear to hurt her by destroying her relationship if she were happy, but if she weren't...if she was running...if she was scared...then I might actually kill the man.

"No, not today. I want to speak to her alone, and I need a moment to think things through."

My mom grabbed my forearm and gave it a gentle squeeze. Who was I kidding? She *was* the best.

"You have that look on your face, Jake, the one that the Devil himself would run from."

"Don't worry. I won't do anything stupid," I said, making sure to leave the word 'yet' off the end of the sentence. I gave her a reassuring smile. "Come on. Let's get home before everyone thinks we're never coming back."

Back at the motorcycle, I got my mom situated before carefully stowing her boxes in the saddlebags. As I pulled my helmet on, I stared across the street at the little bakery and took in the image on the sign once more. It had to be Kat. The rainbow was our calling card. I didn't know what game the fates were playing with me, but I was all in and ready to push my chips to the center of the fucking table.

BEST
FRIENDS

KAT

"THANKS AGAIN FOR COMING," I called out, waving to the last customer of the day. A few had stayed to socialize right until closing, and the entire day had been filled with an incredible, energy-charged atmosphere. I'd never before been so nervous and excited at the same time.

I slumped into the chair across from Olly, who'd been my helper all day. If I stayed this busy, I was going to need to hire someone to help out right away. Olly was slouched down and stretched out, her head back against the wall and her eyes closed.

"That was crazy," I said.

"Girl, it was crazy and incredible, but my feet are *done*. I'm never this busy, not even on new-romance-hotties day." She didn't open her eyes, but she smiled. "I'm really happy for you, and I can't believe there is nothing left even after you made all that stuff." Her bottom lip pushed out, making me laugh.

"Well...that's not one hundred percent accurate. I earmarked one tray of a little something special in the fridge as 'not to be sold' for us to have for a celebration."

Olly cracked open one eye to look at me.

"You'd better not be joking," she said flatly, making me laugh hard.

"No, I'm not joking, and I already ordered some pizza to pick up on the way home so we can just relax and celebrate the day's success."

"I think I love you. Do you mind if I love you?" Olly asked, and we both laughed as I groaned and stood up to get the dessert. When I stepped into the fridge, the cool air felt amazing against my heated skin. I'd stashed the small tray full of the brownies Olly loved on a rack at the back behind some supplies, and as I unearthed it, I found myself stopping and staring.

The tray looked so simple sitting there with its tinfoil cover, but somehow, seeing it suddenly evoked the enormity of the entire day—and the more I looked at it, the more an old longing rose up inside me. I'd thought I'd seen Jake again today.

It was a habit that had become obsessive over the years. Every now and then, I'd think I'd see him sitting in a restaurant, or driving in the next lane, or walking down the sidewalk. I'd even run up to guys and grab an arm to spin them around, only to realize too late to avoid embarrassment that I'd been wrong. Again.

I'd lost count of how many times my heart had soared at the thought he'd finally found me, only to tumble back to earth from the reality that it would never happen. He was off living his fancy, famous lifestyle, and I was no more than a speck in his rearview mirror.

It was stupid that I was still holding on to something that was never going to happen, but my heart still wanted him. I couldn't help picturing how proud he would be of this place and how I'd have to keep smacking at his hands as he tried to steal some of the fresh-baked goods.

My hands reached for the brownies and picked them up, but I no longer saw them or the fridge that surrounded me. All I could picture was his bright green eyes and that smile that made me feel safe. I could picture him wrapping his arms around me and telling me how proud he was of my accomplishment and how much he loved me.

"Oh god, are you sure about this?" I asked, my legs shaking on the wobbly skateboard. When I looked down the tiny ramp, it felt like I was staring down a mountain.

"You've got this. I promise you can do it," Jake said, smiling that smile that made me feel so confident. With that smile in front of me, it felt like I could do anything.

Wiping my hands on my jeans, it was all I could do not to jump off and run away, but Jake's confidence in me was all the encouragement I needed. Rocking a little forward made the front end of the skateboard tip over the lip of the incline, which was almost too small even to be called a ramp. Bending my knees, I prepared myself before leaning forward. Butterflies soared in my stomach as the back wheels made it over, and for a second, there was a rush of intense speed as the skateboard picked up momentum and then came to a stop.

"See! I told you! Now let's try the next size up," Jake said, wiggling his eyebrows at me as I laughed. I could do anything.

Biting my lip, I pushed the old memory down as something deep in my chest began to ache. I'd been so certain that Jake had walked into the store, but my breath had caught and gotten lodged in my throat before I could say anything, and then a customer had stepped in front of me. By the time they stepped out of the way and I could see around them, he was gone.

Just like all the other times, he was simply never really there, and even though I should probably be worried that my mind was conjuring life-like visions of him, I didn't care. Something was better than nothing.

"Hey, are you okay?"

At the sound of Olly's voice, I jumped and gripped the tray of brownies to my chest. I looked in her direction and quickly wiped away the tear that was sneakily making its escape down my cheek.

"Yeah, it's just happy tears," I said. I wasn't lying—I *was* happy, and the nostalgia engrained in practically everything I did would pass until it decided to sneak up on me again.

"Are you sure? You didn't look happy. In fact, you looked pretty sad just now."

"No, I'm happy. I was just reflecting on everything that's happened over the last year and how far I've come in that time." I looked into Olly's worried eyes. "I just realized that I'm a lot stronger than I thought I was."

She smirked as she nodded at me.

"In that case, get your ass in gear. I'm starving, and you don't want to be around me when I'm hangry and my feet are sore."

I made my way out of the fridge and closed the door.

"Oh yeah, you're such a monster," I said, rolling my eyes.

Olly continued to chat excitedly as I turned off the lights and locked the door. Today had been a win and a step forward. Now I just needed Richard to sign the divorce papers and leave me alone forever. It terrified me that he wouldn't, that he might try to hold the papers over my head for the rest of my life, but I wasn't going to let that thought get me down today. One win at a time.

There was only one thing I knew for certain, and that was the fact I wasn't going to let Richard take anything away from me anymore.

JAKE

I stared at the still unfamiliar ceiling in my borrowed bedroom at Tripp's house and once more replayed the scene from when I'd walked into the bakery. Each time the miniature film in my mind played out with a different ending. They'd started out innocent enough, ending with a great conversation and a hug or a passionate kiss, but this one had taken a particularly hot turn.

My hand slid under the blanket and gave my dick a few hard rubs. I could almost taste her lips as I imagined pushing her up against the wall and devouring her mouth the way I always dreamed of doing. She would moan and wrap her arms around my neck as our bodies pressed so tightly together that no space was left in between. As her flavor rolled around in my mouth, I'd lay her out like she was a dessert to be savored.

Just the thought of her eyes staring down at me while I kissed my way up the inside of her thigh until I reached the sweet core of her pussy had every muscle tightening and my cock throwing a fit inside my boxers.

"Shit," I groaned as I gave it a few more tugs. I hadn't felt this worked up in a very long time. Sitting up, I swung my legs over the side of the bed. The new position certainly didn't help as my boxers shifted and the fly parted, allowing my cock to spring defiantly up in the open air.

It had been months since my body last had any real interest in the idea of sex, let alone so strongly that I felt a little wild with the need. I took a deep breath as I tried to rein in the overwhelming sensation that was making me want to drive into town and peek in every window until I found Kat, or Lexi, or whatever name she was going by.

Standing, I paced the room to try and take the edge off and ended up leaning against the frame of the large window that looked out to the back of the house. The water in the distance and the softly blowing trees were peaceful, but they did nothing to calm me tonight. My body continued to heat, and no matter how hard I tried, I couldn't stop envisioning laying my Kat out on the bed and claiming her once and for all.

My eyes were drawn to the empty bed when I turned around. In my mind, the bed was not empty—I could see us. I could see as clearly as if I were watching a movie what her face would look like as I pushed my way inside of her. I could hear what she would sound like gasping as my hands ran over her skin. I could smell what she would smell like as I buried my nose in her hair—but most of all, I could feel what her pussy would feel like squeezing my cock.

I groaned as the image grew in intensity. Giving in to the need, I pushed the boxers down and stretched out on the bed as my hand took a firm hold of my dick, which was now so hard it was painful. Now that I was lying on my back, the image shifted to her riding me as I pushed up into her. Her head would fall back in a scream as her breasts bounced.

My hand sped up, and I could feel the orgasm building at lightning speed. She'd say my name in that sweet, sexy way she could manage without even trying. She'd always been stunning to me, but she'd look ravishing as she came apart on top of me.

My hand sped up—every muscle in my body strained as my back arched off the bed. I'd finally whisper in her ear, 'You are mine, you've always been mine.' In a mad rush to finish, I came, letting out a small yell as the first spurt burst from the tip of my cock and landed on my chest. My hand didn't slow until the last drop of release left my body. Chest heaving, I flopped back onto the bed and groaned as my mind pictured Kat licking the come off my chest. Despite just coming, my dick twitched with interest.

I was tempted to leave cleaning until the morning, but in the end, I got up and made my way to the shower, not willing to chance having Tripp walk in on me all crusty. As I washed, my mind continued to race with even more possibilities that had my body heating up all over again. At this rate, I might as well just move the bed into the shower.

KAT

Stuffed full of cheese and chocolaty goodness and still wide awake, I lay on the bed and stared at the ceiling as I tried to remember what it was like to feel loved or wanted by another. It had been years since Richard had touched me. Well, that wasn't entirely accurate—it had been years since he'd touched me like that. Like he cared.

Richard had started forcing himself on me while I was still recovering from the car accident and couldn't fight him off. I didn't call that a loving or consensual situation. He always wanted to make sure I knew how vulnerable I was, how he could hurt me at any time and I couldn't do a damn thing about it. My body shivered as the memory of him looking down at me while I lay trapped on the bed by my own body flashed through my mind. Clenching my eyes shut, I forced myself to push those toxic images aside and instead remember a time I'd felt safe.

I hated school. All the other kids were jerks, and the teachers weren't much better. I used to be good at school, back before my parents died and I had to move here from the other side of the state to a new school and new classes and new teachers and...and new everything. I sighed as

the toes of my sneakers brushed through the dirt as I slowly swayed on the park swing.

It was hard to remember my parents' smiles anymore. Unless I held a picture of them, I found the images I could conjure up foggy, like my years with them were slipping out of a crack in my brain. A tear slid down my cheek as guilt gripped my stomach. They were my parents. How could I forget them so easily?

"Hey, Washboard."

I groaned at the sound of that jerkface, Steve. I had no idea why he insisted on picking on me, but ever since I'd arrived at this school, he was all over me with the insults. Now it was because I'd started to develop boobs. Last week it had been 'Speedbump,' and this week had progressed to 'Washboard.'

Quickly scrubbing the tears away, I looked over my shoulder to see Steve and one of his buddies heading my way. I'd have to try and run past them to get to the Jones' house. I could try and run for the houses in the other direction, but I didn't know anyone who lived there, and running only seemed to make Steve more aggressive, like he was excited that he scared me.

"What do you want, Steve?"

"You're on my swing. Get off," he said as he stopped next to the swing and grabbed the chain.

There were seven other swings in the park that were all empty, and I could've easily moved over or tried to leave, but I was sick of him. I was sick of all of them.

"I don't see your name on it," I said, glaring at him.

"I said move, Washboard," Steve yelled before grabbing the chains and shaking them, trying to get me to jump off. I stubbornly gripped tighter.

"No. Leave me alone," I yelled, doubly pissed. Steve grabbed the back of the black rubber seat and jerked it up hard. With a thud, I ended up on my ass in the dirt while Steve and his friend laughed.

"See, Washboard. This is what happens when you don't listen," Steve taunted as tears pricked my eyes. I hated this place, and I hated him the most.

"Leave her alone!" My head whipped around at the sound of Jake's voice. I bit my lip as he stomped across the playground, his hands already balled into fists. He looked like he was going to rip Steve's head off, and I couldn't take my eyes off of him. He was like my own personal avenging angel.

"What's it to you?" Steve asked Jake as I stood and dusted myself off.

"She's my girlfriend," Jake said, and my eyes went wide. Was I even allowed to have a boyfriend at eleven? It didn't matter. The fact he'd said the words made my stomach feel all floaty and fluttery.

"You and Washboard?" Steve began to laugh meanly, and I knew I'd never forget the wild look on Jake's face as he lunged for Steve, driving him to the ground with fists flying. Steve's friend took off running rather than trying to help his friend. Steve needed new friends.

As Jake kept whaling on him, Steve screamed and started to cry.

"Oh my god, Jake," I said, wanting to grab him, to stop him, before something really bad happened. "Jake, stop."

Panting, Jake pushed himself off of Steve.

"Make fun of Kat again and I'll break your nose. And this is now her swing. If she wants it, you give it to her," Jake growled like an animal, his green eyes snapping with anger as he wrapped his arm around my waist. Taking me by surprise, he turned and kissed my lips. It was a quick peck, but I felt the jolt from it right down to my toes.

Steve jumped up holding his face and took off running.

"Are you okay?" Jake asked, and I felt a blush spread across my cheeks.

Jake had always made me feel safe. I never worried about what he would do to me or if he would say something mean. Now, almost two decades later, I'd almost forgotten what it was like to be touched by someone with love. I'd forgotten what it was like to feel pretty or be wanted by another.

Truthfully, I didn't want to because it was dangerous. Regardless, my mind still strolled down the same glittering path it always took when I was alone with my thoughts, and that path led to Jake. It was dangerous territory—tantalizing and completely unattainable, yet still as compelling as a siren's song.

Jake in his black leather jacket. Jake lying on the beach in the sand with only his sunglasses and boxers on. Jake on his sexy motorcycle with me on the back just riding around before finding some private place to make out. Jake kissing me with heat and that edge of aggression that I craved to feel from him.

I wanted him to possess me, to storm into my life the way I'd always dreamed and take me away—but I realized now that I didn't need him to save me. For years, I'd convinced myself that I'd never be free unless Jake came knocking on my door, that I was a prisoner and needed him to break me out. But I'd been wrong. All I'd needed was to be strong enough to make the decision to get out. I'd freed myself, and that meant more than anything.

Still, I just couldn't help wanting to know how having that kind of fire smoldering in my belly would feel. Imagining Jake pulling my hair as he slammed his cock into me was the juicy cherries covered in whipped cream that topped the sundae of my fantasies—to have him want me and only me.

With each new image of Jake, I could feel my little sleep shorts getting wetter. I'd never been much for masturbation, but this was a new life and a new me. My fingers dipped inside the loose-fitting shorts to find that I was indeed very wet. With incentive like that, who could blame me?

Running my fingers over my clit, I gasped as I pictured Jake's tongue between my legs swirling and dipping into my folds. Those green eyes, bright as gemstones, would stare up at me as I came on his mouth.

"Oh, god," I mumbled into the quiet room as I got a little more brazen and slipped a finger inside. My other hand had gotten a mind of its own, and I was so preoccupied with what was happening between my thighs that I barely noticed it moving until it pinched my nipple. As it rolled around between my fingers, I imagined it was Jake's hands on my skin, his mouth that was sucking my nipple and driving me wild. It was definitely his hard cock and firm ass pounding into me.

I envisioned him grabbing the headboard as his body worked on top of me, pushing me harder and harder into the mattress. The image of his corded muscles flexing and relaxing as we moved in unison had my fingers working furiously over my body. My orgasm was so close that I could taste it—I wanted the release so bad.

"Oh fuck," I gasped, arching my back off the bed as I pictured him coming inside me and claiming me as his own. I wanted him more than I'd ever wanted anything in my life aside from my freedom. He was the carrot that always dangled just out of reach—the man who could complete my soul like two flames merging together to become one.

I slumped back, my breathing ragged as the last wave of pleasure subsided. As the images drifted back into the recesses of my mind, I sighed and stood from the bed, quickly cleaning up and changing to once more get comfortable. Maybe it was time to try dating. Olly had said that the delivery guy was interested. Maybe that's what I needed to move on from everything that belonged in my past.

Yet, as my mind drifted off into sleep, it was Jake's arms that I pictured wrapping me up and holding me tight.

BEST
FRIENDS

KAT

IT WAS a good thing that I'd decided to open the bakery only two days a week to start. The number of hours I'd already spent in the kitchen making the different squares and cakes and tarts was ridiculous, and I was worried that it wasn't going to be enough with just me.

The phone hadn't stopped ringing with custom orders, and the stress was building from trying to get it all done on my own. Not that I didn't feel blessed to be busy and that people loved what I had to offer, but I was only one person with one used oven, and I wasn't any kind of superhuman.

The front door of the shop jingled, and I peeked around the corner from the kitchen to see the white delivery truck outside. The same delivery guy, Xayne, was standing in the doorway.

"Hi, Xayne. I'm back here. You can just bring it all back like last time," I called out with a wave. He smiled back and then went outside, presumably to get the order. He was back a few minutes later with a loaded dolly cart to push into the kitchen.

"If you can put it on the counter there, that would be great." I nodded toward the empty counter space I'd cleared.

"Umm, congratulations on having a great grand opening? Sorry I didn't make it out," he said as he began placing large paper bags of ingredients on the counter.

"It was amazing. I honestly couldn't have asked for a better turnout, and unless you'd arrived early, you wouldn't have gotten anything anyway. I was sold out by the end of the day and had to promise the last couple of customers that I'd hold some for them this Friday." I paused in kneading out the dough I was making for a crust.

"That's great, though I was kinda hoping you were calling to have more items delivered again so soon just so you could see me again," Xayne said, grinning.

I froze like a deer in headlights and just blinked at him as my mind went blank. My internal monologue was screaming at me to say something, anything, and not seem like a total loser, but instead, I smiled awkwardly and looked down at the dough.

"Sorry. I didn't mean to make you uncomfortable." He leaned on the dolly, waiting. I knew this was my moment, but did I want it?

"It's okay. I'm just not very good at this. The whole flirting thing." I internally groaned as heat traveled up my neck as I flushed in embarrassment.

'Damn you, Olly,' I cursed in my head as I looked up at the man in front of me. He seemed nice enough, with a deep golden tan and short-cut, soft brown hair that matched his eyes and the five o'clock shadow he was sporting. My eyes stole a quick glance at his hands and didn't see a ring, though that didn't necessarily mean anything anymore.

He looked to be a couple of inches taller than I was, and on the whole, he was...cute, but I didn't feel that pull that said this was someone I might want to date seriously. It didn't help that I still struggled not to view every person as a potential threat, thanks to Richard. Kind of put a damper on the whole dating thing.

I immediately kicked myself in the ass mentally as I reminded myself that going on a date didn't mean it had to be the next forever. The next forever might never come, and in the meantime, it was okay to have some fun—to experience life and what it had to offer outside the bounds of the shitty marriage that had kept me trapped. The real issue was my fear factor.

How could I know this guy wouldn't turn out like Richard? How could I know I wouldn't end up on some backcountry road fighting for my life? How could I know if he saw me as a person and not as a notch on his belt? I bit my lip and looked away from his eyes, which seemed amused at something I'd said.

"How about we do dinner? It will give us time to chat. Maybe you'll get better at that flirting thing," Xayne said.

"Oh, I don't know...I...." I let out a sigh. "Okay, one dinner. I'm not promising anything other than that," I said.

"Perfect. How about Friday, and I can pick you up at seven?" He smiled, and I was sure that it was supposed to be flirty and make me feel comfortable, but instead, it made my stomach flip. Just the simple thought of being trapped in a car with a strange man made my heart race, and I had to take a deep breath before it got out of control.

"No, that's okay. I'd prefer to take myself. Where did you have in mind?"

"Are you sure?"

I shifted from one foot to the other, already tempted to call the whole thing off.

"Yeah, I'm sure."

Xayne shrugged and slowly made his way to the door with the empty cart.

"There's a spot just outside of town. It's a cute hole-in-the-wall bar, but they have great food. It's called Rubin's," he said.

"Yo, Xayne. You comin' or what?" the driver from the other day called out as he opened the door, breaking the tension. Xayne waved him off before turning back to me with an expectant look.

"Okay, sounds good. I'll meet you there," I said. As I watched him leave, it suddenly dawned on me that I didn't have a car anymore or any money to purchase one. "Well, shit sticks," I mumbled.

The doorbell chimed again, and Olly's voice boomed out to announce her presence.

"Hello, my friend! How's it going?" she asked as she waltzed in and pulled up a chair.

"Well, the baking is slow and I'm trying not to have a meltdown."

She waved her hand at me and made a face.

"I don't mean with the baked goods, I mean with that piece of sweet eye candy that just left. I noticed he was in here for quite a while," she said, a devious glint in her eye.

"Are you stalking me now?"

"Oh please. I can see that truck from the front of my store, where I happened to be redecorating the window display." She looked at her bright pink nail polish. "This girl is what you call observant."

An idea hit me, and I wasn't sure it was a good one, but I decided to ask anyway.

"Okay, fine. Xayne did ask me out to dinner—." I didn't even get the rest of the sentence out before Olly squealed like she'd just seen a mouse and ran at me. I stood wide-eyed and paralyzed as she crashed into me with an 'oomph' and hugged me hard.

"Oh my god! I'm so excited. When are you going? What are you wearing? How are you going to do your hair? Oh, you have to let me help you get ready. This is so much fun," she shot out so quickly the sentences almost blended together.

I wasn't sure who was more excited about the date as Olly continued to rattle off questions and suggestions without a breath. No—it was definitely Olly. She was a bubbly ball of enthusiastic energy that was merrily rolling along and dragging me with her.

"Well? Speak up, woman. Are you not going to answer any of my questions?" she demanded, finally pausing.

I raised an eyebrow at her.

"I was waiting until you took a breath."

She flushed a bright pink.

"Okay, yeah. I may have rambled, but I can't help it. I'm so excited."

"Well, I'm glad to hear that because I do have a favor to ask." Wiping the flour off my hands with a towel, I tried to lean casually against the counter. "Do you think you could drop me off this Friday at seven for dinner and pick me up after? I'm really sorry, but I just couldn't accept a ride from him when I barely know him, and I only remembered I no longer have a car after I'd already said I'd take myself. I'm sorry if you have plans. I shouldn't have agreed until I'd found a ride first."

"Girl, stop rambling. I don't have plans, and you don't have to explain. Of course I'm in. Where do you need to go?"

"He said some place called Rubin's?" I shrugged. "If I knew how far it was, I could probably walk."

Olly shook her head and held up her hand.

"Wait a sec. He's taking you to Rubin's? Okay, that is the first strike against Mr. Hotness. That place is sketchy. The food is decent, but you could catch a disease from touching the tables—it's that kind of greasy." Olly shuddered, which didn't make me feel very comforted. "You couldn't walk there because it's on some back road. It seriously looks like it's from the beginning scene of some 'stranded in the middle of nowhere with a serial killer' movie."

"Okay, great, that's reassuring. I knew I shouldn't have agreed to a date. It's too soon, this isn't a good time, and I have to get up really early on Saturday."

Olly held up her hands placatingly and walked toward me.

"Whoa. Sorry, girl, I didn't mean to freak you out. It's not really that bad, and if I'm dropping you off and picking you up, what's the worst that can happen?"

I wanted to say that lots can happen, but it was my own anxiety screaming that, not the logical part of my mind. I let out a slow, deep breath as I tried to get my pounding heart under control before it jumped out of my chest.

"Besides, this way, you always have the excuse of work and needing to get up early to call me to come pick you up if things aren't going well. I've got your back. It's just a meal, nothing more. Besides, you can always do the 'fake call' thing. Us girls have to stick together." Olly grabbed my shoulders, shaking them lightly, and I nodded as I swallowed down the lump in my throat.

"You're right. I know you're right," I agreed.

"Perfect. Then I'll help you pick out something to wear. I have the perfect dress for you." Olly let her hands drop and continued on before I could even argue.

"Anyway, I came over to ask you for a favor, not just stalk you. Would you come with me today for a couple of hours? I'm heading up to sign a contract with that local grower now that we have all the boring details hashed out. I wanted to walk around their vineyard a little, maybe sample some places on the way back to add to my growing menu. What do you say?"

My eyes looked at the dough I had just finished making, which needed to be chilled. I could easily find fifty other things I needed to do, but Olly had done so much for me. If it weren't for her, this shop would still be a dream in the back of my mind and not the reality that it was.

"Let me wrap this up and put it in the fridge, and then I'm all yours." I smiled brightly, the earlier anxiety melting away at the prospect of spending a few hours with my new friend.

We were out the door about ten minutes later, and as soon as we got into Olly's Volkswagen, she tuned the radio to an oldies station, cranked it up, and began to sing at the top of her lungs. I held off as long as I could, but as soon as the Beach Boys came on, I couldn't hold back any longer and joined in on the crazy fun.

Olly kept the windows down as we drove, and even though the wind was probably making a mess of my hair, I didn't care. This simple act of driving and singing, something that teens would do, was new to me, and I was savoring every single moment. I didn't even care that we drew stares from the people we passed on the street before we made our way out of town.

"You're crazy, but I love it," I shouted over the music as the song switched again. Olly nodded and smiled, but she reached to turn down the music.

"Oh, I'm out of breath. Who knew singing was so much work? I'm thinking of getting my mom a cat," she said.

Wait, what? I turned to look at Olly in confusion.

"Where did that come from?"

She shrugged the shoulder closest to me and let it drop.

"I'm just busy a lot, and I know my mom stays active between her bingo, walking, church, and having a few meals with Douglas, but I still feel like she gets lonely."

I understood that. I had a lot going on right now, but I had moments where I felt completely alone even when I was surrounded by people on all sides.

"Does she like cats?"

Olly looked at me and started to laugh.

"Not particularly, no."

I burst out laughing along with her and shook my head as we pulled off onto a pretty lane leading to a vineyard. The sign at the beginning of the lane was wooden and classy, with dark purple grapes and a faded cream background that proudly stated 'The Russells.' The large maple trees around the property were just starting to think about changing. Hints of yellow, orange, and fiery red were mixed among the bright green leaves.

"This place is breathtaking," I said. My mouth fell open as we came upon the heart of the farm, which had a big old farmhouse that looked like it had recently been redone standing off to the left next to a large, sparkling pond and a gazebo. On the other side was the vineyard itself, where people were busily moving around and a tractor was slowly driving along one of the rows.

"It's amazing, isn't it? I don't know the Russells well, but they seem like really nice people. They apparently have three sons who I have yet to meet."

"How is it that this place is only thirty minutes outside of town, yet you've never met them?"

"Different district. There is another town not far from here that this is technically a part of, and this whole area is in a different school district as well. Unless you happen to have family on this side of the line, or you meet someone at a special event like a concert, or you step on someone's shoe in a line somewhere, you don't tend to meet many people from out this way."

"Step on someone's shoe in line? That's oddly specific," I teased, and Olly's face blushed a pretty pink. She parked slightly more sharply than needed.

"I may have used that tactic once or twice, but I will deny it if you repeat that to anyone. Now come on. Let's go find the Russells." She jumped out of the car, and her short, fast strides had her halfway to the barn by the time I found my sunglasses and made my own way out of the car. A tall, good-looking man walked up to Olly and held out his hand for her to shake. I wasn't close enough to hear the conversation, but I was pretty sure this was Mr. Russell.

Olly looked like a kid next to the tall man, but he had a warm laugh, and despite his size, I was instantly put at ease by his presence as I stepped up beside Olly.

"Lexi, this is Mr. Russell, and Mr. Russell, this is my good friend, Lexi," Olly said as I held out my hand. His hand absolutely engulfed mine.

"Call me Mark. I hate being called 'Mr. Russell.' Makes me feel like I'm getting old." His blue eyes were as warm as his laugh. This man was the definition of a cinnamon roll, but I still wouldn't want to get on his bad side. I had a feeling he could, and would, flatten you if pushed.

"Nice to meet you, Mark."

His face morphed into excitement as he clasped his other hand on top of where our hands were joined and started shaking my hand so fast I thought he was going to rattle the teeth right out of my head.

"You're the new bakery owner! You're that Lexi, aren't you?"

Heat crept up my neck, making me want to fan myself. I suddenly felt like a very small celebrity.

"Yeah, I am."

"Oh my god, Joy is going to be so happy to meet you. She loved everything she purchased from you, and I know she'd love for you to sample her pirate cookies. She'd never ask, but she'd love to have them carried in your store," he said. His face was lit up with so much enthusiasm that I couldn't find the heart to tell him I wasn't ready to have, or even interested in having, items other than my own in the store.

"What, exactly, is a pirate cookie?" I asked. Mark laughed again and finally let go of my hand.

"That's just what my boys nicknamed it. Trust me, you're going to love them, and it would really mean the world to her to have a small display somewhere. No pressure, of course. I'm just so excited." He began waving to someone behind me, and I turned to see a woman who must be Joy walking in our direction.

I smiled as I instantly recognized the woman. She'd shown up for my grand opening and practically cleaned me out. We'd had a wonderful chat, and she'd seemed genuinely excited that I'd opened the store.

"Lexi, is that you?" Joy asked.

"Hi, Joy. It's nice to see you again."

Olly grabbed my shoulder to get my attention.

"Why don't I leave you two to chat and wander the property, and we can meet up later?"

I nodded as she wandered off toward a door marked 'office' with Mark. In the next moment, I froze up, taken by surprise as Joy gripped me in a hug that was almost as enthusiastic as Mark's handshake had been.

"Oh, my dear, you're even prettier out in the sunlight," she said, beaming.

"Oh, um…ah, thank you," I stammered out as she stepped back.

"Did you want to go for a walk? I can show you around. It's a lovely day," Joy offered.

"Sure, but I'm supposed to try some cookies before I leave. Something about pirate cookies?"

Joy's face went as red as any tomato as she looked away from my eyes.

"Oh geez. Mark shouldn't have said anything. I'm so sorry. I hope he didn't make you feel uncomfortable. Darn men sometimes. I love that man, but I could take him and shake him."

I suddenly wanted to try her cookies right now, no waiting. Her shyness about her abilities was exactly the same way I felt, and there was this kindness about her that made me really hope her cookies were as good as Mark raved. Maybe having one shelf in an area of the shop I wasn't currently filling devoted to local bakers could be a good idea. It would certainly add pull in the community for continued support, and it would be a step toward helping me be seen as a local and not the girl who just moved to town.

Joy linked arms with me and guided me along one of the rows of grapes that had yet to be harvested. There was a very distinct line between the rows that had been fully harvested and the ones where people were still feverishly working. It was kind of fascinating.

We walked quietly for a while, and though it was peaceful, for whatever reason, it felt like someone was staring at us. I could feel eyes on me, but as mine scanned through the rows, I couldn't see any one person who was giving us more than a passing glance.

"Tell me, my dear, what brought you to this sleepy little town?"

The question came out of nowhere, and Joy's soft smile and kind eyes already had my guard down, so I gave her as much of the truth as I dared.

"Just needed a fresh start."

"Boy troubles?" Joy asked. I swallowed hard in response, and she patted my arm. "Don't worry. You don't have to say it. There are only so many reasons a girl needs a fresh start, and a boy who has broken her heart is usually at the top of the list."

She paused and stopped walking. Her eyebrows pushed together in thought.

"I guess I shouldn't be so presumptuous. It could be girl troubles," she said. The worried look on her face made my mouth curl up in a smile.

"No, you were right the first time."

"Oh, phew. For a moment there, I thought I might've put my foot in it and offended you." We continued walking until we reached the end of the row, and I couldn't stop the little gasp that left my mouth as I stared out over the bright green fields of rolling farmland. It was breathtaking, and I had the sudden urge to pull up a chair and sit down to take it all in.

Emotion clogged my throat, and I covered my mouth to try and stifle the sob that was threatening to burst out for no reason. The color of the fields was the *exact* same shade as Jake's eyes, and I could vividly picture him walking through them as he smiled at me. My hand went to my chest as the emotion threatened to bring on a bout of waterworks.

"My dear, are you okay?" Joy gripped my elbow tightly, a worried look in her eyes. I bit my lip hard, not wanting to make any more of a scene than I already was.

"I'm sorry. I don't know what's come over me," I said as levelly as I could. Stepping back, I plastered a wide smile on my face and wiped away the tears.

"Are you sure you're okay? You seemed...I'm not sure, sad, maybe?"

"It's just so beautiful, and I get to enjoy it with such wonderful company. I'm great. I promise that I'm fine. I feel silly for crying."

We turned to walk along the end of the field, and at a flicker of movement, I whipped my head to the left. I could have sworn I'd seen a man out of the corner of my eye, but no one was standing there. A shiver traveled down my spine, and I continued to glance over my shoulder as I searched the gently rustling vines for signs of anyone.

"What's wrong?" Joy asked. She looked back and then at me.

"I thought I saw someone." I shrugged. "It's nothing. I really love your setup here, Joy. It's like a little slice of heaven."

"Thank you. Believe it or not, before this, I worked a corporate job in Vegas for many years in the finance department, and Mark worked as a headhunter."

"Really? I...." I stopped, not sure I should say where I was from, but the look of confusion on Joy's face made me continue. "I used to live there too."

"Well, you have to make sure you follow your heart. That's what we decided to do, and we couldn't be happier. This has been our dream come true, and it was a big step. There were no promises, no fallback plan—we sunk every last dime we had into adopting our boys and then moving out here. The thing is, I don't regret a single hard-working moment, and it was a much better environment for the boys. They'd all had a tough go of it and needed a change of scenery."

I could feel tears welling up in my eyes again, and I hated that I was getting this emotional over someone being kind and brave. It gave me hope for myself, but it also made my heart ache with a longing I'd given up on fulfilling so long ago that it felt like another lifetime.

"I'm so happy there are people like you in the world, Joy. People who are willing to take a chance on kids in the system. I was in the system, too, and I wasn't so lucky." I bit the inside of my cheek to keep from full-out crying.

"Oh sweetie, I'm so sorry. I didn't mean to upset you," Joy said, gripping me a little tighter.

"No, of course you didn't. I'm just really happy, and your story has certainly inspired me. Maybe one day, I'll be as lucky as you and Mark are."

Joy suddenly stumbled slightly on the uneven ground, and I jumped into action, grabbing her by the shoulders to make sure she didn't fall. After a moment, she nodded and patted my arm to show that she was steady again.

"Sorry, dear. I'm not as balanced as I used to be." Despite the sedate pace we'd been keeping, she was breathing a little heavily and her face was flushed.

"Do you want to sit down?" I asked, wrapping my arm around her.

"Oh no no, we're almost back. I'll be fine. Just need to sit this weary body down."

"Mom, are you okay?" I looked up to see a guy jogging down the row toward us. When Joy and Mark had said boys, I'd instantly thought young boys, but this guy was easily in his mid to late twenties and undeniably sexy. His blond hair complimented his tanned skin and soft gray eyes, which could easily have been a match for Joy's. He was fit like one of those guys who swim a lot, and his white T-shirt was clinging to every one of his defined abs. Wowza.

"Jayce, don't make a fuss. I'm fine." Joy waved him off, but he didn't listen and went to his mom's other side. For a second, I thought he was going to pick her up, but one glare from Joy had him halting the action he'd started. "Jayce, don't be rude. This is our guest, Lexi. Lexi, this is my youngest, Jayce, the worrier."

He rolled his eyes in response, making me laugh.

"Is that an official title, 'Jayce the Worrier'?"

"Don't encourage her. I don't need any more nicknames. Nice to meet you," Jayce leaned around his mom to shake my hand as more people rounded the corner of the row.

"Now look what your dramatics has done," Joy huffed out as Mark and Olly ran down to us.

"Sweetheart, what is it? What's wrong?" Mark's eyes were wide as he looked his wife over, and it was the most endearing thing I'd ever seen. That level of commitment was something special. My heart swelled at seeing the couple together even as I longed for something that, up to this point, had only ever been a dream in my mind—nothing more than a fairytale fantasy.

"Oh, don't you start. I'm fine, just winded," Joy said, but her glare didn't have the same effect on Mark as it had on Jayce, as he simply scooped her up and started to walk away. "Hey, put me down. I don't need to be carried," Joy said to absolutely no effect.

I smirked as I watched them go.

"I'll come back another day and try the cookies," I called out, and Joy peered over her husband's shoulder and waved.

"Anytime, my dear, anytime."

When I turned to look at Olly, her face was so red I wondered if she was going to be the next one about to hit the ground. I was about to ask if she was alright but bit my tongue as I noticed how she and Jayce were staring at one another. My eyes darted back and forth between the two, and I suddenly felt very awkward being in their sexually-charged little area.

"I'm going to go wait by the car," I whispered, stepping around Olly.

As I walked the rest of the way to where we'd parked the vehicle, I couldn't keep the stupid smile off my face. But then there it was again—the feeling of being watched was back. I turned in a tight circle and saw movement a couple of rows to the left. Darting over, desperate to find an answer, I rounded the corner to find—a pair of workers picking grapes. They paused what they were doing to stare at me, probably wondering who the new person acting crazy was.

With a muttered apology, I backed away and headed toward the car again, but as I walked, I couldn't stop looking around at the beautiful surroundings...and also looking for something else that I couldn't quite put my finger on. Something about this place felt...I wasn't sure, but it was as if the land was whispering something too quiet for me to hear. Something important.

I shivered and wrapped my arms around myself. Would there ever come a day when a beautiful day could just be that without my mind immediately shifting to Richard and my fear of finding him lurking in every corner of the country, looking for me?

"Are you ready?" Olly asked as she neared where I stood.

"I could ask you the same question," I said, smirking as she blushed again. Olly held out her phone to show that she'd gotten Jayce's number. "A grape contract and a hottie? You're on a roll."

"Right? This place has some awesome vibes." Laughing, we got into the car, and as Olly backed out of the spot, a reflection in the side-view mirror had me looking over my shoulder. Closing my eyes, I gave my head a little shake to clear it. I thought I saw Jake standing at the end of one of the rows.

In the next blink, he was gone. I really needed to stop torturing myself like this. It wasn't healthy for my emotional or mental state, and I was really starting to lose it. On the bright side, there were worse things to lose my mind over than images of Jake.

JAKE

THAT HAD BEEN the closest I'd been to Kat in years. At one point, I could've reached through the grape vines and pulled her into my arms, and the fantasy had been so vivid that I'd almost done just that. The chance to kiss her lips, to truly taste her for the first time, had my pulse jumping wildly. The heat I felt from doing physical labor had nothing on the heat she called up in me with her mere presence. My body felt like it was burning up, and it was hard in all the wrong places to facilitate any logical thought processes.

Her sweet scent, a mix of baked things and spices, was still strong in my nose, and every time I blinked, I saw her stunning blue eyes and that smile that could stop any man in his tracks. It was her. I was sure of it now.

Her voice had floated through my mind and my dreams for so long that hearing her laugh again in the real, waking world had been a dream come true all on its own. I'd had to step away to get control of myself. I didn't think stepping out of the vines like some knock-off version of *Field of Dreams* was a great idea unless I wanted to give her a heart attack. Then again, maybe I was the only one who still thought about us or what could have been.

I didn't want to examine that thought too closely, though. That kind of hole-poking could lead to the fantasy bubble I was doing the backstroke in popping, and I never wanted it to end. There was something else I had to focus on at the moment, anyway. Reaching the house, I jumped up the steps to the porch. The door squeaked loudly as I opened it and stepped into the front hall.

"Mom, are you okay?"

"I'm fine. Did you talk to her?" Mom asked, and both Dad and Jayce's eyes swiveled to find mine. I swallowed hard as the room fell silent.

"Um...."

"You didn't, did you? Son, what is the matter with you?" Mom scolded as she glared at me.

"Whoa, whoa, whoa, back this train up. Who are we talking about?" Jayce piped up to ask. His face had already lit up like a damn Christmas tree—his radar for gossip was finely honed—but before I could tell him to mind his own business, Mom answered.

"The girl that Jake has loved since forever. That was her. She was here, and Jake, you need to follow them and go talk to her."

"Jake loves someone? When did this happen?" Jayce asked. His face twisted in confusion while my dad's morphed into a wide grin that could easily compete with the Cheshire Cat's.

"Which one, Jake? Olivia or Lexi?" my dad asked, and I took a step back from the three of them in defense.

"Okay, see, *this* is exactly why I never tell you guys anything." The heat in my body was quickly changing over to a cold sweat under their stares.

"Lexi, dear," Mom said to Dad, and I groaned at the cat being one hundred percent, irrevocably out of the bag. Jayce wolf whistled.

"Mom, in confidence. Remember?"

"Oh, you mean the girl he wanted us to try and adopt too?"

"You wanted Mom and Dad to adopt a girl," Jayce asked. This was getting out of control.

"Ignore them, Jake. Get on your motorcycle and find that car. Go, now." Mom picked up her bottle of water and flung it at me. I caught it in reflex as my mouth fell open. I took a step back—I couldn't believe she'd done that.

"Go, now, or I'll throw something else, and don't you come back until you've talked to her. You need to stop being scared, Jake. Take the leap, and if you fall, we'll be here. Go!"

"Mom?" I took another step back.

"Don't you 'Mom' me. Get going right this second. You're wasting time."

"I'll take you," Jayce offered, heading for the door with an extra spring in his step, but I held up my hands to stop him in his tracks.

"No, I can do this. I'll go alone. Holy hell, you are a pushy bunch," I teased. As I turned to head out the door, a dish towel hit me squarely in the back of the head. "Oh my god, Mom's lost her mind," I said, laughing as I ran out the door, finally putting some speed into it.

They already had a ten-minute head start, but Mom was right—I needed to do this. I needed to find her, and I needed to man up and speak to the woman who was meant to be mine before I lost her again.

I pulled on my leather jacket and helmet, which I'd thankfully left hanging on the bike, and jumped on, kick starting it. The Harley rumbled to life, echoing loudly in the shed where I had it parked. The lane felt so much longer than usual as I made my way to the end and turned toward town, the direction I figured they'd be heading. As the road stayed Volkswagen-less, it became apparent I might have guessed wrong.

"Shit," I swore, hitting my handlebar as I reached the town limits without seeing a glimpse of the silver car. "Dammit, why didn't I just talk to her?" The universe couldn't have been sending me any clearer of a message, and I'd fucking chickened out.

Veering to the side of the road, I pulled up in front of her bakery and stared at the darkened window and its glowing hours of operation sign. It said she wasn't opening the bakery again until Friday. I had forty-eight hours to get my shit together, and then I was going to speak to her, no excuses this time.

"Mom is going to shoot me," I muttered under my breath. It didn't matter how old I got—I still felt like a bratty teen when she scolded me. Of course, my phone chose that minute to ring. Peering at my watch, I hit the button to put it through to my headset when I saw it was Miles. He always had shitty, shitty timing.

"Hey man, what's going on?" I asked as I pulled the bike back out onto the main road. I loved feeling the cool breeze on my face and the way my jacket fluttered. *This* was the best time of year to take a ride, and I would ride right up until the first snowflake fell.

"Are you sitting down?" Miles asked.

I looked down at the motorcycle under me and shrugged. Technically?

"Yup, what's up?"

"Mr. Russo was so impressed with how the commercial turned out and the unbelievable response it's received that he wants to do a second commercial and a photoshoot spread so he can pick and choose what images to use over the next year. This is fantastic for your brand, and you wanna take a guess at what he's planning on paying?"

I should be hooting and hollering excited, but I felt none of that.

"I will assume by your tone of voice that it's a lot. Is he wanting to do it on the farm again?" I asked, checking my side mirror.

"Man, when did you turn into such a tough audience? This is *great* news, so at least *try* and sound happy."

Rolling my shoulders out, I pushed the bike a little harder down the road, making the motor rumble louder. Maybe if I pushed it hard enough, I wouldn't hear Miles at all.

"Sorry. It is *wonderful* news. I cannot *believe* my luck. Was that better?"

"Only if you were speaking in front of a sixth-grade science class. Fine, whatever. The best part is he's going to rent a trailer and stay for a week with the crew at the farm. They will get everything they need over the course of the week and then you will be done, or at least done until I can find something else you'll actually agree to," Miles snarked, his condescending tone coming thickly through the line. My teeth ground together as I envisioned wrapping my hands around his neck.

"Miles, I can't have an entire crew and Mr. Russo stay at my parents' farm for a week. I don't even know if they would be okay with it." The tightness in my chest, which had been lightening up for the first time in years ever since I'd finally said 'fuck you' to my previous lifestyle, started to return at the thought of my fucked-up life following me here. This was my safe space, my sanctuary. The last thing I wanted was for it to be ruined by all the lights and glamour that I was trying to escape.

"Don't forget the models. They will be coming as well. Look, Jake, I have faith you'll get your family to agree to this. This way, you can schmooze and get a little horizontal action without even having to leave home."

I wanted to bang my head on the handlebars. Repeatedly. It was like I was speaking a different language and Miles couldn't understand me.

"This is not happening," I muttered.

"It's unbelievable, isn't it?"

"No, Miles. I mean they cannot stay at my parents' farm. I will do the ads, but they need to find someplace else to park it."

The heavy breathing as Miles's anger rose on the other end of the line was so strong I could almost feel it blowing into my ear.

"Jake!"

There was no way in hell I was letting him convince me of this.

"Miles! My mom has cancer," I yelled. There was absolute silence on the other end of the line. Shit. Saying it out loud made it far too real—there was a reason I'd been avoiding the word, and fucking Miles had made me say it.

"No one is coming to stay at the farm. I'm not letting the kind of bullshit and pressure that follows me around into her life. Do you understand me? They stay elsewhere or call it all off."

The line was silent for so long that I thought Miles had hung up.

"I'm so sorry. Don't I feel like a fucking prick. Why didn't you just tell me that? Is this why you don't want to travel anymore?"

I could picture the hurt look on Miles's face, and of course, the guilt quickly followed. Sometimes, he made it easy to forget we were friends, and then something like this would happen. Right about now, I could use a stiff drink.

"No, the reason I told you is the truth. It was time to hang up the crazy, but this was another factor that went into making the decision final. She starts treatment next week, and if people are staying at our place, she will try to help out and entertain and be the amazing host she always is, and I'm not putting her through that. It's that simple."

"Okay. I'll sort out other arrangements. You still fine with them arriving Friday? It will simply be a small social the first day, and then I'll take them where they need to stay and be the man of the hour in your place."

I wanted to yell 'no' to Friday—I had plans to stalk the love of my life—but that seemed a bit dramatic even in my own head. I'd make it work. I just needed to make sure that I was out of there and in town before Kat finished with work.

"That works. I'll be there all day and will prep my family, but no more anything at the farm after this, Miles. I really am sorry that I'm being so difficult lately, and I'm sorry I didn't tell you about my mom."

"It's all good. I understand. I'll shoot you a text with all the details." The call clicked off in my ear and was replaced with the rock song I'd been listening to previously.

Even though I'd agreed, there was a sinking pit in my stomach. This didn't seem like a good idea all around. Having Mr. Russo around with his entourage for a day or two was one thing, but a week was a whole different animal. It worried me for reasons I couldn't even put my finger on.

Revving the motorcycle, I let the world streak past as I sped toward home and prayed that my mom didn't kill me for missing Kat and Tripp didn't kill me for the film crew. I sat up straight as an idea came to me. It was an idea that would most likely land me in a shit-storm with Tripp, but I was going to do it anyway because a shit-storm day was exactly the kind of day it had turned out to be.

JAKE

I VEERED into the cul de sac of massive estate homes and eased off the speed. This was the type of neighborhood where people actually called the cops when they didn't recognize a vehicle, and incidentally, exactly the kind of place I never wanted to live.

There were a few people outside tending to their lawns, their golf shorts firmly in place below their long-sleeved shirts. They all paused as I drove by, and I purposely looked in their direction, waving as I made eye contact. It was amazing how quickly they turned around and pretended they hadn't been staring.

I saw the girls before I noticed the giant house behind them that was set back further from the road than the rest. Brianna and Sydney were running around chasing one another on the lawn, and I couldn't keep the smile off my face. They'd gotten so big in the last year, sprouted up so much, that it was like I'd missed their entire lives. They stopped running and stared at me as I pulled the motorcycle up to the curb.

"Uncle Jake!" the girls screamed in unison as I slid off the bike and removed the helmet. Sydney, who somehow was already *eight*, reached me first, and I scooped her up to swing her around in a circle as she laughed.

"My turn, my turn," Bri said, clasping her hands together as her sweet doe eyes stared up at me.

"Okay, fair is fair." Putting Syd back on her feet, I grabbed up a squealing Bri and did the same routine, switching girls again and again until I was dizzy and had to stop. "Okay, girls, that's all I've got," I panted and leaned over, pretending to be completely out of breath for their benefit.

I spotted Lanny coming out of the house, and she looked the same as she always had. Her smile was soft and sweet and her blonde hair was pulled up into a ponytail. It was her clothes and makeup that had changed. Expensive clothes, and I knew exactly how expensive, were on her body, and she had makeup on when she'd never used to wear any before. Her nails were done, and she wore a new aura of importance around her.

I'd always liked Lanny and Tripp together. They had a great balance and the love story of a lifetime—at least, that was what I'd thought. Looking at her now, I wasn't sure what to feel. I wasn't one to promote staying with someone if you weren't happy, but the way she was ending it, and hurting Tripp in the process, made me angry. I masked the anger that was amping up inside me as she got closer and instead put on the mask that I used when I was doing social gigs.

"Hey, Lanny," I said, waving.

As she gave me a smile, a blush crept across her cheeks. Any other time, I would've felt awkward at the fact she was making flirty expressions at me, but I was hoping to use her obvious interest in either me or my lifestyle, or both, to my benefit.

"I try to go by Leanne now, but you can still call me Lanny." She opened her arms for a hug, and I made sure to keep it a single-arm, bodies-separated type. I also kept it short.

"Do you want to play in our new treehouse? It's awesome and so much bigger than the one at Daddy's," Syd said. I kept smiling, but my heart hurt to hear Syd say that. Money wasn't everything, and having the best didn't bring happiness. This new life and attitude that Lanny was sporting was only going to encourage that mentality.

"You know that I can't leave without seeing it." I smiled, giving Bri's shoulder a squeeze as she clung to my leg like a barnacle. "But I need to talk to your mom for a little while first. I promise not to leave without seeing it, though, okay?"

"Okay," Bri chirped. Satisfied, the girls chased one another to the backyard, leaving Lanny and me alone.

Stuffing my hands in my pockets, I took a couple of steps back to lean against the body of the bike. I wanted our conversation to be in full view of everyone who lived here and all the security cameras I was positive they had. What I was about to propose could go either really well or terribly wrong, and at this point, there was no telling which.

"So, you and Tripp are done? I can honestly say I never saw that happening," I said. She crossed her arms, but her face didn't look angry, or at least not yet.

"Yeah. Let me guess. He told you I was a raving bitch trying to steal his kids from him and move to the other side of the world," she said in a dramatic voice, rolling her eyes at the end.

I smirked.

"Not exactly. I don't think the word 'bitch' and your name have ever crossed Tripp's lips together." She had the decency to look ashamed as she looked away. "But he did mention that you and your new *boyfriend* wanted to move." I made sure to emphasize the word boyfriend.

"He also said that he's fighting it, and because of that, you're not letting him see the girls and claiming he hurt you." Lanny looked down at her feet, and I got the impression this wasn't what she'd set out to do—maybe someone had put the idea in her head. I knew all too well what it was like to try and stop a ball you'd already sent tumbling down a hill from rolling.

"Look, Lanny. I'm not here to make you feel bad, but you have to know that lying isn't going to do either of you any good. It's certainly not good for the girls. Syd and Bri love you both so much. They have to be so confused, and what are they going to think if this rumor spreads more and they hear lies at school about their father hurting you?" She made a little noise like she was sniffling back tears. "I know this is not easy for either of you, but this is not the best path to get what you want."

"I wouldn't have done this if he weren't being so fricking stubborn. He's always been like an ox. It's not like he can't come and visit, or the girls can't come back here to stay for a week at a time," she said.

"And if the roles were reversed, would you be okay with him moving halfway across the world and telling you that you can only see the girls when you fly out?"

She sighed and shook her head.

"Is this why you came? To see if you could change my mind for your brother? You doing his dirty work now?"

"Sorta. Tripp doesn't know I'm here. No one does." I let that statement settle on her, and when she looked up, there was a glimmer in her eyes that gave me hope my ploy might work. "I want to make a deal with you."

"A deal? What kind of deal?" Her voice was skeptical, but she dropped her arms to her sides.

"I understand from my manager that you tried to reach me because you were thinking of breaking into the social media and acting landscape. Is that something you still want?"

"I don't know." Her eyes narrowed into thin slits. "Are you going to judge me if I do?"

"Not at all." I shrugged a shoulder and let it drop, hoping a calm and aloof manner would intrigue her more, but she didn't say anything and just continued to stare. "Okay then. I guess I'll go see the treehouse and be on my way." I pushed away from the motorcycle and wasn't surprised at all when she grabbed my arm as I went to walk past.

"Okay, I may be interested." She bit her lip and slid her hand down my arm. "I've followed you since you first started your site. What you do, what you get to see and experience...I've wanted to join you for a while now," she whispered as she slipped her hand into mine and tried to link our fingers. I pulled my hand away, not letting it happen, and her cheeks flamed red as she took a step back.

"I'd never deny that you're a beautiful woman, Lanny, but Tripp is my brother. Flesh and blood have nothing to do with the bond we share, but I'd never do what you're implying."

She quickly crossed her arms over her chest again, and her voice hardened as she spoke.

"Fine. What do you have in mind?"

I slowly stepped away to once more lean back against the bike, crossing my arms and my ankles as I stretched out.

"Are you sure? 'Cause I'm not going to even suggest this unless you're sure. I don't recommend people for almost anything, so it comes highly respected when I do. I'm not putting my neck or reputation on the line for someone who *might be interested.*" I used little finger quotes to make my point.

Lanny bit her lip and looked over her shoulder at the house. I didn't know for sure what was running through her mind, but I was starting to think she wasn't as happy here as she'd been trying to make everyone believe. It was looking like this thing with the gynecologist might have been a landing pad and nothing more.

"Yeah, I'm sure. What do you have in mind?"

"Alright." I cocked my head to the side and flipped my sunglasses up on top of my head. "You have something I want, and I have something you want. I'm thinking a trade." She stood a little straighter, obviously taking my meaning the wrong way.

"Oh, I, um...." She blushed a deep red color and pressed her chest out a little, and for the first time since I'd met Lanny, I was confused by her. I got wanting more from life. I'd be a fucking hypocrite if I said I didn't. The thing was, she was acting like a totally different person, like someone had flipped a switch in her, and there was this odd edge to her that I couldn't quite put my finger on.

She was still my brother's wife, and she was now with a new man, yet she had still openly flirted with me, and more than once. It made my stomach twist in knots for Tripp. He loved Lanny with everything in him. But if Lanny had loved Tripp at all, it was clear as day that she didn't anymore. If he held any hope that they'd find their way back to one another, he was going to need to quickly crush it, or it would only cause more pain.

"What did I just say? I don't mean sex, Lanny." She cleared her throat, but before she could deny what she'd been thinking, I continued. "You want the whole glamorous lifestyle. I'm guessing you want to travel the world and date famous men, or heck, even explore some women." The corner of my lip curled up as she gasped. That wasn't a denial.

"How about dining at five-star restaurants and getting admitted to the most popular clubs and parties around? You might even land yourself on a red carpet or two. Am I wrong?"

"No, I've definitely been interested in doing more with my life before I become some shriveled-up old hag."

"Come now, Lanny. We both know you'd never be that," I said, saying it like I thought she was the most beautiful woman in the world. She was smiling once more—I was on the right path.

"I mean, don't get me wrong. I love my girls, but life with Tripp was like living in a time warp, practically living the same day over and over. He never saw the need to do more, to move or see the world, and he...." She looked off into the distance, her eyes unfocused as she saw what only she could see. "I wasn't happy anymore."

"Okay, I get that," I said, shrugging. I wasn't judging her, but I wanted to make sure that she didn't feel that way, or else this was not going to work. "Since that's the case, then this is what I propose. I will give you all of that. I will open every door you've ever wanted open, and it'll all be served to you on a silver platter, but...."

"But I have to drop the charges against Tripp and give him half custody," she offered.

I shook my head.

"Full custody, but with joint visitation dates that you get to decide. Split holidays, and neither of you ever speaks ill of one another in front of the girls," I said, staring her down.

"No way! How can you think I'd ever agree to that? My girls are my life. I love Syd and Bri," she said, clutching her hands to her chest. It was easy to tell she meant it, but the road and the life I'd been living...and kids? No.

"It's because you love them that you'll agree. Look, Lanny, there is no sugar coating this. The lifestyle I live is not for children, period. You can't drag them from one drunken hotel room stay to another, bouncing them from one school to the next with no stability while leaving them with a nanny twenty-four-seven. Most nights, you'll be living it up with the most famous people around, staying out late at parties and floating around on expensive yachts. That is no life for two young girls, and you know it. If you want this lifestyle, truly want to step into that glamorous party image, then you need to leave the girls here."

"Lots of famous people travel with their kids," she argued.

"That's true, but please be honest with yourself Lanny. Is doing a movie or going to a club and then heading home to your children, what you had in mind?" I lifted my eyebrow and she looked away. "You want the parties, the carefree traveling, the binge drinking, some party drug experimenting and...hours of mindless fucking." I lowered my voice and made sure to draw out the last word and her face flamed red, but a little smile pulled at the corner of her mouth.

Despite hitting the nail on the head, I could still see the worry running around behind her eyes—I knew just what she needed to hear.

"Tripp is not going to keep you from them. To be honest, he still hopes you'll get back together again, but I know the bug that has bitten you and what it makes you want. We both know that getting back together is not happening."

Lanny walked around in a small circle, her agitation obvious.

"I don't know. I need to think about this. Leaving the girls with Tripp full-time was never in my plans. Cutting him out wasn't either, but still…."

"No problem, but this is a limited-time offer. I have a very, very influential man coming to my parents' farm. Not only can I get your new life started with a commercial opportunity on Friday, but I know that if I ask, he will help set your career up for life. If you play your cards right you can leave with him and his crew. Their next stop is the Cayman Islands for a week of fun in the sun before they head to Europe for another commercial shoot."

I didn't tell her that it was probably going to cost me something big, something I wouldn't want to do in the future—to see this happen would be worth the cost. I stood from the bike, and as I got to Lanny's side, I stopped. Her eyes found mine.

"We are talking mega billions here, Lanny. This man is not the type of man you meet at a club, but I respect that you need time to think." I nodded toward the backyard. "I'm going to go see my nieces for a few minutes, and then I'm going to go. If you decide this is what you really want, then I'll make it happen, but only under the conditions I laid out. So, if you decide yes, then get the paperwork to hand over the girls and your terms for visitation in order and meet me at my parent's place at noon on Friday. If you don't show, I'll know what your answer is."

I fixed Lanny with a solemn stare, making sure she could see how serious I was.

"You're not being forced to do this. I want to make that clear. This is simply an opportunity for both you and Tripp to get what you really want. I hope that you both find the happiness you're searching for."

Her blue eyes filled with tears, and I walked away to give her some privacy. Turning my attention to the girls, I followed the same path they'd run down earlier and smiled widely as I spotted them. They were the cutest pair of kids I'd ever seen. I acknowledged that I might be a little biased, being their uncle and all, but they truly reminded me of little fairies as they danced and spun around in the sunlight.

I couldn't remember a time that I'd ever been that carefree and happy. That wasn't a hundred percent true. When I was with Kat, I always felt like that. Light on my feet, a smile on my face and thought that I could conquer the world.

They spotted me coming and dashed over to grab my hands and drag me to a massive structure a story or two in the air that looked more like a nanny's suite than a treehouse. It spanned two trees, had a slide and lookouts, and was decorated with flowers along the outside like a house. I stayed long enough to play a couple of rounds of tag and pretended to be Tarzan as I swung from a climbing rope, making them giggle.

As I explored the treehouse with them, I made sure to make a special fuss over the little additions they'd added to personalize it, like a sitting area filled with their books and a couple of small chairs. Even though I had to admit that this was the coolest treehouse I'd ever seen, I couldn't help wondering if the new man in their lives was trying to buy their love, or maybe their mothers through them.

"Okay, girls. I'm sorry, but I have to get going. It's getting late," I said, kneeling. I held out my fist for the girls to bump. "I'll see you two soon. I've missed you, and I know that everyone else has as well. Grandma Joy is making loads of cookies for when you visit."

"Yay, pirate cookies! Argh," they chimed in together, making me laugh. They would make the cutest darn commercial. Bri gave me a hard hug and ran off, but as Syd stepped close to give me a hug, she leaned in shyly.

"Can you tell Daddy that we miss him?" she whispered in my ear before giving me a kiss on the cheek and skipping off. My heart broke into a million little pieces.

If this didn't work, I didn't know what else I could do, but I wouldn't stand by and let the girls never see their father again. Lanny had to see the light. She just had to.

When I made it back to the front of the house, Lanny was still standing outside. We shared a look, and that conveyed all I needed to know—she would think about it. I caught movement from a window on the second floor of the house, and when I searched it out, I saw a man who looked to be in his fifties watching us. I pointedly made eye contact, and after a few moments, the sheer curtain slid back into place once more, concealing the man from sight.

I didn't get a good vibe about anything I'd seen here today, and I said a silent prayer that Lanny would take the offer for more than one reason.

20

JAKE

"AH! Jake, my boy, you're doing *wonders* for my brand," Mr. Russo said as he stepped out of a large motorhome that looked like something right out of the movies. I wouldn't have been surprised if a pool suddenly popped out of one side with women already in it and a D.J. and bar popped out of the other. It would be on brand for him.

"Good to see you again as well, Mr. Russo." I flashed my million-dollar smile and shook the man's hand before looking over my shoulder to make sure no one else was in earshot. "I'm sorry about the arrangements having to be slightly altered from what you were hoping for."

"First, call me Francisco. I would certainly consider us friends by now. Second, do not worry. Your manager has found the most splendid location. I've already checked it out, and we have lots of space and privacy with a clear view of the water." Mr. Russo stepped in a little closer and lowered his voice. "I was sorry to hear about your mother, though."

"Oh, Miles told you."

"Yes, I hope that's alright?"

"Yes, of course. I just don't want anyone making her feel uncomfortable, is all," I said. Mentally, I was kicking Miles in the ass for saying anything.

"My lips are sealed. Now come. I have lots to talk to you about before we start filming tomorrow."

I followed Mr. Russo to the motorhome and stepped up into the strange, magical world that this man inhabited. Strings of beads of all colors hung over the doors. The seats had all been upholstered with a soft material that looked like satin—it was certainly just as shiny, and there were what looked like hundreds of matching pillows scattered around to accompany the look.

In what looked to be an eating area, bottles of Champagne and flutes were artfully laid out on a table, and in the small kitchen, a chef was busily making something that smelled expensive. The table was already piled high with a wide assortment of exquisite hors d'oeuvres. There was definitely something to this lifestyle that was magical.

Admittedly, it really hadn't been all bad, but as I stared at the elegant décor and lavish extras, I didn't feel anything. No awe or wonder was left in my soul for this sort of extravagance.

I slid across the large bench and waited for Mr. Russo to get settled.

"Before we start, may I ask a favor of you, Mr. Russo?"

"Only if you call me Francisco," he said as he removed the dark sunglasses he was wearing and poured himself a glass of bubbly.

"Francisco, I have a friend who is really wanting to open up her possibilities for...." I paused, not sure how to say it without sounding like I was trying to pimp Lanny out. "For certain luxuries."

Mr. Russo had barely leaned back and relaxed into his seat before the chef was there to serve up the fantastic-smelling items. After the food was placed on the table, Mr. Russo thanked the chef and waved him back to the kitchen with a gesture like some medieval nobleman.

"Eat something, please, and then tell me more about this friend."

I filled a small plate and spent a few minutes nibbling on the food, which was five-star despite being made in a motorhome, while I planned out what to say.

"So, my friend. She is looking for some opportunities, like the yacht party and maybe a commercial or photo shoot. She is uncertain where exactly her talents fall, but she is beautiful, and I've asked her to come and be a part of the commercial. If you're willing, of course," I said.

"What would you like her to do in the commercial?"

"Being an extra is fine to start, just to get her feet wet." I tossed a fluffy pastry filled with cheese and spinach into my mouth—it practically melted all on its own. "Like I said, she's beautiful and looking for opportunities outside of this small town."

Mr. Russo didn't say anything for a long time, and I waited him out. I wasn't going to press or show my hand on just how much I wanted this to happen.

"I can't promise anything specific, but I will definitely meet this friend. I will be calling on you for a favor in the future, though. Maybe a guest appearance at a product launch or something else of that ilk."

Picking up my glass of water, I shot Mr. Russo my most charming smile and held out the glass for him to clink with his own.

"I wouldn't expect anything less. It's a deal," I said. Mr. Russo smiled widely—I knew the sharp *ting* as the glasses came together was as binding as a handshake when it came to this man.

It had become one of my specialties to know exactly what those around me wanted. I'd learned their likes, their dislikes, and, most importantly, what they needed. I'd also made a point of memorizing their families' names, when their birthdays were, and anything else of importance that might help me make a connection with them. Mr. Russo had a few quirks, but all of them were easy to appease, and there hadn't been anything that would cause concern in his history.

About an hour later, a soft knock interrupted the story Mr. Russo was telling. A man came out of nowhere to answer the door. Looking around, I wondered where the heck he'd come from since I'd thought we'd been alone since the chef left.

"Hi, my name is Leanne. I was supposed to meet Jake here," Lanny, or I guess 'Leanne,' said from the door, drawing my attention. I had to admit, she really knew how to turn on the style when she wanted to. She looked amazing.

"Is this who you were talking about, Jake?" Mr. Russo asked as he wiped his mouth and stood to greet his guest.

"Yes, this is Leanne Russell." I stood as she came in and gave her a large smile. "Mr. Russo, I'd like you to meet Leanne, and Leanne, this is Mr. Russo."

Mr. Russo held out his hand and shook Lanny's, hanging on longer than necessary as his gaze fixed on her pretty face.

"Well, Jake, you never disappoint me." He lifted her hand to his lips and gave it a kiss that made her blush a vibrant shade of red.

"It's my pleasure to meet you, Mr. Russo," she said, her voice soft and a little shaky from her obvious nerves.

"Wow, Uncle Jake, is this yours?" Syd asked, her piping voice cutting through the tension as she and Bri came in behind their mother. I tried hard not to look as ecstatic and relieved as I felt—my body was practically shaking with it. Both girls' eyes were as wide as saucers as they took in the massive space that, to a child, probably looked like a wonderland.

"Nope, sorry, kiddo. This amazing house on wheels is Mr. Russo's. Can I speak to you outside for a moment, Leanne?"

As the kids ran down the stairs, Mr. Russo finally dropped Lanny's hand. He waited until she was out of earshot to grab my arm and pull me closer.

"I will do whatever you need me to," he murmured before letting me go and turning back to the table. It helped that Mr. Russo had one particular weakness and that I'd been banking on exploiting, and that was blondes with blue eyes. I jogged down the stairs and guided Lanny over to a shaded area under the large maple tree. It was out of the way enough to provide a little privacy.

"I'm assuming you being here means that you're going to accept my offer?"

Lanny crossed her arms and watched the girls as they ran for the house.

"I don't know if I'm doing the right thing," she said as the girls disappeared inside.

"Lanny, this was a choice that you made—to leave Tripp for a different life. If you want that old life back, you need to speak to him. If you don't and your heart is set on bigger things like you said to me, then this is your opportunity to not settle for some doctor I don't think you're very happy with."

Lanny locked eyes with me, and I could see the struggle raging inside her as she chewed her lower lip.

"Mr. Russo is a very powerful man, and he can open all the doors you want him to, but I can't offer this to you in good conscience if the girls would be with you. If you want to come back and work out joint custody with Tripp later, that is something the two of you can discuss, and you'll never be cut off from them or the family, Lanny."

"You say that now, but what happens six months from now? A year from now?"

I lifted my shoulders in a shrug.

"A lot of that is going to depend on you. If you remain the amazing mom you are and call them and Face Time them and visit them, and they visit you, then there shouldn't be an issue. But if you just disappear for a year and then try to come back into their lives...I can't say how that will go."

Her arms dropped to her sides. It looked like all of the ambivalence had dropped right off of her.

"I wouldn't do that to them. Never."

"Then that's your answer. Have you ever known this family to be vindictive Lanny?"

"No," she said, and looked down.

"Lanny? What's going on here?" Tripp's voice was loud as he came up behind me. "Is this some sort of trick, or are you trying to get me thrown off my parent's property now as well?"

"Don't be so dramatic, Tripp. You're getting everything you want," she bit back.

I put my hand on Tripp's chest and gave him a hard look, but he wasn't paying any attention to me. His eyes were fixed on Lanny's.

"Get what I want? Are you just out to hurt me now? Want to have me arrested in front of the kids? Why? What did I do to you?"

I grabbed Tripp by the front of his shirt and pushed him back.

"Knock it off, Tripp. Let her speak," I whispered, steel in my voice. He couldn't mess this up, not like this.

"Why are you defending her?"

"Shut up a second," I growled. "Take a breath, man." Tripp's eyes narrowed into thin slits, and I could tell we were about a second away from going another round in our own personal MMA. As much as we loved one another, this was something that we did on the regular as teens. It had become our thing to get all fired up and go a round or two and then go back to being best friends a moment later. "Tripp, don't make a scene. The girls are in the house. They don't need to see or hear you two arguing," I urged.

It was like I'd hit a switch. In moments, Tripp's eyes softened and his body relaxed. He ran a hand down his face.

"I'm sorry, but I just don't understand." He held out his hand gesturing toward Lanny. "She tried to get a restraining order against me, man. She had the police come to my house and question me like I was a criminal. I was advised by my lawyer not to go anywhere near her and she knows that, yet she still comes here to my family home, my place of work? The hell is that all about?"

"Lanny is here because I asked her to come," I said, letting my hand drop from Tripp's chest.

"You what?" he demanded.

Before Tripp could start another round of ranting, I wrapped my arm around his shoulders and smiled.

"Lanny here has retracted her original statement to the police and agreed to give you full custody of the girls." I paused to let that sink in and then gave him a nudge when he didn't respond. "This would be a really good time for you to say thank you to Lanny."

I felt like I was talking to someone who didn't speak English who was stuck trying to decipher the words I'd said.

"You need to sign the paperwork and work out a good schedule for Lanny to visit with the girls and the girls to visit her while she travels."

Tripp stood frozen in place, his eyes blinking like he still couldn't comprehend the words I was saying. He stumbled back suddenly—I made a grab for him, but his ass found the grass and his big body started to shake like he had low-grade hypothermia. Shit, was he going into shock?

"Are you serious?" He looked up at Lanny, eyes wide.

Lanny's tears finally spilled from her eyes as she nodded.

"I'm sorry, Tripp. I...I...I'll go get the paperwork." She spun on her heel and walked quickly toward the car.

"What the heck is happening? Am I dreaming?" Tripp asked, hands clasping the back of his head—an old nervous gesture of his. I couldn't answer, however, as the girls chose that moment to run out of the house, laughing and with cookies in hand.

"Daddy! Did Mommy tell you?" Syd asked as both girls jumped on their father.

Lifting a girl under each arm, Tripp stood, making them laugh as he spun around in hectic circles. Their laughter and little shrieks of happiness were infectious, and I couldn't help but smile to myself.

"I just heard. Are you excited?" he asked.

"Yes," they cheered, laughing as Tripp finally set them on their feet. He was practically glowing as he watched them stagger around exaggeratedly and shout about being dizzy. His smile started to dim, though, and I wasn't sure why. Following his gaze, I saw that Lanny was making her way back.

"Girls, why don't you go play on the tire swing for a few minutes while I talk with Mommy," Tripp said, kneeling down to look them in the eyes.

"Okay. We love you, Daddy," the duo of adorable cuteness chimed, and each girl kissed a cheek before running off. They passed by Lanny, who came over with a large brown envelope in her hand.

"You two have a lot to discuss, and to make sure that everything stays amicable, I will sit in on your discussion if both of you are comfortable with that," I offered.

Lanny and Tripp nodded.

"Alright then. I'll be right back. I have to take care of something real quick."

Striding off toward the motorhome, I went to find Mr. Russo to apologize for slipping out on him. Now I just had to hope that I could get Tripp and Lanny to calmly remain in the same room and agree to terms before I needed to leave to speak to Kat.

Being late was not an option.

"You have got to be *kidding* me," I yelled into the wind as I flew down the road. Of *course* Tripp and Lanny couldn't get along for five minutes without sniping at one another. Why would I even have expected that? It's not like they'd been married for years or anything. How did two people manage to go from loving one other unconditionally to not even being able to agree on the weather?

At least Lanny hadn't backed out of the deal, but there were a couple of times I'd wanted to order Tripp out of the fucking room and just take care of the paperwork myself.

To top it all off, now I was running late. I was still ten minutes outside of town, and Kat would be closing up shop in fifteen. Definitely cutting it too close for comfort.

The wail of a siren suddenly broke the countryside stillness, and I looked in my side view mirror to see a Sheriff's car following behind me with its lights flashing. Hanging my head and swearing under my breath, I slowed down and pulled over to the side of the road. Once safely on the shoulder, I cut the engine and continued grumbling quietly but creatively as I stood to reach into my back pocket for my wallet.

The officer sure took his sweet time walking over.

"License and registration," the officer said as he approached, his voice gruff and already angry sounding. Annoyed, I glanced over, trying hard to keep the F-you off my face, and did a double take. I knew this fucker.

"Hey, asshole," Officer-fucking-Karl said, smiling widely. Who'd have thought?

Hopping off the bike, I laughed hard as I gripped Karl in a tight hug.

"You son of a bitch. I thought I was getting a ticket or a gloved hand up my ass."

Karl smiled a shit-eating grin.

"Dude, I don't know where you've been traveling, but if I were going to do that, it wouldn't be roadside," he teased. "Now the ticket, that I *should* give you. You were doing twenty over."

"Aw, come on. Don't be like that." I gave him a teasing jab in the side as I stepped back to take him in fully. "Shit, man, look at you."

My eyes scanned over the wide shoulders, new since I'd last seen him, that filled out his uniform admirably and the totally badass gun at his hip.

"I bet the ladies love the uniform. When did you become a cop?" I settled back against the bike and crossed my arms over my chest, ready for a story.

Karl had been the stereotypical school nerd. Thick glasses, braces, floppy hair that hung in his face, clothes that draped his narrow frame—high school Karl had it all. More importantly, he was also a hell of a great guy.

Karl had a wickedly sly sense of humor that could keep you in stitches, and he would give you the shirt off his back if you ever needed it. He was also super smart. I'd copied from his test in class more than once when I'd forgotten to study, and they were the best scores I'd ever gotten.

I'd always been the tough, *don't fuck with me* type. I usually blamed it on the foster care system, but if I were being honest, I'd had a bit of a chip on my shoulder from before I could even remember. Luckily, that'd never shifted over into me being a bully, and I'd started hanging out with Karl almost the second my family moved here.

The guy had taken some pretty bad licks at school, yet he would always get back up. At the time, I thought he was stupid and should just stay down to buy himself a reprieve, but looking back now, I wanted to cheer for him. That natural toughness inside of Karl was stronger than most and I admired him for it.

That's not to say I didn't know how to stand up for myself or take a stand for others. One year, I got in some pretty hot water, the 'almost-expelled' level of hot, when I broke the nose of a kid who had been bullying Karl. Mom had been so, so pissed, but it was fucking worth it. Now, here Karl was, the same height as me and just as built, and he was a damn cop to boot. He probably threw assholes like his old bully in jail on the regular. I loved the irony.

"When did I get my badge? Not long after you took off for the bright lights. The whole music thing kinda fell apart without our lead guitarist-slash-singer," Karl said. "Not that I really thought we were going to become rock stars by playing all those local joints." He hooked his thumbs in his gun belt, looking every bit the tough guy he'd always been on the inside.

"What are you doing back here, anyway?" he asked. "I didn't think I'd see your face again, what with all the money and the women and the traveling the world. Although, you could've dropped your old friend a line every once in a while, you know."

"Yeah, man. I'm sorry about that. I've been a little self-absorbed." I looked down at my boots and rolled a stone around with the tip of one. "It was time to come home, and I have a lot to make up for with more than one person."

"So does that mean you're sticking around for a while?"

"Means I don't plan on leaving again for a long-ass time," I said with a wry grin.

Karl tilted his head and stared at me searchingly for a moment.

"Seems like there's a story there."

"You fucking mind reading me, man? Seeing into my soul or some shit?" I grinned at him, remembering all too well the number of hours we'd spent watching and re-watching the *Star Wars* movies as we endlessly debated which one was the best and why.

"Naw," Karl said, "I was—."

The radio on his shoulder crackled to life, cutting him off. Stepping away, he spoke briefly into the handset attached to his vest, voice too muffled to hear. He came back over after signing off with an apologetic shrug.

"Looks like you're getting off easy, Russell. I've got to get going. Wanna grab a beer sometime?"

"What? Be seen with a cop?" I screwed up my face and then laughed as he swore. "Where you living these days, anyway?" I asked.

"You remember that old school house that I kept saying I liked? I finally bought it. Drop by and say hi when you can." With a half-assed salute, he marched off and jumped into the cruiser, his face all business. After making a U-turn, he floored it down the road, lights flashing and sirens blaring.

While that had turned out fucking lucky, I was now crazy late. I swung my leg over the seat of the bike and revved up the Harley a moment later. If I had been speeding before, I was about to openly and unapologetically break the law now. Good thing Karl was only a speck in the distance in the opposite direction.

I had just crested the hill that led down to the downtown strip when I spotted Kat walking out of her store and slipping into the passenger side of the same silver Volkswagen as before. Excellent—that meant she was with the girl she'd been with at the farm, her friend. The fact she wasn't getting into a car with some guy sent a flutter of relief washing through me. She wasn't getting away this time.

Keeping my distance, I followed the car as it pulled out into the street. As they traveled down one back road after another, the whole tailing thing got more and more challenging. I had no idea where they were going. This was not an area I was familiar with, and it was becoming increasingly hard to maintain a distance that didn't make me look like some kind of suspicious stalker.

Finally, the car's brake lights glowed brightly in the dark as the car slowed and turned into a parking lot. As I neared the location, I realized it was a bar—one on the seedy end of the spectrum. The glowing neon sign and the middle-of-nowhere location screamed that this was not the type of place you wanted to go to alone. Maybe not even with a group of people.

Kat got out of the car, smiled, and then closed the door before heading inside. The car continued on, pulling out of a second driveway and disappearing down the road. What the *hell* was Kat doing *here*? Was she working a second job?

Shaking my head, I pulled up to the long line of bikes occupying one whole section of the front of the building. A few people stared as I pulled her in at the end, and they were right to stare. It had cost me an arm and a leg, but my baby was a custom-made beauty outfitted with detailing and add-ons that you couldn't find on any other model.

"Nice ride," a woman said as I made my way toward the front doors. She was wearing a club jacket, and that was dangerous territory even if I were interested. You didn't mess with a biker's girl unless you wanted to find yourself strung up by your ball sac somewhere. I really fucking didn't.

"Thanks," I said, but I didn't slow my pace. As I opened the door, the secondhand smoke from the bar punched me in the face and the old craving surfaced. Fuck, I hated trying to be healthy. Why the hell was it that everything that tasted good or felt good to do was bad for you somehow? I was trying to give it all up, but goddamn.

Except for sex, of course. I didn't care if they told me I'd die the next time I had it—I would still jump into that pool no matter what.

My eyes scanned the bar and then the tables, searching for Kat, while my mind worked through the possible reasons she'd come to a place like this. It was as dark and dingy on the inside as it looked from the outside.

The wood of the bar top was so dark brown it was black, and it looked like it had seen more than one bar fight. The walls were decorated in a mix of motorcycle memorabilia, old gas station signs, and glowing beer advertisements, and in one corner, a single, ancient-looking CRT television was showing a football game. There was a stage with a pole set up in the center.

No one was waiting at the door to greet and seat customers, only a bouncer who looked me over briefly before stepping aside so I could continue on my way.

My heart lurched, stopped, and then began thumping wildly inside my chest as I spotted Kat in a booth near the back of the bar. I'd already taken a step or two toward her before I spotted someone sitting across the booth from her. A male someone. My hands instinctively flexed, and I cracked my neck as the urge to march over there raced through my system.

Veering in the opposite direction, I slid into an empty booth that would give me a direct line of sight to Kat and her mystery man. It was definitely not the man the papers and websites had said she was going to marry years ago. That man came from old money and was going to be a doctor. This man looked like he could barely afford the drinks that were on the table, and he had a prison tattoo on the side of his neck.

"What can I get ya?"

I was jarred out of my brooding thoughts as a waitress stepped into my line of sight. I cut the death stare.

"Give me whatever the best thing you have on tap is." The standup menu caught my attention and I snatched it up, tapping on the loaded fries special. "And I'll have one of those."

"You got it. Coming right up."

As soon as she moved, I was once more able to watch Kat. She didn't seem to be having a great time. I'd seen her real smile, and it would light up her whole face and the world around her. Her 'smile' now, a polite lift of one corner of her mouth, screamed that she was uncomfortable, but the dick she was sitting with didn't seem to notice as he rambled on.

Even from across the room, I could tell that he was doing all the talking. I started to make up what he was saying like I was dubbing over a sitcom on mute, and none of what I made him say was good or particularly flattering. It was probably childish of me, but it made me feel a little less murderous.

If I went over there, I knew I would do something stupid. I knew my limitations when it came to Kat, and if that guy said so much as one thing to her that I didn't like, I was going to be seeing Karl again way too soon. I wouldn't get off with a warning, either.

The beer and loaded fries were suddenly on the table, dropped off by the waitress without missing a step on her way to another table. Apparently, service was not what this place was known for. Stuffing one of the fries smothered in melted cheese, ground beef, and jalapenos into my mouth, I grudgingly had to admit that they were tasty. Damnit. One point for the skeezy bar.

As Mr. Dickhead reached across the table and laid his hand on Kat's, my hand clenched the beer glass so tightly I thought it was going to break. She slowly pulled her hand away and laid it on her lap. It took every ounce of self-control I had not to march across the floor and knock the guy on his ass.

"Would you like anything else?" The waitress was back and once more blocking my line of sight.

"No, just the bill."

"Here ya go." She dropped the little white piece of paper, letting it flutter down to the sticky tabletop. It was probably cemented in place.

"Here, I'll pay now," I said, stopping her before she could disappear again. Reaching into my jacket, I took out the cash I had on me—there was enough for a generous tip—and held it out.

"Keep the change."

"Thanks." She stuffed it in her apron without looking at it and then promptly vanished.

My blood pressure skyrocketed as soon as I looked over to see what I'd missed. Kat was standing and not looking very happy as Sir Dicks-a-lot stood in her way. This guy was going to fucking die.

"Lay one finger. Go ahead and do it. See what happens," I growled under my breath.

Kat had it handled, though. After saying something to The Dick sharply, she marched around him and disappeared out the front door, phone in hand. This was my chance. Standing, I crossed the room and rounded the bar just as Dickwipe walked toward me. He was on his phone talking to someone.

"No dice. The girl is a cock tease. I didn't even get a feel. It's all good, though—I know where she works. I'll still get me some, just might not be the way she likes." Dickface laughed, and just as I suspected I would, I snapped.

There was no hesitation as my fist flew in his direction and connected with the side of his face. He rolled backward over a small table where two bikers were sitting. The guy's momentum knocked all the food onto the floor before the table overturned on top of him. He managed to kick one of the bikers in the gut as he fell, too. Multitasking. The two large men stood and looked at me, but I didn't care —I ignored them and rounded the table.

This was the side of me that I'd tried hard to push down over the years, and it was the reason I didn't like to fight. It was way too easy to go from zero to serial killer on the violence scale when someone I cared about was being threatened.

"What the *fuck* is your problem?" Dickhead said as he held his face and stared up at me.

"You stay the fuck away from her." I pointed at the piece of shit on the floor. "If I ever see you near her again, you'll be going home in a body bag."

The biker closest to me tried to grab my arm and told me to 'calm the fuck down,' but I was too enraged to think straight. I hated it when people thought they could grab at me. My knee connected with the biker's gut, closely followed by my right elbow to his face.

Instantly, the bar turned into full-blown chaos, like the fact I was fighting gave the entire place the excuse it needed to punch someone. Glasses shattered and food flew across the room. The standing speakers that had been playing some kind of rock music tipped over and fell with a crash to the floor.

Picking up a wooden chair, I brought it down on top of the motherfucker who had insulted Kat as he tried to crawl away. The chair cracked and broke into two pieces as it flattened the guy to the floor. Tossing the pieces aside, I went to reach for him, but movement out of the corner of my eye had me looking to my left just in time to receive a fist to the face.

Stumbling away from the blow, I wiped at the blood that started oozing from the corner of my mouth and dripping from my nose. My glare found the biker who'd hit me—he had at least fifty pounds on me. Didn't matter. I snarled like a rabid animal as I lunged for the guy and took him out around the middle like a linebacker. We crashed to the floor in a heap.

Kneeling on his chest with a hand around his throat, I drove my other fist into his face, rolling his eyes back in his head. I raised my arm to do it again when I was tackled from behind. My chin slammed into the floor with the impact.

"I don't know what your problem is, asshole, but it's a free fucking country, and if I want to fuck a pretty girl, I will," a voice said.

Dick-for-brains had tackled me. A fresh wave of rage filled me as I pushed myself up with his weight still on my back and yelled as a fist connected with my side. We probably looked like we were playing a fucked-up game of horsey, and at the moment, I was the pissed-off horse. I was gonna trample the fucker.

My muscles flexed as I flipped myself onto my back with Dickwad still attached to it like a fungus, slamming him into the ground.

"Uh," the asshole groaned as my weight pressed the air out of his lungs. In quick succession, I slammed my elbows back into his ribs, and he grunted in my ear with the impact.

The loud bang of a gun going off stilled everyone.

"Enough!" I looked up to see Karl and a half dozen other officers standing by the door. Karl's glare found me, and I could see the questioning look in his eyes as he shook his head back and forth in disappointment.

Great. Just fucking great.

It was like thinking it would happen had made it happen. The waste of space who had been sitting with Kat finally unlocked his arms from around my body, and I peeled myself off of the disgustingly dirty floor.

"You, with me," Karl said as he pointed at me and put his gun away.

"That asshole attacked me for no fucking reason," Dickhead had the nerve to say, and I almost jumped on him again. I would have if it weren't for Karl's hand on my shoulder.

"Don't," was all he said, but his grip was firm. I clenched my jaw and nodded.

"Arrest that fucker," Dickless yelled as he slowly stood. A black mark from where I'd punched him was already showing on his cheek, giving me a feeling of satisfaction.

"How about you shut the fuck up since it was you with your arm around his throat when I walked in?" Karl snarled, and my eyebrow raised at the threatening tone. "Go sit down. I'll speak to you when I'm done with him, got it?" he demanded. Dick-for-brains swore but did as he was asked.

"Outside, now," Karl said to me. I took a deep breath, knowing that I was going to get an earful, if not worse. I had just started a fucking bar brawl.

He ushered me over to a cruiser and away from the gatherings of people scattered around the parking lot.

"Mind telling me what the fuck happened in there?"

"Is this an official interrogation, or are you asking as a friend?"

Karl placed his hands on his hips, his eyes angrier than I'd ever seen them.

"How about we say I'm willing to give you the benefit of the doubt, but man, this is no longer high school. I can't go running home to my mom and ask her to pull some strings to get you out of jail anymore. Don't you fucking smirk at me. It's not funny."

I couldn't help it. I really couldn't. I burst out into laughter until my stomach hurt with it, and Karl was soon laughing along with me. It was like we'd traveled back in time, the image of Karl sitting outside the cell I was being held in flashing before my eyes. Sobering, I looked off into the dark.

"You going to arrest me?"

He took off his hat and smacked it against his leg.

"I don't want to, but you're going to need to tell me what the hell happened in there."

"Can you keep a secret?" I asked.

His eyes grew wide.

"I guess that depends on the secret. I mean, I am a cop now. If you tell me you're secretly a serial killer, I can't exactly let that slide."

I smirked and Karl sighed. "Let's put it this way. Are you about to tell me that 'you buried a body' type of secret, 'cause if so, I don't fucking want to know."

I shook my head, rolling my eyes as I leaned a hip against the cruiser.

"It's not an illegal secret. You remember that girl I used to talk about all the time? The one I wanted to find?"

"Yeah. What of it?"

"I found her. At least, I'm ninety-nine point nine percent sure I have. Anyway, that fuckwad in there was making her uncomfortable, and when she left, he proceeded to get on the phone and start bitching to someone that she was nothing but a cock tease. He acted like he was planning on taking what he wanted at some point, if you know what I mean. No, he didn't *say* the word 'rape, or assault,' but it was insinuated. I'm sure you can use your imagination. I just reacted."

"So you threw the first punch?" Karl asked, and that was definitely judgment in his voice.

I sighed and met his eyes with a wince.

"Do I have to answer that? It seems like an incriminating question."

"What the fuck, man? I see you today for the first time in years, and not only do I catch you speeding way over the limit, now this? You're putting me in a craptastic position. I should take your fucking ass in—would serve you right," Karl muttered as he rubbed at his eyes. "Fuck me. I'll see what I can do, but if I need to charge you, I will."

I held my arm out in the direction of the bar.

"Trust me. If you look into that piece of shit, you're going to find a list of women he's assaulted. He's the type that smiles all sweet until he doesn't get what he wants, which is a piece of ass."

"This isn't the movies, man. It's not that easy to prove unless he was officially charged," Karl said. "I said I will see what I can do, and I meant it, but I want you to know you're a fucking cocksucker. Now get out of here before you cause me any more issues, and for the love of fucking god, don't make me need to see you a third time tonight."

"Consider it karma for all the times I saved your ass."

Karl made a coughing sound that most certainly obscured an insult or two and walked away.

"Get out of here, jerk, and go straight home. If I see your face one more time, I'm going to throw you behind bars just 'cause it will make me feel all warm and fuzzy inside."

Smirking, I made my way to my bike and revved the girl to life. This was certainly not how I'd envisioned tonight going. I mentally groaned as I thought about Mr. Russo and the commercial and prayed I didn't have a black eye. At least there was Photoshop.

"Shit," I swore as I pictured the look on my mom's face when she heard that I was almost arrested. Again. It was a trend I'd broken—or at least thought I'd broken. I guess some habits were harder to kick.

BEST
FRIENDS

KAT

"I'M ASSUMING from the look on your face that things didn't go well," Olly said as I climbed into her car. She coughed and waved her hand at me, making a face. "You smell like an ashtray. No offense."

"As long as you consider him only wanting to hook up and fuck 'a good time,' then yeah, it was great. Other than that, it started off with rude service, and then halfway through the meal, he said, 'You're gonna pay for half of this, right?' and then ordered another beer. The entire time, he talked about himself. Not fun, interesting stories—it was all about how great he was at this and that and how much weight he pressed the last time he was at the gym."

I crossed my arms over my chest, pausing to watch as four police cars flew by going in the opposite direction. I looked over the back of the seat and watched their tail lights disappear, wondering if they were heading to the bar. It wouldn't surprise me.

"He sounds like a real charmer."

"Charmer my ass. Can you believe he had the balls to tell me that all the girls he's ever slept with called him the anaconda because he's so big, so I'd better get ready to worship his cock when I fucked him later?" I spat out.

Olly snickered quietly for a moment before bursting into laughter so strong she had to pull over because tears were pouring down her cheeks.

"Really? That's your response?" As furious as I was, the laughter was contagious, and I found myself laughing along as well. I sobered up quickly, though. Sighing, I stared out the window at the darkened trees and the faint lights of houses in the distance.

"I don't think I'm ready to date anyway, Olly. I mean, I didn't feel comfortable about it right from the first moment. He seemed so nice, but I'm obviously a terrible judge of character. I can't trust myself anymore."

Olly grabbed my hand and gave it a gentle squeeze.

"You'll get there, girl. I may have been a bit too eager to get you back in the saddle again. So, what are you going to do the next time you see him?" she asked.

I covered my face with my hands, wishing I could disappear into the darkness they created.

"I hadn't even thought about that yet," I mumbled as the car started to move again. While Olly turned her attention to driving, I let my mind wander, and of course, it wandered to Jake.

After about ten minutes of Xayne's self-righteous rant about himself, I'd found my mind drifting off and thinking about how I wished it were Jake who had come into my store and asked me out. I wished it were him with me at the table catching up while I quietly prayed that by the end of the night, he'd finally kiss me the way I'd dreamt about so many times. I'd almost convinced myself a time or two that it had actually happened because of those dreams.

Of course, because my imagination had issues, I'd thought I'd seen him again in the middle of one of Xayne's meandering stories, and of course, he'd disappeared again with a blink, nothing there but the back of waitresses and tables full of bikers. Even though I knew it was a fruitless effort, my eyes had scanned the bar, chasing the ghost in my mind. When I couldn't see him anywhere, my stomach had fallen with a disappointment that didn't even make sense. I knew my delusions. This time I could at least blame it on all the fancy motorcycles parked outside of the bar. I'd never be able to look at one again and not think of Jake.

My attention had been drawn back to Mr. Full-of-himself as he laughed obnoxiously at one of his own jokes. Around that time, I'd started trying to figure out in my head how long was too long to endure and how short a time would be considered rude before I made my escape. What a dumpster fire of a date. Time to change the topic.

"What about you?" I suddenly asked, looking over at Olly.

"You're going to need to be more specific." Olly smiled at me, and I realized I'd left her waiting on my plan for seeing Xayne again—which I didn't have.

"Have you contacted Jayce? Are you going on a date of your own?" I asked. Olly squirmed in her seat and then nibbled on her bottom lip. I sat up straight, scenting blood. Payback time.

"No, I haven't called him. I just don't think this is the right time for me to go out with anyone." She looked over at me, but with the darkness in the car, I couldn't make out the expression on her face. It was clear she was holding something back, though.

"Why?"

She sighed, sounding resigned.

"I may have agreed to have lunch with my ex." She spoke so fast that I barely made out what she said.

"Please tell me you're joking?" I turned in my seat to gawk at Olly, my mouth hanging open. "After everything she pulled and how much she hurt you, why would you even think about going down that path?"

"I don't know." Olly gripped the steering wheel hard enough for it to squeak in protest. "I realized when I was talking to her that I, for some stupid reason, still have feelings for her. But you're right. Just because she says she's changed doesn't mean she didn't treat me like shit and break my heart. I don't know. I was caught off guard and agreed."

"Give me your phone." I held out my hand, fully prepared to leave it there for as long as it took to get it.

"What? Why?" she asked.

"Because I'm canceling your lunch with her. Olly, if my ex, god forbid, came to town, would you let me go to lunch with him?"

We'd entered a better-lit area of town a block or two ago, so I could see the nervous, unsure look on her face.

"Well...."

"Be honest."

"No," she sighed before closing her eyes for a moment. I could see the anguish and frustration written all over her face. Snapping out of it, she gave the steering wheel a smack and then looked over at me.

"What if you came with me? She said she wanted to talk business over lunch and wanted to apologize for her actions. What if you came with me and kept me in line?"

"Olly, did you ask if she is still with that other girl?" I crossed my arms over my chest to try and keep myself wrangled and calm. I knew what it was like to feel that pull inside to run back—to give in to what the other person was saying. Giving in to the allure of thinking that they'd changed, that they're different, that they're sorry, that they wanted to be better, that they couldn't live without you...it was a toxic cycle that never ended well.

"She said that they broke up."

"Ah. I see. Did she happen to mention who broke up with who, and why?"

Olly was silent for a long time.

"She's using me, isn't she?" she muttered. I shrugged as we turned off of the main street, unable to prove anything but pretty darn sure of it.

"That would be my assumption. I mean, is it possible that she's changed and regrets how she treated you? Sure, of course it is, but that would mean an entire attitude and personality overhaul. I don't see that as very realistic," I said as kindly as I could.

"Shit and marmalade on toast," Olly said.

"What?" I laughed at the odd cuss.

"Just something my dad used to say. He had a ton of weird ones that I still like to use," she said as she pulled into my driveway. The road was unusually busy tonight—a number of vehicles passed by us before I even had time to take off my seatbelt.

Lately, I was hyper-aware of everything and everyone. I found myself counting things I'd never counted before and paying attention to every person in sight as I searched for Richard in every shadow.

"Okay. I'll come to lunch with you," I said, hoping this wasn't as bad an idea as it seemed. Just seeing her ex again could start a bad spiral, but if Olly was going to insist on going, then I'd go with her.

"You'd do that?"

"Of course I will. I can help you assess if she's being legit, and if she's not, we can say that we're dating and tell her to back off," I said, arching an eyebrow coyly. Olly laughed hard in response, delight clear on her face.

"I can picture that now. You're smokin' hot and she would be totally jealous." Her eyes filled with tears as she looked at me. "I really can't believe you'd do that for me. Thank you."

"My first choice would be you canceling and not going at all, but if this is something you really want to do, then you're not going without me." I grabbed Olly's hand. "You've been a real friend to me when I needed one the most. This is the least I can do to thank you."

Smiling gently, Olly wiped away a tear sliding down her cheek.

"I'm sorry that you had such a shit go of things with your ex, but I'm not sorry you moved here. Now get out of my car. You freaking reek of cigarettes and need a shower bad."

Laughing, I got out, waving goodbye to Olly as I made my way to the door. Olly waited until I was inside the open doorway before turning on the car to make the short journey to the house she shared with her mom. It may have been a wrecking ball kind of night, but at least I could say that I'd gotten out there and given it the old college try—I just wasn't sure I wanted to wander down that road again anytime soon.

A sudden, creeping feeling flowed over me. I paused on my way in and stared up and down the street while the hair stood up on the back of my neck. My eyes searched the darkness and the shadows created by the widely-spaced streetlamps without seeing anything, but I would bet money that I was being watched.

My heartbeat sped up to the point I could feel a panic attack starting to form. Instinctively, my hand clutched the small rainbow on the chain around my neck.

Deep breath in. Think about Jake's piercing green eyes. Slowly let the breath out. Picture him cupping your face and kissing you. The kiss would be slow and deep to start, and then he would turn things up as we got more comfortable together. Deep breath in. He would be here to protect you.

The little mantra helped my pulse slowly return to normal. Giving it another minute, I closed and locked the door when I still didn't see anything waiting to jump out at me from the dark.

I really wanted to hear from Eve that Richard had signed the papers, all was well between us, and he'd moved on. Leaning against the door, I let the trembling settle in the rest of my body before making my way to the bathroom. Who was I kidding? Even if she did call and say that, the likelihood that the fear would ever go away was slim to none.

JAKE

"What the hell am I doing?" I mumbled to myself as I snuck around the bushes of a house just down the street from the one Kat got dropped off at by her friend. The silver car didn't go far afterward—

in fact, it pulled in and parked next door. The friend got out and went inside, so the friend must also be the neighbor.

Kat stood in the doorway looking up and down the street for a moment, and even though the light from inside the house shadowed her face, my heart beat hard in my chest as her eyes unwittingly found mine, not that she knew it. As soon as she closed the door and the front of the house was plunged into darkness, I emerged from my hiding spot and made sure no one noticed me as I slipped from yard to yard.

It had been pure luck that I'd caught up to their car, and my stomach had flipped at the sight of the familiar tail lights. Once more, I'd found myself on a stalk-the-car mission, but this one had ended much more successfully as I'd been able to follow it to this quiet street just off the main road. A childhood spent watching spy movies had me passing the car as it pulled into the driveway so I could park the bike in a cul de sac just down the road and jog back to hide in some handy bushes.

The plan was to speak to her, to do what I'd been planning to do when I'd set out tonight, but then an unexpected feeling snuck up and bit me hard. It was fear. Fear and I were not well acquainted, never had been, but something about the thought of showing up looking like a stray alley cat that had just been in a fight froze me in place. That couldn't be my first impression, could it? It wasn't like I thought she'd mind, or did I?

Why was I so terrified to speak to her? It wasn't like I didn't want to—I'd been dreaming about it for years. The small voice in the back of my head screamed at me, shouting, 'But what if she hates you and never wants to see you again after this? You didn't speak to her years ago, and now here she is, quite possibly hiding from that life when you could have prevented it from happening if you'd only manned up and talked to her.'

Would she forgive me? Could she? I'd promised her that I'd find her, and when I finally did, I just walked away. In all the ways that mattered, I'd broken my promise.

Closing my eyes, I shook my head as the real and irrational fears converged in my system, almost drowning me. Pulling the hood of my hoodie up and staying low, I jogged behind the decorative bushes that created a low privacy barrier along the sidewalk.

"I'm losing my mind. That's the only explanation for this," I said, berating myself as I peeked through the bushes and looked around. Positive that no one was out lingering on the sidewalk or peeking through their curtains, I stepped through a gap in the small hedge and made my way toward Kat's house.

Heart hammering so loudly that it sounded like a drum in my ears, I silently opened the latch on the gate to the backyard. I kept my eyes peeled for cameras and motion detectors, but I really wasn't sure what to do about it if I found one. I may have landed small acting roles as a badass agent a time or two, but my sleuthing skills were not exactly featured at the top of my resume.

If you wanted someone to shoot a gun, chug a bottle of whiskey, or ride a bike into the sunset, then I was your man. Becoming as light on my feet as a ballerina in these combat boots, well, that was not happening. Subtlety was not my strong suit.

A single light was on in a window at the back of the small bungalow, and I crept toward it slowly. When I got close enough, I shifted from side to side, trying to see through the thick sheers behind the glass, but I was just a little too far away to make out anything.

Agitated, I stared at the freaking rose bush growing right in front of the window.

"It had to be roses," I muttered. I knew I was going to regret the decision later, but I pushed my way through the sharp thorns, which immediately dug into my legs through the jean material. It got me closer to the window, though.

"Shit," I hissed as a thorn jabbed my hands and scraped the front of my shirt. I stuck my finger in my mouth and sucked on the little droplet of blood forming. Now it was *really* going to look like I'd thrown down with a large cat.

Humming reached my ears, and then everything ceased to exist but Kat. She walked into what I realized was her bedroom with a towel wrapped around her body. Another one held her hair up on top of her head in that twist that all women seemed to do. Except for my eyes tracking her every movement, I was frozen in place. I didn't dare to move—I didn't even breathe for fear she would disappear before my eyes.

Kat lifted her leg up onto the bed to rub some lotion on it, and I couldn't stop the smirk that crossed my lips as the towel slipped up her leg. I wanted to be that lotion. Within seconds, my cock was hard and begging to be released. Unable to stand it any longer, I released the air I'd been holding in my lungs in a shaky, ragged breath. Goddamn, Kat.

The towel on her head slipped to the side and she grabbed for it, pulling it off and laying it on the bed. Her dark hair was long and wavy, the damp strands hanging around her face like a curtain only accentuating her beautiful features. As she switched legs to perform the same ritual on the other one, my body began to shake and I broke out in a sweat. It didn't matter that it was only sixty-six degrees outside—I felt like I was in the middle of the desert on a record-high day.

My dick kicked in my jeans, making me let out an involuntary groan. An unfortunately loud involuntary groan. I froze as she stood up straight and looked at the window. The pulse pounded harder in my veins as I saw her face clearly. I took a deep breath, my nose filling with the scent of roses—I knew that the scent would remind me of her from now on. She'd been like a mirage in my mind for so long—something I'd been grasping for that was always just out of reach. To have her so close and still not be able to touch her was torture.

"Oh crap," I whispered, stumbling backward to get out of the bush as she began walking in my direction. The thorns cut deeply, and I held back the swear words I wanted to shout as I made it out just as her hand reached for the curtain. I turned and ran for the darkness of the backyard.

In a fluid motion that James Bond himself would've been impressed with, I dove over the fence and rolled to a stop on the other side. I ended up on my back and just took a moment to smile widely up at the stars. Why I hadn't just gone for the gate, I have no freaking idea, but I felt like a total badass. Panting hard, I slowly flipped myself over to get back up, but the sound of a chain rattling had me looking around the dark yard like a character in a horror movie.

A deep growl came from one corner of the yard just as my eyes fixed on a dog house and the large shadow that had stepped out from inside it. Swallowing hard, I stared nervously at the dog, which looked more like something that had clawed its way straight out of Hell than any breed from a store that I'd ever seen.

"Nice puppy," I whispered. White teeth flashed as it growled louder and darted toward me. "Oh fuck me!"

Bolting to my feet, I ran like my ass was on fire. The dog snarled and barked loudly as it chased me across the yard, its teeth grazing my leg as I once more did a Superman dive over a fence to escape the yard.

I landed hard and awkwardly, skidding along the unforgiving sidewalk with a force that pushed a loud grunt out of me. I half expected the beast to come sailing over the fence after me, but the chain must be good for something after all, as Cujo just rattled the wooden boards, barking so loudly it was definitely going to draw attention.

"This is not my night," I mumbled before I started the painful process of pulling myself up off the ground. "You sure have a funny sense of humor," I said to the sky and the world at large as I limped down the sidewalk, trying hard to look as normal as I could.

Over the years, I'd had a lot of embarrassing nights where I'd questioned my sanity, but this one was taking the cake and running away with it. If Karl saw me again tonight, especially looking like this, he was going to throw me in a cell and maybe even swallow the key.

"Fuck," I growled as I reached my motorcycle. Catching sight of my face in the side view mirror, I shook my head in despair at the fresh sidewalk rash. Even through the dark shadows cast by my hood, I could clearly see the cuts and bruises lining the other side of my face. My hands and legs were not fairing any better—gashes split my knuckles in several places, and the tears in my jeans were damp with blood. Thank god for the leather jacket I was wearing. I had a horrible realization of how much worse it could've been and what the make-up artists were going to say.

"Shit. Miles is going to kill me."

BEST
FRIENDS

22

KAT

MY HANDS SHOOK as I whipped back the white sheers to peer into the backyard, and a moment later, I let out a yelp. Someone was out there, I think. What I saw was just a flash, but now I could only see my own reflection. My gut told me someone had been standing there a moment ago. Someone had been watching me, but I couldn't be sure. I hated this, all I could think was that Richard had found me and was finding new ways to torture me.

Was this just my imagination and my fear getting the better of me?

"Shit, shit, shit." I grabbed an armful of clothes out of the dresser and ran for the kitchen. In a frantic dance, I dropped the towel and pulled on the clothes as I stayed as close to the large butcher block of knives as possible.

"Dammit. My phone." Looking around, I realized it must be back in the bedroom because it sure as heck wasn't anywhere convenient like the kitchen counter or the coffee table. I hadn't heard any glass shatter, so the window was probably still secure, but I pulled the longest knife out of the block just in case before slowly venturing toward the bedroom.

I could hear the dog next door barking loudly, which didn't calm my nerves. All of my limbs were trembling as I passed the back door —I stared at the handle like it was going to suddenly turn, opening the door to reveal Richard standing there like some monster. He *was* a monster, just the kind that walked around in a tailored suit with no one the wiser. The most dangerous kind.

Swallowing hard, I darted into the bedroom and grabbed my phone off the nightstand, cursing as I jerked the charger out of the wall in my haste. It almost made me drop the phone and ended up fumbling it like a bad juggler.

"Calm yourself, Kat. It's nothing. If it were Richard, he wouldn't hesitate to barge into the place. It was probably some kids goofing around," I mumbled to myself as my heart continued to flutter wildly in my chest. "Come on, you're just being stupid," I said, trying to sound as decisive as I could, but I still unlocked the phone and hit Olly's number. So much for self-therapy and self-soothing.

"Hey girl, what's wrong?" Olly asked, voice groggy like she'd already been in bed.

"I'm really sorry, but can you come over and stay the night? I know I'm being stupid, but I could've sworn someone was in the backyard just now, and I'm kinda freaking out, and—."

"Whoa, girl, stop right there. I'm on my way." There was a rustling sound and then the slam of a door closing. A minute later, there was a knock on my door. Not trusting myself to run with a knife in my hand, I tossed it onto the counter before bolting for the door. I fumbled with the lock with shaking fingers until it opened to let Olly inside.

As soon as she stepped inside, I pulled her into a hard hug, relieved beyond words that she was there. Olly patted my back, and it felt so comforting.

"Wow, Lexi, you're really shaking. Okay, tell me exactly what happened," she said as I stepped back and wrapped my arms around my body.

"I got out of the shower and went into my room, and I just, I could've sworn I saw a large shadow in the window, and I started feeling all creeped out." I was shaking so uncontrollably now that my voice was wavering with it. "I grabbed the sheers and opened them wide open to look, and no one was there, but...Olly, I promise I'm not going crazy, but I think someone was out there."

"Hey, it's okay." She pulled me into another hug, and I wanted nothing more than to keep clinging to her as the panic clawed at my throat.

"Wait here. I'm going to go check it out." She tried to pull away, but I latched on to her arms.

"No. You can't go out there," I said, not getting why she would even suggest that. Going to investigate scary shit is how people died.

Olly grabbed my arms right back and stared into my eyes.

"Breathe with me, Lexi. Deep breath in...deep breath out." I did as she asked a few more times and then closed my eyes, forcing myself to regain control. This feeling was too much like what life with Richard had been like. It was why I'd run, and why I was far, far away from him now.

I'd secretly and legally changed my name. I hadn't used any of my old I.D. or credit cards. I hadn't left a trail. I had to remember that.

"Good, there you go. Now, I'm going to go check, or else neither one of us is going to get any sleep," Olly said, giving me a smile. I stood near the doorway and watched as she walked outside and wandered around the side of the house. This was how horror movies started, except in this case, my life was the horror movie, and I was already well into it.

"Oh shit," Olly shouted, and I lurched towards the door, already about ready to faint. "Sorry, I'm okay. Just caught my flip flop on a crack and stubbed my toe," she called out a second later, and I sagged against the doorframe in relief. There were no more frantic screams, and by the time Olly came back around the corner a few minutes later, my nerves had finally begun to settle. She shook her head as she got close.

"I don't see anything, but it's dark. I'll look again in the morning."

I felt ridiculous about hauling Olly out of bed for nothing. Rubbing my eyes, I stepped inside so Olly could follow me into the house and close the door.

"I'm so sorry. I could've sworn...the dog from the house behind me was barking like crazy and...." I stopped, shaking my head. I could feel the prickle of tears forming, but I wasn't going to cry. Richard had gotten too many of my tears already, and he didn't deserve any more.

"I'll stay on the couch. You're going to be fine, Lexi," Olly said, wrapping her arm around my shoulders to give them a squeeze. Pulling the sweater I'd put on tighter around myself, I nodded.

"Thank you. I promise I won't bother you again like this."

"Don't be ridiculous. I'd be pissed off if you didn't. Now go to bed—we have a long day ahead of us tomorrow."

I quickly helped make up the couch, grateful again that so much had been left behind by the previous tenant, and then made my way down the short hall to my room and mostly closed the door, leaving it open just a sliver. Just in case.

Unable to help myself, I made my way over to the window and moved the sheers out of the way to stare at the rose bush and the dark, quiet backyard. Not even the neighbor's dog was barking now. Letting the material fall into place, I flicked off the light and got into bed, but all I could do after settling down was stare at the ceiling. *That* brought back some memories.

I swore in my head as I lost count of the dots in the ceiling tile of my hospital room. No matter how many times I tried to get them all counted, I either lost count or someone would interrupt me, and then I'd have to start all over again. Not that I had anything better to do, but it really would be nice to get them all counted at least once. It had become a personal challenge.

The doctor had just left after telling me that I was going to go home with Richard tomorrow—all the necessary preparations had been made for me to continue my recovery at home. He'd smiled at me like that was the best news he could ever say and then proceeded to practically gush about what a great guy Richard was and how lucky I was to have him as my support system. That single sentence had squashed all lingering thoughts I'd had about trying to ask for his help.

For most patients, it probably was great to be sent home to their loved ones, where they'd be able to sleep soundly in their own beds. I imagined that many would even call it a blessing, but for me, it felt like a jail sentence. When I crashed and ended up in here, I'd been running from the home they were sending me back to so cheerfully. I'd already felt helpless before, like a trapped animal about to be tortured, but now....

A hot tear slid down my cheek, and anger rolled through my system when I couldn't move my arm to wipe it away. The progress I'd made over the last month was undoubtable. I mean, I could wiggle my toes and fingers. I could even clench my hand and feel when I needed to pee—but what good did that do me when I couldn't get up to relieve myself? Not much.

I turned my head as much as I was able to, breaking out in a sweat with even that little bit of effort. At least it let me look out the window at the large tree, which always had a bird of some sort sitting on the nearby branches. I'd walk again—I was determined to walk again—but to do that, I needed to come up with a plan. To successfully get away from Richard, he couldn't see me as a flight risk.

Richard had always been controlling, but the weeks leading up to my mad escape attempt had been horrible. I'd walked on eggshells every second he was home and was scared to leave the house when he wasn't there in case he arrived back home while I was gone. I'd made that mistake once, and that was the first and last time I ever wanted to feel the crack of his hand. Squeezing my hand into a fist, I took a deep breath. Staying calm was supposed to help my recovery.

"Oh, that is great news, Montgomery," Richard said, his voice floating into the room from somewhere down the hall.

Of course Richard had made friends with my doctor. Yesterday, they'd stood at the end of my bed and talked about what a great golf game they'd had, and I'd wanted to vomit. Richard fawned all over me in a big perfor-

mance, lying about how much fun we had going to the course together. In truth, I'd wanted to learn how to play, but I wasn't allowed to go. Richard had said it was the guys' time to unwind and I'd just humiliate him at his fancy club. I shouldn't have been surprised or angry, but I was.

Rage had burned in my chest over the fact he had once more found a way to not only keep me under his power, but also make it look like he was a doting husband trying to help his flighty wife while doing it. Words like 'unstable' and 'emotional' were tossed around between Richard and his doctor friend like they were in a tennis match as they spoke in front of me as if I couldn't hear them.

After the doctor had left, Richard had leaned in close to my ear.

"Be a good girl or I'll have to say this isn't the first time you've tried to kill yourself. I'll have the good doctor recommend that you're locked up for your own safety." After kissing my forehead, he left, and I knew that I could never let him know about my true level of progress—and that meant hiding it from the nurses, doctors, and anyone else who could be manipulated by Richard and his shitty charm. This was one battle I was going to have to do on my own.

"Yes, I'm extremely confident that with the right physical therapy, she will regain full mobility," 'Montgomery' replied in the hallway. It sounded like they were getting closer. "The last surgery repaired the remaining damage and now she needs to heal."

As quickly as I was able, I relaxed my hand and turned my head to look back up at the ceiling. There was no point in pretending I was asleep because the stupid little monitor that read my heartbeat gave me away every time. It spiked as soon as Richard was near, and I could see the glee in his eyes that my reaction to his presence was terror—and that I couldn't get away.

It was a dream come true for him and my worst fucking nightmare.

Both men laughed over something that I couldn't hear, but it probably had to do with them fucking some unsuspecting and impressionable girl together. The fact that I couldn't talk or move had made Richard bold, far bolder than I ever thought he would become. He'd gone so far as to fuck one of the nurses in my fucking hospital bathroom. If looks could kill, they both would've been dead as soon as they stepped out of the small space. Alas I didn't have such powers, but I sure wished that I did.

She'd at least had the decency to look ashamed as my eyes followed them, but not Richard. Nope. He welcomed my anger like it was a badge of pride. It was something else to use to push me down and make me feel worse about myself— just another way to show me that he and he alone held all the power.

I looked at the men as they came over to the bed, Richard doing his fake smile. The one that used to make me think I was special. The one that made me feel loved and safe. The one I'd since learned was nothing more than a mask to hide the true intentions of the monster that lived underneath.

"Hi there, Buttercup. It's so good to hear that you're going to come home tomorrow. I'm making special preparations to have around-the-clock nurses with you, and a physiotherapist is going to come in every day. Nothing but the best for you." He brushed the bangs, which had gotten long, away from my face and kissed my cheek.

What the hell was up with the terrible nickname? He'd never called me 'buttercup' once in the last seven years. And I would bet everything I had, which admittedly wasn't much, that the nurses would all be young, pretty, and easily fuckable with a little of his persuasion and his ability to open doors for them in the medical field.

Great. Just what I'd always wanted—to be able to hear him having sex every chance he got all over the house and not be able to move. At least before the accident, he'd kept it in the office or just not come home.

"There are a few more things I'd like to go over for Kate's recovery," the doctor said, but I'd already tuned them out. What he said didn't matter. I knew what I needed to do.

How had this become my life? I had no real answer to that, but I had to do whatever I could to either get away from it or die trying.

BEST
FRIENDS

# 23

KAT

"THANK YOU, AND HAVE A GREAT DAY." I waved my last customer off from the front door of the bakery before reaching over to flick off the 'open' sign. I'd never felt so bone tired yet invigorated in all my life. Running my own business was certainly not what I'd expected it to be in so many ways, but it was also so much more than I'd thought it would be.

I only got about three feet away from the door before a knock had me turning around to see the other delivery guy, not Xayne, standing outside the door with the delivery cart. That was awesome, as I still didn't know what to do about Xayne, but I was unsure why I was getting a delivery again so soon.

Unlocking the door, I pushed it open and gestured for the man to enter. Without a word, he pushed the cart inside, which was weird, as I remembered him being a lot friendlier the other times we'd met. If nothing else, he hadn't looked like he wished he were anywhere else.

"Hi. I didn't expect to see you so soon this week," I said.

"Where do you want this?" he asked, voice gruff. He wouldn't look me in the eyes.

"Oh, just right this way. Sorry, but I didn't catch your name." I tried to keep my tone light and pleasant, but the look on his face said he had no interest in idle chit-chat.

"Name's Brad. Is here fine?" he asked, stopping just inside the kitchen.

"Yes, that's great. Thank you." The following silence as he unloaded the delivery was incredibly awkward. Unable to help myself, I decided to ask about what had happened to Xayne. This whole encounter was going very strangely, and I had to know why.

"Is Xayne no longer doing the route?"

Brad made a disgusted sound in response, and I almost expected him to spit on the floor.

"This will be the last delivery you get from my company. I only brought it because you pre-paid. Find a new company to deal with." He marched to the door, leaving me with my mouth hanging open.

"Wait! What did I do to upset you?" I asked, following Brad out to the store area.

"Ask your boyfriend. I don't know why you'd agree to go on a date if you already had a guy, but whatever. That's for your morals to deal with," Brad fumed, looking me up and down with a conde-scending glare.

"Whoa, wait, what?" I asked. I couldn't have heard right.

"That asshole man of yours messed up Xayne real good, and now he's refusing to do your store anymore, which means I have to do this whole section of the route on my own. I'm too old to be doing this on my own, thank you very much, so I hope you're happy." Brad pushed open the door and left—the silence after the little bell above the door stopped jingling was deafening. I stared after him, unable to force down the bubble of panic that was rising up in my throat and making me want to throw up.

It had to be Richard. That was the only logical explanation, but the fact Richard wouldn't have called me his girlfriend gave me pause and the one thread of hope I could desperately clutch. He was always adamant about calling me his 'wife' or his 'sweet little wife' or something else that claimed me when we were around others. In private, he'd called me his possession. 'Girlfriend' was not a term he'd use— he'd see that as a step back.

I locked the door before backing up until I found a seat to park myself in before my legs gave out. Dropping my head between my knees, I practiced the breathing technique my psychologist had told me to do whenever an attack hit.

It couldn't be him, could it? I could've sworn someone was staring in my window last night, and though it had seemed to be nothing, maybe it really was something. Maybe that something was Richard.

Another knock on the glass had me jerking upright in the chair and grabbing for my chest to try to hold back my galloping heart. Olly stood on the other side of the door, her expression concerned as she pointed to the lock. Jumping up, I flipped it open. She immediately pushed through the door.

"What is it? What's wrong? Do you feel sick?" Olly asked, reaching for my forehead like a mom, which made me smile weakly.

"No, I'm not sick. It's...it's probably nothing, just a strange coincidence, but I'm kinda having a panic attack over it." I sat back down and sighed as I rubbed my hand over my face. This whole thing was going to give me gray hairs early.

"Tell me what happened." Olly sat across from me with her hands folded on the table, and she looked so professional like that, so formidable. Her face was serious, mouth slightly pursed as if she were ready to rip someone's head off, if not physically, then at least verbally.

"I need to find a new supplier. Xayne's saying that some guy beat him up, and that the guy who did it was my boyfriend. Now Brad, the owner, doesn't want to have to deliver to me, so he's cutting me off," I moaned. Looking at Olly and feeling very small, I revealed my true worry. "What if the 'boyfriend' was my ex?"

Olly's mouth relaxed as she listened, and by the end, she was full-on laughing. I had no idea what I'd said that was so funny, as I was kind of baring my soul over here, and just waited until she was done with her outburst to say anything more.

"Did I say something funny?" I asked, more than a little peeved, when she finally stopped.

"Sweetie, the look on your face is priceless. Listen. Brad and his jerk behavior aside, Xayne probably ended up getting drunk and in a fight and is simply using you and the bad date as his scapegoat. The guy was a total jerk to you, and he knew you wouldn't have anything nice to say about him in front of his boss. He might even have wanted to make sure he never had to deliver to you again after how rude he was."

Olly took a deep breath and signaled for me to do the same. I did as she asked and felt my pulse start to slow.

"Let's look at this logically. It seems very unlikely that your ex wouldn't have tried to drag you out of the bar in the middle of the date instead of hanging around after to beat up some rando guy. Besides, didn't you tell me he is all about image? That he cultivates his 'perfect doctor' persona? Just the idea of him bloodying his knuckles in public seems unlikely." She sat back in the chair, crossing her arms over her chest.

"You do have a point there."

Olly snorted before smiling widely.

"Of course I do. Xayne is not exactly guy-of-the-year material. Do you really think it would be below him to lie?"

Although I knew Olly was right about everything, I just couldn't shake the feeling that there was more going on. Maybe Richard wasn't behind any of it, but Olly's analysis still didn't explain the creepy feeling I'd had on a few different occasions that someone was watching me. It also didn't explain seeing someone in the backyard last night, although in all fairness, I couldn't be certain someone had actually been there, either.

Rubbing my face, I sat back in the chair and stared at the vibrant picture of cupcakes that I'd purchased to decorate the store. The rich-looking little cakes topped with their decorative icing and whimsical trimmings made me smile. It was like looking at a rainbow of sugary sweetness. It made me feel strangely better.

"You're right. I'm probably being ridiculous."

"No, you're not ridiculous. Stop putting yourself down, girl. Look. The thing is, you ran to have freedom, but it seems like every time you start to feel a semblance of calm, you allow the memories to lock you back up. You need to find a way to stay vigilant without being wary of every single thing that happens."

That...actually made a lot of sense. I nodded at Olly, encouraging her to continue.

"You're giving him too much credit when you do that, and you shouldn't give him that power." Olly stood and came around the table to squeeze my shoulder. "I'm about to close up, so do what you need to here and then I'll take you home. You can have a glass of wine, a bubble bath, and relax. Tomorrow we'll worry about looking for another supplier."

"Thanks, Olly."

She was right. I needed to stop letting Richard control me. I'd spent years living with his abuse as I rehabbed my body on my own. I'd focused on leaving and didn't let anything stop me. Now was not the time to become weak, and if Richard *did* show up here, I'd fight him all over again until my last dying breath. Standing, I headed to the back to finish cleaning up.

JAKE

"Man, you look like a pile of dog crap that got stepped on by a boot, scraped off with a stick, and then run over by a tractor," Tripp said as he wandered over to the tent that had been set up for filming. "When Jayce said you went a round or two last night, I thought he was kidding."

I pulled my sunglasses off and stared at my dear brother, way too tempted to punch him in the face simply because it would make me feel better. After an hour with the makeup artists, I looked amazing and knew it.

"No, he wasn't joking. How are the girls settling back in?" I asked, quickly changing the topic before it could turn into a Jake-bashing session. Tripp was very good at working those in.

"They're great. It's like a dream having them home." He looked over to where the girls were fawning all over the tent that held the makeup artists. Syd giggled as one of the artists drew something on her cheek. I followed Tripp's line of sight to where Lanny sat—she was smiling and laughing as she got her makeup done.

"I didn't need you stepping in and fixing everything with all your fancy money, you know? I had it handled."

I pinched the bridge of my nose so I didn't reach out and crack him in the face for real. I just thought about it really hard and hoped he could feel it.

"A simple 'thank you' would suffice." Crossing my arms, I stared out at where the last of the filming was being done for today.

Uh oh.

I internally groaned as I saw Miles marching my way. I was in for it now.

"What the *hell* did you do to your face?" I opened my mouth to answer but then snapped it shut again as Miles continued without stopping for a breath. "I can't *believe* this. The whole shoot may have to be rescheduled because you got in a freaking fistfight with a local." He wagged his finger in my face angrily for emphasis as he spoke. His face was so flushed it looked like he was about to have a heart attack.

"Miles, relax. I kept an ice pack on my face all night so there was minimal swelling, luckily, and the makeup artists did their thing and made me look as good as new." I pointed at my face to demonstrate. "Seriously, relax. You're going to give yourself an ulcer."

"Too fucking late for that," Miles said. A bottle of pink liquid appeared in his hand from nowhere like magic, and he proceeded to chug it down like he was downing a beer. I cringed. Even Tripp made a gagging noise, and he would eat anything.

"Okay, I've got this." Miles shot daggers at me with his eyes. "Can we just get through with filming without any more issues? Please? Pretty fucking please?"

His piece said, Miles marched away. I shook my head as Tripp piped up.

"Jesus. I thought I was wound tight, but he's definitely next level."

"You have no idea," I muttered.

I really wanted to get back to the new life I was trying to forge—and also go back to Kat's house. Should I just show up? Should I make a grand gesture? Should I show up at her work instead so it wouldn't be so private? The questions and wondering wouldn't leave me alone.

I hadn't gotten a single second of sleep after seeing her in nothing but a towel. Even now, my mind wanted to drift off into la-la-land thinking about what her skin would taste like with water droplets from her shower still damp on her skin. I sucked in a deep breath and tried for some semblance of focus.

Tripp turned and settled into the same relaxed pose I was in.

"I don't ask for help. You know that," he said. I blinked, totally confused by the conversation switch.

"What?"

"Before Miles walked up, I said that you didn't need to use your money to help me. I don't ask for help."

My brain caught up with Tripp and his train of thought.

"Oh, I know," I said, glaring. "Before you ask, I don't want anything in return. The girls deserve stability, and Lanny wants something different right now." I looked at the side of Tripp's face. Even though we weren't blood-related, as teens, we'd been mistaken for full-blooded brothers all the time.

Maybe it was our similarly-shaped jaws and black hair, or maybe it was because we'd had the same bad attitude and had stuck up for one another at any cost. Whatever it was, I'd felt like Tripp was my blood long before I bonded with Jayce, or even with Mom and Dad.

"We know better than anyone what having a stable home can do to shape your life. I still cringe to think how our lives would've turned out without Mom and Dad."

"I know, but I still *had* it, I...fuck. Thank you. That's what I'm failing at trying to say," Tripp said.

"That was the most painful 'thank you' I've ever heard. I don't even know if I can call it that in good faith." I smirked as Tripp glared at me.

"You're still a fucknut, but...I love you." Before I could respond, Tripp pushed away and walked toward the house. Over near the cameras, Mr. Russo held up his hand to wave me over. Showtime.

It was dark by the time I made my way to Kat's. I'd tried to do a little sleuthing, but anything social media-related that she had was either gone or hadn't been active in months. Parking my bike down the street to give myself a few moments to compose myself, I stared at the small house and its weather-beaten door as my heart hammered hard in my chest.

"This is not difficult, man. Get off the bike and go talk to her," I said, giving myself a much needed pep talk. Pushing down all of my fears that this was going to go terribly wrong somehow, I made my way up the sidewalk and to the door. I held my knuckles up to knock but then froze in place on the welcome mat.

Was I really going to do this? I hadn't even gotten her flowers or chocolates or...the decision was made for me when the door swung open in front of me, and there she was. Kat was talking on the phone, looking down, but as soon as she caught sight of my boots, she jerked her head up, screamed, and slammed the door in my face.

"Well, that couldn't have gone any better," I mumbled as I rubbed the back of my neck.

The curtain hanging over the glass panel beside the door moved to the side, and I lifted my hand in a wave as she peered out at me.

Hi, I mouthed. There was a soft click before the door reopened with horror movie slowness.

"J...J...Jake?" Kat's eyes were as wide as saucers as her shaking hand reached out the door and poked me in the chest. Huh.

I couldn't help but smirk and then smile. I knew exactly how she felt. How many times had I thought I'd seen Kat somewhere only to be mistaken?

"Hey, Kit Kat," I said softly. "I've missed you."

"Oh my god. It really is you." Her face flushed a beautiful shade of pink, and I couldn't help staring at her. She was so beautiful. She was a graceful butterfly that was unique and spectacular. "You can't come in. I—I need to clean up."

"No, it's...." The door slammed in my face again. "Okay."

Well, this was not how I'd foreseen the reunion going. Turning around, I parked myself on the lone step. At least she hadn't told me to get the fuck away from her, so I was one step in the right direction. I wiped my hands on my jeans to remove the bit of dampness on them and to help with the building nervousness.

I could hear her thumping around inside the small house and smirked as the thudding of her feet closed in on the door again.

"Okay, you can come in now," she said as soon as the door was open. Her voice sounded shy and she was still blushing, which had me feeling hot all over. Dear god, it was not fair. She was even more beautiful than the last time I'd seen her, and it was all I could do to keep my heart from beating out of control in my chest.

"I still can't believe it's you, like actually *you*," she said as I slowly stood to face her. She was fidgeting with the bottom of her sweater, and my lips curled up at seeing the old habit.

She'd let her hair down to fall in long waves around her face and changed from the simple hoodie she'd been wearing to a pretty dark blue sweater that matched her eyes.

"Are you sure you don't want to slam the door in my face again? I've never had it happen three times in one night—you would beat the current record."

"Oh, shut it and get in here," she said, rolling her eyes. As I stepped inside, she looked down at her sock-covered feet, and I had to resist the urge to grab her and push her up against the wall.

"Did you want coffee, or tea, or something cold, maybe water, or I have some brownies and—," she rambled as she went to walk past me, but I quickly grabbed her wrist, bringing her to a halt. She sucked in a sharp breath like she was afraid I might hurt her, and I instantly wanted to kill whoever had made her feel so fearful.

I could feel her pulse pounding hard under my fingertips. She seemed as nervous as I was, and there was a strange comfort in that. As her big blue eyes slowly lifted to mine, I stepped forward and wrapped her up in a hug. She felt as delicate as the butterfly I'd pictured her as. At first, she remained stiff, but as I continued to just hold her and bury my nose in the soft waves of her hair, she sighed and melted into my body.

Ironically, she smelled like roses—like roses and rich cherries. The scent was sweet and completely intoxicating. Her arms slipped inside my open jacket to wrap around my waist and hold me tight. My world became nothing but her.

The feel of her pressed up against me, the way she held me tight, the scent of her in my nose, and even the little sigh she made —it all felt like coming home. I lapped it up and soaked in every ounce of her. My earlier nervousness had completely washed away. I was once more holding my Kat.

Nothing I'd seen or done in all the time I'd spent on the road could compare to this moment right now.

"God, I've missed you so much, Kat. I didn't know if it was you for sure at first, what with you using the name Lexi and all."

"That's a long story. Is this really happening?" Her voice was soft and muffled from where she had her face buried in my leather jacket. It was almost like she was a real cat tucking herself into my warmth. I never wanted to let her go.

"Doesn't feel real to me either. I've dreamed about this moment so many times," I whispered into her ear, smirking as her body shivered against mine and her hands balled my shirt up in her fists.

"I don't want to let go. I don't want you to disappear again. I'm afraid that if I let go, you're going to vanish like every other time I thought I'd seen you," she said. Her voice sounded like she was on the verge of tears. She turned her face up to mine, and even though I knew I shouldn't, I couldn't stop myself as I dropped my lips to hers.

I'd waited seventeen years to taste her properly—I wasn't waiting another second. I'd known she was mine from the moment we met, and I knew now that she'd be the only woman for me.

She froze and sucked in a sharp breath, and I held still to see what she'd do. We stood there, lips touching—hers were so, so soft. When she didn't pull away or smack me, I deepened the kiss, my tongue running along her lips to ask for access. She moaned and opened her mouth for me, and the logical part of my brain shut down.

All I'd planned on doing was talking to her, getting reacquainted with her, and finding out why she was here in this small town and not in Nevada. But not anymore. That all got tossed in a box and thrown out, and the door definitely slammed behind it.

Every bottled emotion, every desire I'd buried by drinking, partying, and sleeping around, reared up and took control. She was what I'd been endlessly searching for but could never find. Is it possible for someone to own your soul? If so, Kat had always owned mine.

As the kiss deepened and her hands gripped my waist, I knew that I had to have Kat. There was no other option. From this moment on, I would do whatever it took to make her officially mine.

"I'm trying really hard to be good," I mumbled against her lips.

Her hands traveled up my body, lighting a fire everywhere she touched until she wrapped her hands behind my neck. With a gentle tug on my hair, she brought my lips back to hers, and my control slipped a little more. My body shook with a desire that I couldn't fully explain—I just needed to have her.

She moaned as I pulled her closer, our tongues moving in sync, and it was the sweetest sound I'd ever heard. Kat ran her fingers through my hair and gave it a tug again, driving me wild and pushing me closer to the ledge. Unless she shoved me away, I was making love to her tonight. I was going to lay her out and savor every last inch of her body like she was a decadent dessert to show her how I felt and convey all the emotions inside me that I couldn't even name.

I could feel every part of her rubbing against me as she softly squirmed in my hold, and my cock was enjoying the feel of her pushing up against it way too much to not worry about a little premature relief happening if it continued. Breaking the kiss on a gasp, I laid my forehead against hers.

"Tell me to stop or I'm not going to. For me, it was always meant to be us, and I've waited for this moment for too long. I'm barely holding my shit together, Kat."

I loved that she looked like she was dreaming, like she was caught up in some amazing fantasy. Her eyes were closed and her slightly swollen lips parted, and the flush on her skin painted her a dusky rose.

"Please, Kat. Tell me what I need to hear so I can stop this if you don't feel the same," I said—even to me, my voice sounded pained. The heart beating away in my chest physically hurt as I waited for her to answer. She'd been all I'd ever wanted, all I dreamed about, all I fantasized about for so long, and now that she was finally here in my arms, all of those hopes and dreams were converging.

With a shuddering breath, she opened those stunning eyes to stare into mine.

"You want *me*?" she asked, her tone laced with confusion like she couldn't understand why I would.

"Yes. More than anything. I've always wanted you." I lifted my forehead from hers and smoothed the long strands of hair away from her face. "God, you're so beautiful. You're more stunning now than I could ever have imagined, and I've never wanted anything more than I want you right now."

She licked her lips as her eyes searched my face. Her fingers were still driving me crazy from where they swirled little designs on the back of my neck.

"We probably should stop," she said. My heart plummeted, but I closed my eyes, prepared to back away and push the beast raging inside of me down. A gentle touch on my cheek made me open them again. Her eyes were pools of need that I knew mirrored my own.

"But it's always been us for me, too. I've never stopped wanting you or thinking about you, and it might be wrong, but I don't want you to stop. Even if this is a fantasy for one night only, I want it. I want you."

The corners of my mouth lifted in relief.

"It's going to be more than one night, Angel, if you let me. I plan on making you mine."

"Yours?" Her lips curved up in a sexy smile. "I love the sound of that," she whispered, cheeks flaming red.

Oh fuck, was she in trouble now.

BEST
FRIENDS

KAT

I HAD no idea if I was dreaming or not. I'd lost count of how many times I'd prayed for Jake to randomly show up at my door, and the last place on earth I'd expected that to happen was here, where I was doing my best to hide from the world.

I should've been terrified that Jake had found me because it meant that Richard could as well, but while Jake was near me, while he was kissing me and holding me in his arms, nothing else was real to me but him. I knew I'd missed him, knew I loved him, but it was almost incomprehensible how desperate and out of control I felt, how much I craved more as his lips moved against mine. The fact he said he felt the same way was like a drug straight into my veins.

A part of my brain was screaming that I didn't know him anymore. He'd turned into someone who I barely recognized and who I really couldn't trust. The thing was, the moment I saw those green eyes again was the first time since we were separated that the world felt right. It was like I'd been stuck on a bad rollercoaster for years and was finally able to get off.

Maybe he was lying. Maybe he'd fuck me and then walk out the door and I'd never see him again, but I honestly didn't care. There wasn't a part of me that didn't want this and whatever it may or may not entail.

Jake pushed me up against the wall, and what would've terrified me with anyone else only made me ravenous for more of his touch. If this really was some elaborate figment of my imagination, then I never wanted it to end. It would be better to live forever locked in this steamy little corner of my brain than to wake up again to the constant state of emptiness I inhabited.

My blood roared through my system, lighting my body on fire, and my heart sang with so much joy that I thought it might burst right out of my chest and take flight.

As Jake broke the kiss and began sucking on my neck with as much passion as he had my lips, I gripped his wide shoulders through his sexy leather jacket. If it wasn't for the wall and his tall, hard body holding me up, I would've melted into the floor. *This* was definitely not the boy who had kissed me when we were kids.

We stood to watch the last of the fireworks. The Joneses had given up on trying to get us to come in, and as I looked up at Jake, I couldn't help but smile.

"Why are you looking at me like that?" he asked, eyebrow cocked.

My face heated as soon as he caught me staring.

"No reason," I said as I turned my gaze away. Out of the corner of my eye, I could see that Jake had begun to rub at his neck, a nervous gesture he had, but I pretended not to notice. After a moment, he cleared his throat like he was trying to get my attention, which made me look over at him again.

Jake looked upset, and his eyes kept darting between the inside of the treehouse and the fireworks and my face.

"Are you okay," I asked.

"Yeah, um...okay, so I want to try something."

I shrugged and leaned back against the large post keeping the treehouse up in the tree. Jake had good ideas, and I was usually open to them.

"Okay, what do you want to do?"

"You have to promise me first not to get mad or all weird."

"You're the one acting weird." Tossing my braid, which I'd been playing with the end of, over my shoulder and crossed my arms over my chest. "I already told you I'm not jumping down, though, so if that's what you're gonna say, then you can forget it."

"No, that's not it." Jake licked his lips and stepped a little closer. He cupped my cheek, and I sucked in a sharp breath—I knew what he was going to do. I wasn't sure I wanted him to kiss me, but I also didn't want him to stop. He looked into my eyes, and my heart beat fast like a rabbit's, the thumping echoing in my ears louder than the fireworks still banging away in the distance.

Leaning in, he paused just before our lips touched. "We're still friends after this, right?"

"Duh." It was all I could think to say in the moment before his lips pressed against mine. This wasn't like the brief touch of lips that had

taken me by surprise when he pretended to be my boyfriend at the park.

Butterflies took flight in my stomach, making me feel jittery as we stood still, neither of us ready to do anything more. Jake slowly broke the kiss and leaned back.

"Why did you do that?" I asked, voice breathy.

Jake shrugged his much wider shoulders.

"Just wanted us to be each other's first real kiss. Come on. We'd better head in before we get grounded or something."

I touched my fingers to my lips and smiled as he climbed down the ladder. A little shadow crossed my mind—it felt like I should maybe tell him what had happened to me, but I didn't want anyone to know. I really didn't want Jake to see me as anything other than Kit Kat, the girl he was forced to room with who was now his best friend.

"You coming?" Jake called up to me.

"Yeah, pushy. I'm coming."

In the mad scramble of grasping arms and flying clothing, I couldn't really say when I'd ended up in nothing but my sweater with my legs wrapped around Jake's waist. His leather belt and the stiff material of his jeans chaffed in a strangely delightful way as he thrust his hips toward me like he was trying to fuck me right through his clothes.

A tiny bit of fear threaded through my mind as Jake groaned, bracing his hands on either side of the wall to cage me in with his body.

"Wait," I panted out. His body flexed hard, but he stilled like I'd pushed a button. Panting, he lifted his head and looked at me—those green eyes were so intense that I had to swallow down the sudden lump in my throat.

"Are you okay? We can stop," he said, voice strained. I could tell how much trouble he was having with holding back, and there was something about the juxtaposition between the intensity with which he wanted me and the fact he was giving me space to breathe that calmed the little bubble of fear.

"No, I don't want to stop. I just needed to catch my breath." When I offered him a smile, he stared into my eyes like he didn't believe me, but I wasn't letting Richard ruin one more thing for me, especially not this moment. Grabbing his head, I crushed our lips together, becoming the aggressor, until he shuddered and caved under my touch.

Jake grabbed my ass and gave it a hard squeeze as he hitched me up a little higher on his body until I was staring down at his sexy face. I suddenly understood all those women who liked their men to take control and carry them around. I felt completely out of control in his hold, but there was no more panic and the fear evaporated. I trusted him like I'd never trusted another.

Jake was my home. He always had been. I had no idea how this moment had happened, and I wasn't going to stop to ask—instead, I was going to take it for the miracle that it was.

With a heave, Jake pushed me up the wall until my head almost hit the ceiling, making me scream in surprise. His eyes were practically feral as he put my legs over his shoulders.

"Oh my god, Jake," I cried out as he nipped the inside of my leg. I suddenly felt a bit shy and nervous—I mean, his face was *right there*

—but there was no time to contemplate it as he gripped my ass and his tongue swirled around my clit.

"Mmm," he growled, and my breath jerked in and out in ragged gasps as I gripped his hair tightly. The black strands I'd dreamed about ran through my fingers as his tongue assaulted my clit with wild abandon. My back arched off the wall as he stole the air from my lungs with waves of pleasure that my body hadn't been prepared to feel.

"Jake, oh fuck, yes. Right there," I managed to gasp out a second before I came at a blinding speed. He didn't slow—if anything, it only encouraged him to lick faster until I was a twitching mess.

A zipper jingled somewhere close by, but what that meant didn't penetrate the lust-induced fog in my brain until Jake slid me down his body and I felt the slick head of his cock rub against me. Jake's lips latched on to the side of my neck as he pushed inside.

As he continued his advance into my body, the moan I let out rose in volume to almost become a scream. It was proving to be a very tight fit for him regardless of our little pre-game session. His groans of pleasure and the flex of his muscles under my hand sent a ripple of need through my body once more.

"Oh fuck, Angel. You're so tight, " Jake bit out, breaking the seal of his lips on my neck. His eyes were closed tightly, and the tendons in his neck strained as he clenched his jaw. My own mouth hung open, stuck between a scream of pleasure and desperate pants for air.

With a guttural sound, almost a growl, Jake pushed in hard until there was nowhere left for him to go. Every inch of him had stretched me deliciously wide, and it felt like he had sunk in so impossibly deep that my body couldn't possibly take any more. His much larger frame pinned me to the wall like he was trying to push us both right through the drywall.

For a moment, we stood there panting and just stared at one another like neither of us could believe that this thing we'd wanted for so long was actually happening. I know I couldn't. Somehow, it still felt like this was exactly where I was always meant to be.

"You're mine, Kat," he said. I would've answered with a very emphatic 'yes,' but instead, the word came out as a mindless yell as he pulled his cock out slowly, stealing my breath, and then thrust himself back inside. The soft thud of my back hitting the wall as he bottomed out heightened every sensation running rampant through my system. "You've always been mine."

Jake repeated the action, and I had to wrap my arms around his neck and hang on for the powerful ride as we banged against the wall at a rhythmic pace. His hot mouth latched back on to the skin on the side of my neck, and this time, his hot groan rumbled right in my ear.

My brain was already so scrambled that I couldn't remember if it was day or night, but the last bit of my sanity flew right out the window as Jake began sucking on the side of my neck like he was a teenager hoping to leave his mark for the world to see.

I cried out as Jake's teeth nipped at my skin and another orgasm began to rise. In a moment that was pure fire, he licked up the side of my neck before cupping my face to dive in for a kiss. We kissed like it might be our only chance ever to do so, giving and taking everything we could to and from each other.

"Say it. Say you're mine. Say you've always been mine," he ordered, lips still touching mine. I opened my mouth to try and say the words, but only incoherent sounds tumbled out as his pace picked up. Each one of his thrusts was more frenzied than the last.

"Open your eyes and look at me," he said, voice demanding, and my eyes snapped open in response. His intense stare seemed to pierce into my soul, not letting me focus on anything else, and everything inside me crumbled in on itself. I simultaneously felt like I was drowning and being thrown a life preserver.

"Say it, Kat," he said in a gravelly growl. The sound of it sent a tingle all the way down my spine, making my body shiver.

"Yes," I managed to gasp out on half a breath. "Yes," I said, trying again, wanting it to be clear, and Jake smirked at me and my efforts.

"Not good enough, Kat," he said. My eyes rolled back in my head as his hand slipped between our bodies, his thumb finding my swollen clit. He began rubbing it in time with his powerful thrusts.

"Oh dear god!" I shouted. A thrust later, I was screaming his name as I came harder than I ever had before. Nothing could compare to him, to this right now between us. Unable to help myself, I dug my nails into his shoulders as he continued to pump into me until my orgasm subsided.

Jake slowed to a stop but continued running soft kisses along the base of my neck. Each one of them was as soft as a feather's touch, yet they seared my already hypersensitive skin.

"I'm...yours," I managed to get out before my body collapsed onto his. Everything felt heavy and weak, but my heart soared as it pounded away in my chest.

"I was hoping to have a cup of coffee and a conversation, but this is way better," Jake said, amusement clear in his voice. I nodded in agreement with my head still on his shoulder. His deep chuckle vibrated against my chest as he began to walk. I didn't particularly care where he carried me, but I let out a deep sigh of satisfaction when he laid me down gently on my bed.

I couldn't remember any other time I'd felt this deeply satisfied yet wanton for more—I wanted everything he had to offer. My head lulled to the side, and I was treated to the sight of the sexiest man I'd ever seen pulling off his black T-shirt one-handed to show off the full length of the tattoos that covered both of his arms.

Jake held out his right arm for me to see, and my mouth curled up in a smile as I looked at the initials 'K and J' surrounded by the other artwork. Not saying a word, he turned around, and I couldn't do anything but stare as I saw the roman numerals that stretched across his back.

To anyone else, they would have no meaning, but not to me. My hand flew to my mouth as my eyes traced the numbers that made up the exact day and time when we'd been separated. I'd memorized everything about that day—the clock of my life had seemed to stop with the hands at 8:07 p.m. seventeen years ago.

Jake turned to face me, and his eyes became concerned as he noticed my tears. One strong finger reached out to trace the tear trailing down my cheek.

"What's wrong?" he asked.

My emotions were all over the place—even through my tears, I couldn't help but drink in the vision he made. He'd lost his jeans at some point, and every inch of him was now on display. My eyes roamed over very cut one of his abs and ridges of definition in his shoulders before sliding up to find his sexy green eyes.

"The date and time on your back." I covered my mouth for a moment to keep myself from crying any harder. "I memorized it too. I had it inscribed on the back of this."

My finger lifted up the little rainbow he'd given me. I still clearly remembered the disgusted look on the jeweler's face when I'd asked him to engrave the piece. He'd tried to sell me something new, but I didn't want something new. I wanted the old pendant and only the old pendant, as if hanging onto it would somehow always keep Jake with me.

His lips curled up in that wicked smile that only Jake could do—a look that could melt any pair of panties that walked through the door. It had certainly melted mine.

"I told you. You've always been mine, Kat. That's not a line—I mean it. And it looks like you never gave up on me, either," he said, pointing to the pendant I'd lifted up to show him.

The predatory look on Jake's face as he knelt on the edge of the bed had me wondering if I should be running for my life, not spreading my legs wider so he could crawl up my body.

"You're so fucking beautiful that it hurts to look at you, Kat," Jake murmured. I didn't think it was possible to feel any hotter than I already did, but the blood rushed to my face at his compliment, and I had to look away. Reaching up, he used one finger to turn my head until I was looking him in the eyes.

"Don't look away from me. I've dreamed of this moment, of being with you again, day in and day out since the night we were separated. You're like an exquisite, exotic flower—rare and impossible to replicate. Don't you ever forget it."

I didn't know what to say. I'd spent almost my entire life feeling like there was something wrong with me. Aside from my short time spent with Jake in foster care, I'd never felt special or loved on any level. At times, it had gotten to the point I honestly believed I was not worth loving at all—but this man, this *amazing* man, was here telling me that I was special. That he'd never stopped thinking about me or wanting me.

It was like my brain couldn't compute the words. If it had been any man but Jake saying them, I would've called him a liar, but it *was* Jake, and the look he was giving me was achingly sincere. It was the kind of look that said you were their whole world, the kind of look that you dream about but never expect to receive.

"Sit up," he ordered, and I did as he asked. "Lift your arms up."

I shivered as he grabbed the soft sweater I was still wearing and pulled it off over my head. Jake's heated stare traveled over my body, taking in every detail like I'd done with his, but his eyes paused on the long scar that curved out from my belly button and wrapped behind my back. I bit my lip hard as he traced the scar with his thumb.

His eyes snapped up to mine, and the anger burning in their green depths froze me in place like I'd been encased in ice.

"What happened?"

Swallowing hard, I looked between his intense stare and where his thumb was still softly tracing the line.

"I don't want to talk about it. Not right now, anyway."

My pulse pounded hard as his eyes narrowed into slits—he looked dangerous, more dangerous than I could've ever pictured Jake becoming, and I instantly trembled under his stare. He reached out, and I instinctively flinched, but he gently cupped my cheek, his thumb running over my bottom lip.

"Hey, you don't need to pull away from me, Kat. You never, ever have to be afraid of me. No matter what you might've heard about me, or seen, or anything else, I want you to know that I'd never hurt you."

Like everyone who followed him on social media, I knew about his short stints in jail, which had helped with his 'bad boy' image, but I didn't really know the story behind them—only that it was a few days here or a weekend there. That information wasn't really posted in his profiles.

His thumb pressed a little harder into my bottom lip as he tilted my head from side to side like he was looking for more marks, but then he stopped and fixed me with that hard stare.

"But if I find out that sniveling piece of shit of an ex of yours did this to you…I'll kill him with my bare hands."

That one sentence rocked me senseless, and considering all the shocks I'd had so far, that was saying something. How did he know about my ex? Before I could form a response, Jake cupped the back of my neck and laid a soft kiss on my lips.

"I want to taste every last inch of your body all over again," he whispered as his hands slid up my legs, making me moan. "But I've waited too long to have you under me." Jake slowly crawled up until he was hovering over me, arms braced on either side, and I was lying back, panting hard with anticipation.

"So I'm going to fuck you senseless first, and then I'm going to worship you the way you deserve," he said. He dropped his mouth to mine, and it took only a few moments of his ministrations to feel lightheaded.

I yelped as he reared back and pulled me down the bed with a hard, quick tug.

"Are you a good kitty or a bad kitty?" he asked, cocking a sexy brow as he traced lines down my legs with his fingertips. I giggled nervously at hearing the silly nickname he'd teased me with years ago. I suddenly felt like I was a teen all over again. How could just one look from this man make every part of me so nervous? It wasn't like I hadn't done this before. It hadn't even been an hour.

His very prominent dick was lying against my stomach, and I

couldn't stop staring at it like it was about to attack. My core clenched tight at the memory of how good it'd felt inside of me, and I licked my lips, suddenly wanting to be caught. Jake moved his soft touches to my hips.

"Cause if you're a *good* kitty, I'm going to shove this cock in you just like this, but if you're a *bad* kitty…well, those ones have to get on their knees and beg," he said.

"I'm an *everything* kind of kitty," I said, voice low, before laughing at how quickly his eyes lit up. "But right now, I'm feeling *very* bad."

Jake's eyes flared with a heat I was sure would sear me from the inside out. He slid off the bed and stood, giving me his patented sly look.

"Then get on your hands and knees," he ordered. Feeling way too naughty and loving it, I did just that. Taking my time, I languidly flipped myself over and pushed my ass into the air. I looked over my shoulder to fix him with a coy look, and even though I watched him reach for my hips, I still squealed when he gripped them hard to pull me closer to him. He was very strong, and that thought was both sexy as hell and unnerving at the same time.

"Oh god," I moaned as his fingers reached between my legs and gripped my already hardening clit. He rolled it around between his fingers while his thumb dipped inside my pussy.

"I'm going to have each of these holes, Kat. This little rosebud of yours is very tempting to ravage tonight," he said.

Jake gave my ass a soft slap, and even though it didn't hurt, I tried to lurch away from him. His hands held me firm. The movement only pushed his finger, still rubbing small circles on my clit, deeper into the sensitive flesh, making me moan and my legs shake.

"Oh," I gasped out, hanging my head as his thumb left me quaking. When he removed it, the reprieve only lasted a moment before he began rubbing circles around the sensitive flesh of my ass, zeroing in on my opening.

"Is this a virgin hole?" Jake asked, and I groaned as he applied a little bit of pressure. "Because if this is a virgin hole, then one day real soon, I'm going to pop that cherry and make you scream with a whole new kind of pleasure. So is it, Angel?"

Even though I couldn't see him, I could feel every little touch. Another finger pushed deep into my core and gave a few delightful thrusts—I was definitely wet again—before he pulled it out and ran it over the 'rosebud' he'd just mentioned. I bit my lip as he applied a little more pressure.

"Answer me, Kat. Is this a virgin hole?" Jake asked, his voice having a distinct and very pleasurable effect on my clenching core.

"Yes," I panted out, and the deep groan Jake made, along with those incredible fingers working me over, was turning me into a wiggling, panting mess.

"So tempting, but not tonight. I'm going to save that," he murmured. The promise of more nights like this was not lost on me, and the fluttering in my stomach and chest got stronger—it felt like a whole flock of butterflies had taken flight inside me.

"You want this, Kat? You want me to fuck you so hard that you will never think of another man?" Jake rubbed his cock all over my ass before running it up and down my very wet pussy. I hung my head and wiggled my ass at him, silently begging him to take me. "Say it, Kat. I want to hear the words."

"Yes," I whispered. And then barely a second later....

"Oh fuck!"

I couldn't hold in my yell as he did exactly what he'd promised and slammed himself into me so hard that the sound of our skin coming together made a slap that rang throughout the otherwise quiet house. We both froze as he held himself as deep as he could go. I'd never felt so full, so complete.

He wiggled his hips around in a circle, hitting all the right places inside my body, and my arms shook as my body quivered at the sensation.

"I couldn't hear you, Kat. Was that a yes?" Jake asked as he pulled himself out at an agonizingly slow pace.

"Yes," I said, louder this time.

He once more slammed home only to stay perfectly still—he was trying to drive me crazy. It was working. I tried to wiggle, but his firm hands held me still.

"I still can't hear you, Kat. I'm starting to feel like you don't want this."

As he started to withdraw again, a strange kernel of panic that he was really going to stop, was going to leave and never come back, burst open in my chest.

"Yes! Yes! Yes! I want it! I want *you*!" I yelled, panting hard.

"Much better," he said, and I could hear his smirk.

This time when he thrust his hips forward, he started up a quick pace that had my mouth hanging open in a silent scream as the most amazing pleasure I could ever imagine spread through me.

"Oh fuck, Angel, you feel so fucking good. Be a good girl and rub your clit for me. Come all over my cock again. I want to feel you come."

My hand instantly reached between my legs, and I was momentarily stunned to feel his balls smack into my hand. I needed to feel that this was real. Slipping my fingers around his slick cock, I tightened them into a ring so I could feel him slide through with every thrust into my body. The cock was too big for my fingers to meet around it, but Jake groaned as I squeezed the hard shaft that was stretching me wider with every thrust.

"Come on me, Kat. Soak me, give yourself over to it." Jake's voice sounded strained, and I loved hearing him like that. I did as he asked, removing my fingers from around his cock to begin furiously rubbing at my clit.

"Oh god! Oh Jake! Yes, I'm going to come. Holy...." My back arched and every muscle tensed as another release hit, wracking my body with what felt like tsunami waves of pleasure.

"Oh shit! Kat!" Jake's hips bucked faster and harder into me at such a blinding pace that the orgasm I'd been riding got drawn out into one that felt impossibly long. "Fuck, I'm gonna come," he gritted out.

I could tell he was getting ready to pull out, and I didn't want that. I wanted it all—every last drop that he could give was mine. I pushed back onto him hard as he tried to withdraw.

"No, come in me."

"Are you sure?" he asked, voice straining.

"Yes. Come in me, Jake."

"Oh fuck!" With a final thrust, he pushed his cock in as deep as possible, and I could feel every single drop he pulsed into me. Unfortunately, like all good things, it eventually stopped.

"Oh my god, that was amazing." Jake leaned forward, pressing us together until I could all but feel the heat of his pleasure-warmed body sink into my bones. He kissed the middle of my back. "You're amazing."

I swallowed hard as his finger suddenly traced the long, thin scar from my back surgery that ran along the side of my spine.

"What the hell happened, Kat?" he asked. He sounded so concerned, but I didn't want that—I wanted him to go back to being sexy and seductive Jake. I didn't want to talk about what had happened.

"I was in a car accident," I said, looking over my shoulder to see his face. When I went to push the sweaty strands of hair out of my eyes, I realized my arms were shaking so badly that I could barely hold myself up, and it wasn't from exhaustion. I was suddenly and inexplicably terrified.

"I don't want you to leave," I blurted. I had to look away from him—I couldn't bear to meet his eyes.

"I'm not going anywhere, not ever again." He slowly stepped back from the bed but walked around until he could reach the edge of the blanket to pull it down. "Now come on and get under the covers. I'll worship you when we get up," he said, giving me a wink, and I couldn't have stopped the blush from creeping up my neck if I'd tried. How could three little sentences make me feel all better?

Crawling up the bed, I got under the covers and smiled widely as Jake turned off the light and crawled into bed behind me. After pulling me flush against his body, he softly kissed my neck. The butterflies in my stomach went wild again. His hand moved down to touch the skin there like he somehow knew the effect he had on me and wiggled around, making me laugh.

"Little different than the last time we slept together," Jake said before he proceeded to put his leg over mine like he was penning me in.

"Yeah, just a little. I don't remember us being naked."

"Trust me. Even at fourteen, I thought about you naked."

"Perv," I said, unable to hold back a smile. Jake made a rumbling, growl-like noise into the side of my neck and ramped up his tickling, making me squeal and laugh and try to escape his hold. He'd always tickled me to get his way when we argued about anything.

"Yield. I yield," I called out, laughing as he stopped to nip at the skin of my neck, making me wiggle for a totally different reason. "Is it weird that it feels like yesterday and forever ago that I saw you last?"

Running my fingers up and down his muscled forearm, I took a deep breath and relaxed into his hold. It had been so long since the last time I could let my guard down and feel safe that I wanted to cry all over again. Even if it was just for tonight, to be able to get a good night's sleep—it felt like he was giving me the world.

"No, I feel the same. God, I've missed you so much. I can't say that enough." Jake buried his nose in my hair and took a deep breath. "You smell like roses and cherries...and cookies, I think," he said, making me giggle.

"Is that a bad thing?"

"Nope. Other than a tire store and my whiskey, those are now my favorite smells." He laughed, and the deep sound vibrated against my back. My smile slipped, and I didn't want to say it, but I knew I had to.

"We have a lot to talk about, Jake." I whispered.

"I know, and we will, but for now, go to sleep." He kissed my cheek. "I'm not going anywhere."

I smiled into the dark as silent tears slipped from my eyes.

"I love you, Jake. I always have."

He snuggled in tighter even though there was no more space between us.

"I know. And I have loved you from the moment you stomped into our room at the Joneses' house and claimed half the space."

"I did no such thing," I huffed. I could feel him smiling into my neck at his joke. I'd been more mouse than girl when we first met, but the annoyingly cute, green-eyed boy who became my roommate had taught that girl to stand up for herself. If only that girl could've seen through Richard before she married him.

"Go to sleep. I've got you now."

I lay there awake for what felt like hours, waiting until I was sure he was asleep and not about to disappear before letting my eyes close. Was it possible for my beaten and terrified heart to mend? Would it be able to heal with this man? I'd always loved Jake, but this almost felt like our fairytale ending rather than our beginning because we were now very different people on very different paths.

I mentally kicked myself as I started to picture all kinds of worst-case scenarios—there was plenty of time for that later. If I'd learned one thing from being with Richard, it was to appreciate the good moments because you never knew when they would come to an end.

25

JAKE

I STRETCHED, reaching for Kat, but her side of the bed was cold. My eyes snapped open to stare at the empty spot next to me for a moment as I ran through what had happened last night to make sure I wasn't having another alcohol-induced moment of memory loss or some incredibly realistic dream. Looking around the small bedroom full of cream and grey everything, which would've looked plain except for the splashes of sunflower yellow scattered about, I spotted the sweater Kat had been wearing when she'd answered the door. Not a dream.

Slipping from the bed, I bent and picked up the sweater, bringing it to my nose to take a deep breath of the scent I wanted to commit to memory. It was stupid, but even though I was undeniably standing in a strange house after waking up in a strange bed, I still hadn't believed it was all real until this second.

Wanting to find and hold the real thing, I tossed the sweater on a chair and pulled on my boxers. They somehow were more or less still clean even after everything. Poking my head out the door, I could hear the shower running—I was tempted to sneak in and join Kat, but when I gripped the knob of the bathroom door to give it a turn, it was locked. I rapped my knuckle on the door instead.

"Kat, you okay?"

I could hear the shower curtain move, and the sound of the water changed like she'd stepped out of the stream.

"Yeah, sorry. It's just a habit to lock the door. I'll be out in a minute—I put the coffee on if you want some."

God, I loved her sexy, sexy voice. It sent shivers down my spine, and looking down at myself, it was more than apparent that I was already raring for more of last night's action. I decided it would be safer to put my jeans on before venturing any further to create at least some kind of barrier against temptation. Amazingly, they were still clean, too. Go me.

The scent of the coffee drew me down the hall to the pot sitting on the counter. Kat had already set out two cups, a bowl of sugar cubes, and a carton of creamer. Even as a kid, she had always been considerate, always worrying about what everyone else would like or think, and it seemed that her nature hadn't changed. Pouring some coffee, I dropped in a cube and a splash of creamer before leaning against the counter to look around the small home.

There wasn't a personal item to be found. No matter what corner my eyes searched, I couldn't see a single photo, or even a knickknack, that showed this space was hers. I couldn't help thinking about the scars on her body.

She'd said the big one on her stomach was from a car accident, but I'd always been able to tell when she was lying or holding back. There was more to the story, and my blood boiled hotter than the coffee I was sipping at the thought of the fucker she'd married hurting her. The image of killing him was clear in my mind. I didn't care if I spent the rest of my life behind bars for it—I would find him, and I would make him pay.

"Whoa, is the coffee that bad?"

I jerked my head up at the sound of Kat's voice, and there she was, standing just inside the small kitchen while rubbing at her long, wet hair with a towel. The morning wood I hadn't managed to get rid of throbbed behind the confines of my jeans. Kat looked like a meal that needed to be devoured, and I was more than ready for the buffet.

My eyes raked over her body, seeking out every little detail. What should've seemed like simple sleep attire had my mouth watering. The soft pink tank top and flower-patterned boxer shorts looked sexy as hell, no lace or peekaboo cutouts needed.

"The coffee is great," I said with a smile.

I set the cup down and held out my hand to her. She stared at it tentatively, and I hated seeing that subtle timidness in her. She'd been the same way when she'd first arrived at the Joneses' place—I saw that same fear from back then in her eyes now.

"I promise that everything is fine," I said, trying to push every ounce of sincerity I possessed into the words, and something deep inside of me unclenched when she started over to me. As soon as she was in arm's reach, I pulled her in close and cupped her face.

"Fuck, you're beautiful. Do you know that? Do you understand what you do to me?"

Kat's cheeks flamed bright red. She opened her mouth, but nothing came out. So many images flashed through my mind as I took a moment to savor the sight of her blue eyes. They were even more beautiful in the daylight, and as I looked, I lost myself in them.

Like so many times before, I wondered what our lives would've looked like if I'd chosen to be selfish eleven years ago and spoken to her rather than letting her and her friend disappear down the street.

Her body trembled slightly as we stood staring at one another, and I couldn't take it any longer—I dropped my lips to hers, ravenous for her. The taste of her lips was amazing, a combination of fresh coffee, mint, and everything clean and sweet that was her. Kat moaned and opened her mouth for me to deepen the kiss, and as I did, I grabbed her around the waist and lifted her up to place her on the island.

"I'm...," she started, but I stopped her next words with a kiss. She rallied after a very hot minute, pulling back with a gasp. "I'm supposed...," she panted, and I moved in to kiss her again, unwilling to end the moment. Unfortunately, she moved her lips out of the way. "I need to get ready for work," she finally finished, smiling and eyes alight.

"Not until I get my breakfast," I said with a wicked smirk.

"I can make you pancakes," she offered, and I had to laugh at the sweet, innocent remark.

"No, Angel. Everything I want to eat has already been served." Grabbing the adorable boxers she was wearing, I gave them a hard tug that made Kat squeal as she slid toward me on the island. Her hands grabbed for the edge to stay on the surface.

"Jake, I really need to...oh dear *god*," she gasped out as I dove face first into her pussy with the boxers barely past her knees, tongue swirling around her quickly hardening clit. I wasn't waiting even a moment longer to get back to where I wanted to be.

Keeping my tongue deep inside her folds, I grabbed her ankle and placed her foot up on the island to give me better access. She tasted like the sweetest of grapes and the richest of wines all at once. I sucked on her harder, and if she had any reservations left, they definitely seemed to disappear as I took my fill.

"Oh Jake, oh god, don't stop," Kat shouted. Her hands found my hair and pulled my face harder into her—I was all too happy to oblige. Using my middle finger, I slid into her tight core and searched out her G-spot. As I rubbed my finger over the sensitive spot, she fell backward onto the countertop. Her back arched off the island until only her head and shoulders still touched, creating an intense curve that screamed sexy. Fuck everything she did made me hard all over. She yelled my name again, which had never sounded sweeter coming from a pair of lips.

"Oh my god, Jake. Oh god," Kat moaned.

She was right on the edge. I could feel her body twitching with her building release, and I quickly pulled away.

"What are you doing? Please don't stop." Her eyes were wide and feral as I stepped back from her body.

Grabbing my belt buckle, I pulled the two ends of the strip of leather apart and let them hang with a jingle.

"You only get to come if it's on me," I said. Kat's eyes followed my hand as I reached out and gave her mound a smack. She yelped at the sudden action but then bit her lip and moaned. "You liked that? My, my, you are a *naughty* girl."

I smacked her mound again, making sure her clit, darkly flushed and clearly on display, got most of the attention. This time, Kat dropped her head back and groaned.

"This sexy pussy doesn't get to come anymore unless I make it come, unless it's filled by me. Do you understand?" I growled.

Her lust-filled eyes, hooded by thick lashes and damp with tears of overstimulation, found mine, and I had to have her. I couldn't wait any longer. Stepping between her legs, I braced myself on the counter and leaned into her body as I pushed her shirt up over her breasts.

"Fuck, you smell good," I said, burying my head between the two perfect globes, unsure which one I wanted to suck on first. Choosing the left, I swirled my tongue around the pink bud at its crest before sucking hard.

"Do you want me to stop? Let you get ready for work?" I asked as I switched nipples, drawing a groan from her lips. I knew it was an unfair question, but I didn't care. I wanted to hear her beg for me to continue. I had to know that she needed me as much as I needed her —because fuck me, I needed her in every way possible.

She was my drug, my life's essence, my end of the fucking rainbow. Was it unnatural to be so consumed with another the way I was with her? Maybe, but I really didn't care. This was one addiction I'd die before giving up.

"No, don't stop. *Please* don't stop." Kat ran her hands through my hair, which I loved. Tightening her fists, she gripped hard and pulled my head closer to her chest. I smiled against her skin, loving the effect I had on her.

"Alright, Angel. You got it." With the sweep of an arm, I pushed everything I could reach on the island onto the floor and out of the way. Kat jerked upright and covered her mouth in shock, wincing as a wooden bowl full of fruit clattered as it hit the floor and rolled. She'd probably be finding stray grapes under things for a week.

Bracing my arms on the edge of the island once more, I flexed them, enjoying Kat's appreciative looks, before I slowly pulled myself up between her legs like an animal stalking its prey. She *was* my prey.

She was the one who had gotten away, and that was never happening again.

Kat pushed herself away from the edge and further across the countertop. She stared at me as I reached out and pushed a small stack of magazines off the island. They landed with a heavy smack on the tile floor.

"What are you doing?" Kat asked. Her eyes grew wide as I flicked a neat pile of cloth napkins off the island as I continued to chase her across the shiny surface slowly but steadily. The colorful little squares of fabric fluttered to the ground like confetti like we were at a party. In a way, we were—we were at our reconnection party, and I planned on reconnecting with her on every surface of this place.

"What does it look like I'm doing?" I asked as I undid the zipper on my jeans and reached inside to pull out my cock, which had been ready for this moment since I'd opened my eyes. Kat had backed herself up until she had to grip the edge of the island tightly to stay on top or risk rolling backward off the counter.

"It looks like you plan on us doing it right here," she said, her eyes darting from my eyes to what was coming for her between my legs.

"You'd better believe it."

"Jake, I cook on this island."

I shrugged as I settled myself between her thighs, which spread wider to accommodate me despite her unsure expression.

"Do you never clean your counters?"

Her cheeks flushed a brighter shade of red as she stammered adorably.

"Well...yes...of course I do."

Lowering my head, I captured her lips before she could come up with another excuse.

"Then what does it matter?" I asked. Deepening the kiss, I pushed my hips toward her, rubbing myself between her folds. I groaned as the tip of my cock found her opening, and Kat inhaled sharply as I slowly pushed myself into her slick heat.

"Fuck, you feel amazing," I mumbled against her lips. She became the aggressor as we kissed, and her quick panting breaths and incoherent responses rang through me like a clarion call, urging me onward. My ass flexed tightly, and with one last thrust of my hips, I bottomed out inside the sweetest fucking pussy that had ever walked the earth.

Universal truth or not, it was my truth. She was made for me and always had been, and like two puzzle pieces, we'd finally slotted back together the way we always should have been.

Wrapping her arms around my neck, Kat wiggled beneath me and gave herself over to our union. I remained still, loving the feeling as her walls clenched my cock in a choke hold over and over as she quietly begged for more. Ready to turn things up a notch or seven, I gave a quick, hard thrust and circled my hips.

"You want more?" I asked.

"Yes," Kat hissed.

"Beg for it. Beg for my cock to make you come hard all over your little island." I gave her two short thrusts this time, and she bucked her hips up into me to try to get more.

"Please, make me come," she panted.

"Where?"

"Here, there, everywhere. I don't care."

"That sounded fucking hot. Wrap your legs around my waist and hang on tight," I instructed. With a groan, she did as I asked, and her legs looping around my waist allowed me to sink even deeper into her.

"Oh god. Kat," I groaned as I let go and started to really fuck her hard. Her arms and legs locked around my body were the only things keeping her from being pushed off the island. The sound of her skin squeaking against the smooth surface mixed with her low, throaty moans as I rammed my cock into her tight pussy, and it was like having a whole fucking choir of angels singing in my ear.

"Be a good girl and stick your finger in your pussy with my cock."

Kat hesitated for a brief moment and then unlocked one of her hands from its death grip to slip it between our bodies. A full-body shiver ran over me as I felt her fingers caress the root of my cock before one adventurous digit slid down and started to squeeze in next to it.

"Yeah, that's it. Shove that finger in and find your G-spot. Damn that feels so fucking good."

"Oh sweet *hell*," Kat moaned as she got her finger in position—it made her already tight pussy feel that much tighter, and my balls drew up tight and began to throb at the stimulation. It was incredible. I picked up the pace, leaving Kat struggling to take a deep breath.

"Oh, oh, oh, oh fuck, Jake!" she wailed.

Kat came on a scream that shot through my body and straight to the source of our joined pleasure.

"That's it, Kat. Come for me. Keep coming," I encouraged as her walls clenched me tighter.

Her first climax seemed to roll into a larger one as I continued to fuck her hard. She shuddered and whimpered beneath me as the distinct feeling of her release flooded over me. Her body arched up into mine, and I gladly picked up the pace. Lost to my own need to come, to claim her as mine, I pounded my hips into her with full abandon.

Kat's nails dug into my skin as she cried out my name, legs tightening around my waist as she rode out her orgasm. I couldn't hold back any longer. The first shot of my release had every muscle in my body straining with the explosion of unbelievable pleasure.

"Fuck, Kat, ah!" I hollered as the second shot fired more powerfully than the first. I felt paralyzed and frozen as my body strained, but Kat had taken over and was bucking her hips up against my body. The sensation of me coming must have extended her orgasm—that thought, along with Kat's wild thrusts and steady contractions, drew out the rest of my load like she was sucking me with her mouth.

"Holy fuck," I groaned. Spent, I collapsed on top of her, only lifting my body enough for Kat to remove her hand from her pussy. She completely shocked me when she locked eyes with me, brought the digit to her mouth, and sucked it clean. Jesus *Christ*.

Even spent, my cock twitched at the sight, and I suddenly wanted to fuck her ass while she shoved a dildo in her pussy so, so badly. The image made me shiver with excitement. I wanted to try everything with her. Anything she wanted, anything she'd let me try, I was here for it.

Reaching out to remove the finger from her mouth, I immediately opened mine to suck it in slowly. I loved the smile that spread across her face as I gave the finger the same attention she had.

"I've never felt like this before," she whispered solemnly as she watched her finger disappear into my mouth.

"What exactly do you mean?" I asked before playfully nipping at her other fingers to make her smile again.

"So wanton, so desired. So free." She gave me a shy smile. "And so satisfied."

"No sweeter words have ever been spoken." I kissed the tip of her nose and then her lips. "Do you have a dildo?"

She shook her head at the sudden question and the even more sudden change in topic.

"What?"

"Do you have a dildo?"

"Um...." She looked away from my eyes and shifted nervously. "My ex wouldn't allow me to have something like that." The way she said that made my hackles rise. "So no, I don't."

I wanted to ask why not. I wanted to ask what the fuck the guy's problem was and why she looked so ashamed, but I didn't want to ruin the moment, so I sucked in all the questions and forced them down to smile at her instead.

"Well, we're going to rectify that. I want you to have a lineup of your favorite toys—anything you want to try, you tell me and we'll get it. If you want to swing like Tarzan from a harness in your room while I make love to you, Angel, then I'm so there."

Kat laughed, and as she did, I groaned at the feeling of her tightening around me all over again.

"You're serious? You're not just pulling my leg?"

"Of course I'm serious. We're going to use them to play with, or not—whatever mood hits." I smoothed back her hair and loved how her eyes were glittering with humor. "I am yours to do whatever you want with and wherever you want to do it," I growled, making her laugh again as I rumbled right into her neck, tickling her with the vibration. "I hate to do it, but I'd better move or I'll keep you on here all day."

As I slowly withdrew from her body, I sucked in a sharp breath. I was still mostly hard despite the incredible release that had left my legs feeling like Jell-O. If she wanted, I'd be happy to service her for hours.

"You're really serious about all of that, aren't you?" she asked as she tilted her head to stare at me. "Like you plan on this not being just a one time thing." I pushed back from the counter and smirked.

"One time thing? Oh, hell no, you'll be lucky if you can get rid of me now. As for the toys, yeah. I am serious." I scooped Kat up and set her on her feet. "We'll go online and pick out whatever you want to try. I really love the idea of you having something with a remote that I get to control. So many possibilities." I sent her a wink as all those delicious ideas crossed my mind.

Kat's mouth dropped open, but before I could find out what she was about to say, a knock sounded at the door. She looked at the clock over the stove and her eyes widened to perfect circles.

"Oh shit, that's Olly." I watched in amusement as Kat darted into the bedroom to find some clothes. I, on the other hand, needed to know who this 'Olly' was and marched for the door. If Olly was a guy and not the girl I'd seen at the farm, well...there was a distinct possibility that Karl would need to stop by and mop up some blood.

I stuffed my cock back in my jeans and carefully did up the zipper, but I made sure to leave the belt unclasped. I wasn't leaving any doubt about what we had been doing.

"No, Jake...shit," Kat said when she stuck her head out of the bedroom door and saw where I was heading. She took a step toward me while still trying to get her other arm through an arm hole, but I didn't bother to listen as I whipped open the door to reveal a short blonde. Relief washed over me as I recognized the woman from the other day. She was the one who Jayce was whining about because she hadn't called him yet. I looked her up and down as she did the same to me, only with her mouth hanging open.

"Can I help you?" I asked as I leaned against the door frame and crossed my arms. A raised eyebrow seemed like it might be overkill, but I did it anyways.

"What the hell is going on here? Are you Lexi's ex? You'd better get out of this house right this minute!" the small blonde growled. Yikes. She was a lot scarier than the package she came in would suggest.

"I'm not going anywhere," I said, moving to block her as she tried to peer around my body into the house. It was jarring to hear someone call Kat 'Lexi.' I knew she was going by the name, and I suspected why, but to hear it out loud felt strange.

"Get out of my way." Olly pushed on my chest as she proceeded to step around me and into the home. "Where is she? What did you do to her? I'll fucking kill you if you hurt her!" She stabbed a finger at me as she threatened, eyes full of fire. Honestly, I was very behind her protectiveness, but it wasn't needed. Protecting Kat was *my* job.

"I'm fine," Kat said as she darted back out into the living room from the bedroom. She was now wearing an adorable skirt and blouse that made me have a whole lot of teacher/student role-playing ideas, or maybe librarian ones. Both were hot options. Even the sexy short heels were making me hard all over again.

"Oh my god, Lexi. Are you okay?" Olly ran to Kat, and I cocked a brow at the two women as Olly looked Kat over like I might've beaten her, which said a lot about what Kat was running from so desperately—I flexed my fist at the thought. "He didn't hurt you, did he? He's not taking you from here, not even over my dead body," Olly said, shooting daggers at me.

I had to give it to the pint-sized woman—she was a spitfire.

"Her real name is Kat, not Lexi," I said. Kat's mouth dropped open before she sent me a hard look. "What? It's true, and I don't know if I can get used to calling you by that fake name. I was going to slip up, and you know it," I said.

"Shit, okay. Look, I don't have time for this right now. I need to get to the bakery to open, so let's do this *real* quick. Olly, this is Jake, not my ex. Jake, this is Olly, my friend, and can we please put a pin in everything else until tonight? I guess it's time I tell the both of you what's going on."

"Oh...." Olly looked between the two of us and then finally seemed to notice the suggestively unbuckled belt. "Oh! Um...okay, tonight it is."

"I hate to rush you out the door, Jake, but I really need to go," Kat said. A few things lying next to her purse got shoved inside it before she grabbed it up and swung it over her shoulder.

"You know I'm not great at waiting. Can I come with you to work?" I asked.

"If it were a baking day, I'd say yes, but I have customers coming. There will be no good time to tell you what needs to be said." She walked over and wrapped her arms around my waist. Her eyes looking up at me just about brought me to my knees. "Please?"

"For you, I'd wait a lifetime." Cupping her face, I captured her lips softly. "Mmm, so damn good." I loved that her eyes stayed closed after I broke the kiss like she was inviting me in for more. "Leave me your key and I'll clean up the mess we made and lock up. What time do you get off work? I'll swing by and pick you up."

"Really?"

I didn't care if Olly or anyone else—even my own mom—was in the room to see. I bent down to kiss her again, this time slow and deep. I made sure she knew exactly how much I wanted this.

"What time?" I asked again.

"Six. No, seven. Six-thirty?"

I laughed and gave her a kiss on the cheek.

"I'll arrive at six, and if you need to take some time to finish up, you can have all the time in the world. Maybe I'll find another shiny surface to utilize." Kat's cheeks went cherry red as she cleared her throat. Olly's eyebrows shot up.

Stepping away, I stuffed my hands into my pockets before I did something to try to convince her to stay longer and gave her a wink.

"Key?" I asked. Kat dug around in her purse and produced a small ring of keys, which I caught as they sailed at me in a gentle arc through the air.

"No stealing my underwear, you perv," she teased with a sassy grin that warmed my heart straight through. That was the Kat I knew —that sweet and sassy personality that could give as good as it got, that smile that could light up a room.

"No promises," I said, unable to hold back a smirk.

Kat gave a very stunned-looking Olly a nudge to get her moving. The two women made their way out the door, and I snickered to myself when I heard Olly demand to know the whole-freaking-hot story, and *right that minute*, as she closed it behind them.

In the following silence, I stared around at what I could see of the small house. I would keep up my end of the bargain, as I fully intended on cleaning and making myself useful, but I also intended to snoop around and see if I could find out more about the ex who had her so fucking scared. Kat was tough, far tougher than she gave herself credit for, so whatever he'd done had to be very, very bad.

Once I found out what that was…. I cracked my neck and ground my teeth together. The ex was going to see the other side of my personality, the one I hid from the world. The one that would gladly break his fucking neck and spit on his twitching corpse.

That prick was mine.

BEST
FRIENDS

26

KAT

THE BELL JINGLED as another customer left, and I smiled widely as Olly's mom walked in to take his place. She was so well dressed and stylish that she could've passed for a European countess, or duchess, or something equally as fancy. Her bright white hair was in perfectly styled, lush curls, and while a long dress coat covered most of it, she was clearly wearing a stunning dress underneath.

"Marie, what a wonderful surprise," I said with a big smile.

Her answering smile was just as warm as on the day I first met her. That had hands-down turned out to be one of the luckiest days of my life.

"This doesn't even look like the bookstore anymore, not even a little. I simply can't get over what you've done with the place," Marie said.

"Thanks. I couldn't have done it without Olly. I can't tell you how blessed I am to have met you and Olly when I came here."

"Oh stop, hun. We did nothing special other than be friends to you. Besides, I haven't seen Olly this happy and animated in a very long time. You've had your own effect on her."

Laying down the cloth I was using to wipe off the counter, I got out one of the pink bakery boxes from under the counter. My eyes snagged on the little rainbow logo in the corner, and I took a moment to stare at it in wonder.

I'd already done this multiple times over the day, but I couldn't help but do it again. I had to wonder if the symbol really did hold some magical power, if putting it up had acted as my own version of the bat signal and summoned Jake back to me. If so, I wish I'd done it a long time ago.

"What can I get you?" I asked, shaking my thoughts off and grabbing a set of tongs.

"Oh, I only came in to say hi while I waited for Douglas," Marie answered. I paused in reaching for one of the German chocolate brownies and gave her my full attention. "Don't you be looking at me like that. It's not what you think." She fussed with her coat and wouldn't meet my eyes, which told me an entirely different story.

"Now, *why* is it that I don't believe that?" I asked. I quickly loaded up the box with an assortment of treats, ignoring her sputtering until I'd taped up the box.

"Well, you can think whatever you want, but it's a simple dinner. Nothing more than two friends having a meal. I just wanted to stick my head in and say hi and tell you that I'm very happy to see you've made this town your home. I knew you'd fit in just fine the first moment I met you."

"I appreciate that, Marie. Thank you. Now here. You can take these with you to add a little sweetness to your dinner plans. Maybe share a nightcap together over them?"

Marie's cheeks flamed red and she opened her mouth to spout out what I was sure would be another denial, but before she could get out a word, the bell jingled again and the man of the hour stepped inside.

"There you are. Olly said you'd be in the bakery," Douglas said as he stepped inside.

Grabbing the box, Marie sent me a look that made it clear my scolding was not over before she smiled and turned to face Douglas.

"I came in to get some dessert for later. What do I owe you, dear?" Marie asked.

"This box is on the house. It is the least I can do as thanks for your kindness."

"Well now. Thank you, dear." Marie smiled widely, and I returned the gesture.

"How thoughtful. Nice to see you again, Lexi," Douglas said before waving as the two made their way out the door.

I shook my head in wonder at the adorable older couple. Just as I turned to head into the kitchen, the loud roar of a motorcycle reached my ears, drawing my eyes to the front window. My heart stopped in my chest and then jumped right out of it as I watched a black motorcycle pull up out front.

In what felt like a dream, I watched Jake slide smoothly off the bike. Black jeans, a black T-shirt, and a black leather jacket adorned his body, making him look very much the badass. The sunglasses definitely didn't hurt, either. *Lord* have mercy.

Was it suddenly unusually hot in here?

I had the strongest urge to fan myself as Jake walked into the store. He was so unbelievably sexy that it almost didn't make sense that it wasn't illegal.

This still didn't feel real. Even as he took off the shades and smiled, his green eyes twinkling with that perfect combination of mischief and sexiness, it didn't feel real. Even as he stepped around the counter and wrapped his arms around my waist, making my body heat up at his touch, it didn't feel real.

"Hello, my sexy Angel."

The strange bubble of doubt in my mind popped as Jake's lips found mine. He kissed me until I was lightheaded and barely remembered my own name. Either of them. How was he able to do that?

"I know it's only been a few hours, but I missed you," he said, breaking the kiss and pulling me into a tight hug.

"I missed you too," I said, unable to hide the slight waver in my voice. I couldn't make up my mind whether I wanted to cry, cheer, or do both at the same time. It was stupid to feel like we'd never been apart and yet that was exactly how I felt. Being near him was like slipping on a favorite sweater and wrapping myself up in the comfort.

"You ready to go?" Jake asked. The door jingled again, and he moved a step back as Olly stepped inside. I blushed and cleared my throat as she narrowed her eyes at Jake, who didn't seem to be overly happy to see Olly and glared right back. So glad no one was being awkward about this. Clearing my throat, I stepped out of Jake's hold and reached to turn off the lights inside the display counters.

"I just need to pack up the bit left that didn't sell. I hate the idea of throwing it out."

"Oh, you're *so* not doing that. If my mom knew you threw out some of her favorite treats, she'd die of a heart attack. Pack up whatever is left, and I'll buy it," Jake said.

"There's at least three boxes' worth," I said, flabbergasted.

"I have two brothers, my parents, and two nieces to feed. That lot is like a school of piranha. Trust me. It won't go to waste."

I'd been reaching into the counter for the tongs I'd left there, but at that, I paused to look up at Jake.

"You have a family?" I asked.

His look softened as he stepped forward and pulled me into a hug.

"Yeah, and I can't wait for you to meet them. I was going to fill you in on everything that's happened to me since I last saw you when we had our chat tonight," he said. I nodded but was unable to respond. A whole family.

Reaching into the display shelves, I began packing the boxes to keep my hands busy. I felt so...thrown off. I was happy for him, of course. I mean, I wouldn't ever want him to have ended up in a bad situation, but I couldn't help feeling sad.

I guess I'd just always thought we were both somewhere suffering alone after we were separated, which was an admittedly stupid and selfish idea. Instead, he'd found this perfect family to join while I'd ended up moving around so much that it had felt safer to sleep on a wooden pallet in the back of an ice cream parlor with cockroaches than at any of my foster placements.

"Hey Angel, don't be upset. I'm sorry," Jake said, worry written all over his face.

Stepping back from the counter, I wiped the stupid tears away and shook my head at the concerned expressions I was getting from both Jake and Olly.

"I'll be fine. That was just a shock. A lot of shocks in twenty-four hours. Come on. We have a lot to discuss," I said, absolutely not ready to unpack any of that at the moment. As much as I loved the bakery, I was suddenly more than ready to go home.

At least the store would be closed for the next three days, so I could do a thorough cleaning tomorrow without any problems. Flicking off the lights, I stepped outside into the darkening dusk and immediately shivered in the cool breeze.

"Here, put this on." Jake took off his jacket and held it open for me.

"It's okay. I can go with Olly in her car."

"No. Now that I've found you again, I'm spending as much time with you as I can get, so get your adorable ass in my jacket and on my bike so I can take you home."

I could see Olly standing off to the side behind Jake, and she rolled her eyes in response before marching off toward her car. It was becoming clear that Olly didn't think much of Jake, which didn't sit well with me. That would have to be dealt with, and sooner rather than later.

Stepping forward, I slipped my arms into the way-too-large jacket and brought the flaps of the collar to my nose to breathe in the scent of leather and cologne that lingered. Jake zipped up the jacket for me like I was a kid again before walking to his bike and opening a saddlebag flap to fish out a helmet.

"What about you?" I asked, taking the offering and pulling the black helmet on to clip into place.

"I don't need one. This head is hard enough," he said, shrugging off my concern. I gave him my best 'don't be an idiot' look, but he just laughed as he got on the motorcycle. "Come on. Get on behind me and hold on tight."

A thrill of excitement raced through my system—this would be my first ride, and it was with Jake. This was one of my fantasies come true. My blood practically sang as I pulled up my skirt enough that it wouldn't get caught and mounted the bike behind him. He patted my hand as I linked my arms around his waist in a death grip.

"Oh my," I whispered as the bike roared to life and proceeded to rumble away between my legs. I bit my lip hard as Jake pulled away from the curb and did a U-turn to head toward my house. As we parked in my driveway, I had to admit I was disappointed that it had been such a short trip.

Olly was already wandering up the sidewalk from next door as Jake and I made our way to the front door. There was a tension in the air that felt like two animals getting ready to fight, and I had no interest in being the bone caught in the middle. I was finding it strange that Olly had more than encouraged me to go out with Xayne, yet her reaction to Jake so far was visceral anger.

After placing Jake's jacket on the back of a chair, I stepped into the kitchen and pulled out a few beers from the fridge. Making my way back, I paused at the even higher level of tension in the room. Olly was sitting at one end of the couch while Jake had found his way to the large reclining chair. The two of them were staring at one another like they were in the middle of the standoff at the O.K. Corral. They looked a bit like two feuding royals, or at least rival CEOs.

I handed them each a bottle and then sat down on the couch with Olly, but the two still didn't look in my direction. Awkward.

"What's your problem with me?" Jake asked, breaking the heavy silence and asking the question that I'd just been thinking. Olly leaned forward, arms on knees, apparently more than ready to get into it.

"I don't like you. Actually, I don't like your type," she said.

Jake's eyebrow rose.

"Oh really? And what the fuck have I ever done to you?"

"Um...*guys,*" I said, trying to interject, but it was like I wasn't even in the room.

"I know your type, and I don't think you're good for Lexi. She's just gotten out of a terrible relationship, and the last thing she needs is to be hitching her wagon to the likes of you."

"Oh really? You think you know me?" Jake said as he leaned forward to mirror Olly's position.

"Yeah, I do. When you answered the door, I thought I recognized you. Then Lexi called you 'Jake' and I just *knew* it had to be you, so I did a little looking, and wouldn't you know, I was right." Olly crossed her arms and slumped back into the couch.

"You're the *famous* Jake Russell who was already in and out of jail even when you were just a local teen. The Jake Russell who probably broke more hearts than every other guy around these parts combined. And now here you are all these years later—the Jake Russell with twenty million followers whose bad boy ways are still very much intact," Olly practically spit out. She jumped to her feet to pace the small space between the couch and the front door as if she just couldn't sit still anymore.

"Let me count the reasons that you shouldn't be near Lexi. Number one, the partying and drinking that is obviously way out of control. In the last video you put up, you could barely speak you were so hammered. You even asked, 'Where am I? Does anyone know which way my motorcycle is?' before the camera cut out. Real classy."

Olly held up a second finger, actually serious about the counting.

"Then there's the fact that you're obviously a man whore. Now, I don't care how often you dip your wick, or with who, but I won't let you hurt my friend—or rather, another friend. You already broke my best friend's heart in high school. Do you remember Laurel?"

Jake didn't say anything. In fact, his face was completely unreadable except for his eyes, which were fuming.

"Don't worry, though. After you callously broke up with her and I had to listen to her cry over you for months, she moved out of town and got married. She's very happy."

As Olly dramatically held up another finger, the first sparks of doubt began to seep into the happiness I'd wrapped myself in since Jake had landed on my doorstep last night. I already knew about all his escapades, but to hear someone else voice all the concerns I'd had about reaching out to Jake in the first place made me sick to my stomach.

"Lastly, you're a nomad," Olly continued. "You travel around wherever the wind takes you, and you party with and then fuck whoever you can get your hands on until you get bored and move on to do it all over again somewhere else. It will be over my dead body that I let you treat Lexi like a piece of trash to be used hard and then tossed aside when the next wind blows into port."

My gaze darted to Jake. I expected to see him burst up from the seat and start yelling—he always did have a temper—but instead, he sunk back further as his eyes found mine. They held so much emotion that I couldn't even figure out what I was seeing, and with each second that passed in silence, my heart pounded harder.

"Nothing to say for yourself?" Olly came to stand by my side like she was guarding me, and Jake's gaze turned up to meet hers.

"Just collecting my thoughts. Give me a moment," he said, his voice holding the same mixed emotions his eyes did.

"Please sit down, Olly," I said, reaching out to touch her arm softly. She sighed and uncrossed her arms as she returned to her seat on the couch.

"I can't argue with anything that you found out about me, or even what your friend Laurel probably said about me. I was all those things and sometimes more," Jake said to Olly, but then he turned his head and his eyes found mine. His gaze was piercing.

"But there is a lot more to those stories that you don't know. There is also the fact that I no longer want that life and had already moved back home for good to be with my family before I even found you, Kat. I've also told my manager that I won't be traveling or doing any of the social parties anymore, so he'll have to find a new way for me to promote. I didn't like the version of myself that I'd become."

Jake broke the intense look he was giving me to look at Olly again.

"You also don't know the history that Kat and I share. She is my everything—my best friend, the person my soul has longed for ever since we were separated. When that happened, it felt like I'd lost a piece of my heart, and it is also why I never dated seriously, like with your friend Laurel."

Jake paused to take a sip of the beer that had been dangling, ignored, between his fingers before giving Olly a sardonic smile.

"Who I do remember, incidentally, and the part you're not mentioning is that I told Laurel I didn't want anything serious. She agreed at first, but then when *she* wanted things to get serious and I broke it off instead, she said I'd led her on. Which I didn't."

He took another sip, but this time, there was no smile.

"What you don't understand, Olly, is that I actually *like* how protective you are of your friend. Kat needs someone like you in her corner. But don't paint the mistakes of my past onto who I am now. Those colors don't match me anymore."

Jake leaned forward again, and if glares actually had real heat to them, his would've lit Olly on fire where she sat.

"So, let's get one thing straight before we continue this chat. Kat is mine as I'm hers—we always have been. Now that we've finally found one another again after all these years, I'm not letting go, so you'd better get used to seeing my face around whether you like me or not because I'm not going anywhere. No matter how many fits you throw or how many times you trumpet that I'm a terrible guy, I'm here to stay."

Olly's face went bright red. I couldn't tell if she was angry or embarrassed, or both, but it was time for me to interject before blood started flying. I stood so I could face them at the same time.

"Okay, enough. Both of you. You each got to say your piece, but now it's my turn, and this is my life, so what I say is what matters," I said with as much authority as I could muster. They crossed their arms, unintentionally mirroring each other as I looked back and forth between them.

"Let's start with the name thing. Jake, you can't call me Kat out in public here. The man I got married to is not a nice man, and...." I looked away from his stare to make it easier to get the next part out past the tightness in my throat. "I'm hiding from him while the divorce is happening so I can get my life back on track."

"Yeah, I kinda guessed that. My mom says people usually only change their name for a couple of reasons, and one of them, especially for women, is to disappear. I'm sorry that he made you feel so scared that you've had to do that. Maybe that's why I'm stubbornly calling you Kat. It's not just that—that is how I see you—but I hate the idea of embracing something that he forced you to do." Jake's voice was so soft that I could feel tears pricking the backs of my eyes and threatening to fall.

I had to clear the emotion from my throat before I could speak.

"I'll talk to you more about that later, okay?" I asked, voice equally soft. Jake nodded, so I turned my attention to Olly.

"Olly, Jake is telling the truth that I've known him since we were kids, and we have...a special bond that I can't even explain. Kate is my real name, but Jake has always called me Kat. When I came here, I came with the intention of starting over, and that meant leaving every part of who I was in the past, which included a legal name change. I didn't mention it to you because I simply hoped to never need to. If I needed to, it would mean my past had caught up with me. Mind you, I was assuming my past would be my ex, not Jake."

Bringing my own beer to my lips, I chugged back the drink but had to set the bottle down as a nervous shaking started in my body. My eyes found Olly's concerned expression, and I understood where she was coming from because I'd seen the same look on Eve's face time and time again, but Jake was different. At least, I believed he was different. Maybe that was foolish, but I genuinely believed every word he said.

"Olly, I promise to tell you all about Jake and me another night and why it is that I'm willing to give him a chance." I held up my hands as her mouth opened—I just knew she was going to argue. "I'm not saying your concerns are not valid, but this is different than my ex, or even your ex. I promise we can sip wine while I tell you all the cute stories everyone has forgotten about to balance out the bad, but right now, I need to talk to him."

Olly stood and shook her head.

"I don't trust him. I don't trust anyone that's like him. They can't settle down. They try, but it never lasts. He also hasn't proven he's really this great new version of himself. How does he, let alone anyone, even know that it will last, that he won't just get bored and pick up where he left off?" she asked.

Jake mumbled something under his breath as he stood and marched for the kitchen.

"I know that's what you think, Olly, but what we see on social media is not the whole story. We both know that." I lowered my voice so only she could hear. "My ex started telling everyone I was mentally ill, that I was depressed and suicidal, and he was seen as some pillar of the community because he was by my side during the 'tough times' as he supported me." I had to pause for a moment—those had been some dark, infuriating days.

"He began posting self-help videos and using fake health issues that I supposedly had to support his own cause. I have no proof, but I just know he was getting ready to either have me locked up or kill me, and everyone would've praised him while crying with him and his crocodile tears over his loss. It took all my strength to leave and start over."

Olly's eyes, filled with equal parts horror and compassion, were hard to meet.

"My life has turned into living each day with a different level of terrified. I'm never at peace, always looking over my shoulder and jumping at every sound."

I rubbed at my face to wipe away the tears as Olly put her hand on my shoulder.

"I know what the eyes of a monster look like, Olly. I know them because I lived with them for ten years. I need you to trust me when I say that the first good night of sleep I've had in years, I had last night. With him. Please let that be enough for you right now and don't worry about all the other stuff," I requested, just a little bit desperate. I needed Olly, and I needed Jake. I needed them to be okay with each other.

"Jesus Christ, why didn't you tell me that? Someone that unhinged can't be trusted. I should have you stay with me and my mom, and we can get ten guard dogs, and I'll work with you at the bakery, and—."

"No. That's the point, Olly," I cut in. "I don't want to live my life like that anymore. This is my fresh start, and I want to treat it like that."

Olly shook her head as she gnawed on her lower lip like a dog with a bone.

"I'm sorry I didn't say anything. I know I should've said something, but I didn't want to give my ex any more power over me, and honestly, I didn't want to bring anyone else into my mess," I said. The irony of that was painful because here my mess was, getting all over everything anyways—as usual. It felt like I'd never be free of the looming shadow of Richard no matter what I did.

"All I can say is that every one of those posts my ex made about me is fake, but he played the part of the bleeding-heart husband so well that anyone who sees them who doesn't know the real me would believe him. So I'm going to ask you to please give Jake a chance if I decide to, for my sake, because you and my friend Eve are the only friends I have in this world, and I don't want to lose you over this."

Olly pulled me into a quick hug.

"That won't happen. I've got your back, and I'd never turn my back on you, girl. You need to know that." She lowered her voice. "I can't guarantee I won't stab Jake if he hurts you, though." She gave me a wink and then looked over her shoulder. Jake was watching us closely as he leaned against the island.

Olly took a deep breath and then sighed like she was resolving herself and coming to terms with the argument being over for the night. Turning, she set the rest of her beer down on the table before staring back at Jake.

"If you hurt her, you'll have to deal with me, and I'll kick your ass," she bit out before turning and making her way to the door. She gave me a hard look as she pulled it open. "If you need me, I'm right next door." I waited until the door was closed before looking over at Jake.

"She makes some valid points, Jake. I haven't seen you in a very long time, last night excluded, and I know nothing about the person you've become since the night we were separated other than the persona you had in your posts."

"I know, and...wait you saw my posts?"

I swallowed hard. "Yeah, how could I not? I thought about reaching out so many times, but you lived this life that I just wasn't interested in and you seemed so happy. I honestly didn't think you'd even remember my name."

"Shit, Kat. Of course, I'd remember you. Part of the reason I started the account was so that if you ever saw me, it would give you a way to reach out."

I shook my head, a sad smile lifting my lip. "Well, aren't we a pair."

Jake sighed. "Look, like I said, I can't and won't deny that I was who you saw in the pictures and videos. To some degree, I still am. I love my bike, and I like to travel and sing and photograph the world and all its wonders. I make no apologies about that," Jake said.

Wrapping my arms around myself, I looked away to gaze at the picture of a large wave hanging on the wall. I felt like a small ship in the harbor staring down that wave as it came for me. Jake's mere presence threatened to suck me up and drag me along with him.

Out of the corner of my eye, I could see Jake moving closer, and I hated that I wanted him to wrap me up in his arms and hold me, but I did. He was the one thing in my life that I'd always clung to fiercely. I'd clung first to the real him and then to his memory, and I had the tarnished pendant to prove it.

I closed my eyes as he pulled me in close just as I'd hoped, immediately melting into the strong hold and letting him guide me to the couch. We ended up with me curled up on his lap, and god, did it feel good. Laying my head against his chest, all I could hear was the thump of his heart—there was something so soothing about the rhythmic sound. He was so warm that all I wanted to do was close my eyes and let myself be swept away by the feel of him, by the calmness he brought simply by being in the same room.

"I want to know what he did to you, Kat. I want to know why you're so scared."

"I don't want to tell you. I'm so ashamed," I said, wishing I could just sink into him and avoid all this—wishing that he, of all people, never had to know any of this. Jake nudged me away from his chest so he could look into my eyes, but I couldn't hold his stare.

"Look at me." Grabbing my chin, he gently lifted my face to look at him. "This is not you. The girl I know has a heart of gold but a back of steel," he said, and I just couldn't. I scooted off his lap and stepped away, a bitter laugh escaping my lips as a horror show of the accident and all that ensued afterward crossed my mind. It felt like the girl in Jake's memories had died long ago.

"Kat, I'm serious. If you don't start talking, then I'll be forced to find out another way, and yes, I'm a fucking asshole for pushing, but one way or another, I will find out what he did. I'd just prefer to hear it from you," Jake said, and I saw red. I spun on him, the anger over everything that happened to me bubbling to the surface in a rush like a geyser.

"You don't want to know, not really. You don't want to hear all the gory details of what he did because all it will do is force you to see how weak and pathetic I really am," I said, practically spitting it out between my clenched teeth.

Jake stood and took a step toward me, but I took a step back. I needed to keep some space between us. The emotions swirling around in my chest were volatile and painful, and I didn't want to say something I'd regret.

"I could never see you as weak, Kat. You've always been so strong, so fearless in pushing for what you want and living your life to the fullest."

"Stop. Just stop." My hands balled into fists.

"Kat, stop beating yourself up," he said, his voice too kind for what I deserved.

"Fine, you want to know? I married Richard just before my twentieth birthday, and I thought I was happy. I easily believed it because after you and I were separated, I ended up in one home after another

—had my arm broken by a girl at one, then I got beaten up at the school I went to every day. Sometimes, it was really bad."

I couldn't even look at Jake to gauge his reaction. Now that the floodgates had opened, it was all pouring out in one big, toxic flood, and I couldn't have stopped if I'd tried.

"I tricked the older woman who ran this little ice cream shop where I worked into signing a letter that said I stayed with her so I could transfer schools. She had terrible eyesight, and I told her that I'd forgotten to get permission for a field trip and begged her to sign. That was horrible of me, who does that to someone?"

I walked around in a small circle, unable to keep still.

"The school accepted the letter and the change of address, and I left foster care and never looked back. It was safer to live out of an ice cream shop. I was sixteen with nowhere to go and lived like a rat, hiding out and begging for everything I had." God, I sounded pathetic even to myself.

"So yes, when Richard suddenly started to pay attention to me in my senior year, I was that typical, gullible girl who fell for it hook, line, and sinker. I was that girl who saw only the charisma and the house bigger than any I'd ever seen, let alone lived in. He always had food on the table without having to beg for it or count every fucking cent. It was the closest to happy I'd been in years, because I felt like I wasn't in a constant state of hyper anxiety over everything."

Needing to get a little more distance, I stomped over to the fridge and pulled out a second beer. Cracking the lid, I took a huge swig. I needed to get this story out. Not even Eve knew all the details of what Richard had done, and I didn't know how much I could get through before I broke down. Jake followed me into the kitchen but stayed on the other side of the island, quietly waiting for me to continue.

"The first few years, it started with things that I didn't even notice as issues—subtle ways he'd make fun of me in front of our friends, like he was being cute. It's hard to explain, but the point is we didn't get married and then the next day he was hitting me, it wasn't like that. Anyway, then it became insults to my face, like telling me that I looked like a slut or that he didn't dare take me out in public because I'd humiliate him. I heard it all. I was pathetic, a loser, a piece of garbage, that I was lucky to be with him, that he didn't know how he put up with me. The list is endless."

I could feel Jake's anger starting to build from across the island, but he'd wanted to know, so he was going to hear about it now.

"Things got really bad when I caught him cheating on me with his secretary, though I'd already had my suspicions before that. I mean, he'd go out and be gone two or three nights in a row and say he was working, but he'd come home smelling like someone else's perfume, and he never wanted to have sex unless he happened to come home drunk and was horny."

Jake made a sound that I could have sworn was a growl, and I looked up to see the anger dancing in his eyes as he gripped the counter.

"Is this too much for you? Because you wanted to know. I told you that you didn't—I told you that you'd see me differently, and you still pushed." I was quickly building up a wall around myself, waiting for him to run for the door and say that I was too damaged and weak and he didn't want anything to do with me. "Now you're seeing the real me, the one that was too weak to stand up for myself. I guess it's better that you know now so you can use the door before..."

I stopped before I said that I fell in love with him all over again. It was pointless to say that, I'd never stopped loving him. One night together and it felt like home and my forever and I didn't want it to end even though it had barely been twenty-four hours since he knocked on my door.

"I don't know if I want to have anything to do with myself, so why should I expect you to be any different?" I took another sip of the beer.

"I don't see you any differently, Kat. Nothing you say will change that. Just continue. Please. I want to know," Jake said.

I took another long sip of the beer before stepping back to lean against the counter behind me.

"It got to the point that I tried to leave him. We ended up in this huge fight that lasted most of the night, and I finally packed a bag while he took a work call. I was heading for the door when he saw me. We struggled and...I fell and hit this decorative marble table in the hall. The scar on my side is not from the car accident, it's from the fact that I practically gutted myself when I fell. It was bad, like I didn't even really know how bad because I was so scared and all I could think was that I needed to get out of the house and run as far as possible."

"Holy shit, Kat." Jake came around the island, but I held up my hand to stop him.

"Don't touch me, not yet, or I won't be able to finish this," I said, meaning every word. I gripped the counter for something to hold on to, absently hoping my nails wouldn't break from how hard they were digging into the underside. Jake looked like he was going to argue but managed to stay put.

"Richard went to get stuff to help, and he was on the phone with 911, but I got up and took off in the car. I know it was stupid, but like I said I was scared. I'd been scared for a long time by then, and all

I could see was my escape narrowing. I realized in that moment just how terrified of him I was, and I needed to get away from the prison he had me in."

I pinched the bridge of my nose to force the tears back. This next part was the really hard part.

"I crashed the car. Thankfully, I didn't hurt anyone other than myself, but I ended up having to have surgery on my spine. I was paralyzed for months. My ex is a doctor, someone everyone idolizes, and the whole time, he had my doctor fooled and the nurses under his spell. I became more trapped than I had been before. In a blink, I'd put myself in a cage and at his mercy. I eventually started getting better, but I didn't dare show Richard my progress. Making him underestimate me was my only hope."

I quickly finished chugging down the beer. This story needed liquid courage and I was thankful for the light buzz that was starting to take effect. My hands were shaking as I set the bottle down, and the sound of it rattling on the counter was loud in the quiet room.

"It got so much worse than I ever could've imagined. It was like a switch was flipped in him, like the accident gave him all the permission he needed to fully become the monster that had always lurked beneath the surface."

I stopped talking, my mouth opening and closing uselessly. I couldn't seem to form the words I needed to say, like saying them out loud to someone would make everything more real somehow. I'd already lived through the nightmare, but I'd managed to push most of it aside to protect myself. I'd been so focused on my goal of escaping that it was all that had occupied my mind, and now that I was actually having to deal with it, I wasn't sure I was ready. To say it now, to form the words....

"Hey, look at me," Jake said as he stepped in front of me and gently placed his hands on my shoulders. I lifted my eyes to his. They were so different from Richard's, so filled with compassion and worry, and I could feel how genuine the emotions radiating off of Jake were. "I'm here now, not him. He can't hurt you, and I'll never let him near you again. No one will ever hurt you again, Kat. I'd kill anyone who tried."

I believed him, and while I should've been terrified that Jake could so easily claim that he'd take someone's life in my name, I couldn't bring myself to care after everything I'd been put through by that man. Jake leaned forward and kissed my forehead.

"I've got you," he said, and I could no longer hold everything inside in the face of his tenderness. The tears burst free and spilled over to trail down my cheeks as my mind traveled back.

"He...he liked the fact that I was paralyzed. He liked that I couldn't move and couldn't fight back. He loved that I couldn't run and had to take whatever he dished out. The look in his eyes was terrifying, Jake. He genuinely enjoyed hurting me," I sobbed. Jake wiped away the tears with his thumbs and remained quiet as I sucked in a deep breath.

"Oh fuck, yes!" The girl hollered like a porn star. For all I knew, she was one. I stared at the ceiling and continued counting backward from a thousand in my head. I needed to find something new to focus on because I could practically sing the numbers now.

Finally finished, the girl lowered her little white tennis skirt and pulled her panties back up. She gave me a smile, and I managed to keep my face neutral until my eyes found Richard. Him, I couldn't help but glare at as the latest girl he'd fucked in front of me made her way to the door.

"I'll be right back, Love Muffin. I just need to walk our guest out." He smiled, and it took everything in me not to scream in rage. Guest? I sucked in a deep breath as my chest heaved with the barely contained anger coursing through me.

I wanted so badly to swing my legs out of bed and show him just how much I'd advanced, maybe punch him in the face and tell him I was filing for a divorce, but if I did that, he'd strap me down—or worse, he'd lock me up in a room I couldn't escape. He was only being blasé with me because he believed I was trapped by my own body. I deserved a fucking Oscar for this performance.

I had no idea what he got out of bringing a new girl to the room at least twice a week for a quick fuck. Did it make him feel powerful that his paralyzed wife couldn't stop him? Yeah, he wasn't powerful—he was a sniveling excuse for a man. As far as I was concerned, the women were no better.

Each one allowed him, a man everyone knew was married, to walk them into the bedroom. The look on their faces when they saw me lying on the medical bed was always comically shocked. They'd gasp and their hands would go up to their pretty mouths in horror or even a little outrage. A few professed to be concerned about doing anything in front of me, like doing it behind my back was any better. That was some moral gymnastics I couldn't even wrap my head around.

Of course, when Richard whispered promises of money or advancement at wherever they worked, they would soften. Their eyes would find mine and then look up at Richard's handsome face, and their shift in priorities was almost palpable. If they could only see past the golden-haired model's face they were captivated by to the ugliness of the real person underneath, they'd spit on it instead of worship it. Probably.

Richards's dutiful speech was always the same. He'd shed a crocodile tear and place his hand over his heart as he poured on the charm. This particular girl's eyes had lit up with excitement as Richard spoke to spin his web of lies.

"My wife always liked to watch. It was kind of our thing. Doing this for her is the least I can do."

"Really? That's so kinky. I'd never have thought it of you, Dr.," she'd tittered.

"I'm just being a good husband. I love my wife and only her, but I want to satisfy all her desires, and right now, this is what I can do for her."

Her hands had flown to her chest as a tear shined in her eye. I'd rolled mine.

"Oh my gosh, that's just so sweet. You have an amazing husband," the girl had said as she looked at me with her big, doe eyes. I still couldn't tell if she was naive or just willfully blind.

Of course, and as always, he'd made sure to drop their used condom into the trash bin right beside my bed so I'd have to stare at it. Sometimes he'd leave them there for days. I knew it was a mind game, just another in the long list that was constantly growing, so I couldn't let it get to me.

I wanted to yell after the girl, ask her how she could believe this crap? It was all lies. If I'd ever even thought about adding a person to our relationship like he went on about, he would've smacked me across the face and called me a cheating whore. He'd flat out said on multiple occasions that he would ruin me if I ever tried to step out on or leave him, that he'd have me locked up in a hospital where I'd never see the outside again.

That was one thing he'd said that I did believe wholeheartedly. He was evil enough, had the Dr., in front of his name and had the money to back him up.

I watched the hands of the clock on the wall slowly tick away. A minute turned into five turned into ten, and then it was already an hour. Taking a deep breath, I figured that Richard had decided to go out for the night and I might be able to relax for a change. By relax I meant work on my exercises until I couldn't lift my arms for real and continue to plan my escape.

Suddenly, I heard feet on the stairs—his feet. It took everything in me to turn my eyes back up to the ceiling and once more mask my real feelings and the internal fury that kept building. I only needed to last a few more months.

Eve had managed to sneak in while Richard was at work a couple of times, and surprisingly, the nurse who stayed with me all day had allowed her to sit at my bed and read. In those moments, we'd planned my escape. It was slow and painful getting everything in place, but the lawyer was close to having my new identity made, and I was almost strong enough to handle a trip.

"Well, what did you think, Kate? Was that fun to watch?" Richard asked as he sauntered over to the bed. He leaned against the mattress, and I couldn't stop myself from glaring at him. He just smirked in response.

"Is that a no? What are you trying to tell me, Kate, that you don't like the little shows? I work very hard to put those on for you, you know."

He used his finger to tuck a strand of hair behind my ear, and I wanted so badly to turn my head and bite it off. Instead, I turned my gaze away from his smug face to stare at the expensive but ugly piece of art hanging on the wall. I'd hated the piece ever since he'd gotten it, and of course, as soon as I'd mentioned I didn't like it, Richard had put it up in our bedroom. Now that I was currently in the spare bedroom, he'd moved the thing in here for me to have to look at all day and night.

"I don't like this attitude from you, Kate," he growled.

I continued to look away from him. I hated him, and I knew that what I was thinking would be burning in my eyes even if I didn't say a word.

"Fine. You want to be a bitch, then I'll treat you like one." Richard straightened up, and fear rippled through my body. "You always were a decent-looking woman." He grabbed the blanket covering me and gave it a hard yank. "Such a shame you did this to yourself. And you did do this to yourself, you know?"

All I could think as he reached for the bottoms of the scrubs I was wearing to yank them down, jerking my body harshly in the process, was that this had to be a movie. This couldn't really be happening to me. The police would storm the door to stop the bad guy, or the director would yell cut, but this couldn't be my life. My heart hammered inside my chest, the elevated blood pressure making me feel lightheaded. 'Don't panic, don't move, keep your shit together, Kat,' I chanted to myself over and over in my head.

Goosebumps rose up all over my body, and I involuntarily shivered as his finger trailed up my legs. I wanted to be sick.

"Still the prettiest pair of legs I've ever seen." He grabbed one ankle and moved it to the side of the bed before doing the same with the other. With everything that had happened, with everything he'd already done to me, I'd never felt more exposed than in that moment. "Maybe what

you need is to get fucked. Is that what you're missing, Kate? My cock being stuffed into your slut hole?"

'Fuck you, you fucking prick,' I screamed inside. I glared at him, willing my eyes to scream out exactly what I was thinking.

"See, that is the look I'm talking about. You're an ungrateful bitch, and you need to be taught your place," Richard said as he unzipped his khakis and revealed his cock to me for the second time that night. Bile rose in my throat.

I was still slow and lumbering. If I tried to fight him now, I knew what would happen. Richard had proven how sick he could be—that there was no low he wouldn't stoop to, no new pain he wouldn't happily inflict. When I failed, I'd experience the full scope of his sickness, and it would be forever.

As he crawled onto the bed between my legs, I pictured him bleeding. I pictured ripping his dick off with my bare hands. Nothing I imagined could hurt him enough to satisfy my fury—but all I could do was lie there and take whatever he decided to do to me.

Traitorous tears spilled over and slid down my cheeks as he pushed himself into me with a hard grunt. Pain ripped through my body at the unexpected assault, and my back seized with the intensity of it. The scream in my mind was loud and unending as I forced myself to lie there as still as a discarded puppet.

"Oh, you're tight," Richard said as he stared down into my eyes. He almost sounded surprised. I couldn't stand looking at him anymore. Letting go of the ego I'd been holding onto, I let my eyes flutter closed. With each press of his hips, my body revolted as my mind tried to crumble. I let my mind wander to anywhere but that room and what was happening to me.

"I like you better like this, Kate," he panted, and a drop of his sweat

hit my cheek. "Oh, so now you cry?" He slammed his hips into me harder. "You can't lie to me, Kate. I know...."

Slam.

"You fucking...."

Slam.

"Love it, you little slut."

Slam.

Against my best efforts, my lower lip trembled in the face of the onslaught. My good hand slowly clenched into a fist as I gripped the sheet, desperate for something to anchor myself with as the bed jolted back and hit the wall with each jerk. Not screaming took every ounce of strength I had, but I was determined—I wouldn't give him that. Richard could try and break me, but I'd never break for him. Not ever again.

"Oh yeah, fuck. Take what I give you, you bitch, take it all," he yelled as he came. The feel of him coming used to be something sexy, something special between us as a couple—something that spoke of a possible family. Now, all it did was make me want to bawl as I prayed to God to not let me get pregnant if he was on my side at all. I couldn't have this monster's child. I just couldn't.

My mind replayed what happened like it was some kind of demonic movie projector shining a gruesome video on the walls. It repeated over and over, just like the real thing had.

"He'd get on the bed...," I forced out, determined to finish now that I'd started. My heart was beating so fast that I could barely catch my breath. "He was so smug as he smirked at me, and he'd say all these terrible things, like how he liked that I was unable to move, as he undressed. He'd sneer that I was his personal rape toy and had to take him as he forced himself between my legs."

Jake's hands tightened on my shoulders. I closed my eyes like it might actually help block out the images of what Richard had done —how he'd grunt in my ear and tell me I was his good little trophy wife as he came.

"He raped me, Jake, over and over, and I just lay there and had to take it." I gasped in a few gulps of air before I managed to make myself pass out. My body just kept trembling. "I couldn't let him know I was healing, couldn't let him know that when he was at work, I was getting stronger and planning to run, but he started to come home every night to torture me. I was his new-found favorite toy—a monster had always lived inside of him, and I'd set it free. I...."

I broke down in sobs. The sheer scope of it all was hitting me, really hitting me, for the first time.

"If he wasn't raping me, he was fucking someone in the room so I had to watch. Please understand that I had to get strong enough first. Please," I begged, covering my face. The shame pressed down on me like a lead weight, and my knees gave way as the pain and terror that had been bottled up tight in my chest burst free.

I clung to Jake as he scooped me up before I could hit the ground and buried my face in his neck. I let it all out. I knew he was speaking to me, something calm and soothing sounding, but I couldn't have repeated a single word he said.

How had I not seen Richard for what he was?

"I hate myself, Jake. I hate that I stayed with him even when he started to treat me like crap. I hate that I didn't leave sooner when I could've. I hate that I married him at all, but most of all, I hate that I didn't try harder to find you, or been brave enough to reach out when I had," I blubbered, unable to see through the tears. It didn't really matter. I knew we were sitting somewhere and that Jake had his arms wrapped around me—that's all I needed to know. "I'd seen your posts. I could've gone to you, but you just seemed so happy, and I...I was so broken...."

Jake cupped my face and gently touched his lips to mine, which wouldn't stop trembling.

"Stop, Kat. You need to breathe before you pass out." He forced me to stare at him and take a few steadying breaths. I could tell he was still angry, but his face showed only concern. It was the calm I needed as I mirrored Jake in taking slow, deep breaths. "Shh, Kat. None of this is your fault."

I shook my head back and forth.

"You don't understand. *Me* of all people—I should've seen the signs. He had the same charismatic smile and glint in his eye that my fucking uncle did. That look that promised pain. Once I saw past it... it was like I'd peeled back his skin to see the lying snake underneath, the kind that promises love to get you close enough to sink his fangs in and rip you apart."

"Whoa, what?" Jake interrupted.

Blinking, I remembered that Jake had never heard how I ended up in foster care. Sure, why not go there, too?

"You never asked how I ended up at the Joneses' with you, did you?" I asked. Looking down at his chest, I saw that it was now wet with my tears.

"I always assumed you were forced into foster care after your parents were killed in the car crash. I mean, you never talked about that time, and I wasn't about to ask. My past wasn't something I liked to share, either, but I never thought that...." Jake's green eyes searched my face. He looked like he'd been punched in the gut. "Kat? Please, please tell me I'm wrong. Please tell me it's not what I'm thinking."

My eyes, unable to hold his any longer, darted away from his pleading stare.

"I wanted to tell you so many times, but I couldn't get the words out. He never...it never got as far as full penetration, but he made me do things, and he touched me and he hit me. I had bruises everywhere. I went to the counselor at my school about it. I thought they'd find a cousin for me to stay with, or something, but that didn't happen. I don't even know why, maybe morbid curiosity, but I looked him up years after I'd been married and found an obituary of him." I remembered clearly staring at the screen and reading the small description that said he had no living relatives. I hadn't cried, but instead was angry. On some level it felt like he'd set me on the path to Richard and maybe I'd been looking for someone to blame for my own shitty actions and decisions.

Jake didn't say anything else. He just grabbed the blanket I had laid across the back of the couch and wrapped it around my shoulders as I shivered. He felt like home as he wrapped me tighter in his arms. He felt like a warm cup of coffee on a cold morning or a good book while curled up by the fire. Jake had always been my everything, even when my life had been at its worst, my heart and mind would always come back to him and long for what had been lost.

"I'm so sorry, Kat. I'm so sorry, and I wish I...god, I wish so many things had been different for you. I love you, and that will never change. Nothing you've said will ever change that—I need you to know that, Kat. I've got you now." Jake kissed the top of my head. "You're not weak. Don't ever say that again, okay?"

I nodded, but it was hard to see the strength in all those bad choices.

"Jake?"

"Yeah, Angel?"

"I love you so much it scares me." I lifted my head to look at him, and he leaned in to kiss my damp cheeks and then my lips.

"Don't ever fear loving me. I won't hurt you, not ever. I pinky promise," he said, making me laugh as he held up his little finger. After I entwined my finger with his, he brought our fingers to his lips to kiss.

"Take a nap, and when you wake up, we'll have dinner," he said.

"That sounds good," I said, already letting my eyes close. I hadn't realized how drained I felt, but in a blink, sleep was already pulling me under into its embrace.

JAKE

IT WAS easy to tell that retelling that story had taken everything out of Kat. As soon as she was asleep, I laid her down on the couch and tucked her in. I couldn't sit still any longer—the anger that had begun at the first inkling of abuse was now a raging bull in my system. It was happening. I was going to kill him. I was going to find the fucking piece of shit and kill him.

My teeth ground together painfully, and only the fact that I was in *Kat's* house was stopping me from putting my fist through the wall. That's just what I needed—to fuck things up for her even more or hell, scare her. She'd had more than any one person should have to live through.

I could've stopped so much of that from happening, and I didn't. I chose to be a coward instead. The memory of Kat walking away from the bridal shop with her friend as I sat there and let her go was seared into my brain like a brand that could never be removed. I didn't deserve to remove it.

Dropping to the floor, I punched out as many pushups as I could before my arms refused to do another. Breathing hard, I flopped over onto my back and stared at the soft cream color of the ceiling.

"Shit," I muttered as I hauled my ass off the floor. Like a moth to a flame, my eyes were drawn to Kat's sleeping face, her features finally relaxed as she rested. Pulling my phone from my pocket, I ignored the thousands of notifications I'd been refusing to check to pull up a search engine.

It took me a minute to remember what Richard's last name was, but as I pictured their wedding announcement, which had always haunted my memories like a ghost, it came to me. As I punched in his name, it felt like I was coating my thumbs in filth.

Kat was getting my last name as soon as she was able to re-marry, and then I'd yell it for every single fucking person to hear. I only wished there were a way to scrub him from her mind the same way I intended to scrub him from the earth—I'd happily do both.

Richard Baldwin. The 'pretty boy' doctor, with his crisp white lab coat and million-dollar smile, appeared immediately at the top of the search. His teeth were so white that he could've been the poster child for a dentist's office—all that was missing was a little sparkle animation. If I were honest with myself, I would never have pegged him for an abuser, and that fact sickened me. Somehow, I should have known. Everyone that has ever come into contact with him should have known. How does his family not know? Was he simply that good at hiding it or were people so unsuspecting that they wrote off the evil that lurked under the surface?

But then again, that was his superpower. Flying under the radar, coming off as the doting husband and hardworking doctor, was the cover for the piece of shit that lay beneath those bright blue eyes. It was the modus operandi for raping bastards like him. As I scrolled to see what I could find out about him without too much effort, the phone buzzed and displayed Tripp's name.

Great. Perfect timing brother. After walking into the kitchen to create a little distance from Kat, I hit talk.

"Hey, I can't deal with you and Lanny stuff right now. I don't even want to know if the two of you have fucked up the plans I made," I snarked.

"Don't be a dick, we got that shit sorted out. It's Mom," Tripp said, which shocked me out of my rage as effectively as if an actual bucket of cold water had been dumped on my head. I felt just as chilled. "She's having a bad reaction to the chemo," he continued. "I don't know all the details. Dad took her to the hospital and asked if I could let everyone know."

"Shit, okay. I'll be there as soon as I can." After ending the call, I closed my eyes and just stood there for a moment as I battled the fear that my mom wasn't going to be okay. I knew it wouldn't be easy, but I didn't think it would be this difficult to see her going through all this. I just felt so useless and unable to help. 'Feeling useless' and I were not friends, but I was experiencing a severe double dose of it tonight.

Hands slipped around my waist as Kat pressed herself against me. I must not have been as quiet as I'd thought.

"Are you okay?" she asked.

Turning in her arms, I kissed her forehead, already feeling calmer with her touch, and pulled her tighter against me. How was it that she'd always been the steadying force in my life even when we'd been so far apart? This woman had a power over me that I'd never be able to explain to anyone.

"It's my mom. She's in the hospital."

Kat's eyes went wide and she pulled away sharply, breaking my hold on her. I stared after her as she dashed from the room, but a moment later, she was back in jeans and a sweater and stuffing her arms into a jacket. I hadn't even known it was humanly possible to get changed that fast, and I'd seen models backstage at a fashion show. They had nothing on Kat.

"Well, what are you standing around for? Let's go," she said. Stunned, I opened my mouth and then closed it again as she grabbed her purse off the island and jogged to the door.

"You want to come to the hospital?" I asked. The second the words left my mouth, I knew it was a stupid question. Of course my perfect Kat did. That was exactly the kind of person she'd always been.

"Do you not want me to come? Oh, I guess I should've made sure you were okay with it...maybe you don't want me to meet your family yet, or ever, or...," she mumbled, hands on the collar of her jacket like she was debating pulling it off again. God, I loved her. The chill that had engulfed me lifted as I met her at the door and laid my hands on her shoulders to stop the panicked rant.

"I want you to meet my family. I just didn't think you'd want this to be the way you meet them," I said. She looked so fucking adorable when she nibbled on her lip like that when she was nervous—unable to help myself, I dropped my lips to hers.

"You're mine, Kat, and that means that whatever is mine is yours, including my crazy-ass family." Her cheeks pinked in a blush, and my one-track mind could only picture pushing her over the arm of the couch for a quickie, but I reigned in the urge. "You may regret wanting to meet them, but it's too late now 'cause you're stuck with me."

"I'd never regret anything with you," she whispered, and I grabbed her hand, running my thumb over her naked ring finger. I had to get her out of the house before I did something that would end with us naked.

"Are you sure after what you just shared that you're up for this? Just so you know, my mom is fighting cancer. She's having a reaction to the chemo."

"Oh my god, Jake. I'm so sorry." Kat hugged me hard. Wrapped up in her arms like that, I never wanted to leave these four walls—just let them keep all the crap and worry out there and us inside. "I feel better now that you know."

I kissed the top of her head taking an extra moment. "We'd better go," I said.

After pulling on my jacket, I took her hand again, and then we were off and out the door. The chill in the early fall air was noticeable during the short walk to the bike, and as Kat climbed on behind me, I knew the first thing I needed to buy her was her own leather jacket. I had a need to take care of my girl.

Old school, over the top protective? Maybe, but it was who I was when I was around her. She made me want to do things that I never felt with anyone else. Like feed her in bed, massage her body after a long day and draw her a hot bath. I wanted to cook her meals that didn't taste like cardboard and make her laugh until her stomach hurt. She needed more smiles in her life and I was the one who wanted to put them on her face. I was all in and that meant whatever Kat needed me to do phys-ically, emotionally, financially and of course sexually, I was here for.

The drive to the hospital took over half an hour, and I could tell Kat was getting pretty cold by the end of it. When she snuggled in, tucking herself tighter against me, I could feel her body shivering against mine. That wasn't the kind of shivering I wanted to share with her.

"We're almost there," I yelled over my shoulder, and her head nodded against my shoulder in response.

The glowing blue H shone like a beacon on the multi-story building as I crested the last rise to the hospital. This late at night, the lot was practically vacant, so I was able to get a spot close to the door. Kat hopped off quickly, probably ready for some warmth, but her hands were shaking so badly that she couldn't undo the strap on the helmet. Taking her hands in mine, I blew on them—it was like a punch to the heart seeing her shudder and smile at me in gratitude.

Once her hands were no longer little blocks of ice, I undid the clasp myself and stuffed the helmet in the side saddlebag before wrapping my arm around Kat to walk inside. As soon as the automatic doors slid open, I did some shivering of my own, and not because of the cold. Ever since the night that had landed me in foster care, I'd never liked hospitals.

I ran down the hall to our apartment, skidding to a stop outside the door. Mom was going to kill me for being late for dinner. Again. Grabbing the handle, I gave it a turn, but unlike every other day when I

came home, it wouldn't budge. Weird. Putting both hands on the handle, I tried again, but it still wouldn't turn.

Clutching my Wolverine backpack to my chest, I knocked on the door and then pressed my ear against it. I tried to hear if Mom or Dad were coming, but all I could hear was the television. It sounded like one of those shouty news stations.

"Man," I grumbled before knocking as hard as I could. If they were ignoring me, I was in a lot more trouble than I'd thought. My heart thundered in my chest as I winced at the thought. I hated getting spanked, and my butt still hurt from the last round even if it had been Dad doing the spanking. Dad's hand hurt less than Mom's, but I wouldn't tell her that because she thought Dad's was worse.

When there was still no answer, or even any movement, I looked around at all the closed doors along the hallway. Nibbling on my bottom lip, I wondered what to do. A check under the mat revealed no key, just an old stain and a dead ant. I quickly dug around in my backpack, but I couldn't find my spare key either. When had I lost that?

I tried knocking again. This time, my fist thudded against the wood loudly enough to make it echo all up and down the hall.

"Mom! Dad!" I shouted.

"What the hell is all the yelling for?" a gruff voice suddenly demanded.

Shoot. Cringing, I turned to look at our grouchiest neighbor, Mr. Brown, and stared up at his old wrinkly face and the mean look he was giving me. He placed his hands on his hips as he glared.

"Well, don't just stand there staring at me like you're daft. Why are you yelling?" Mr. Brown asked.

"Um...I can't get into my apartment," I whispered.

"What did you say, boy? I'm old, can't you see that? You need to speak up so I can hear you."

Clearing my throat, I gripped my backpack a little tighter for courage and tried again.

"I can't get in. My mom and dad are home, I think, but no one is coming to unlock it." I pointed to the door, which was still stubbornly shut.

"Humph. Alright, come on in, kid. I'll call the Super." Mr. Brown stepped to the side and held open his door for me to enter.

I didn't want to go into Mr. Brown's apartment—it smelled like mothballs and old people in there—but looking back at my own door, I realized my only options were to go with him or try to find someone else to help. That probably wasn't happening.

As I stepped into the dark and smelly apartment, my nose wrinkled up at the stench. Mr. Brown shuffled slowly across the orange, fur-like carpet, which covered every room that I could see and looked just as old as he was, to get to the phone sitting on the table beside his couch. He practically collapsed onto the ugly gold and black monstrosity. He picked up the receiver to dial but then stopped and looked over to where I was still standing in the doorway.

"You gonna come in or just stand there lookin' stupid?"

"I'm not stupid," I said, lifting my chin. What a butthead.

"I didn't say you are stupid, I said you look stupid—there's a differ-ence," he said as he poked at the buttons on the phone and then held the receiver to his ear. Yeah, total butthead.

"Hey, Gary. It's Martin Brown callin'. We have a little situation. The Bentley's kid...." He covered the receiver and looked at me. "What's your name again?"

"Jake."

"The Bentley's kid, Jake, can't get into his apartment. I don't know. How am I supposed to know that? Just come open the door so he'll stop screaming the hallway down."

"I wasn't," I huffed, glaring.

"Alright, I'll let 'em know." Mr. Brown hung up the phone and stared at me where I was still standing. "Gary's on his way up."

"Thanks," I said, turning to slip out into the hallway and wait.

"Geez, kid, what's your hell-fired hurry?" Mr. Brown groaned as he stood. Even when he got all the way up, he was still slightly bent over. He probably needed a cane or something.

"I can wait alone."

"Fat chance. If you got sold, I'd be to blame. I'm too damn old for that to be on my conscience."

I wasn't sure what that meant, but I nodded anyway and waited for him before going out the door.

A few minutes later, the Super arrived with the ding of the elevator. He didn't look any happier than Mr. Brown had about helping me—his scowling face was as red as a tomato as he stared at the handful of keys he was sorting through one by one. When he reached where we were standing, he glanced up and looked me over like I'd been doing something bad.

"You know if your parents are home, kid?" the Super asked. I nodded, too scared to open my mouth. "Do they let you wander around alone a lot?" I shrugged, not sure what to say to that.

"How old are you?"

"Eight. Why?"

"No reason," he said before turning to the door with a key in hand.

As the lock clicked and the door swung open, my life changed forever. There were some moments you never wanted to forget and others you wished you could , but they were seared into your brain for all time.

I bolted through the open door, blood pounding hard in my ears, and stared down at my mom. She was lying in what looked like a pool of blood. It was everywhere. As I lifted my shoe to step closer, I heard a squelching sound, and I realized I was standing in it.

I could hear a lot of noise behind me, but it didn't matter. All I could focus on was my mother's still face and the blood that soaked her shirt. Dropping to my knees, I grabbed her shirt and shook her.

"Mom, wake up!" I shouted. When I pulled harder, her head rolled toward me. Her soft green eyes stared at me, but they didn't blink.

The room became even louder and filled with people. Someone pulled on me, forcing me to let go of my mom even though I tried my best to hold on tight. I screamed for her in desperation, then realized I'd been screaming for her the whole time. She hadn't answered.

Tears poured down my cheeks as a police officer sat with me in a patrol car parked by an ambulance and asked me questions. I didn't look at him or speak—I had no answers to give. I just stared at the flashing lights on the other patrol cars, and I barely registered the drive to the hospital.

At the hospital, a woman in a pants suit holding a clipboard sat with me for a long time, but all my focus was on my blood-stained hands. No matter how many times they'd washed them for me or what they'd used, I could still see the red. The harsh smell of the strong cleaners the hospital used irritated my nose, and the unending sound of walking feet and beeping machines hurt my ears.

"Can I see my mom?" I asked.

"I'm sorry, sweetie, but your mom has passed away," she said. She *laid her hand on my shoulder, but it didn't feel good. Her hand didn't feel right.*

"Where's my dad?" I asked, desperate for something familiar. She didn't answer as she looked away and removed her hand.

"Why don't we get you some food and find you a place to sleep for the night? We can talk about the rest once you've had some sleep." The lady—I couldn't remember her name—stood and held out her hand to me. Reaching forward, I put my hand in hers.

"Hey."

That was Kat's voice. Kat was shaking my arm.

"You okay?" she asked softly.

I looked down into her worried expression and realized that I was holding her tightly and hadn't taken a step further inside. In fact, the doors were trying to close, but we were standing just close enough that they reopened each time they tried. Several people in the admission area were staring. Swallowing hard, I sucked down the emotion making its way up my throat.

"Yeah, I'm sorry. I just...I'm not a big fan of hospitals."

The corners of her mouth pulled down.

"Neither am I," she murmured. Her voice sounded sad, and I realized that being here like this had to be even harder for her. Caught up in my own thoughts, I hadn't even taken a moment to consider how she might feel about coming here because of what happened to her after the accident, and then everything after that with Richard.

"Oh shit. Kat, I'm sorry. I wasn't even thinking. Are you okay? You don't have to come any further."

"Yeah, I'm good. The hospital sucked, but it wasn't the hospital I had a problem with, just the man I was married to. Let's go see your mom." She pulled on my hand as she stepped forward, and that seemed to kick my feet into gear. I tucked her in tight beside my body.

"You haven't changed. Always looking out for everyone," I said. I hated seeing the sadness hidden behind the smile she gave me in response.

"I've changed, but I'm trying to be a better, smarter version of myself. Not sure if I'm even close yet, but I'm getting there," she said with a wry grin. The room we were passing, some kind of examination room, was empty, and Kat squealed as I dragged her inside and closed the door. "What are you doing?"

I trapped her against the door with an arm on either side of her—tossing her on the examination table was tempting, but someone could come knocking at any time. Dropping my mouth down to Kat's, I kissed her like I thought it was going to be the last time. She melted into my hold, her soft moans making my body sing.

"Life is only filled with small moments, and we can't cling to any of them. That is the nature of life," I said against her lips. "I'm not taking another moment for granted. From now on, I'm going to be greedy about our time. I don't want us to miss another single moment when we could be happy together." I kissed her long and slow for an eternity before finally breaking the kiss to lay my forehead against hers.

"I'd get prepared for just about anything if I were you, because you make me want to do a wide assortment of naughty things to you," I whispered. Kat full-body shivered from head to toe, but this time it was in the good way and made me smirk

"I'd forgotten what it was like to live in the moment," she whispered, and my heart ached all over again.

"Well, my mom has been preaching to me for years that I need to start doing things that actually make me happy. She and my dad are big believers in living in the moment, so I'm going to take a page out of their book. Are you with me?" I asked, lifting my head to stare into the prettiest pair of blue eyes that had ever walked the earth.

"Yeah, I always have been," she said, and my legs shook. I wanted to drop to my knees, grip her tightly, and never let go. I didn't deserve her, but there was no way I was letting her go.

"I have something I need to tell you after we leave, and I don't know if you'll ever be able to forgive me, but...." My thumb ran across her bottom lip. "I need to tell you."

"Oh, okay. Oh crap, do you have a girlfriend? Are you married?" There was no holding back my smile or the chuckle that burst out of me.

"No, there is no girlfriend or secret marriage. There has only ever been one woman I wanted to marry, and she's in this room." The dark blush that crossed her cheeks had me smiling wider. "No, it's something else. Just, please, remember that I was twenty, okay?"

Kat's eyebrow lifted as she searched my face for answers.

"Alright. You're kind of freaking me out, though," she said, evidently satisfied to wait.

Kissing the tip of her nose, I stepped away from the door so she could follow my lead. Opening the door, I peered out carefully, only to receive a strange look from one of the nurses further down the hall. His expression made us both laugh as we scooted out and continued on our way.

If I could go back in time, there were so many things that I'd do differently. Living with regrets in your soul was a terrible thing, and there was a lot that I regretted. But I planned on making at least one thing right.

BEST
FRIENDS

28

KAT

AS WE ROUNDED the corner and five pairs of eyes swung in our direction, I suddenly wasn't feeling so confident about meeting Jake's family. I recognized two of the men leaning up against the wall —they'd been at the vineyard the day that Olly and I had been there. One of them had even hit on Olly. He had the type of face you didn't forget easily. That meant the lovely woman I'd been walking with....

"What's your mom's name?" I whispered.

"That's one of the things I need to talk to you about. My mom is Joy Russell. You already met her when you came to the family farm," Jake said. He rubbed the back of his neck as I stared at him with my mouth wide open.

"You saw me? You saw me at the vineyard and didn't say anything?"

His face morphed into the expression he'd worn when he'd done something I wasn't going to like when we were kids. That was not helping my anxiety.

"Yeah...can we talk about it later?" he asked with a grimace. I wanted nothing more than to poke at him and make him tell me everything, but I packed it away for later as we reached the waiting group. All their eyes went to our linked fingers, and I wanted to squirm under their inquiring stares.

"Kat...shoot. I mean Lexi." Jake paused and looked at me, his eyes worried. He hadn't been kidding when he said he'd mess up with my name.

"It's okay. Your family can know," I whispered close to Jake's ear before turning back to face the small crowd. "My name was Kate, or Kat, but I'm going by Lexi now," I said, not offering any more explanation. People changed names all the time, after all.

"This is my family. You might remember my dad, Mark. The two jokers here are my younger brother, Jayce, and my older brother, Tripp, and these two rug rats are Tripp's girls, Sydney and Brianna," Jake said, pointing out each person in turn as we took turns shaking hands.

When it was Sydney's turn, she grabbed on and gave my hand a hard shake. Her grip was so much stronger than I would've expected for a girl her age.

"You can call me Syd, and my sister prefers Bri. Who are you, and how do you know my uncle?" Syd asked, finally releasing my hand only to put her small fists on her hips. It was freaking adorable.

"Sydney Russell, that was very rude. You apologize right this instant," Tripp said, giving his daughter a hard stare. The young girl pulled her long blonde hair over her shoulder and played with the ends as she pushed out her bottom lip.

"I'm sorry," she said, voice small and eyes downcast.

"Actually, it is a fair question." I knelt down so I was the same height as her. "I'm a longtime friend of your Uncle Jake, but...we lost touch years ago and only just found each other again."

"Are you going to have kids so we can have cousins?"

Jesus Christ. I...*what*?

"Oookay, that's enough with the questioning, Syd," Jake said, and I was happy he'd taken that question head-on, as my brain had stalled. I had no idea how in the world to answer that question. I was expecting do you like my outfit or want to know what I learned in school, but having kids with Jake...that came out of left field.

"It's nice to meet you, Lexi." Mark stepped forward and pulled me into a hug. My initial impression of him hadn't changed. He was as tall as Jake but built like a bear, and I felt like he could crush all my bones with a single squeeze if he wanted to—I was just as certain that he never would.

"Anyone who can make my Jakey-boy smile like that is family to me. Welcome." Mark took a step back but kept his hands on my shoulders, and after a moment, his face lit up even more. "Wait, I *do* know you. You're the one who owns the bakery. That's what Jake meant when he said you might remember. Gosh, I thought I recognized you. I'm sorry, my mind is so scattered right now, what with Joy not doing well. She is going to be so excited to see you."

"It's perfectly fine, and no worries at all. This must be so hard on all of you. How is she?" I asked. Mark sighed and proceeded to take a seat in one of the chairs lining the wall.

"She's tough. She never wants us to see her struggling, but this was different. She's been really weak lately, and then she started throwing up non-stop and fell over and hit the wall." Mark raised a shaking hand to point to the room across the hall. "She's in there right now, but she refused to have any of us in there with her while the doctor is examining her."

I could see the pain on his face as clearly as I could see that the hospital's walls were painted a soft yellow. He very obviously didn't like being shut out, which was understandable, but I got where Joy was coming from as well. When you were a tough, independent woman used to taking care of everyone else, you hated being the one who needed to be looked after.

"Has the doctor been out?" I asked.

"Not yet," Mark said.

"I need some air. I'll be back," Jayce abruptly said before he pushed away from the wall and left the group.

"I'd better go talk to him," Jake said, giving my hand a squeeze before he left to follow his brother.

After I took a seat beside Mark, the two girls slowly made their way over like they wanted to inspect me up close. It was kind of like being inside a fish bowl, but with the most adorable people watching me.

"Would you like me to braid your hair?" I asked, figuring it would make a good peace gesture. I really wanted these girls to like me.

"Fench baid, pease," Bri cried, clapping her hands together in excitement.

Syd rolled her eyes.

"Don't mind her. She just lost a tooth, and now she sounds funny."

"I do ot," Bri protested before plopping herself down in front of me. Luckily, both she and her sister were already wearing hair ties that I could repurpose.

I laughed and lifted my eyes to look over at Tripp as I started finger combing his daughter's hair. If Jake hadn't said that Tripp was also adopted, I would've thought he was related to Mark by blood. He hadn't said anything so far aside from when he'd said hello and scolded Syd. His eyes seemed to be carrying the weight of the world in them.

I wanted to say something, make some conversation to ease the tension in the air, but I wasn't sure what to say. What words could make any of this better? As my fingers worked at putting a French braid into Bri's hair, I had a thought.

"I think Joy had a great idea," I blurted out, and both Tripp and Mark's eyes swung around to find mine. "After giving it some consideration, I love the idea of showcasing some local talents in my store, and Joy's pirate cookies are going to be the first to have a space. They come highly recommended."

"Really? Grandma Joy's cookies are going to be in a store? That's so cool!" Syd smiled widely, clearly delighted with the news.

"Mmm, I want pirate cookies," Bri offered as she ran her fingers over her braid. I finished up and tied off the end. "Do they have them here?"

"No, silly, we're in a hospital, not at Grandma's," Syd said, shaking out her thick blonde locks for me to braid as she nudged her sister over to take her place.

It was easy to see how close this family was, how much they were there for one another and loved each other, and a part of me couldn't help but wish that I'd found something resembling this when I'd been separated from Jake all those years ago.

Maybe then, I wouldn't have married someone as toxic as Richard. Maybe I wouldn't have been scared enough to cling to the first man who came along promising to be real despite the eventual warning flags, and maybe I wouldn't have lost who I was while trying to please someone else. If I hadn't been so damn desperate, who knows how different things could've been?

"That's really nice…," Mark started before stopping to clear his throat. It looked like he was trying to swallow down the overwhelming emotions. "Joy will love that."

The sound of Jake's voice reached my ears from down the hall just as my fingers finished twisting a hair tie, complete with fashionable bobbles, around the end of Syd's braid. I turned to look for him as she bounced up, obviously pleased.

"I love it," Syd squealed before she dashed toward Jake to show off her new hairstyle. Bri was tailing her in seconds, and as they reached him, Jake scooped up both girls with little effort. He listened to them as they chattered animatedly and showed off their braids as if what they were saying was the most important thing to have ever happened to him.

Just as their small party reached the group, Joy's door opened and the doctor, a middle-aged man with glasses, stepped out into the hall.

"How is she?" Mark asked as he stood, his height making him tower over the doctor.

"How could you let this happen?" Tripp growled, edging closer.

"Do you know what caused this?" Jake piped in, placing a restraining hand on Tripp's shoulder.

"Can we take her home?" Jayce asked.

The doctor looked between all four men and seemed unsure which question to answer first. He apparently decided to go with the husband's and turned slightly toward Mark.

"Joy is stable and resting comfortably. The loss of balance and falling she experienced were always a possibility. It's a condition called neuropathy. I spoke to Joy at length about the side effects that could occur, and unfortunately, this is one of them. It's where nerve damage occurs in the extremities, and in her case, her feet."

"But she'll be okay, right?" Jake asked as he took my hand in his like he needed the support.

"Yes. She didn't wait and came straight in, so it is my professional opinion that she will make a full recovery. However, we will keep a close eye on her. I'm going to be changing her medication, and I'm going to give you a list of things she needs to be careful while doing to avoid injury."

The doctor held up a hand as all the guys tried to ask more questions. Amazingly, they stopped.

"Yes, she can go home, and I'll be giving her a new medication to help with the vomiting. If her symptoms persist, then I've instructed her to come in right away."

"I'll make sure she comes in," Mark said. "Can we go in and see her now?"

"Yes, you...." The poor doctor didn't get any more out before he was almost run over by the stampede of concerned family members racing to get into the room.

"Sorry about that," I offered with a shrug, not sure if I should follow the group or not.

"Don't be sorry. I'd rather see patients have this kind of support than no one." He pushed his glasses farther up his nose before turning and making his way down the hall. I knew all too well how true that statement was. If it hadn't been for Eve, I would've been completely alone in my personal hell. Richard's false claims of love and worry didn't count as real affection.

The door opened again and Jake stuck his head out.

"Are you coming in?"

Swallowing down the small bubble of fear that had decided to float up and get lodged in my chest, I took a step toward the door. Everyone had been great so far, or as great as a group of seriously stressed-out people can be, but my past experiences kept me waiting for the other shoe to drop.

My introduction to Richard's family hadn't gone very well. They hadn't seemed to like a single thing about me and had made sure to let me know all the ways I'd never be good enough to marry their son. Nothing says 'warm and fuzzy welcome' like being told straight to your face that you'd never really be part of the family.

With all the large men filling it up, the decently sized hospital room felt small. It was a good thing no one was in the second bed, or there wouldn't have been any room left at all.

"Well, as I live and breathe. Lexi?" Joy asked, visibly perking up from having an unexpected visitor.

"Hi, Mrs. Russell. It's good to see you again. I just wish it were under better circumstances," I said as I made my way to the side of the bed. She held out her hand for me to take. Syd and Bri were curled up on the bed with her like a pair of cats, and Bri already looked to be fast asleep.

"First of all, you call me Joy, and I mean it. Mrs. Russell sounds too formal, and it definitely sounds way too old. Second, I'm just happy that this stubborn oaf finally spoke to you. Would you believe he's been scared to talk to you?" She pulled on my wrist until I had to sit on the edge of the bed or risk toppling over her.

Glancing up at Jake to check the veracity of her claim was enlightening. He immediately looked away as his face turned a healthy shade of red. He crossed his arms over his chest and refused to meet my stare. Very telling.

"Really? This is news to me," I said, grinning.

"Oh yes. He's been pining after you for *years*."

"Okay, Mom. We can put a pin in this topic now," Jake said, and there was a collective snicker from around the room. The warmth of Jake's family was infectious, and there was no holding back from smiling along with them. Never in a million years could I picture the social media mogul Jake Russell being nervous to talk to me—the idea had a certain appeal.

"We'll talk later when it's just us girls and I'm feeling a bit more myself. I have tons of embarrassing stories for you," Joy said, giving me a wink as Jake shook his head in a horrified no.

Joy winced as she leaned forward, probably to push herself up further on the bed, and Mark was right there fluffing Joy's pillow as soon as she'd moved even slightly. The little gesture would've seemed insignificant to anyone else, but to me, it spoke of how in tune they were with each other and how much love was shared between them. They were the relationship that people strived for, the one they could only hope they would be lucky enough to find.

I hadn't had many of those special kinds of moments, but the ones I did have, I clung to with both hands and appreciated on a level most others took for granted. Jake casually placing his hand on my shoulder as everyone continued talking while waiting for the doctor to return was one of those moments for me. It was so natural and uncomplicated. So perfect.

Against all odds, we'd finally found one another again. There was no telling how long it would last, and there were so many things about Jake's life I still didn't know, but I'd learned never to take gifts from the universe for granted. As Jake and I said our goodbyes to everyone for the night a little later, it really felt like, for once, I'd been truly blessed.

"Kat." Jake pulled on my hand, bringing me to a halt as we reached his motorcycle. "Thank you for coming with me and...." He sighed and looked at the ground like he was gathering himself for something. When he looked back up, he reached out to tuck a few strands of hair behind my ears. His thumbs lingered as soft as kisses on my cheeks.

"I don't know what I ever did to deserve finding you again, but I'm hoping that what I need to tell you won't ruin this."

"You keep saying that. What's going on?" I asked. The nervous butterflies that always fluttered around my stomach when he was near took full flight as my fear of what Jake might say ratcheted. What could be so terrible that he'd be this scared to tell me?

Jake rubbed at his face as he began pacing a line between a nearby bench and me. The breeze had picked up, and while the cool air made me shiver and pull the jacket tighter around myself, I wasn't entirely sure how much of my body's reaction actually had to do with the weather. The coldness I was feeling was more than skin deep.

Good things didn't seem to stick for me. It was like I was allergic to them—inevitably, they would eventually disappear, warp, or turn against me—so standing there staring at Jake's terrified face, my instinct was to prepare for the worst. The worst meant he had decided we were over before we'd even really gotten going.

"So, first, I need to tell you about what my mom was referring to." He stopped pacing and turned to face me. "I saw you the day of your bakery's grand opening. I was there with my mom and had no idea the new owner was you until I walked in the door. I just froze and couldn't bring myself to speak to you." He scrubbed at the back of his head sheepishly.

"Then, you showed up on the family farm. I was busy working and spotted you. I thought my mind was playing tricks on me at first, but even when I knew it was you, I once more slunk away like a damn coward." He placed his hands on his chest. "I'm such a fucking idiot."

"Oh...." My initial fear plummeted, and I couldn't help but laugh. "That's what you were worried about telling me? I mean, I probably would've done the same thing." Smiling, I took a step in his direction, but he held up his hand.

"No, that's not everything."

"Okay, enough, Jake. Just spit it out already. You're freaking me out." Crossing my arms over my chest. I was going to pass out if he kept making my blood pressure yo-yo like this.

"I'm sorry. I'm just nervous. You make me nervous—you always have," Jake said, shocking me. I'd never seen Jake act like this. He'd always come across as cool and in control, even in foster care, so I had no idea what he meant by that.

"Don't look at me like that," he muttered. "You *know* how I've always felt about you. You've always been able to make me melt with a single look."

Stepping forward, I grabbed his hands, and he immediately pulled me against his body and enveloped me in his warmth.

"Just tell me, Jake."

"It's my fault," he said so quietly that I barely heard him.

"What's your fault?"

"That you married Richard, that everything you experienced

happened and all you endured—and I don't know if I can forgive myself for it, let alone expect you to forgive me."

Taking a step back, I stared up at his troubled face and the worry etched in his eyes.

"Okay. You're going to have to explain that one to me," I said.

He swallowed loudly enough that I could hear it over the rustling leaves.

"I found you before you got married. I actually saw the wedding announcement that was plastered all over the Las Vegas social sites and hunted you down. I saw you leave the wedding dress store with your friend, and you looked so happy," he said. There was a faint ringing in my ears.

"From what I'd read, the guy you were going to marry had it all— the looks, the family, the money. He could give you the life you'd always deserved, but I had nothing to offer. I was surfing couches while I tried to make a career for myself as an actor, and it wasn't going anywhere," he continued.

My mind was blank. I didn't even know how to process the information, let alone what to say, and stepped back to begin my own pacing.

"Kat, I can't tell you how many times I've replayed that day over in my mind and thought about what might've happened if I'd just not cared about your happiness. I know that sounds stupid, but if I'd been as selfish then as I am now, I would've stormed across the street and told you not to marry him. I thought I was doing the noble thing. Please say something."

"I don't know what to say." My eyes locked with his as a whirlwind of emotions swirled up in my chest and dragged me through the gauntlet. How did you even break something like that down? I was confused and hurt, and the hurt was dumb because it wasn't like he'd done it to hurt me or could've known how Richard would turn out. "I need time to process this," I whispered.

"Shit. Kat...."

Holding up my hand, I stopped whatever it was he was going to say. My emotions were so all over the place that I was worried I was going to burst into a round of hysterical tears. In the past, I'd always leaned on my memories of Jake for support when I had a problem, but this time, Jake himself was part of the problem.

"I'm not saying that I suddenly don't want us to be together or anything like that, but I need some time to process. And please, I know you find it hard, but please call me Lexi in public."

He opened his mouth like he wanted to argue but then snapped it shut and nodded.

"Okay. Let's get you home."

The ride back to my small house felt a lot colder. It was like someone had stolen the warm light that had begun burning in my life the last couple of days from having Jake in it. It wasn't fair. Everything that had happened to me was because of my choices, and I couldn't pretend otherwise, but it was a kick in the teeth to think that everything I'd been through could've been avoided if just one thing had gone differently.

When we finally got there, we walked together along the path to the front door of my house, and every step felt heavier. My stomach churned and my heart hurt. Old scars from what Richard had done twinged, and my body had started to tremble. That was the problem with trauma—I could never seem to pinpoint what would set me off, what would bring it all back or make it feel like a vice was tightening around my throat.

Unlocking the door, I turned to face Jake.

"I think I need to be alone tonight." As hard as it was to stare into his worried eyes, I forced myself to lift my chin. I couldn't read the expression on his face as his spring-green eyes searched my own. "I'm not angry. I just really want to deal with this news on my own. I...."

"It's okay, I understand." Jake wrapped his arms around me to give me a hug, which still felt amazing, before his lips grazed my forehead. I hugged back, balling my hands into fists to resist the urge to grip him tight and not let go. "Good night, Kat."

Breaking the hug, Jake walked away, but he waited until I had my door open before he waved and revved his motorcycle to life. A terrible feeling welled up inside me, making my chest ache as the red taillight disappeared down the street.

Of all the things I thought Jake might say, nothing could've prepared me for the knowledge that the hell I'd lived through had almost been avoided. Lip trembling, I marched for the bedroom. It was too much. Dropping onto the bed, I buried my head in my pillow to drown out a scream that would've brought the neighbors running. It felt like I might die if I didn't let this feeling inside of me out somehow.

Rolling over, I let my eyes blearily focus on the lines of the tongue and groove ceiling. Like a movie playing out before me, images of Jake and me getting married, having kids, and living the life I'd always fantasized about danced vividly across the cream-colored wood.

I'd have worn eggshell to my wedding instead of the stark white that Richard's mother had insisted on even though it washed me out. I would've chosen green to match Jake's eyes for my main color instead of the vibrant red that, once again, Richard's mother had insisted on, and I would've carried the spring flowers I'd wanted, fun tulips and pretty daisies or pansies, instead of red and white roses that didn't say one thing about me.

I would've had Jake wear his black jeans instead of some over-priced tux—I didn't care if they were unorthodox, they were him. Our wedding would have been *real*, not some caricature of one that just went along ticking off other people's boxes.

Tears ran freely down my cheeks as more images formed in my mind. What would our children have been like...what would they *be* like now? Would our home be filled with just as much laughter as I'd always pictured rather than the fear and coldness I'd experienced?

Back then, confronted with the boy of my childhood dreams, would I have left Richard to run off with Jake? I didn't really know for sure—after all, nineteen-year-old me had thought she was in love. Despite that, the anger I felt was almost palpable, like sucking on sour lemons.

Limbs heavy and heart aching from the emotional weight of the day, I managed to get myself peeled off the bed for a quick shower. By the time I made it back, there were simply no more tears left to cry. The streams of sadness had run like taps stuck on full for so long that by the time I crawled under the blankets, all that remained was a desert in my soul that left me numb.

29

JAKE

MY BIKE ROARED as I flew down the road at a breakneck pace. I kept berating myself for telling Kat so soon, while things were still so fragile. I should have at least waited until we'd spent more time together—but I knew I couldn't have looked her in the eyes and kept it secret. I couldn't do that to my Kat.

The gravel crunched as I pulled into Tripp's driveway. A slithering white fog parted before the motorcycle as I wove my way under the dense canopy of the surrounding trees, which blocked out most of the moon's weak light. It was a haunting, ghostly effect, but I wasn't exactly in the mood to appreciate it.

While Tripp's truck was in the driveway, the house was dark, so my arrival probably hadn't been noticed. I sat on the bike for a moment to collect myself before going inside. I wanted to text Kat to say something, anything, but what? What would make the knowledge that both of our lives could've been completely different had I simply *spoken* to her any better?

Lights pulled into the driveway as I hopped off the bike, and I shaded my eyes to try to see better as a vehicle I didn't recognize got closer. The vehicle stopped a few car lengths away, making it impossible to see who was inside. The passenger side door opened and Lanny stumbled out, laughing and clinging to the door just to stand.

What the fuck?

"Lanny, what the hell are you doing?" I bit out in a harsh whisper. The last thing that Tripp or the girls needed to see right now was Lanny like this. She could barely stand, for starters, and had makeup smeared across her face. Her hair looked like she'd just been fucked in the back of a car. Probably that one.

"I'mmm heeere to visit my girrrlss," she managed to slur out and then began to laugh. She walked toward me, but about halfway there she tripped, and I lurched forward to grab her so she wouldn't hit the ground face first. The last thing anyone needed was a midnight ambulance visit because Lanny managed to break her face.

"Myyy knight," she said. Before I realized what she was doing, Lanny had grabbed the front of my leather jacket and hauled herself up me like some kind of crazed koala bear. Arms wrapped around my neck and legs wrapped around my waist, she crashed her lips into mine.

"What the *fuck*," I spat as I tried to turn my head away. "Lanny, get the hell off of me. What the fuck are you doing?" I growled out. I didn't want to hurt her—that was the last thing I wanted or hell, needed—so I just pushed at her waist to try to get her to let go. That failed spectacularly. She just clung tighter and laughed like this was all so funny and just a game, but it wasn't funny or a game to me. There was nothing funny about it.

"I said get off of me," I snarled. Fed up, I pushed her away hard enough that she was forced to let go and ended up sliding down onto her ass on the ground. As I glared at her, she laughed hysterically adding in little snorts as she held her stomach. At least one of us was amused.

"Don't you ever do that again," I snarled as I wiped my mouth off with the back of my hand. I was tempted to pick her up and throw her back into the car. Seriously, who was even in there driving? "I should have you charged with assault for that."

Lanny laughed so hard she began to cough and gag. She covered her mouth like she might throw up but managed to keep everything down. Yay.

"You're funny. Who would believe you, with...with.... Um, with...your history," she slurred out, and I saw red. I really saw red.

"What the fuck did you just say to me? Was that a threat, Lanny?" I asked as I took a step toward her.

Lanny grabbed the front of her blouse, and ripped open the top two buttons as she gave me what I guessed was supposed to be a seductive look. I'd never been less turned on in my life.

"Soooorrry," she said in a stupid, sing-song voice. "What? You don't want any of this?" she asked and then laughed again. "These are new, you know," she added with a wink before she shook her boobs back and forth.

"How dare you do something like this after what I did to try and help you?" I snarled.

"Oh *please*, don't give me that line." She waved her hand at me and made a face like she'd just sucked on a lemon. It was deeply unattractive. "You wouldn't be helping me if it didn't also help Tripp."

It sounded like she was jealous that I wanted to help my brother, which made no sense at all. Why would she expect any differently? I found this very confusing among all the other things that Lanny had said and done lately.

"You couldn't even be bothered to give me a call back when I left you a message. Mr. Jake Russell, all high and mighty. Too good for the rest of us peons," she sneered. Her anger seemed to be sobering her up a bit—the glare she fixed on me was steady, and she was barely wavering where she sat. Thank god for small favors.

By this point, my own temper was more than flaring, and I could hear my teeth making a squeaking noise as they ground together. Lanny was acting like she was some jealous girlfriend, and while I had no idea what had spurred this on, I was done with the conversation.

"I don't know what's gotten into you or what kind of game you're playing, but get up and get your friend, or whoever that is, to get you the fuck out of here before you wake up your daughters and they see you lying on the driveway. Or is your plan to push them away completely so they don't want anything to do with you anymore?" I force out through gritted teeth.

Lanny's smile slowly fell and the laughter died out as she stared up at me.

"What did you just say to me? Are you threatening to take away my girls?"

"You fucking heard me, and don't turn this around like your actions are what I want to see happen. Do you really want your girls to see you like this? Throwing yourself on their uncle, not able to stand, and looking like you were dragged through the garbage dump?" I shook my head, disgusted.

"Seriously, Lanny. I don't know what you're going through, but this...." I pointed to her on the ground. "This is not healthy, and you certainly don't look happy. Trust me. I know from experience that whatever you have going on is up *here*." I tapped the side of my head. "And in *here*." I tapped over my heart. "You need to find a way to deal with it that doesn't involve alcohol or drugs or sex or fancy operations."

Lanny rolled herself over onto all fours. I thought she was going to throw up, but with what I knew was a great deal of effort, she managed to get herself standing. I'd been there myself plenty of times, but I certainly wasn't offering to help after the stunt she'd just pulled. She'd regret this once she sobered up—or at least, I hoped she would. I always regretted the shit I did.

I was beginning to wonder if I'd done the right thing by making that deal with her. It may have helped Tripp, but I suddenly wasn't too sure it wouldn't hurt Lanny.

"You don't know what I want," she said as she straightened up to her full height. Her face turned a sickly shade of green, and I realized she was finally going to puke about a second before she turned her head to throw up in the grass. Just great. My stomach churned at the smell. It was like my body had PTSD and revolted as the smell brought up old memories of all my nights with my head stuffed in a toilet. I'd lost count how many times I prayed to the porcelain god as my stomach turned inside out.

I waited until she was done and had started trying to wipe her mouth off on the bottom of her flapping blouse to respond. I wanted her to hear this.

"Oh really? Okay then. How about I go get the girls right now? I'm sure that Syd and Bri would love to see their mother plastered out of her skull with puke running down her face. That's going to be very memorable for them."

When she didn't say anything, I turned toward the house. I only took two strides before Lanny grabbed my arm.

"Don't. Please," she said, voice pleading.

My eyes turned down to meet hers, and some of the glassed-over look that had been there a few moments ago was now gone. She was finally hearing what I was saying.

"Then get out of here, and I'll pretend this never happened for your girls' sake. The last thing they need is for you and Tripp to begin arguing all over again. But Lanny, if you ever pull a stunt like that again...." I narrowed my eyes and leaned in closer to her face. "Let's just say you'll find out what happens when I'm pushed too far."

I held up a finger as she opened her mouth to say something that was going to piss me off further. I could just tell.

"Don't even bother. Get out of here and sleep this off. I never want to talk about it again," I said.

Her hands uncurled from the tight, clawed grip she had on my arm. Stepping back, she nodded and turned to stumble over to the passenger side of the car. Raising my hand, I tried to block out the light from the high beams to see who had brought Lanny here in the first place. Based on the hands on the steering wheel, it was a guy, but before I could get a better look, Lanny closed the door and whoever was driving started backing down the driveway.

I stared after the vehicle, waiting until I couldn't hear the sound of the motor any longer before I moved.

"That was fucking weird," I muttered. I'd done some messed up stuff, but purposely stalking and hitting on one of my brother's girls? Never. What the hell was going on in Lanny's head? The thought that her feelings might be based on more than simple attraction crossed my mind, making me stop and pinch the bridge of my nose.

No, it couldn't be that." I'd known her since she was sixteen, and there had never been any sexual chemistry between us. At least, not on my part. Why was everything so fucked up tonight? Kat and her reveal that still churned my stomach. Then my mom. Then I tell Kat I was a huge reason she was assaulted and now Lanny. I was on a roll and not one that I liked.

My mind was all over the board, but it was my heart that hurt as I thought about Kat. Seeing the pained look on her face had been worse than any physical blow. Standing in the driveway, I looked between the dark home and my wheels.

"Fuck it. I can't do it."

Grabbing the motorcycle, I walked it to the end of the driveway and fired her back up. It roared loudly as I flew along the road back to town.

KAT

Banging jerked me right out of an exhausted sleep and straight into full-blown panic. It took a moment to process what was even happening, but then a few more brain cells came online and I realized that someone was at the front door. My heart went wild as the loud pounding started again, and I jumped up out of bed.

Grabbing a knit sweater off the chair on my way out of the room, I shoved my arms into it while my eyes searched the living room for a weapon. Success. Running over to the small fireplace, I wrapped my hand around the poker before I quietly padded to the front door.

Bang, bang, bang.

I felt each one of the knocks in my chest. Flicking on the outside light, I peeked through the curtain and sighed in relief before opening the door.

"Jake, what are you doing? You just about gave me a heart...." The words were stilled in my throat, the rest of the sentence lost to the strong breeze, as Jake wrapped me up in his arms and crashed his lips to mine. Much like the first night he'd come here, Jake pushed me up against the wall as his mouth moved in time with my own.

"I'm sorry. I'm sorrier than I can ever make up for, but I can't leave. I know you said you wanted the night and that you needed to think. I just can't do it. I can't go—not again, not ever again. I know it's selfish, but please don't make me," he said. His thumb ran along my trembling lip. "I have too much to make up for, too much that I want for us, and life is way too short. With every fiber of...."

"Shut up, Jake," I said, interrupting him, and his eyes went wide. Gripping his jacket in my fists, I pulled him closer. "Just stop talking and make love to me already."

"Only under one condition," he said before laying his lips softly on mine.

My eyes fluttered closed as my body responded to his touch.

"What's that?"

"You give me the fire poker. You're kinda scaring me," he said. I hadn't even noticed I was still gripping it as I clung to him and laughed as I let him take it from my hand.

"I thought you were someone else," I said as he set it aside. His eyes darkened at my words, the intensity making it hard for me to breathe.

"I know, but he'll have to go through me to get to you, Kat, and that's not happening." Jake cupped my face, and it felt like my blood was singing with just that simple touch.

"Marry me."

"But...what?" I asked, dumbfounded.

"I know it can't be official until your divorce is complete, but I'm not wasting another moment of my life without you in it. Agree to marry me, and as soon as we're able to, we can have whatever kind of wedding you want. It can be on the beach in Italy or a simple barbecue here—I don't care. All that matters is that we're together for however long we have left."

I'd already decided that I couldn't change the past and that coming here was my new start, whatever that looked like. I couldn't determine for certain that my life wouldn't have gone the same way— that I wouldn't have chosen Richard over Jake even if he had spoken to me.

I was young and dumb and craved love and security more than anything in the world, and I'd thought Richard would give me both. Looking into Jake's eyes now, I understood that my past pain made me appreciate what we had between us so much more.

"Yes. Yes, I want to marry you," I answered, never more sure of anything in my life.

A wide smile broke out across his face a second before he grabbed my hand and pulled me toward the bedroom. Or rather, I thought it was going to be the bedroom, but we veered into the bathroom instead.

"Get the water to the temperature you like," he said, shrugging off his heavy leather jacket and dropping it onto the floor. I stood motionless, momentarily stunned by the sight. The black T-shirt that fit like a second skin was next. He peeled it off his body, and with each new inch of skin shown, my mouth salivated more. It was my own personal strip show.

"I love that you look at me like that," Jake chuckled. Reaching out, he spread my sweater open to show off the satin sleep outfit I was wearing. He bit his lip as he groaned, and the sound traveled through my body like a small electrical current. "Mmm, *fuck*, you're beautiful. Now, be a good girl and turn on the water so I can fuck you until you can't stand."

Turning, I reached for the tap. My hands were shaking. He made me nervous, but not scared nervous—this was different. It was an 'in the best way possible' kind of nervous.

I wanted to sound sexy. I wanted to say something erotic back the same way the words seemed to come so easily to him, but my tongue felt frozen and my brain was blank.

When I checked, the water was cool to the touch, but I could feel it warming as I held my hand under the spray. Warm hands grabbed my shoulders, and I jumped a little at the sudden touch—some habits were harder to break than others—but it was just Jake, and Jake meant safety. His breath blew hot against my neck, and goosebumps rose all over my body in response.

"Do you know how beautiful you are?" he asked. I tilted my head into his words. The passion-laced fog in my brain was thickening from my body's heady response. I didn't answer the question, assuming it was rhetorical, and Jake slowly pulled the sweater off my shoulders as he asked again.

"Do you know how beautiful you are?"

I slowly turned around in his arms, and somehow, the low light filtering through the steam from the steadily warming shower only added to his sexiness. He literally could have put a paper bag on his head and still found a way to make it ooze sex.

"Say it," Jake demanded.

"Say what?"

"Tell me you're beautiful."

I smirked and avoided his eyes as I teased him back.

"You're beautiful," I repeated, laughing, but Jake snatched my chin, making me gasp as he gently forced me to look at him.

"No, Kat. Don't do that. I want you to say it. Say, 'I'm beautiful.'"

"I...I...this is silly." I tried to turn my head from his hold, but I wasn't getting away that easily. "Jake...."

"No more running, right? You came here for a new beginning and to heal. So then, say it. Tell me even though you don't feel it—because you need to start to understand that it's true." He laid his forehead against my own, and in that moment, I'd never felt more connected to another living person.

I felt whole with him. I felt myself with him. I felt like I could be goofy, could tell him a stupid story or spill flour all over the floor, and it would all be fine.

The understanding that Jake really saw me flowed through me. No matter how many years we'd spent apart, no matter how many miles had separated us or how our lives had differed, he was the one constant in my life—and I was the one constant in his.

"I love you, and...." I took a deep breath. "I am beautiful."

"Not bad. It needs work, don't get me wrong, but since you added in that you love me, I'll let it slide." Jake stood straight, a hint of a smile playing on his lips. "Now strip for me, and I want it to be sexy."

Stepping back, he leaned against the door, and my pulse kicked it up to eleven. With a pose like that, he could do an ad for literally any product and still make it mouth watering, hot *damn*. I was not even close to his league. Swallowing past the lump in my throat, I gripped the bottom of the silky tank top and froze, hands shaking.

"Angel, don't be nervous. Just be you. You're sexy no matter what you do," Jake soothed. I chewed my lip as I looked at him, and good lord, it wasn't fair for him to look so calm while I was a bundle of nerves. "You've got this, trust me."

This was so out of my element. I felt lost, yet I still wanted to try. My movements were stiff at first as my body began a little back-and-forth sway, but my confidence built with each passing second, and soon, I was dancing to a song that only I could hear.

Working the top up, I teased him by showing off one nipple and then the other, and the hungry look in his eyes and tension in his muscles, like he was getting ready to pounce, had me growing bolder. With a final flourish, I pulled the top off over my head and tossed it in his direction. Running my hands up my body, I tweaked my hardened nipples—there was a distinct intake of air from Jake's direction.

"Fuck yes, Kat. Touch yourself. I want to watch you explore every inch of your body." He pushed away from the door, and the heat coming off his skin felt like a pulse throbbing in time to the need in my own body. "Every place you put those hands is where I'm going to trace with my tongue. If I were you, I'd be smart about where I touched myself and make sure I was thorough so I wouldn't be left wanting."

A challenge had been tossed down, and even though he didn't say the words outright, I knew he was pushing me out of my comfort zone on purpose. Turning slowly so my back was to him, I continued with my little dance, dramatically bending over at the waist until my ass was almost pressed up against the bulge in his jeans. Hooking my thumbs in the little satin sleep shorts, I wiggled my hips around in a circle, daring him to keep his hands off me as the shorts slid over my ass and down my legs.

He groaned as I remained bent over and ran my hands all over my legs before sliding a finger between my thighs. I wanted to make sure he could see what I was doing. The sound of a zipper lowering had me peering around my leg, and I got a mouthwatering view of him pulling out his cock to stroke.

With each passing second, my confidence notched higher until I found myself stepping into the shower to lean up against the wall facing Jake. Lifting a foot onto the ledge of the tub put me on full display, and I watched his eyes as he watched my hand move lower. He seemed entranced by my movements.

I'd never been so bold in my life, but standing naked before Jake, there was no shame. I felt no fear of being judged or told a hundred different, terrible things.

"Oh yeah, Angel, that's it. Touch yourself for me," he said as his jeans finally hit the floor. "Show me how you like it."

Grabbing the body wash, I lathered up my hands and ran them over my body. The white bubbles slid over my skin, and I let my hands do what they wanted. Every groan that Jake let out, his heated stare, his hand stroking himself—it all mixed together, making me more brazen. It felt like I was finding myself for the first time in my life.

Moving under the spray, I let all the little bubbles rinse off, and I couldn't stop a smirk from forming as Jake's eyes traced their path down my body. With new confidence, I leaned against the wall again and slid the fingers of one hand down my skin until they dipped down and pressed into my core. I moaned. Both hands got into the action, and my eyes closed as I pleasured myself while thinking about the man in front of me. Somehow, it didn't feel real despite the fact it undeniably was. Few things in my life had been so real.

"Fuck, that's hot. You're so fucking hot that I can barely control myself," Jake said. He stepped into the shower with me. "Everything about you is perfect, I never want you to think or say otherwise," he commanded. "Not anymore. It's time you were free to be you." Even though his voice was low, there was weight to his words and my heart sputtered.

I started to stand up straight, but Jake wrapped his hands around my wrists, holding them in place.

"No. You keep doing exactly what you're doing, Angel. I love seeing you pleasure yourself."

If the ability to combust into flames were real, I certainly would've done so when he got down on his knees in front of me. His hands felt so large on my thighs as he gripped them firmly.

"That's it. Just like that," Jake said right before his tongue joined my fingers. If he hadn't had a firm hold on my legs, I would've slipped right down the wall with the first lick. My fingers brushed against the rough five o'clock shadow on his chin as he buried his face and latched on to my clit.

"Ah, yes, oh god," I cried.

"Say my name when you come as I drink you down," he growled against the sensitive skin, making me whimper. "Do you understand?"

"Yes, Jake, I...." I cried out again as his finger joined mine and sank in deeply. His rhythm matched my own, and our fingers rubbed against each other's as we pushed me closer to my climax. When he slipped his finger out, I wanted to cry out for him not to stop, but my objection turned into a moan as he dipped the tip of his finger into my rosebud.

"Oh, you like that, do you, Angel?" he said, smirking. I nodded furiously, unable to form words any longer as he continued to work over my pussy while licking at my clit and fingering my ass. Nothing had ever felt so good. "Did you want me to pop this virgin ass's cherry? Fuck your tight little ass while I finger your pussy?"

Little murmured noises were the only answer to tumble from my lips as he picked up the pace and went a little deeper.

"Mmm, you're so tight. Do you have lube, Angel?" Jake asked. Once again, I nodded, swallowing hard as I pointed to the vanity.

"It's only petroleum jelly, though."

"That will work just fine," Jake said. He slowly stood, his teeth grazing up my stomach until his mouth found my nipple. My hands clung to his wet hair as the forgotten shower continued beating water down on us.

"You taste so good that I want to devour every inch of you," he murmured against my skin. Wrapping his hand around the back of my neck, he held my head firmly in place to stare into my eyes in a way that reminded me of a wild animal. As he blocked out the light, I felt subsumed, and my throat instantly turned as dry as a hot summer day in the desert.

"Are you scared of me?" Jake asked, still staring deeply into my eyes.

I shook my head, but my pulse pounded even harder through my veins at the question.

"No."

"Are you sure?"

"Yes."

"Good. I'd never hurt you, and I will bury anyone who tries to touch you again."

Why were those words so hot? My knees were shaking so badly from the sheer amount of arousal flowing through me that I was surprised they weren't knocking together. The tattoos that ran the lengths of his arms stood out more darkly in the dim light of the bathroom. The skulls, knives, and snakes embedded in the tribal artwork patterns all seemed to be screaming the same promise of protection and retribution.

Without warning, Jake's lips crashed down onto mine, stealing the air from my chest. Before I could regain my balance, he pulled away and grabbed for the bar of soap. I felt like I was getting emotional whiplash.

"You make me high," I blurted out as I eyed up the delicious muscles in his back. He turned to look over his shoulder at me, and it took every ounce of control not to jump onto his back and ride him to the ground. He scrambled every wire in my brain until all that was left was this raw need that was demanding and unpredictable.

The corner of his mouth pulled up, showing off his sexy dimple.

"Good. I want to keep you addicted," he said. Smirk still in place, he turned to look at me as he slowly ran the bar all over his body, mimicking what I'd done when he was watching. God, it was hot. His eyes darted to where my hand was slowly making its way down my stomach to where my body was demanding more.

"Go ahead and touch yourself. I won't stop you." Jake's expression shifted from mischievous to serious in the blink of an eye. "But you don't come until I say you can."

The rest of the shower felt like it was over both in a blink and after a thousand hours of small, teasing touches and heated glances. I wanted to run to the bedroom and throw myself on the bed, but I also wanted to board up the door and stay locked away with Jake in the small bathroom forever. It was as if this tiny space had become our safe haven, our place where the rest of the world couldn't touch us.

After stepping out of the tub, Jake wrapped one of the large towels around my shoulders. The cool air didn't seem to affect him in the slightest. He bent down and rummaged around in the vanity for a moment before grabbing the lube and, once he straightened, my hand as well. Prepared, we headed to the bedroom.

"Come on. Tonight, we're turning you into my sexy, dirty angel," Jake whispered in my ear. My mouth fell open, and he laughed in response. I still had no idea how to respond to comments like that.

"You're crazy." I blushed and then bit my lip as I looked toward the bed.

"You're right, I am. I really, really am," Jake said, repeating the same words to me that he'd said years earlier. When he pulled me to his body, his cock pressed into my stomach, instantly spiking the desire that had subsided to a simmer.

Taking hold of the edges of my towel, he tugged it away from my hands until it fell to the floor. Placing a finger under my chin, he lifted my head so I was forced to stare him in the eyes.

"I'm only crazy for you, though. I know you still have trouble believing that, but it's the truth. I feel like I've been living with one lung this whole time, struggling for each gasp of air. But, when I'm with you, I'm able to take a real breath again." He ran his thumb over my bottom lip. "You've always been my twin flame and as essential to my life as the air I breathe."

It was such an intimate moment, so *of course* tears pricked at my eyes, but I tried to hold them back. It still felt like a dream for Jake to be here, let alone feeling the same way I did. Swallowing down the emotions, I smiled widely and wrapped my arms around his neck to rise up on my tiptoes and place a soft kiss on his lips.

"I wish I had your way with words. I guess I'll have to show you how I feel instead," I said, and before he could come up with something else clever to say, I kissed him hard, pouring every ounce of how I felt into the act.

Anyone else would probably say we were moving too fast—that we needed to get to know one another again first, or a million other warnings that were all equally valid. The thing was, to me, it felt like we'd never been apart, not where it mattered. It felt like I'd been coasting along in a life that wasn't my own just waiting for this moment. Jake was the mirror to my soul, and as far as I was concerned, 'anyone else' and all of their warnings could go suck it.

30

JAKE

"OH FUCK," I yelled as my cock finally made it all the way into Kat's tight ass. The muffled scream from Kat told me that she was at her limit. She looked so fucking sexy with her face pressed into the pillow and her ass in the air, and my hands shook from the exertion of that final thrust as they gripped her hips.

Sweat had already been trickling off our bodies even before I'd started preparing her ass, and now I felt like I'd never left the shower, but holy *fuck* had I found a new slice of heaven.

"Just relax," I said through clenched teeth as her passage clenched hard around my cock. It throbbed inside of her body just begging for release, and the rhythmic pulse of her ass gripping me tight and relaxing was a sweet, sweet torture. Every ounce of my focus was directed into holding still and letting her adjust.

"Just relax, Angel," I said, through gritted teeth as I held off my own desire.

Kat's head sagged down and I could feel her breathing deeply and watched as her muscles in her back and ass began to release.

Taking it slow, I reached around her body to gently rub her clit and roll it between my fingers. Kat shuddered and gasped as she began to react to the extra stimulation. Adding a finger to the mix, I slipped into her pussy and pressed firmly. She moaned loudly in response, making me smirk.

"That's it," I cooed to her softly.

"Holy fuck, Jake," she yelled a second before she came. After that first orgasm, I'd decided there was nothing sweeter than making her come. The adorable noises she made, how sexy she looked, and of course, how her body responded all because of me—that shit checked off every fucking box I had. The overly territorial side of my personality had been dormant for years, but it was roaring to life with a renewed vengeance.

Kat slumped, body twitching as she bathed in the glowing aftermath of her orgasm.

"*Fuck*, you're sexy, Angel," I said, still only daring to move back and forth an inch at a time. After feeling her come all over me, I was so turned on and ready for the final act that I might fucking explode before I even had a chance to enjoy her. Tentatively, my thrusts got a little longer, and when she didn't tell me to stop or whimper in pain, I pulled almost all the way out and slowly sank deep into her body again.

"Oh, my *god*, Jake," Kat panted as she pushed herself up onto her hands. The slight change in position allowed me to slip in easier, and I increased the pace.

"Can you come for me again?"

"Fuck yes. Make me come again," she moaned out.

"You've never said sexier words to me." Taking to the challenge, my hips thrust harder, and the sound of our breathing grew loud in the otherwise quiet room. "Can you move with me to the edge of the bed?" I asked, and when she nodded, we moved in slow, synchronous movements to the edge.

After placing my feet on the floor, I pulled Kat into the perfect position and gave her ass a playful slap. She jumped and then moaned as she looked over her shoulder at me.

"Fuck. I want to bottle that look and take it everywhere with me," I said, slapping her ass again.

"That feels so good," she said as she wiggled her ass, making me groan. Leaning forward, I held out my finger to her.

"Suck on my finger," I said, loving that she didn't hesitate to open her mouth for me. "You're so good at that," I praised. My eyes were glued to her hollowed-out cheeks as she sucked on my finger. "Now two," I ordered, adding a second one to her hot mouth.

They felt good and wet after a few more sucks, so I pulled them free. I couldn't help smiling at the pout she sent me, but I made it worth it when I pushed them into her pussy, making her yell out a series of curse words I never thought I'd hear coming from her.

"I'll take it you liked that?" I teased.

Not waiting for a response, I pulled back and thrust forward with both my body and my fingers.

"Oh, *fuck*." Kat's scream, muffled from how she'd dropped her face to bury it in a pillow, but the sound still rang out through the room. I shuddered with the knowledge that I was the one to bring her this level of pleasure.

As my pace increased, my head fell back, and I badly wanted a strap-on so I could fuck her with two cocks at the same time. The sound of skin against skin and our mutual moans grew until Kat was pushed over the brink for a third time.

"Ah, oh fuck, *yes*, keep fucking me," she yelled.

I pulled my fingers from her pussy grudgingly so I could get a better grip on her hips, and only then did I let loose. The full power of my building desire took control as I slammed home over and over.

With a roaring yell, I thrust into her a final time, and my fingers dug into the soft skin of her hips as my body froze with the shock of release.

"Fuck," I screamed. It was the only comprehensible word that would form in my mouth as wave after wave of relief poured out of me. Catching my breath, I rubbed at the smooth skin of Kat's back and ass until my eyes landed on the long scar from her surgery. It struck me only then just how close I'd come to losing this, losing her, forever.

My decision to stay away could have cost her life. A shiver of terror traveled down my spine, wiping away the euphoric feelings I'd been enjoying. All I could picture was an obituary with her name and a sharp pain stabbed me in the chest.

"You okay?" Kat asked as she turned her head enough to look at me, obviously sensing that something had changed.

"Yeah, Angel, I'm better than okay. I just never want to move," I lied before I slowly pulled out of her. She gasped at the sensation. "I'll be right back. Just going to get some stuff to clean us up."

"I can come," she said, but as soon as she tried to move, she winced.

"No, trust me. Just relax." Bracing myself on the bed, I leaned over to kiss her temple before I backed away and slipped out of the room.

Once in the bathroom my hands gripped the edge of the counter hard as fear and rage mingled in a toxic combination in my chest. Images of a mangled car, of Kat lying paralyzed as Richard tortured her, kept running through my mind on a dangerous loop that was bringing all my dark inner demons to the surface.

If I didn't get a grip on myself, I was either going to break something or break down, and that couldn't happen here—not in front of Kat. She didn't need to see me like that. Closing my eyes and taking a few deep breaths, I rolled out my shoulders and focused on breathing until I felt a little less like killing something.

After cleaning myself up and splashing some cold water on my face, I managed to push the images aside, but I knew they would come back to torture me again. That kind of fear was like a PTSD episode all on its own. If I'd seen the car, if I'd known.... I had to shake my head to stop the spiral that was insistently trying to take over my mind.

Grabbing the jeans I'd discarded earlier, I pulled them on before squatting down to dig through the vanity for a second time. Right at the very back, I found what I was hoping to find—a carton of Epsom salt. Turning on the water, I set the temperature and let the tub start filling. I poured in a healthy dose of salt before going on the hunt for some painkillers.

Kat may not feel it right now, but she was going to be sore tomorrow, and I wanted to ease as much of that for her as I could. I wanted to care for her like this all the time until she wanted to smack me for hovering. I hit the jackpot in the second drawer I checked and quickly grabbed the little red and white bottle and a glass of water.

As I headed back to the bedroom with my loot, a flash of light caught my attention. Stopping to look outside through the gap in the curtains of the window next to me, I saw the bright lights of what had to be a car parked in front of the house. The glowing clock above the oven revealed the time to be four-thirty in the morning—a pretty strange time for someone to be around unless they were up to no good.

Placing the items for Kat on the kitchen counter, I made my way to the living room window and pulled back the curtain to get a clearer look. A car was definitely idling in the road right in front of Kat's house. I whipped open the door to ask what the fuck the person thought they were doing, whoever it was drove off. It was too dark to see inside the tinted windows, but I managed to memorize the license plate number before they turned the corner.

"Jake, is everything okay?" Kat called out from the bedroom.

"Yeah, just getting some fresh air. Everything is good," I called back as my eyes scanned the street for anything else unusual. It seemed quiet, but my eyes lingered on all the bushes and shadowed corners.

Closing the door and locking it, I did a quick sweep of the house to check the windows and back door before continuing on with my original mission. Shutting off the water in the tub, which thankfully hadn't overflowed, I finally made my way back to the bedroom.

Kat hadn't moved from the spot she'd flopped over into when I left. Bending down, I smoothed her hair away from her face.

"You okay?"

"I'm great. This is the best pain I've ever had," she said. "Wait. I guess that's kind of a bad way to put it. I'm simply great," she said, eyes shining as she smiled widely.

"As flattering as that is, I want to make sure you'll still be saying that tomorrow. Can you sit up?" I asked. After nodding, Kat swung her legs over the edge of the bed with a grimace, but she never cried out. My tough girl. I held out two of the white pills and the water. "Here, take these."

She looked at them for a breath and a ghost of something crossed her face, but in a blink it was gone. "Thanks," she said, grabbing them and knocking them back.

"I'm not done yet." I bent to scoop her up into my arms, laughing as she let out a surprised squeak, and carried her into the bathroom. She sighed as I slowly sat her in the warm water.

"Jake, you didn't have to do this," she said, gripping my hand. I brought her knuckles to my lips to kiss.

"Yeah, I did. Just try to relax. I'll make us some tea, and then we should get some rest. Do you have work tomorrow?"

"The store isn't open, but I do have to figure a few things out. There's no rush to go in."

"Good. I'll need to leave in a few hours. Today is the last day of filming with the commercial crew I was telling you about, and then they will finally be gone." I stood, but Kat kept a tight grip on my hand.

"Jake...." Her eyes filled up with tears before she blinked and looked away. "Thank you." It felt like she wanted to say more, but it was late and had been a long, emotional day all around, so when she didn't continue, it seemed better to let it go and not press.

"Always, Angel. I'll give you some privacy and come get you in a bit." After opening the door, I looked back at Kat, who already had her head leaned back against the tile and her eyes closed. "Oh, and Kat? Don't try to get out by yourself. That's an order."

She smirked as she waved me out, eyes still closed. "There's chamomile above the stove," she mumbled.

As soon as I got the tea steeping, I perched myself on a chair in the living room to keep watch out the window like a pit bull.

I hated that a guy thousands of miles away was making me paranoid, but I didn't want to take a chance with Kat's life. Richard was a real threat, and even going as far as hiring a P.I. seemed like it might be a good idea—anything that would give Kat leverage over the guy.

I could kill him, of course. I could find him, take him out into the middle of nowhere, and kill him. Unfortunately, while that thought was very tempting, if I were caught, then Kat and I would lose one another again.

Taking a moment, I looked up some P.I. services and sent the long list to Miles. *Hey man can you look into these companies or recommend a good one? Don't ask, it's better if you don't know, I just need someone good and discreet.*

It took a minute, but the little bubble showed Miles was answering back. *What the fuck man? It's like five in the morning for you...never mind don't tell me why you're awake. All I want to know is do I dare ask if I need to get ready for any negative publicity?*

No, nothing like that.

Fine, I'll look when it's normal people hours.

Thanks.

Don't mention it.

Smirking, I thumbed through my contacts until I found the number Karl had given me and hit talk. The phone rang five times, and I was getting ready to have to leave a voicemail message instead when a groggy voice finally answered.

"Sheriff Carr speaking."

"Hey Karl, it's Jake."

"Jake, what the fuck. This better be important. It's my day off," Karl griped.

"I thought a sheriff never got a day off?"

"Exactly my fucking point. To sleep until the sun comes up is a luxury." I could hear him moving around as he got up. He probably wasn't going to like this next part.

"I'm sorry, man, but I need you to run a plate."

There was a laugh on the other end of the line, and then all went silent.

"Oh, you're serious. I thought there was a punchline coming."

"No punchline. Can you do it?" I asked, trying not to sound impatient.

"Jake, you do know that real life is not like television? I can't just run a plate for fun. I have to have a legit reason."

"I do have a good reason. I think the car was casing a neighborhood," I offered. The sound of running water hitting a long drop came over the line, and I screwed up my face and pulled my phone away from my ear to look at it. "Are you pissing with me on the phone?"

"Nothin' you haven't heard or seen before. Besides, you woke me up in the middle of the night. What do you expect?" Karl grumbled, voice tiny.

Pinching the bridge of my nose, I shook my head and brought the phone back to my ear. Seriously.

"Can you do it or not?"

There was a deep sigh as a toilet flushed, making me shake my head.

"What's the real reason you want me to check the plate, Jake? I'm not stupid and I wasn't born yesterday. You haven't suddenly joined a neighborhood watch, so what gives?" The sound of running water started again and I could tell he was now washing his hands. It was like I'd stepped back in time when we all shared a changeroom in school.

"You wouldn't believe me if I told you, and I don't have time to go into the story right now, but let's just say it's important, and I need you to believe me," I said, trying to push as much sincerity as I could into my voice.

"Fuck. I forgot how annoying you are. Yes, fine, I'll fucking look into it—but Jake, in all seriousness, if you're in some kind of trouble, it's better if I know upfront. You understand? I don't need to be blindsided by some crap. I can't just break you out of jail or not arrest you because you're my friend."

"Yeah, I know. I'll tell you the whole story over that beer I promised." I could almost feel Karl glaring at me through the phone. The thick silence was pretty impressive and made me squirm.

"Okay, whatever you say. Text me the plate number, and I'll call you back when I know something."

"Thanks, Karl."

Karl yawned in my ear, the charmer.

"Yeah, yeah," he grumbled before the line went dead.

After firing off the text, I stuffed the phone back in my pocket and went to grab the tea to take it to the bathroom. Trying not to startle Kat, I rapped softly on the door and then opened it a crack when she didn't answer. She was sleeping. Not very safe, but adorable.

Unable to help myself, I walked in and leaned against the counter to watch her rest. She looked so peaceful, so perfect. As my eyes fell on the rainbow pendant around her neck, which had faded to a solid gold color over time, I decided it was time to get her a new one.

That pendant marked the last time we'd seen each other. We needed one that marked our new beginning.

Kat shivered, and I pushed off the counter and into action. Pulling a large, fluffy towel free from the rack, I knelt down and touched her shoulder. Waking, she blinked a few times, her thick lashes fluttering before she looked at me with her big blue eyes.

"Did you want your tea?"

She slowly shook her head. "Too tired."

"Okay. Come on, then. Let's get you to bed," I said. Reaching into the tub, I let Kat wrap her arm around my neck so I could pick her up and place her on her feet. I made as fast a job of drying her off —I didn't want her to have to stand tonight—before picking her up again.

"I can walk, you know," she mumbled into the side of my neck.

"I know, but I want to carry you. I'd carry you everywhere like a queen if you'd let me."

"You really are crazy, but I love you for it," she said as I laid her down in bed. Stripping down quickly to get my now significantly damp clothes off, I got into bed behind her and held her as close as I possibly could.

"I love you too, Kat."

"Jake?"

"Yeah?"

"Is there anything else I should know? Like any more secrets that are going to pop up one day?"

"I don't think...oh, I guess there is one." I could feel her breathing stop, and I laid a soft kiss on her neck to reassure her that it wasn't that terrible. At least, I didn't think it was that terrible.

"I was kind of following you around after the bakery. I was going to speak to you—I promise I'm not normally a stalker—but it kept not working out for one reason or another. But yeah, I followed you to the bar when you went on that date with that idiot. I laid him out good, too. He was such a dick," I said, not even a little sorry about that last part.

Kat snickered, and then it turned into a full-on laugh. Her body vibrated against mine, making me smile.

"It was you..." She stopped like she was going to say more and I had a feeling she was going to mention she thought it had been her ex that hit the dick.

"You're not mad?"

"No, but no more following me around. I thought I was losing my mind when I kept seeing you in places. Turns out, you actually *were* there," she said, still laughing.

We lapsed into silence, and I was just starting to drift off when she spoke.

"Jake, you still awake?"

"Yeah, Angel, I'm awake."

"Can I ask you to call me Alexis or Lexi?"

"You really want me to?" I asked, leaning up on my elbow so I could stare down at the side of her face. Even in the dark, I could make out her features, and my chest constricted with how much I loved this woman.

She rolled her head back far enough that she could look up at me.

"Yeah, I do. Kate was a girl who was abused and scared and grew up into a woman who became so desperate she married a man just as abusive. I don't want to be that girl anymore. Coming here and changing my name was done as much as a symbol for myself, something to show that I was no longer that girl, as it was done so that Richard couldn't find me. I want to be the person I'm learning to become and not go backward, if that makes sense?" She sighed like the weight of the world was on her shoulders. "Kat was broken."

I hated that she thought she was weak and wanted to forget who she'd been, but I also understood that the pain of her scars, inside and out, weighed heavily on her.

"Alright, but there's no guarantee I won't call you Licksy," I teased, making her giggle. "Fine. 'Lexi' it is, then. But just so you know, Kat...Lexi, you might have been lost, but you were never broken. You might have been adrift in an ocean of darkness, like I was, but you were and are the furthest thing from broken. Never doubt that."

Her body began shaking slightly, and then the sound of her soft sobs reached my ears. It felt like a physical blow to my chest. Gathering her close, I whispered that I loved her over and over in her ear. It was the only way I knew to let her know that I had her back now.

"You always know what to say to make me feel better. I love you, Jake. I always have."

"I love you too, Angel. Now get some sleep."

BEST
FRIENDS

KAT

THERE WERE two things about having a bakery that I'd never expected, the constant negotiations with suppliers and the sheer amount of garbage produced. I'd managed to find a new supplier for flour and my other baking needs, but the garbage situation...that was proving to be trickier to handle.

The back door to the store, which never wanted to move, squeaked loudly as I leaned my full weight against it to push it open. Stupid thing. Okay, now there were *three* things on my list—those hinges were always a battle to deal with. Locking the door open, I grabbed up the two heaping bags of garbage and took them out to the dumpster.

Taking a moment, I stared out at the water down the soft slope of the hill, with its pretty speckling of trees, that led to the water's edge. There was no denying that this place was stunning.

Lost but never broken. Lost and adrift in an ocean of darkness.

Jake's words had been playing on repeat in my mind, and the

thing was, they felt like truth. With those few words, he'd described exactly what my life had felt like for so long—like I was drowning and couldn't find the surface in the darkness

Focused on wiping my hands off on my apron, I turned a little too quickly to go in and had to wince at the bright flare of discomfort in my backside. That ache had literally been following me around from behind all day. I couldn't deny that I'd had the best sex ever last night, and I wouldn't even try to, but it would be a while before my back door was on the menu again.

Stepping back into the bakery, I battled with the door in the opposite direction to try to get it back into place. When Olly had mentioned that the thing needed fixing, I didn't realize she meant it was going to require a wrestling match that made me break out in a sweat every time I wanted to move the darn thing.

I'd just gotten it latched when the front door jingled.

"Hello, stranger," Olly called out.

"I'm in the back," I shouted as I made my way to the sink. The apron just hadn't cut it—I needed some serious soap.

"You know, it's been like forever. Do you even remember what I look like?" Olly asked as she walked in and immediately made a beeline for the fresh brownies sitting on the table.

"So dramatic. What's it been? A couple of days? And don't you dare," I said, stepping forward to block Olly and give her hand a hard glare as it froze over one of the little chocolate sweets. Her lower lip pushed out, and I laughed at the adorable expression, which somehow still suited her despite her being well past the pouting-like-a-child stage of life.

"I made you your own box. It's over there." I nodded toward the pink box waiting on the far counter, and her face lit up as she made her way around to her treasure. In three seconds flat, she had the box open and half a brownie bulging out her cheeks.

"Oh my *god*, these are *sooo* good. I swear they're better than sex," Olly said. My face flamed red, making me focus very intently on drying off my hands.

Not if you had the sex I did last night.

"How's the bookstore doing?" I asked, turning to watch Olly as she pulled out a second brownie and moaned as she took a bite.

"Good. Sales are up with the latest T. L. Hodel release—everyone has been waiting for this book for months. Holy dear *god*, I swear you put crack in these," she said as she eagerly licked her fingers clean. She was employing some serious tongue action.

I was suddenly tempted to film her and turn it into an advertisement for the bakery, but I had a feeling any video featuring Olly with that look on her face and her finger in her mouth would bring in the wrong kind of clientele. Shaking my head to banish the thought, I made my way over to the large trays of brownies that still needed to be cooled and picked one up.

"Can you open the fridge for me?"

Olly jumped into action and held the door as I traveled back and forth with the large trays. As I set down the last one, I once more forgot my little predicament and tried to turn around too fast. My wince was not subtle.

"Shit, Lexi, are you alright? Did someone hurt you? Did *Jake* hurt you? If he hurt you, I'm going to rip him a new one," Olly declared with a steely glare.

My face felt so hot that I knew I was blushing without having to look in a mirror.

"Oh, he hurt me alright. Just not in the way you're thinking," I said before giving her a smile and walking past her to go clean up. After a few steps, I looked over my shoulder at Olly, whose face had twisted up in confusion, to see how long it would take to click. Suddenly, her mouth dropped open as her brain registered what I'd said.

There it is.

"Oh. Ooohh. Oh my. Well now, then tell me more." She flung the fridge closed and smiled widely, making me laugh.

"Let's just say he's really, really good."

"I'm not surprised with all the women he's been with." Olly smacked a hand over her mouth. "Shit, Lexi. I'm sorry. I shouldn't have said that—it just slipped out."

The fuzzy, bubbly sensation in my chest dwindled a little with the jab, which hurt a lot more than it should've since it wasn't even aimed at me. Grabbing a rag, I began cleaning the counters.

"It's fine, Olly. I know he has a past. He hasn't tried to hide it, and even if he wanted to, he couldn't. Not with it all over social media. I mean, millions of people know what he used to spend his time doing."

"I know, but it was a snotty, bitchy thing to say...shit. Me and my big mouth. Sometimes I just say things before I think—I really didn't mean to upset you. Look, why don't we all go out to dinner tonight? I want to spend time with you, and this will give me a chance to get to know Jake better."

After I finished wiping flour and droplets of chocolate off the counter, I turned to look at Olly. She genuinely looked terrified that I was going to throw her out as she stood there clutching her box of goodies to her chest.

"Olly, I'm not angry. I promise. Jake has lived a life I can't imagine, and to be honest, I probably don't want to know too much about certain parts of it. But I love him, I've always loved him, so I'm choosing not to focus on the things that I can't change. Way too much of my life has been made up of things that I wish I could change but can't. What we have right now is something I can focus on, and that's what I'm choosing to do."

"That is not only very mature, it is super zen of you, and I don't know if I could do it, but.... Wait, did you say you *love* him? Like as in *real* love, love?" Olly asked.

Laughing hard, I pulled my apron off and hung it up on its hook. It needed to be washed, but that was as good a place as any to keep it until I got around to it tomorrow. I didn't like to leave the small washer running overnight and then things sitting there damp all night.

"Yes, as in *love*, love."

"Wow, I...I didn't realize things had gotten that serious. And so quickly. Are you sure you're ready for that?"

I leaned against the door frame, crossed my arms over my chest, and thought about how to answer the question. What would make Olly understand? What would make anyone understand what we shared?

"I've been ready from the day Jake and I first met. Now that we've reconnected...." I shrugged. "I'm ready to throw caution to the wind. It's like we have finally come home. I know that sounds crazy, but it's the only way to explain it. He's my other half and always has been. It's like my heart was sitting in stasis and has finally started to beat."

My eyes went wide as Olly marched toward me and gripped me

in a hard hug. Before her face disappeared into my shoulder, it looked like she was crying.

"That was beautiful. I'm so happy for you, Lexi. Just so you know, though, I'll still be keeping my eyes open for anything shady he decides to do."

I wrapped my arms around her and hugged her back.

"I wouldn't expect anything less." Pulling back from the hug, I once more wondered how I'd gotten so lucky as to find Olly, especially with my luck. A person was lucky if they found one amazing friend in their life, so I considered myself blessed to now have her and Eve.

At the thought of Eve, my heart hurt. I hated not being able to call all the time or see her smiling face.

"Okay, dinner sounds great. Let's do it. I'll call Jake and let him know," I said, breaking the hug. Olly practically bounced on the balls of her feet in response.

"Great! Usual spot in town, and how about seven-thirty?"

"Perfect," I said as I grabbed the keys to lock up. "By the way, what did you decide about the lunch with your ex?"

Olly filled her cheeks with air in a pretty decent chipmunk impression before she let it all out in a rush like a deflating balloon.

"I sent her a message and said that I'd decided against it, and then I had to block her because she kept insisting that we meet. It was really weird, actually. I had to block her on all my social media—it kinda felt a little stalkerish or overly desperate. I don't know." Olly shrugged as we made our way outside. "Anyway, it's in the past now, and I need to stop thinking or worrying about her."

"I'm happy you canceled. I would've gone no matter what, but I had visions of ending up on the nightly news because someone filmed the fistfight I had with her when she tried to pull a fast one," I said with a laugh. With a few turns of the key, I finished locking up, and we strolled along the sidewalk to Olly's bookstore.

"See, *this* is why we were made to be friends, 'cause I'd be the exact same way. Did you want me to drive you home? I can come back and lock up after," Olly asked, pausing at her door.

"No, don't be silly. It's a bright, beautiful day with people everywhere, and it's practically just around the corner. I'll be completely fine." I smiled even though half of my bravery was forced bravado. There's no way I'd ever feel safe in public without having Jake, Olly, or Eve by my side until I knew for certain that Richard was no longer a threat.

"Only if you insist," Olly pressed.

"I do. I'll be fine. I'll see you at the restaurant, then?"

"Sounds good. See you soon," Olly said before making her way into the bookstore.

As I started down the sidewalk and a few large clouds moved in front of the sun, I realized just how much cooler it had been getting day by day. Pulling my thin coat tightly around myself, I made a mental note to get some winter clothes before the bad weather hit. Coming from a place like Nevada, it was hard to imagine what I knew was coming.

Someone honked their horn and I jumped, my heart hammering in my chest. Spinning I spotted the car responsible and the woman inside waving at another person walking down the street. Taking a deep breath I chided myself. It was sad, but I realized that out here, walking by myself on the empty sidewalk, my head would forever be on a swivel—every little noise seemed amplified and made my heart race. Would I ever truly be free?

Realistically, even if he *did* sign off on the papers, would he actually let me go? I had my doubts, but I couldn't let myself go there. I had to believe there was an end in sight.

Partway up the path toward the front door of the house, I caught sight of something that had me slowing to a stop. There was a box wrapped in cellophane on the front stoop, and I slowly stepped closer as if it might bite. With my luck, it would come alive and do just that.

After stepping up onto the landing, I was able to peer through the plastic and smiled as I spotted a beautiful bouquet of flowers. There didn't seem to be a note, but this had to be Jake—he was always so thoughtful. Images of the nail polish and the bath, of how he simply knew how to make me feel special, came to mind and made me smile widely.

Fumbling with the keys, I finally got the door open and bent to pick them up. They were *heavy*. I whistled as I set them on the kitchen counter and proceeded to get them out of their packaging. I had no idea how Jake knew all my favorites, but the flowers were stunning, and I bent closer to take in their fragrant scent. Positioning them on the counter, I took a quick photo and sent it off to Jake.

L: Look what I got.

J: They're stunning, but not as beautiful as you. (winky face)

L: Thank you! You really brightened my day.

J: Always. We're just finishing up filming for the day, and then I'll be by.

L: Speaking of...How do you feel about dinner with Olly? The three of us can go out to the pub in town, and this will give the two of you a chance to get to know one another better.

The little typing bubble appeared and disappeared so many times that I could picture him trying to find a way of gracefully getting out of it. Time to play a little dirty pool.

L: It would mean a lot to me.

J: Okay...since you put it that way, what time?

The smile on my face couldn't have gotten any wider as my thumbs typed out the necessary information. Laying down the phone, I went to change my clothes—it was time to look *good*...or at least not covered in flour.

After pulling open the closet doors, I grabbed a pair of jeans and a cute top with a warm sweater to go with it. I was putting silver hoops in my ears as I made my way into the kitchen when I froze and stared at the countertop. A black widow spider was sitting there.

"*Oh my god*," I breathed before running across the kitchen like a mad woman and grabbing an empty water glass. With a scream, I put the glass down to trap the poisonous spider under it. God, it was giving me the heebie-jeebies. How the hell had that got in here?

As the spider walked around the perimeter of its small prison on its way too many legs, I couldn't take my eyes off of it—it felt like it might disappear if I did. The roar of Jake's motorcycle shaking the house announced that he'd arrived, and I said a silent prayer of thanks. He'd know what to do.

"Come in," I called out as a knock sounded. I was not losing sight of this spider.

"Hey, Angel...what are you doing?" he asked as I ran to him as soon as he cleared the doorway and pulled him across the kitchen. With a shaking hand, I pointed at the glass, and it lifted one of its legs like it was pointing back which only horrified me further.

I *hated* spiders. I knew it was irrational and that they were more scared of me than I was of them, but it didn't matter. I was full-on freaking out.

"What is that doing in my *house*?" I demanded.

Jake walked closer and bent down to look at the spider, which seemed to be turning to keep an eye on Jake, which was totally freaking me out.

"I mean, we *do* get them in this area, but not this late in the year. The only thing I can think of is that it was hiding out somewhere warm in here, and you're just seeing it for the first time now," he answered. The traitor looked intrigued by the eight-legged menace.

"Oh my god, don't say that to me. I'm already freaking out enough without you telling me I've been sleeping with it here like a pet for weeks."

Jake smirked over the glass at me.

"I'll take it you still don't like spiders?"

"I swear to god, if you try to scare me...."

He laughed as he placed his hands on the counter, and I watched his hands like the spider was watching him.

"No, I won't try and scare you, but this does need to go outside."

"Yeah, like outside in the next county over."

"Do you have a piece of paper and a hardcover book?" he asked, attention once more on the spider.

I took off like my ass had been lit on fire and came back with what he'd requested. Jake slowly and carefully took the paper and slid it under the glass until the spider was forced to stand on top of it. While I performed my patented freakout dance, which was mostly me squealing and jogging on the spot, he slid the glass, paper, and spider onto the hardcover book.

"I'll get the door," I said before jogging to the door to hold it open. I was ready to do anything to get rid of it faster—anything aside from touching it myself, of course.

"Have I told you how adorable you are and how manly this is making me feel?" He paused next to me like he expected me to give his spider-holding self a kiss, but I pointed out the door, making him laugh.

"Take it *really* far away. I don't care if we're late for dinner."

As Jake did whatever with the spider out of sight and out of mind, my eyes darted to every corner or crevice I could find to check for movement, and any dark spots on the old wooden floor got a suspicious stare. I was trying really hard not to think about the old 'where there's one' adage. I was failing equally hard.

"Crisis averted," Jake said as he walked back up the path sans spider. "Your knight has saved you." At his teasing, I was instantly transported back in time.

As the giant, hairy tarantula walked toward me across the floor, I could do nothing but shriek and cower in the corner. Again. The freaky thing belonged to one of the other foster kids who lived here, and he loved to let it out to 'stretch its legs.'

I hated the thing. Whenever he took it out, it always found me like I was some freaking spider beacon. Were spiders like cats? Could they tell when you didn't like them?

I'd only been here three months, and I was already begging my case worker to find a new home for me. One where I didn't have to share a room with a boy. One that didn't have spiders the size of my face wandering around.

"Get him away from me!" I screamed. In a moment, footsteps pounded nearer, making me hopeful that help was coming.

Jake raced into the room and skidded across the smooth floor on his sock covered feet.

"What is it? What's...oh, it's Harry," Jake said, relaxing like the crisis was averted. Some help.

"I know that. Get him away from me," I yelled, pushing myself harder into the wall as 'Harry' took another step toward me. I swear the stupid thing was laughing at me.

"Harry won't hurt you. He just wants to be friends." Jake shrugged, which was absolutely no help at all. As if Jake's words had spurred the furry spider onward, it crept closer until it was only a couple of feet away.

"Please, just get him away. Please. I'll vacuum your side of the room for two weeks," I begged, beyond caring about appearances.

"Vacuum for two weeks and my dishes for a week," Jake said before smiling widely.

"Fine, it's a deal."

Laughing, Jake knelt down and tapped his finger on the tile. The spider turned at the sound and started walking toward Jake like it was a dog and not a tarantula. I wanted to throw up as Jake held out his hand so it could crawl into his palm.

"Don't worry. I'll be your knight in shining armor." He gave me a wink and laughed as he walked out of the room.

Yeah, I didn't need a white knight. All they ever did was let you down or go away—it only ever worked out in fairytales. I mean, look at *my dad. I'd loved my dad and he'd loved me, and he'd sworn to protect me always and forever—and he left.*

Sure, I guess dying wasn't his choice, but he still left, and as a result, I ended up at my uncle's. My time at my uncle's was something I never wanted to think about again, so no—no more white knights for me. The fairytale stories were all lies.

As I sat on the edge of the bed and stared at where the spider had been, I just wanted to cry, but there was no point. My parents were dead, my uncle had hurt me, and now I was stuck here. Nothing I said or did would ever make any of that right.

Jake was so quiet when he walked back in that I didn't hear him until he sat down on the bed next to me. Startling, I jerked around and tensed. Was this when he changed, too?

Jake had never been mean to me even though I'd tried everything to get him kicked out of our room. I'd even gone so far as to lie and tell Mrs. Jones that he'd pulled my hair and called me rude names—but he never got angry with me. I didn't understand it.

He laid his hand out on the bed palm up, and I looked between it and his profile. He didn't look at me and didn't say a word. I couldn't explain why I did it, but I reached out and laid my hand in his—and in that moment, for the first time since my parents had died, I felt safe.

Jake wrapped his arms around my waist and pulled me to his body for a kiss. He still seemed ridiculously pleased with himself, the big goof.

"I see some things haven't changed," he said before nipping at my bottom lip. "Go grab your jacket or we're going to be late. Not that I mind." He kissed my neck and then stepped back. As I walked into the house to grab the jacket, I heard something that made me pause.

"By the way, I invited my brother to dinner."

"Which brother," I asked, making my way back toward him, jacket in hand.

"Jayce."

Well, this should be an interesting dinner.

JAKE

SOME OF MY ideas are fucking brilliant, and this was one of them. As soon as we pulled up to the pub, I could see Lexi's friend Olly waiting out front with Jayce. By the looks on their faces and all the finger-pointing, they were not getting along very well. Excellent.

"Well, that doesn't look very good," Lexi said, nodding her chin in the direction of our dinner partners. No longer able to be contained, the smirk instantly spread across my face.

"You did this on purpose, didn't you?" Lexi asked before she swatted my arm and laughed.

"Let's just say that I figured it was a win-win either way. Jayce has been twisted in knots because Olly never called him, so I know he will be entertaining. He couldn't keep his foot out of his mouth if he tried. Also, Olly won't feel compelled to treat me like I need to be interrogated if she's busy battling Jayce's annoying poking. Besides, maybe this is the push they needed to go for it."

"Devious. You're truly devious," she said as I grabbed her hand. Together, we started walking.

"So many new things you're learning about me." I gave her a wink and loved the blush that spread across her face.

"Hey, guys. What's going on?" Lexi asked once we were in earshot.

"You mean other than the fact that *Jayce* here is arrogant and self-absorbed?" Olly asked, obviously irritated. I wanted to shake my brother's hand.

Don't get me wrong, I genuinely loved my brother with all my heart, but he was a fucking pest of the first order. He could crawl under your skin and say just the right thing to set you off and make you want to smack him. I wasn't even sure he realized when he did it most of the time or if it just came naturally to him.

"For doing what? Thinking that you'd call me when you said you wanted my number? How is that self-absorbed? If anything, you're inconsiderate of other people's feelings and rude," Jayce said. He shrugged nonchalantly and casually stuffed his hands into his pockets. "It's your loss, though. I had a great date planned."

"How about we just go in and eat, and we can discuss something else? Anything else?" Lexi smiled widely and clapped her hands together like she was herding cats or kindergartners along, which surprisingly seemed to work.

I held the door for the other three to walk inside, and as soon as I stepped in and the waitress greeting us saw me, her face lit up. I was used to that look—it was the 'oh my fucking god, it's *you*' look. It was not a look I was in the mood to appreciate.

At one point, I would've puffed out my chest and glowed from the attention and recognition. Now, all I wanted was a meal with the woman I loved. The waitress pulled out her cell phone, and I knew she was going to ask for a picture before she even opened her mouth.

"Oh. My. God. Jake Russell. It's you!" The pitch she got as she squealed the last word sent a shiver up my spine. It was like she didn't even see the three people I was with—she pushed past them as if they were invisible. *That* I did not appreciate. That was a problem.

I held up a finger, and she stopped moving like I'd pushed a button.

"I'm not doing pictures tonight. I'm sorry to disappoint you, but maybe another time."

"Please, just one. My younger sister loves your songs, and it's her thirteenth birthday tomorrow, and she would literally die if you wished her a happy birthday." She clasped her hands together, very openly begging.

My eyes searched out Jayce and Olly's before locking with Lexi's. She seemed to know what I was silently trying to ask and nodded.

"Please, I'm begging you. She has your song lyrics written out and posted on her walls like wallpaper," the waitress pleaded.

"Alright, but this is the only one I'm doing."

"Eek! Okay, I can't believe this."

"What is your sister's name?" I asked as I ran a quick hand through my hair.

"Amanda," the waitress said, bouncing.

I held out my hand for her phone, and she quickly brought up the camera option. Taking the phone from her, I switched it to video and cleared my throat. It had been weeks since I'd sung anything, and I felt a bit rusty.

"Hi there, Amanda. I understand you have a special birthday coming up, so this song is for you." I sang the usual birthday song and gave the camera a wink before handing it back to the beaming waitress. A round of applause sounded throughout the pub.

Jayce was used to this and was taking it all in stride, while Olly looked annoyed and Lexi terrified. I had no idea why she was practically hiding in the coat rack area with her back to everyone—then I realized that more than just myself had been recording the impromptu birthday greeting. It wasn't a sea of cameras, but the number of customers with their phones up was not small, and they were recording from multiple directions.

Oh shit. Protectiveness surged through me, and I quickly but casually moved over to better block Lexi from view. Smiling, I waved to the customers, and even a few staff, still filming.

"The show is over, everyone. Thank you. Just a quiet night out tonight. Okay?" When people realized I was serious, they began to put their phones down. My muscles relaxed, and I peeked over my shoulder to make sure Lexi was okay.

"Thank you so much. She's going to *freak* when she sees this. Here, I'll take you to our *best* booth." The waitress grabbed a stack of menus and started walking, and Lexi dashed out from behind me to follow, keeping her head down the entire way.

Guilt clawed at me that she was having to hide her face because my fame had gotten in the way, but that guilt was quickly replaced with anger when I remembered why she was hiding in the first place. It was insane that she couldn't even go out for a simple dinner without worrying that he'd find her—and what he'd do once he did. It wasn't right and it wasn't fair, and I wanted to crush him.

"Here you go," the waitress said as she stopped at a large round booth in the far corner of the restaurant and placed the menus down on the tabletop.

As Lexi slid in, her eyes darted from one person in the restaurant to the next. Turning around, I noticed that a couple of people were still filming like they thought they were the fucking paparazzi. Jesus Christ.

"I'll be right back," I said before marching over to the first table. I did not give the people the chance to speak, just calmly and firmly asked them not to film me anymore this evening and offered to do a single picture with the couple. Heading to the next table, I did the same thing until all the cameras were put away.

"So much for a quiet and uneventful meal. Doesn't look like you can go anywhere without drawing a crowd," Olly said, obviously more than ready to pick at me. "Is this going to be a problem all night?"

"I hope not, but I can't control what everyone does any more than you can," I said, hoping to shut her down. I was already annoyed enough for both of us.

"Olly, I can fight my own battles," Lexi said, and Olly sighed but nodded.

"Lexi, I'm so sorry. I didn't even think about all the cameras around," I whispered and started to grab for her hand, but she shook her head and picked up a menu to use like a shield.

"There are still people watching," she said from behind her makeshift wall.

"There are always people watching, even if I wasn't me, but don't worry—they've put their phones away. You're good." I offered her an encouraging smile. Hopefully, the evening wouldn't be ruined for her from this.

It really burned my ass that she felt like she needed to act like a skittish mouse, though I wasn't mad at her. I *couldn't* be mad at her, not for being scared, but I was fucking pissed at the man who did this to her. That fucking ass had molded her into the woman shaking beside me because a few people had made some recordings, although she was trying so hard to hide it. Something needed to be done, and soon.

I'd heard back from Miles about a P.I. that I could hire and had sent him a message with the information that I wanted. So far, the only thing the guy had come back and said was that he'd let me know what he found when he had something. Not exactly what I was hoping to hear. Patience and I were not well acquainted.

Slipping my hand under the table, I laid it on her leg, and I heard her sigh as her muscles relaxed under my touch. Peaking at Jayce and Olly, who were consumed with their own somewhat heated discussion over the menu items, I took the opportunity to lean toward Lexi.

"What did I promise you?" I whispered. Those amazing blue eyes of hers found mine, and some of the worry in them melted away like an icicle on a warm day. The sight melted my heart.

"That he'd have to go through you, and that would never happen. That he'd never hurt me again," she mouthed quietly.

"I intend to keep my promise," I said, and Lexi nodded, the last of the worry melting off her face. Sitting up straight, I turned to watch the exchange between our dinner companions like I was at a tennis match.

"You like *ketchup* on your mashed potatoes? Are you a heathen?" Olly asked and screwed up her face like she was going to be sick.

"It would probably pair wonderfully with your wine," Jayce snipped back, and Lexi choked on her water.

"Wow, you two should just get married. You bicker like you

already have been for twenty years," I said. Lexi couldn't hold it back anymore and laughed, earning a glare from her friend while Jayce just rolled his eyes.

"Please, spare me. I'm never getting married. Only stupid people tie themselves down like that," Jayce said, the absolute dumbass. Foot and mouth disease was most certainly his thing, and the conversation got a lot more heated as Lexi got in on the argument.

A new waitress came to the table, and I was thankful when she either didn't know who I was or didn't care as she did her job with polite efficiency. Lexi was back to being her relaxed self, and she even leaned into me when I dared to wrap my arm around her shoulders.

This was what I'd been missing out on for years, and Richard had another thing coming if he thought he was going to ruin this for me. Let him come for me, let him try to take his anger out on me, and he'd find out the depths I was willing to go to for Lexi to be safe.

I had to admit that by the end of the meal, Olly had moderately grown on me—kind of like a fungus. She was a fierce friend, which I respected, and she was smart with a wicked sense of humor. Watching Jayce and Olly talk was the equivalent of watching cats hiss and spit at one another, but there was a spark there. It was almost as if they were too much alike yet still perfect for one another—I could see it even if they refused to acknowledge it.

"I'm sure I'll see you again soon," I said, holding out my hand for Olly to shake as we made our way outside.

"Is this your way of calling a truce?" she hedged as she tentatively placed her hand in mine.

"I didn't realize we needed one, but sure. If that will make Lexi happy, then a truce it is," I said. Smirking, I let go of her hand and stepped back to give Lexi her turn. The girls hugged, and as Lexi and I began to walk away, I had to stifle a laugh at the conversation that started up behind us.

"So, you actually going to call me this time?" Jayce asked.

"I haven't decided yet. I'm not sure why I'd want to," Olly quipped back.

"Do you think they'll ever get along?" Lexi asked as she sneaked a look over her shoulder. My own shoulders lifted lazily.

"Not sure, but if I were a betting man, I'd say they will have sex within a month."

"Really? They seem to hate one another," Lexi said as I veered us away from the motorcycle—the ice cream shop was still open. It was a seasonal luxury that would be coming to an end soon, and my mouth was watering for one of their mixed-flavor bowls.

"Did you not feel the sexual tension between them? Trust me. If my brother has anything to say about it, he'll have her in the back of his truck sooner rather than later."

Pulling open the door, I let Lexi go in before me as I took a deep breath of the cool air rushing outside. It held hints of several flavors all mingled together, creating its own unique, memorable scent. Going to the beach and getting to eat ice cream from a spot just like this had been a summer highlight every year. Nothing said 'summer' to me like this little ice cream shop, which had glass cases filled with a rainbow of choices lining half the space and a wall that looked like a toddler had painted on it.

"You know my weak spot," Lexi said, her eyes lighting up as she made her way to the long cases.

Wrapping my hand around her waist, I dropped my voice so only she could hear.

"I thought *I* was your weak spot?" My lips brushed her ear, and she shivered at the light touch. "If I'm not, I will be after I take you home and remind you all night why I should be." Her cheeks flamed a delicious shade of red that just happened to match the cherry ice cream in the case in front of us.

"The things I could do with this ice cream." I groaned softly in her ear, making her shiver. "The places I want to rub it on your body and lick it off. Swirl my tongue deep inside your...." A soft jab from her elbow cut me off for a moment, but that wasn't going to deter me. "Make you a whipped cream bikini, maybe?" I softly kissed the side of her neck as more ideas began to dance before my eyes.

"Hi there. What can I get for you?" the girl behind the counter asked.

"Um...I think...," Lexi started to say as she stared at the wide variety of flavors, trying valiantly to concentrate. I couldn't have that.

"I want to lay you out like a dessert, lick my way up between your legs," I breathed in her ear.

"Gravy," Lexi blurted out. She immediately shook her head and covered her face before she burst out laughing. A playful glare was sent my way over my shoulder.

"You. Knock it off," she said before she cleared her throat and turned back to the confused girl.

"Um, I'm sorry, but we don't sell gravy." The girl tilted her head and crinkled her nose up—she looked like a confused little bird, or maybe a bunny.

Lexi tried to step away, but I was having none of it and kept my hand firmly on her waist. The ability to make Lexi nervous in all the good ways made me feel like I had a Marvel superpower, and the satisfaction of it ran through my system. My chest brushed against her back as I leaned close to her ear once more.

"Didn't you say how much you liked double p...." Lexi whipped around and placed a finger delicately but firmly on my lips. I furrowed my brow and arched an eyebrow as the girl gave the two of us an inquisitive look.

"I was only going to say peanut butter and chocolate," I mumbled around her finger before giving her a quick wink. "You know, flavors to satisfy two cravings?" I smirked as Lexi's face deepened to the darkest shade of red I'd ever seen and her eyes snapped with anger like she was planning on killing me.

I was enjoying every fucking second of this. Lexi plastered a smile on her face and turned to face the girl behind the counter again. As soon as her back was turned, I gave her ass a squeeze that caused her to yelp and my cock to stand at attention. Every fucking thing she did made me want her more.

"Chocolate, anything chocolate," Lexi managed to get out.

"Oh, you want chocolate again tonight?" I asked, pulling her a little closer so I could rub my hips against her soft curves.

"Would you like sprinkles?" the girl asked, thankfully still blissfully unaware.

"She definitely wants sprinkles, lots of them," I said, smirking. I jerked and had to swallow a loud groan as Lexi grabbed my cock through my jeans. In one single movement, she rendered me speechless.

"And whipped cream, loads of whipped cream," Lexi said, and I had to bite my lip hard as she gave me another squeeze. Holy hell, she was killing me. All I could think about was getting her home and naked.

"And what would you like?" the perky girl asked as she handed over Lexi's cup.

"Yeah, sweetie, what would you like?" the sexy devil beside me asked as she rubbed her hand in a circle. My body shuddered as all the blood rushed from my brain to focus solely on completing one goal, and while tongues were involved, licking ice cream was not it.

After making sure I was watching, Lexi slowly licked a dollop of whipped cream off the top of her cup. I briefly wondered how much it would cost to pay the girl to go and just leave the key so I could lay Lexi out on the counter.

"What's the matter, hun? Are you unsure what you want?" Lexi's hand was strategic as she subtly stroked me harder out of view of the counter. She was pulling off a fabulous innocent act with her big doe eyes opened wide and her mouth pushed out just enough that it made her look sweet and innocent—and not at all like a girl grabbing my hard shaft.

"No, I know exactly what I want. It's just where I want it that's becoming the issue," I said. My eyes watched her tongue as it licked away a speck of whip cream I was pretty certain she'd left on the corner of her mouth on purpose just so she could do that.

"Mmm, this is sooo good," she said, licking the sweet white topping again, and it was suddenly me who was panting and flushed. "You'd better order, snookums. The nice girl is waiting." With a devilish smile that lit up her whole face, Lexi let go, and I simultaneously took a deep breath and wanted to yell for her never to stop.

Oh, I was *so* making her scream when we got back to her place.

"I'll have your quad sundae with all the toppings."

A few minutes later, Lexi gasped in shock at the massive sundae as the girl handed it over, making me grin.

"Oh my god. Look at that thing," Lexi said, wide-eyed.

"I really want to make a joke right now, but I'll behave," I said as we made our way outside.

"Behave? You call what you did in there behaving?" Her tongue swirled around the top of her chocolate treat, and I had to look away. I was too close to my don't-give-a-fuck meter being tapped out, and there was no telling what I'd do.

That was one bonus to living the life I'd lived for so long—you really didn't give a shit anymore what people saw you do. Being all over the internet for fucking her in this very nice, absolutely not private park would almost be a dream come true, considering that I'd had similar daydreams for years.

I seriously have issues.

We sat down at one of the empty picnic tables and stared out at the dark water, which sparkled from the light of the moon reflecting off the surface. Lexi shifted closer to me like she always used to do, making those tiny movements she seemed to think I didn't notice until, like magic, she was right next to me.

I used to love it when she did that, although I never dared to say a word. I didn't want her to stop—I never wanted her to stop seeking me out. Wrapping my arm around her now, I was thrilled as Lexi snuggled into my open jacket and laid her head on my chest.

"I love the little lights and the way they sway back and forth," Lexi said, pointing to the white decorative lights that had been strung from tree to tree like little swings. She shivered slightly, and I decided to abandon my ice cream and get Lexi home despite how I would've loved to have sat in the same spot all night with her.

"Let's get going," I said, nudging her gently.

She turned her head up to look at me, and I couldn't help but drop my lips to hers for a quick kiss. She tasted like rich, dark chocolate, and her tongue was still cool from the last bites she'd eaten.

"What about your ice cream?" she asked. "Why don't I go see if they have a lid so we can take it with us?"

"Sure, if you want," I said and smiled as she jumped up and took off.

I heard the voices of several women before I could see them walking along the sidewalk, but as soon as we caught sight of each other and they screamed like fan girls, I knew I wouldn't like where this encounter was going.

"Oh my god, *oh my god*, what are the *chances*?"

"Is it really *you*?"

"Fuck, you're *so* much hotter in person. I told you it was a good idea to leave that shitty concert and explore."

"This *can't* be happening. Quick, where's your phone?"

I tried to back away from the four women as they rushed toward me, but *damn*, they were fast. In a moment, they had me surrounded. I hadn't been noticed once since I'd moved home, and this was now twice in one night that I was going to be accosted.

One of the women slid her arm around my waist, and I pulled away only to have my ass grabbed by one of the other women. What a fucking perfect time for teamwork.

"Ladies, I'm happy to take a picture with you, but lay off the merch with your hands," I growled out, my annoyance spiking. This shit was only mildly entertaining when I was black-out drunk. Sober, it was just fucking irritating.

The third girl, wobbling in her fancy sandals, managed to successfully get her phone out of her purse only to trip and crash into me. She didn't waste any time in utilizing the opportunity to cop a feel of my dick.

"Okay, that's enough," I barked out, and they all froze. "Get off of me, now."

Like I'd dumped a bucket of ice water on their heads, they shut up and, in an impressive maneuver, took a step back in unison. All four women stared up at me and blinked their red, glossy eyes like it might help my words make more sense. I was guessing it wasn't going to help.

"Wow, you seem so much nicer in your videos," the one who had grabbed my dick said, crossing her arms over her chest.

I bit the inside of my cheek hard to stop the sarcastic comment that wanted to slip loose, but one of the women had her phone up like she was filming me and waiting for me to lose my cool.

"I don't take kindly to being sexually assaulted. If you'd like a photo, I'm happy to take one with each of you, but that's it. And no touching."

"Oh, is that your newest girlfriend way over there?" one of them asked before trying to step around me for a better look. I quickly blocked her way. Even though I couldn't see Lexi, if she was really there, I wasn't letting this turn into a three-ring circus. There were already too many elephants, lions, and clowns in my life—the last thing I needed was to add this fiasco to my ever-growing list.

"Did you want the picture or not? If not, please move along," I said.

The woman made a noise like a surprised horse, and the droplets spewing from her mouth hit me right in the face. I quickly wiped them off my cheek and chin as she pointed a finger at my chest.

"You're nothing like your videos, and I'm gonna tell all my friends what an asshole you are."

I smiled, but it didn't reach my eyes. The old me would've said something sarcastic like. "Oh like I'm sure your cat will really care." But, this was the new me, this was the me trying to stay out of trouble. "I'm sorry you feel that way, have a nice night," I said instead and wanted to spit on the ground because that tasted so bad in my mouth.

Ten. Nine. Eight. Seven.

I counted backward in my head, making sure that no emotion showed on my face as the small group wandered away until I was finally alone again. Slumping, I turned around and spotted Lexi standing in the shadows of the trees.

Shit.

"Hey, I'm sorry about that." I walked toward her, but when she held up a hand to stop me, I halted. "What's wrong?"

"What's wrong? Jake, twice tonight, I've almost ended up in a video out in social media land. I'm in hiding...I can't do this," she said, pacing a small line from the tree to me and back again. She had her arms wrapped around herself, and her eyes were so large that I could almost see the fear spinning in them like a tilt-a-whirl.

"I'm already scared most of every day. I can't add this to it too, Jake. I just...should I move again? Maybe I should go to Canada. Richard hates the cold. I could move way up north where he wouldn't want to go," she rambled as she continued to pace the small line.

Fear gripped my throat as I stared at her terrified expression, but she had another thing coming if she thought I was letting her go that easily. As Lexi turned to march away from me again, I reached out and grabbed her shoulders, forcing her to come to a halt.

"Stop, Lexi. Just stop and breathe." I gripped her upper arms firmly as she shuddered and looked around in the darkness, checking for monsters that only she could see. "Look at me." Giving her arms a soft rub, I waited until she locked eyes with me. "Are you saying you want us to end?"

I didn't think she could look more scared, but at my question, her face drained of all color.

"No, never. It's just...this...." She held out her hand to where I'd been standing before. "I can't be seen in public with you. God, this whole situation is crazy, but he can't find me, Jake. You don't under-stand what a sadistic...." She lifted her hands and laid them on my chest like she was pleading with me to understand. "I can't explain how evil he is."

Cupping her face in my hands, I took a deep breath and waited until she did the same.

"Lexi, you can't hide forever. At some point, you're going to slip and end up featured in a local paper, or your picture will be in a social media post for your bakery."

"I know, but this feels too soon, like I'm dangling something red in front of a bull. It's only been a few months since I took off." She wrung her hands together. "Jake, I believe you that you'll keep me safe when I'm with you, but you can't start babysitting me every minute of the day."

"Lexi, look at me." Her eyes lifted from staring at my chest, and I gave her a smile. "You're right. Maybe in a year from now, you'll be ready, or five years from now, but that would mean living every single day in constant fear of what he may or may not do that entire time. Is that how you want to spend your life? Spend our life together?"

"No, it's not, but...."

"No buts. I'm in this for the long haul now, and you're not getting rid of me easily. I plan on sticking to you worse than a toe fungus."

Lexi smirked and then laughed, the sound as hypnotic as the tinkling of a wind chime. "Wow, that has got to be the least sexy thing I think I've ever heard, and yet oddly fitting."

Pulling her close to my body, I kissed the top of her head.

"You're not the same woman, Lexi. You've re-found your strength. You left as soon as you could, which is brave all on its own, but now look at you. You're starting your life over and building a business from nothing. You need to believe in yourself and know that I have you now."

She lifted her head up higher, and my lips hovered over hers.

"You keep saying that," she said.

"I'm hoping one of these times it will start to sink in how much you mean to me," I whispered before letting my lips brush against hers. "I have you, Lexi. I. Have. You."

Lexi grabbed the front of my shirt and slammed her lips to mine. The searing desire behind the act melted every organ in my body.

"Take me home right now," she said, breaking the kiss.

"Yes ma'am, and just so you know, I'm going to get cameras installed in and around your place and mine, okay?"

"Thank you, Jake."

"No need to thank me. I want to do whatever I can to not only keep you safe, but make you feel safer."

Linking our fingers, I teasingly tugged her toward the motorcycle, but Lexi pulled me to a halt, her face serious once more.

"I'm sorry. I'm sorry for the panic attacks and the weak moments and...I'm just sorry for all the crap. I feel like I have nothing to offer our relationship other than drama and baggage."

"First, you have nothing to be sorry for. Don't ever be afraid to be yourself with me. Second, did you see what happened tonight? If anyone has drama and a steaming pile of baggage swirling around them, it's me. Now come on, I have ice cream to play with and a woman I want to use it on." My lip curled up. Lexi laughed like I was joking, but I fully intended to have her screaming while I ate my dessert off the best dessert of all.

BEST
FRIENDS

33

KAT

"**WHAT DO** you mean the order was canceled?" I demanded as I paced the floor of the bakery. Between being put on hold and continuously transferred from one person to the next, I was surprised I hadn't yet worn a track into the tiled floor. What the heck was with this new, never speak to a live person crap?

"No, I understand what the words mean, but I didn't cancel my order. If I don't have those supplies, I can't make anything, and then I have nothing to sell." I stopped pacing, my mouth falling open at what I was hearing.

"Of *course* it's your problem. Someone at your place made an error, and now me, the customer, is paying the price. I would say that is most certainly a 'you' problem." The line went dead, and I brought it down from my ear to stare at it. "Are you *kidding* me," I yelled. I felt like tossing the cell across the room.

My heart pounded hard as my disbelief mingled with white-hot anger. How the heck was I going to get enough supplies to finish my custom orders this week? The store was open tomorrow. Not fulfilling orders and being understocked so soon after opening would be a disaster my bakery might never recover from fully.

There was only one chance I could think of, but it was a long shot. Grabbing my purse, I fished out my phone and locked the door as I hit Jake's number. It went to voicemail.

"Hey, Jake. I need to ask you for a favor. I don't know if you can help, but...anyway, I'm going to borrow Olly's car and head to your parent's farm, so I'll see you there." Hanging up, I pulled open the door to Olly's bookstore. She smiled and waved as soon as the door dinged.

"Hey girl...whoa, what's up with your face?"

"My face?"

"Yeah, you look like you're going to kill someone."

Rubbing my face, I sighed. I certainly *wanted* to kill a few people, not that it would help.

"I feel like it. Can I borrow your car? I promise I know how to drive."

She snorted and shook her head, obviously amused.

"Like you even have to ask. Here," she said, holding out the keys.

"Thanks. I need to go see Jake. I'm hoping he can help me out with something."

"I could—."

Holding up my hands, I waved her off.

"Nope. You've done more than enough to help me already. I've got this," I said, smiling. "Promise. It's not an Olly sized crisis," I teased, making her smile.

"Okay. Well, you know where the car is parked, so have at it. Should I plan to walk home?"

I paused on the way to the door and looked back over my shoulder at her as guilt gnawed at my stomach. She kept giving, and I kept taking.

"Yeah, probably a good idea."

Olly laughed and shooed me out the door when I hesitated, about two seconds away from calling it off and giving her back her keys.

"I see your brain over thinking and don't even bother. Get out that damn door, girl."

After retracing my steps to where we'd left the car that morning, I unlocked the door and slid in. It felt good to be behind the wheel of a car again. I hadn't been sure how I'd feel about driving because of the accident, but once the initial bout of palm sweating got out of the way after the first five minutes of white-knuckled nervousness, I started to relax. It helped that this area seemed to have the quietest roads in the country and even those driving along didn't seem to be in a rush.

Like with riding a bike, the muscle memory returned as I continued past the town limits. I opened the windows some and let the cool air flow into the car as I sang to whatever song came on the radio. It was exhilarating to feel such freedom again. I could go anywhere, but where I was going was exactly where I wanted to be—with Jake.

When I reached the Russell farm, a couple of cars pulled out of the driveway while I waited to turn in. I could see that tents were still set up and a couple of RVs still parked, but it looked like everyone was working away at packing up. Jake was standing under one of the tents talking to a small group of people I didn't recognize. My palms began to sweat all over again for a totally different reason.

After parking, I took a deep breath to ground myself, stepped out of the car, and made my way toward Jake. He looked over his shoulder, and when he saw me, his face lit up. The initial nervousness was wiped out of my mind, along with the rest of the people standing there, as he walked toward me.

He didn't bother saying hello as he wrapped his arms around me and kissed me like he hadn't seen me for years. The desire I felt was instant and spread like a wildfire fanned by a hot summer breeze.

"This is a pleasant surprise," Jake said, breaking the kiss but keeping his arms wrapped around my waist. It took me a moment to remember why I was there in the first place. I hadn't thought it was possible to feel this loved or special, yet Jake managed it.

"Yeah, sorry. I tried to call, but you must have still been filming," I said. At my words, Jake immediately pulled out his phone to check it, and his face scrunched up into a frown.

"Huh. I thought I turned it off mute. Anyway, you don't need a reason to come see me, and you certainly don't need to apologize," Jake said. He started to pull me closer, but it was hard not to notice the whispers and furtive glances we were now receiving from the people who were definitely still standing there, no matter what my lust-addled mind thought. "Ignore them. They don't exist."

My blood pressure rose with the blush creeping up my neck, making me wish I had a fan to try and cool myself off with because *damn*—Jake needed to come with his own heat advisory.

"That's easier said than done, but...I actually came because I was hoping you either might know someone who could be my new supplier or know someone who knows someone."

Jake cocked a brow at me.

"Um, supplier of *what*, exactly?"

It took a second for the light to go on, and then I couldn't hold back a laugh.

"Sorry. Flour, sugar, yeast—definitely not what you were thinking."

Jake took a small step back to see my face better.

"Why, what happened?" he asked, brows furrowed.

"I really don't know. There was some sort of mix-up, and my order got canceled. They said I canceled it, but I never called them. Now they don't have enough product or anyone to deliver it even if they did," I said, lifting my shoulder and letting it drop despondently.

"That's strange," Jake said right before our phones dinged at the same time.

I looked down at the notification that had popped up from some gossip site, and my heart sank through the floor at the sight of Jake kissing a pretty blonde who looked like she was climbing his body.

"What the fuck," Jake said as he stared at his phone.

"Funny, I was thinking the same thing." I held up my phone to show him the picture.

"You're a *fucking* asshole!" a male voice yelled. I looked over as Jake's older brother, Tripp, began stomping in our direction.

"Oh shit," Jake muttered as he held up his hands to ward off his fuming brother. "Dude, calm down."

"You didn't have enough women to fuck. You had to take my wife too," Tripp yelled, drawing the attention of everyone who wasn't already staring. My mouth couldn't have hit the floor any harder at his words. "I invited you into my home, and *this* is how you repay me?!"

"Whoa! Man, it's not what it looks like." Jake looked at me with pleading eyes, but I was still stuck in the 'holy shit' stage and too confused to offer any encouragement. "I mean it. It wasn't like that."

Jake took a step back as Tripp got closer, and suddenly Jayce was there, putting himself in between Jake and Tripp with a hand on each of their chests.

"Hold up, Tripp. Damn bull in a crystal shop," Jayce said.

"What the fuck? That's *not* how the saying goes, and get out of my way so I can break his fucking nose," Tripp growled, his large fists balling just as all of our phones dinged again.

I was terrified to look, but I lifted the screen, hands shaking, and stumbled back as I stared at two images. There was a picture of Jake and the four women from the park as they draped themselves all over him, but I already knew what had happened there. It was the picture of him and me kissing and holding one another as clear as day that had panic gripping my chest.

The pictures were part of an article. The title read, "The Player Jake Russell Is at It Again." Bracing myself, I scrolled down.

Well, it didn't take long for the well known playboy influencer, Jake Russell, to go back to his old ways. Are we saddened by the news? Not in the slightest. This juicy and very delicious social media mogul just keeps on giving the content. Seen in these three images are a group of fans he couldn't keep his hands off of and a secret girlfriend we didn't know anything about. If that wasn't scandalous enough, the girlfriend is reportedly married to another man. Who is this poor man whose wife ran off on him to be with a social media star? I don't know, but we will make sure to let you know that juicy tidbit soon. Now for the real whale of this story, folks. I wonder if Jake Russell's mystery girlfriend knows that he's also sleeping with his sister-in-law? You know what they say—don't cheat unless you want to be cheated on.

A short interview clip embedded in the article began to play, and I recognized Xayne right away.

"That girl likes to play games. She asked me out on a date, and then her boyfriend came in and beat the shit out of me. I think it's some sort of joke to them that they get off on playing, but it's not very funny. I think they both should be arrested."

It just doesn't get any better than this. Keep it coming, Jake Russell. You know we love it when you fall off the good-boy wagon to return to your bad-boy ways. All I can say is that this is certainly going to make family dinners a little awkward. Until next time, my Sexy Heathens.

"Oh fuck," Jake said as his eyes found mine. "Lexi." He reached for me as I clutched at my chest and futilely tried to take a deep breath. It was like breathing through a straw. Before he could touch me, Tripp lurched forward and went to grab for him again, but Jake jerked away angrily.

"Fuck off, Tripp! It's not what you think. Just give me the fucking benefit of the doubt, for fucks sake!"

Whipping around, Jake grabbed me as I stumbled backward and eased me down to the grass.

"You're okay, Lexi, you're okay. Just breathe." He cupped my face, and I couldn't stop the tears from welling up and spilling over. "I know this looks bad, but it's not what it looks like."

I shook my head back and forth as the air barely wheezed into my lungs. He was going to find me. Richard was going to find me. It was all I could think about.

"Who...wha...."

"Don't try to talk," Jake cut in. "Just use your calming thoughts or words or whatever you have. It's going to be okay."

He was trying to help. I could hear the obvious worry in his voice as he rubbed my cheeks with his thumbs, but no amount of calming words was going to stop the world from seeing that post. Richard would see it—I could feel it in my bones as surely as I could feel Jake's hands on my skin, and a cold sweat broke out all over my body.

I couldn't get a sentence out as the panic gripped my chest tighter. It felt like a boulder was sitting on my rib cage, crushing it, and the searing pain from the lack of air made it feel like I was having a heart attack.

"Can't...breathe...," I gasped, needing Jake to understand.

Jake picked me up and began marching away from the steadily growing group of onlookers, who were somehow managing to make the panic even worse just by being there. I felt like my world was narrowing in on top of me.

Someone opened the door to the house for Jake to walk through, and I could hear Joy and several other people, but their voices were no longer making sense.

"Jake...," I said right before his face blurred and everything went dark.

JAKE

"Shit, she blacked out. Someone get me a cool cloth," I said as I laid Lexi, down and stuffed pillows under her legs. "You're okay, Angel." I felt for a pulse and made sure her chest was rising and falling, which seemed to be happening more smoothly now that she wasn't conscious.

"I'm going to get to the bottom of this, Angel. I'm so, so sorry." After giving Lexi's forehead a kiss, I looked up at my mom. "Can you look after her for a few minutes? I don't want to leave her, but I need to go sort this shit out."

"Of course. You don't even have to ask," she answered.

I wrapped my arm around my mom for a quick hug on my way past her, thankful that she was there. Her steadying presence helped me push down my panic so I could focus on the cold rage running through me. Rage, not panic, was going to get me the answers I needed.

"Thank you. I'll be right back. If she wakes up...."

"Go, Jake. I've got her. We'll be fine," my mom said, giving me a reassuring smile.

Jayce was waiting outside the door and followed me as I stormed across the veranda. Stripping off my leather jacket, I tossed it onto a wooden lounge chair as I went. Blood. I wanted the blood of whoever did this.

Whoever did this knew me—knew where I was, knew about my past, and worst of all, knew how to get money out of doing this. A cheap story and pictures like that would bring a nice payday for someone, and I had a feeling I knew exactly who would want to cash in.

Tripp was waiting for me at the start of the gravel driveway. I did not need his issues right now.

"We need to talk," he said.

"Get the fuck out of my way, Tripp."

He grabbed my arm and I stopped, glaring at his hand.

"Let go. Now," I growled out as my eyes met his. For the first time in our lives together, he looked unsure and let go of my bicep. "Good call. Follow me," I said, resuming my march across the gravel, stones crunching under each heavy footfall. I reached the trailer that had arrived today to help take some of the cleanup, but it was also the trailer that I knew the girls from the shoot had been staying in and began pounding on the door.

"Lanny! Get the fuck out here." My fist hit the door so hard that I was leaving small dents in the metal frame.

"Oh my *god*, stop the pounding," came Lanny's voice from inside before the main door opened and Lanny's face peered blearily through the screen door. She blinked and yawned, but as her eyes focused, she froze. "What's going on?"

"What do you think is going on?"

She looked around like the air was going to give her the answer before clearing her throat.

"I don't know."

"Look at your fucking phone," I said, my voice coming out more of a snarl than as words. "I told you. I warned you that if you ever pulled a stunt like the other night again, I'd ruin you." Placing my fist against the wall of the trailer, I leaned toward the thin screen separating us. "You've made a big mistake."

"Jake, I swear. I don't know what you're talking about." Her eyes darted to something behind me, and I knew she was looking at Tripp and hoping he'd step in. The fucking nerve. The trailer rocked as I smacked both hands on the side of it.

"Look at your phone, now!"

It had been a really long time since I'd been this mad, and very bad things happened when I was this angry. I forced myself to step away from the side of the trailer, chest heaving with every breath and hands clenched into fists as I fought the swirling, volatile rage.

"Oh my god," Lanny whispered. She pushed open the trailer door, but her eyes were glued to the screen. "I didn't do this, Jake. I swear I didn't."

"You denying that's you?" I asked, pointing at the phone.

"No. I remember the kiss, but barely. Shit, I was so drunk and...." She stopped and looked at Tripp as she swallowed. "High. I was really high."

"So you remember doing this? Why? Why the fuck did you do this? You said you wanted this life, and I fucking gave it to you on a silver platter, and then you do this to me?" I demanded.

The anger was simmering white-hot again, and Jayce must have felt it because he pulled me further away from Lanny and squeezed my shoulder. I wouldn't have hit her—I didn't do that kind of shit, but he was right—it was safer to put distance between us.

"I...it was a dare, a stupid prank. I thought it was funny at the time, but Jake, I didn't take a photo, and I didn't set out to cause trouble," Lanny pleaded.

A sarcastic laugh ripped its way out of me as I turned and stomped a few strides away to cool off. I had never heard such bull-shit before.

"You did this? You kissed my brother at our old home for a prank?" Tripp asked. I'd never heard his voice sound so hurt, and I turned just in time to see Lanny reach out as Tripp backed away from her like her fingertips were coated in poison. "I don't know who you are anymore. What would you have done if our girls had seen you?"

Lanny covered her mouth as tears streamed down her face. She shook her head back and forth.

"I...I was drunk. I wasn't thinking about—."

"You weren't thinking at all, apparently," Tripp bit out. He shook his head and turned to look at me. "Jake...."

"Don't!" I ran my hand through my hair. "I know your life has fallen apart, and I'm fucking sorry about that, but you believing this crap...." I shook my head. "Man, you should fucking know me better than that. I'll forgive you in time, but right now...I can't fucking believe you'd automatically think I'd do something like that to you," I said. "I would never, you hear me? Never."

I wasn't even sure what more there was to say.

"Look at the picture again. Does it look like I'm enjoying the kiss?" I asked.

Tripp looked at the photo again and shook his head.

"You were ready to rip my head off over this. Fuck this. The two of you are fucked up. Figure out your own shit, but I'm out. I want nothing to do with either of you." Spinning on my heel, I started back to the house and the person I actually cared about right now.

I could hear Lanny's feet crunching the gravel behind me before she grabbed my arm.

"Jake, please believe me. I didn't know this was what would happen."

Glaring down at her, she took the hint and let my arm go.

"What exactly do you think is going to happen when someone offers you a large sum of money for a *joke*? You think they have good intentions?" Her eyes darted to the ground, and that was all I needed to see to confirm that she'd taken cash to do this.

I'd given her an out. I told her I would let the whole thing go, and I hadn't said anything to anyone for the girls' sake because they deserved better than having their mother's name slandered—but now...now, the gloves were off.

"I mean, Lanny. Come on. Did it seem like a normal prank for someone to drive you to your ex's house in the middle of the night to try and accost his brother as a *dare*?" I paused as I thought of something and shook my head. "Wait a minute. I didn't get home until two in the morning. How did you even know when I'd be there? You pulled in a couple of minutes after me."

She bit her lip as Tripp, Jayce, and I all stared at her. I heard the door to the house open and looked over my shoulder to see Lexi step outside. Relief washed over me at seeing her standing with the color back in her face, but her sad look stabbed me in the gut worse than any physical blow ever could. Turning my eyes back to Lanny, who looked like she was ready to rabbit right out of there, I posed the question again.

"Answer me, Lanny. How did you know?"

"We were waiting," she finally said.

"Who is *we*?"

She shrugged.

"I don't know. He said he was from some magazine, but honestly, I was so out of it by then that I barely remember. I can't even tell you what he looks like."

I took a step toward her, and Lanny sucked in her lower lip as she shrank away from my dark look.

"If it wasn't for your two daughters...." I needed to get away from her before my head exploded. "Don't ever talk to me again. Get off my family's property and never look in my direction for anything ever again. I don't want to hear your name, I don't want to see you at family events, and the last fifteen years of friendship are no more." I pointed my finger at her and then at myself. "We are no longer friends, and we're certainly no longer family."

I could hear her sobbing as I turned and walked away, and I didn't care. I had another call to make. Yanking my phone from my pocket, I swiped past the images that were making my blood boil and saw the twenty messages and calls that I'd missed from Miles. Hitting redial, I put the phone to my ear. He answered on the first ring.

"It wasn't me," he said before I could ask the question.

"Then who the hell did this? Someone has set me up, Miles, and I fucking want to know who," I said as I reached Lexi and wrapped an arm around her waist. When I looked into her eyes, she didn't seem angry, and I took that as a good sign and gave her waist a gentle squeeze. Her grounding presence was very welcome, as Miles' explanations and excuses were not making me any happier.

"I don't care if it seems impossible," I barked into the phone. Closing my eyes as I listened to Miles talk, only half listening, I laid my lips on Lexi's temple and was beyond thankful that she didn't pull away. The look that had come across her face when those pictures first popped up had put my heart in a vice.

"Yes, I'm well aware that the trash magazines are pissed that I'm not giving them easy headlines anymore. It doesn't give them the right to set something like this up. They almost ruined my relationship with my brother, not to mention my fiancé...yes, I know you didn't know. Just find out who. Follow the money."

I hit the end button and took a shuddering breath as I stared down into Lexi's blue eyes. I still had a hard time thinking of her as Lexi, but it was what she wanted so that was what I'd do. Now that the rage was subsiding, my muscles were shaking, and I wrapped her up in both arms.

"Please tell me this hasn't ruined us, that you don't believe I'd do that to you?" I begged.

She gripped my shirt tighter in her fists.

"At first glance, I thought so—but I know your heart, Jake." I hugged her tighter and sagged with relief. "I was also in there studying the image, and your face was shocked. Besides, if you were going to cheat—."

"I never would, not in a thousand years," I said, cutting in. I couldn't bear her thinking I would, not even hypothetically.

Her body relaxed into mine, and I took my first deep breath since this had all started. Only minutes had gone by, but I would swear that years had just been shaved off my life.

"All I'm saying is that if you did, I think you'd be smarter than to get caught by a tabloid," Lexi finished saying, and I leaned back to force her to look at me.

"Never." I held her gaze until she nodded. "I will find out who did this, and I know I can't stop Richard from seeing the image, but I will do whatever I can to keep you safe."

Lexi nodded in response, but as she looked toward the gazebo, a lone tear trickled down her cheek. With a sniff, she wiped it away.

"I know, but like you said, I can't hide forever." Lexi tilted her head to look up at me. "If he finds me, he finds me. I'm so tired of being scared all the time, Jake. The terror has made me numb, it has made me feel crazy, and I'm ready for it to be over. All I know for certain is that I love you, and I'm never going back, and I'm never backing down again. It's time I faced my fear."

I'd never felt more pride for anyone in my entire life. She amazed me. Everything about her had always made me feel unworthy of her attention, and after those words, I felt even less like I deserved her. The thing was, I was still never letting her go.

"Jake, why didn't you tell me about this happening? Did you think I wouldn't understand?" she asked, brows pressed together.

"No, Angel, it wasn't anything like that. It just happened the other night, and honestly, I wasn't planning on saying anything because she was wasted out of her mind and I didn't want it getting back to Syd and Bri. I figured she'd sleep it off, feel stupid, and apologize. I never expected it to turn into this, but I should have. Living the life I have, I never know who I can trust, but I promise you that if anything like this ever happens again in the future—and I'm praying it doesn't, but if it does—I will tell you right away."

She nodded as she looked up at me and then laid her head on my chest.

"I've been lied to so much, Jake. I believe you, but I don't want to start doubting you," she said, and I held her tighter.

"*We* are my number one priority—not screwing that up is number two on the list. This is on me. I should've thought that something was up, but I just didn't expect it from Lanny. Shows you how stupid I am. So no secrets between us. I'll never keep anything from you, and you never, never, ever have to worry about me cheating on you," I said with a kiss to the top of her head. It felt wonderful to feel her hug me tight and sigh as she relaxed.

I looked toward the house to see my mom smiling as she wiped her hands on a tea towel, and I knew that we were all going to be okay. We had to be...I'd make sure of it.

BEST
FRIENDS

34

KAT

MY PHONE RINGING woke me up with a jolt, and I sat up in a temporary state of confusion about where I was. The light pooling in from the window revealed a pastel blue room with a decorative flower border and white trim. I wasn't in my little house...I was in Jake's parent's house.

I turned my head to look for Jake as I grabbed for the phone. My tired eyes were having trouble focusing on the number, so I gave up and hit accept.

"Hello?" I asked.

"Oh thank god. When you didn't come home last night, I thought you'd taken off," Olly said, and I could hear her take a deep, loud breath.

"I wouldn't do that. It was just a really long day, and I crashed at the Russell house with Jake for the night."

"What? You're still with him? Girl, what the hell?" Olly squawked. That was the only word for it.

Swinging my legs over the side of the bed, I stretched and rubbed at my face as I tried to formulate a coherent sentence.

"I'll assume you're referring to the post that went out yesterday?"

"Um, *yeah*. Lexi. You just got out of a horrible situation—for the love of *all* the fur babies in the world, *why* would you jump right back into this kind of drama?"

"It was a setup, Olly. It's a long story, and I'll give you all the details, but now that I'm awake, I'll get home and...shit, the store. What time is it?" Frantic, I looked at the clock on the nightstand. "Oh god, I have to get going. The store is open today, and now I'm going to be late to open. On top of that, the new supplier that Jake got lined up is set to arrive soon with an order."

"Don't sweat it. I'll go open. I know how to run a cash register and pack boxes with the best of them, and I can point the guy with your stuff to the back. Mind you, I would never suggest leaving me to bake," Olly said.

"Really?"

"Yes, of course *really*. Take your time. I've got it under control, and this way, you won't be tempted to try and avoid telling me what the hell you're thinking. Because I'm totally confused."

To laugh felt so good—it was something that I cherished having in my life again.

"Thanks, Olly. I'll see you soon."

Hanging up, I quickly scanned the area for my clothes and found them neatly folded in a chair in the corner. Picking up the shirt, I gave it a tentative sniff. Sure enough, my suspicions were confirmed —someone had washed my clothes while I slept. I could definitely get used to having magic laundry fairies.

A quiet knock sounded at the door, and a moment later, Jake's head popped through the crack. When he saw me by the chair, he smiled a huge, beaming smile.

"Oh, good. You're awake and you found your clothes," Jake said as he entered the room. As soon as I saw his tousled hair and the impish grin on his face, I couldn't stop a flurry of images of last night and the sweet way he'd made love to me from running through my brain.

He was like so many different versions of the same man all rolled up into one, and every version was mine. I had no idea how I'd gotten so lucky, but I was taking it.

"I brought you coffee, but if you keep staring at me like that, then I'm never letting you leave the room again," he teased.

Smiling, I took the steaming mug from his hands and raised myself up onto my tiptoes to plant a soft kiss on his lips.

"Thank you for the coffee, and as much as I love the idea of staying in here all day, I'd better get going. The store is open today, and if I'm going to 'face my demons,' as you put it, then step one is to go about my life as I normally would." I took a sip of the coffee and moaned—it tasted so good.

"Besides, now that I have a new supplier thanks to your magic yesterday, I have to be around to accept the ingredients when they arrive, and I'm still not sure if I can get everything made once the store closes this afternoon," I said.

"I can help with that," he offered as I set down the coffee to pull on my sweater.

"You bake? And asking someone to make them for you doesn't count," I teased, knowing full well that the cookies he'd made when we were kids were more Mrs. Jones's work than his.

He shrugged, unconcerned by my culinary dig at him.

"I wouldn't go so far as to say I bake, but I can stir ingredients with the best of them. I'm also great with heavy lifting, and besides, I look pretty damn sexy in an apron. Especially when it's the only thing I have on," he said, making my cheeks warm.

"I have a feeling that I'd definitely get more clientele that way, just not the kind looking for brownies and tarts," I giggled. "But yes, I could certainly use the help if you're up for it." Walking toward him, I bit my lip and batted my eyes. "The pay isn't great, but I'm sure I can find a way to make it worth your while," I said as I ran my finger down his chest.

"Are you propositioning me for my sexy services?" Jake wrapped his arms around my waist and pulled me tightly against his body. It felt great. He was always so hot, not just to look at but physically as well. He was a walking furnace, and I wanted to cuddle into the comforting feel of him.

"I might be. Is it working?"

"Angel, there are many terrible and depraved things that I'd do to get a taste of you," he said before dropping his lips to mine.

He tasted like coffee, and I was suddenly a lot more tempted than I should've been to pull him down onto the bed and take him up on staying in here all day. Jake had an uncanny way of always saying or doing the exact right thing to make butterflies take flight and flit around in my stomach while also making me want to throw caution to the wind.

Breaking the kiss with a groan, Jake lifted his head and licked at his lips like he was savoring our kiss. Okay, why was that so hot? I seemed to be asking myself that a lot lately.

"You'd better get going. I'm really close to locking the door," Jake said as he stepped back, making me grin. "What time do you want me to come by?"

"Anytime this afternoon would be great." I finished off the coffee in one large gulp and handed the empty mug over to Jake, who stared at it with wide eyes. He should never underestimate my caffeine-consumption abilities. "Oh, and I should warn you that Olly may be there, and she was pretty fired up that I was still with you."

"Oh great." He tapped his chin. "Maybe I can talk Jayce into coming to run interference again."

"I'm pretty sure you can handle yourself just fine. That tongue lashing you gave Tripp and Lanny was pretty fierce," I smiled widely and gave him a quick kiss before escaping out the open bedroom door.

"Is 'fierce' good?" he called after me.

Reaching the top of the stairs, I paused with my hand on the railing.

"Fierce is sexy."

I laughed as I heard a faint *yes* as I jogged down the stairs.

"Hi, Joy. That smells wonderful," I said, poking my head into the kitchen as I pulled on my shoes.

"Fresh biscuits, grits, bacon, and gravy. Are you not staying for some?" she asked as she turned my way, and I felt terrible as her sweet smile fell.

"Can I take a rain check? The bakery is open today, and I'm already running late."

"That's right. It's Friday. I'm so sorry, dear. These meds give me brain fog," she said while looking at the counter, which was full of food. I had no idea who all she'd planned on feeding, but there was enough there for two armies.

Walking into the kitchen, I grabbed a paper towel and laid it out. Picking out a few of the still warm biscuits, which were so fluffy they were making my mouth water, I quickly slathered them up with a generous amount of butter and jam.

"I'll take these for the road," I said before giving her a hug. "Don't worry. I have a feeling that with the men you have hanging around here, none of this is going to go to waste."

"Isn't that the truth? They're goats," she said, smiling. "I'm really happy you listened to Jake and decided to believe him. Many wouldn't have given him the benefit of the doubt with his history, but I tell you right now, with God as my witness, that boy loves you more than his own life. Plus, he wouldn't do that to you or Tripp. I'm still pissed with my oldest for believing such nonsense." Joy shook her head, and I could see the disappointment in her eyes.

"My personal opinion, for what it's worth, is that Tripp is just angry in general, and Jake and that photo made a good target to take his anger out on. He just seems so sad, and I don't think he really believed it, if that makes sense?" I gave a little shrug. "I do hope they work this out, though. I've seen the way Jake talks about Tripp, and I think he'd be lost without him."

"Yeah, you're right. I'll see if I can talk some sense into my two knuckleheads. You'd better go, dear." Joy shocked me as she pulled me into a hard hug and then just as quickly released me. "Okay. Get on out of here before I talk your ear off some more."

Laughing, I took my biscuits and made my way to Olly's car. The farm looked so open without the tents, cars, and RVs lined up every-where. I preferred it like this—the beauty and tranquility were breathtaking.

The drive back to town seemed to take longer than getting to the farm had, probably because I was running late, but I still wanted to stop at home to get changed. On Fridays, I liked to wear my soft pink blouse with the little rainbow on the pocket. It was silly, but it was my version of a uniform for now until I could afford a proper one.

Running up the walkway to the house, I shoved my key in the door and pulled it open. I came to a screeching halt as a deluge of water came rushing out. I gingerly stepped inside—the water was almost up to my ankles.

"What the heck?"

I quickly dialed Marie's number, but when it rang, I heard it ringing both in my ear and somewhere behind me. Looking outside, I saw her walking down the street. Lifting my arm in the air, I waved and called her name. The initial smile on her face fell as she saw my expression.

"What's wrong?"

"I think a pipe burst. Has this happened before?"

Marie stepped up and covered her mouth with her hands as we watched a pen float past as more water rushed out across our feet.

"Oh dear lord. I'll call the plumber right away, but I'm more worried about the water reaching something electrical than the water damage. This place is still done up with fuses and not breakers."

Marie pulled out her phone and began making calls while I stepped out, not daring to test my luck with standing in the water after what she'd said. I looked down at my wet sneakers and jeans and shook my head—how things change so rapidly.

I was just getting used to my calmer life when Jake had all but stormed into it. I loved it, and I loved him, but it seemed like he'd brought a literal storm with him. I couldn't exactly blame him for a burst pipe, but the last forty-eight hours had certainly taken a strange turn. The question was, would I trade it all away or take what we had, ups and downs included?

No. That would never be a real question—not in a million years. Bring on the storm.

"So I think I've called everyone under the sun to come by, but you might as well head to work, and I can keep you posted," Marie said, sighing as she looked toward the water that was still creating a stream out the front door. "Nothing like this has ever happened. I'm so sorry, Lexi."

"Don't apologize. You couldn't have anticipated this. Are you sure you're fine with me heading to work?"

"Of course. It's my job and there is not much to do other than wait. Now go on, get out of here."

By the time I made it to the bakery, I felt like I'd been running on some strange hamster wheel all morning. After I parked and stepped out of the car, I noticed that Olly was standing outside the bakery and washing the window and there wasn't the usual lineup outside. Now what?

"Hey, what's going on?" I asked as I made my way across the street. Olly looked over her shoulder, and she looked caught between furious and on the verge of tears. Shit. "Do I even want to know?" I looked inside the store, which was still dark, and then at Olly. "What's going on?"

She dropped the sponge she was using into the bucket of soapy water and pulled me into a hug.

"I'm so sorry," she murmured.

"Yup. I'm officially freaked out."

"Are you *sure* this Jake guy is worth it?"

My brow furrowed at the question.

"Yes, I'm sure. *Why?*"

Olly held out her hand toward the window.

"Someone spray painted 'cheating whore' on the window, and I'm presuming it was the same people who broke in the back door and trashed everything that was stored in the fridge." Olly looked like she was on the verge of tears. I could relate—I was, too.

"I'm so sorry. I should've had that door fixed before you took over. It looks like it was never latched properly, so all they had to do was pull hard enough to open it. God, Lexi, I'm so very sorry, but I had to send everyone who was waiting home—and Lexi, there were definitely fewer people here, on top of everything."

I stumbled back and had to sit down on a bench.

"Who the hell would do this? Who would be so cruel to another human when they don't even know them? They have no idea what I've been through. They have no idea that I've had to fight to find a semblance of a normal life after all the loss and abuse and...." I was getting angry. The shock was rendering my legs weak, but the rage over this attack, which seemed so petty and pointless, was coursing through me.

"I'm sorry, Lexi. I wish there was something I could say to make this better or take all this away...." She waved her hand at the window, which was still smeared with red. Honestly, the fact Olly had managed to clean it as much as she had was probably pretty incredible. "I already had Sheriff Karl out to take photos. He said he'd drop by again later to talk to you."

"Thank you, Olly. Do you mind if I just sit here a moment before I go in and start to clean up?"

"Of course. Take your time, girl. I'll finish this window, and then will head on in."

I watched Olly swipe over the red streaks of smeared paint until, bit by bit, it disappeared. At the moment, nothing felt more like a representation of my life—but there was no way I was letting someone scare me off of what I wanted, not anymore.

This was my home now, and I fully intended to make a life here, so they could throw my food on the floor and paint my windows with obscene things, but I wasn't going anywhere.

My phone began to ring, and I pulled it out to see Jake's smiling face. I had no idea when he'd put a picture in for his number, the little sneak.

"Hey there," I said, answering.

"Why do you sound upset?"

"I'll explain when I see you later."

"I don't like you keeping things from me," Jake said, and while I was tempted to tell him everything, he had work to do, and so did I. As much as I wanted to lean on him for every little thing, this was something I had to do on my own.

"I'm not keeping anything from you, just delaying the relay time. Was there a reason you were calling, or did you just miss me already?" I asked, hoping to deter him with teasing.

"I always miss you, that's a given, but I forgot to tell you that a courier will be by at some point with something for you."

"Well, that's all very cryptic," I said, laughing.

Jake chuckled into the phone, his deep voice making me wiggle on the bench.

"You'll understand when you see."

"Okay. I'll wait to find out as you will wait to find out. I guess fair is fair."

"I love you, Lexi," he breathed.

"I love you too, Jake," I responded just as quietly.

"I'll never grow tired of hearing that. Talk to you later."

"Bye." I hung up the phone and looked up at Olly, who had turned to watch me. She sighed and picked up the bucket now that her job was complete. The window looked great.

"I may not like some of the drama he's brought into your life, but to see that smile on your face makes the load of feces that follows him more bearable," she said.

"Is that your way of saying you like us together? I'm not sure with all the shit talk."

Olly laughed hard as I stood up from the bench, ready to get on with things.

"Let's not talk crazy. 'Like' is a strong word, but I have to admit that Jake is doing something right. I just hope the storm quiets before it carries you away."

I grabbed her arm before she could walk away. I didn't like that flash of worry in her eyes.

"I'm not going anywhere. I'm not saying I'm not scared anymore —I'm just saying that I'm done running, and that's partly because of you." I looked up at the storefront. "This place is my home now, and you are like family. I honestly don't know where I would've been without you, Olly. You've been crucial to me getting my life on the right track, so thank you."

Olly wiped at her eyes with her free hand.

"Well shit. Now you've gone and made me cry. Come on. Let's go in before I turn into a sobbing mess on the sidewalk."

The wind picked up and blew my hair around my face, and I turned into it to look at the quiet street and the few cars parked on it. No one looked my way while they walked down the sidewalk or stepped out of a shop, yet I shivered. As illogical as it was, the feeling of being watched was hard to shake.

No matter how bright, the sun would never be able to warm the type of cold that came with the fear that Richard would find me, but it didn't matter. I wouldn't run despite how much my fear was telling me to hightail it out of town. This spot, these people and Jake, were my home now, and no social media bully, vandalism, or even Richard himself was going to take this from me.

My hands balled into fists as I let the anger take over and drive. Richard had repressed me long enough, and I wasn't going to take it anymore.

Jake had said I was never weak, and maybe he was right, but the one thing I did know for certain was that I wasn't anymore.

BEST
FRIENDS

35

KAT

I WAS MOPPING THE FLOOR, trying to scrub out the last little bits of food from where the vandals had ground it into the grout, when the jingle of the bell announced that someone had walked inside the front door. Poking my head around the corner, I spotted a man who stood out as badly as city folk in a country bar. His tailor-made suit was cut to fit, rings donned each of his fingers, and he stood with his back straighter than a ballerina's.

"I'll be right with you," I said. I had been expecting the Sheriff, and I quickly tried to clean myself up. Pushing the wild strands of hair out of my face, I could only imagine how much of a disaster I must look. Stepping out from the back area, mop still in hand, I went to greet the impeccably dressed man, who clearly sucked at either reading or following directions to have ignored the 'closed' sign on the door.

"Are you Katelin Baldwin?" he asked as he stepped forward.

I straightened my own spine at the sound of the name I'd abandoned when I'd moved here to become Alexis Dupree. Scanning the man closer, I forced my throat to work and my voice to sound firm even though my insides had turned to jelly. What fresh hell was this?

"And what is it to you if I am?" My eyes darted to my phone, which was sitting on a counter near the door to the back room in arm's reach.

The man stepped further into the bakery, and it was only as he turned to close the door that I realized he was holding a large brown envelope.

"I have paperwork that needs to be signed to finalize your divorce," he said.

I knew this wasn't the lawyer that Eve had hired. I'd met the man once, and he was in his early seventies with vibrant white hair and a distinctive pot belly. Although this man had a dusting of gray in his hair, he looked like a GQ model ready to do a silver fox edition.

"Is that so?" I replied, making sure not to give away any of my building nervousness.

"My name is Jonathan Lewis, and I'm a lawyer." He held a business card up between his fingers. "I represent Mr. Baldwin in your divorce matters, and he wishes to get the proceedings over with as soon as possible."

My eyebrow raised, and I couldn't stop the sarcastic laugh that bubbled up.

"Obviously, you don't know Mr. Baldwin well if that is what you think."

He held up the envelope and pulled out a thick stack of white papers with colorful little tabs sticking out along the edges.

This couldn't really be happening, could it?

"What's the catch?" I asked.

"First, I must get confirmation that you really are Katelin Baldwin," he said, and my lips curled up at his tone. What an ass.

"And I'd like proof that aliens exist, but I guess today is not going to be that day for either of us," I said.

I could see him analyzing me as he looked me over. This 'Mr. Lewis' knew damn well who I was, and if he was here, then Richard knew where I was. He'd obviously seen the picture and sent his henchman to do his dirty work. The problem was, I wasn't sure whether to believe that this guy was an actual lawyer, an information collector, or both.

Who was in the store with me right now? The thought terrified me to my core and made my bones feel brittle under my skin, but I wasn't letting Richard and his fucking scare tactics win again. If this guy really was who he said he was, then he needed to prove it first.

"Mr. Baldwin said you might be difficult to deal with," he said with a drawl like I was boring him and this was all a waste of his way-too-valuable time. "I have a flight in four hours, so I don't have much time. Are you going to confirm you're Katelin Baldwin or not?"

Mr. Lewis openly looked down at the flashy gold watch on his wrist, and even though I normally wasn't one for making quick assumptions about people, I absolutely didn't like this man very much. My hands tightened on the mop handle as fantasies of swinging it at the man's head crossed my mind.

"Are you going to show me the paperwork? If not, you can leave my bakery at any time to catch your oh-so-important flight." I held my arm out toward the door invitingly and offered a smile I knew didn't reach my eyes.

He took out his phone, and before I realized what he was doing, he took a picture. You'd have to be an idiot not to know who he was busy sending the picture to, and a cold sweat trickled down my spine. The phone buzzed a moment later.

"Mr. Baldwin says it is you, Mrs. Baldwin."

"Please do not call me that," I said, teeth clenched.

"Very well. Please come look at the paperwork so that we can proceed," Mr. Lewis said as he pulled out a chair at the nearest table. The freaking gall.

Could this actually be real? Could Richard have come to his senses and decided that he wants me gone from his life as much as I want him gone from mine?

I didn't dare hope for such a thing because there was always a catch when it came to Richard. Grabbing my phone, I was tempted to call Jake, or at least Olly, to come over, but I was a big girl capable of handling her own problems. My whole new life had been about rediscovering that for myself.

Instead, I just brought it with me to have it close by in case the jerk decided to try something. I brought the mop along to the table as well, just in case. You never knew when you needed to clean up a mess and something told me this man would run from a dirty bucket of water being dumped near him.

Mr. Lewis set the thick stack of paper in front of me as I sat down and then proceeded to hand over a pen that looked like it cost more than everything I owned.

"All the tabs that are marked with a pink tab are for you to sign or initial," he said as I flipped to the first tab. Yeah, right. I wasn't signing anything until I'd had a chance to read it over carefully.

"I will read it over now, but I hope you don't expect me to simply sign this without it being looked over by my lawyer. I'm not exactly up on all the legal jargon and would hate to miss an important clause."

"I wasn't aware you had a lawyer, but yes, by all means, take all the time you need to read it over. Would you like me to come back?"

What a snake. This guy had to know that I had my own lawyer. I was the one who filed for divorce, not the other way around.

"No, stay until I'm done in case I need any clarification on what Mr. Baldwin is asking for. Don't worry. I'm sure you'll still be out of here in plenty of time to catch your flight," I said and began reading. There was a certain appeal to making the man miss his flight.

Thumbing through the pages, I wasn't surprised to see that he didn't plan on giving me anything. Not that I wanted a dime of his money, but after ten-plus years and all the shit he'd pulled, you'd think he'd feel some sort of compassion. Figures.

By the time I got to the last tab, I was going cross-eyed from the extremely small print. What the last appendix said, though, had me focusing in and sitting up straight. I read the page three times before I looked up at Mr. Lewis.

"Are you kidding me?" I asked, flipping the pages around so he could see what I was talking about and pointing to a certain, very troubling part. "He wants me to admit that I was, and am, clinically depressed and suicidal due to my mental state. Then he wants me to write a formal apology to him and his family for embarrassing them in the media after everything they did to try and help me with my issues?"

The sentences all ran together in front of me as my pent-up hurt and betrayal poked their heads up from the sand to join my burning rage. Richard had beaten me down emotionally and mentally before he'd started physically abusing me. He'd crushed my spirit and then kept me hostage in my own home, turning it into a prison with him as the warden while he tortured and raped me when I couldn't fight back or run, and *now* he wanted me to say that I was *clinically insane?* He wanted to absolve himself of any wrong doing and have it in print for the courts...forever?

Oh *hell* no. I may have run to escape his grasp, but I sure as hell wasn't giving this asshole carte blanche to do it to someone else.

"Let me guess. This also comes with an NDA or something?"

"Yes, of course. Considering how you abandoned your family with not so much as a word and embarrassed them when all they did was try to help you, it seems very reasonable to me," Mr. Lewis said.

I stood so fast that the chair I'd been sitting in skidded backward across the floor. Leaning my hands on the table, I glared straight into his eyes.

"So manly of you to come here and talk about things that you know nothing about. Maybe, Mr. Lewis, if it had been your paralyzed body he raped repeatedly while you laid there helpless, you wouldn't look so smug," I gritted out, and his eyes went as wide as saucers. "I'm *never* signing that. You can go back to *Mr. Baldwin* and tell him to shove that paperwork so far up his ass that they can never get it out."

Seething, I snatched the business card off the table. I was tempted to tear it in half, but I put it in my pocket instead.

"I'm not sure why you didn't receive my lawyer's documents, but I'll have him draw up an agreement that is fair and get it sent directly over to you right away."

"Mr. Baldwin was very clear that everything was negotiable except the last appendix," he said, but his voice didn't sound quite as certain now. Good. He needed to know what kind of slime he was really representing.

I felt like I was a dragon ready to blow fire. Of *course* Richard would say that. He didn't care about giving me money if I wanted it—he had more than enough for ten wives. No, what he wanted was to humiliate me right to the very end of our marriage. It was his final play, a chance to make sure he had the upper hand and try to force me to sign off on something that would crush my soul to sign. If I didn't, then he got to continue holding the strings of his little puppet.

I hated the thought of a long, drawn-out battle in court, but I wasn't letting him do this to me. I'd handed over my love, my body, and then my soul, and he'd taken them all and twisted them into dark and depraved things. He wasn't going to turn the years of abuse into something that was my fault—something that was all in my head. No. *Never*. At some point, you had to fight back.

"Get out," I said, barely holding it together. When Mr. Lewis didn't move, I snapped. "Get the fuck out of my bakery! Now!"

Eyes going wide, he jumped up and grabbed his paperwork before making a break for the door.

"And take your stupid pen," I shouted. Grabbing it off the table, I flung it at Mr. Lewis and felt a moment of satisfaction as it hit him in the back.

He snatched the pen off the floor and fled like I was going to leap over the table and tackle him. *This* was what Richard wanted—to get under my skin, to let me know that even when he wasn't near me, he could make me feel trapped. Fuming, I started stomping toward the kitchen when the door jingled again.

"What did I just say," I yelled as I whipped around, but instead of Mr. Lewis standing there, it was a young delivery guy. "Oh dear. I'm so sorry. I thought you were someone else."

"Um, I have a package for Lexi?" he said, looking down at the top of a simply-wrapped box.

"That's me." I walked forward and held out my hand to take the package. I felt really guilty as the poor guy took off as soon as it was out of his hands, looking very much like Mr. Lewis had. I was on a roll, apparently.

Feeling utterly deflated and with my insides still jumping around, I sat down to open the package. It didn't say who it was from, but I assumed it was the delivery that Jake had mentioned.

But what if it's from Richard?

Staring at the box like it might bite, I momentarily froze, not sure if I wanted to open it.

"Nope. This is what Richard wants—for me to feel terrified to do simple actions. Don't give him the power." Nodding to myself after my little pep talk, I ripped off the paper. I had to open a series of boxes—so very Jake—until I finally got to one that was made of black velvet. Suddenly, the front door was flung open.

"Wait," Jake yelled as I screamed.

"Oh my god, Jake. Jesus H and all that is holy," I said between pants as I tried to get my heart back under control. While I clutched at my chest, he laughed and wandered toward me looking as calm and cool as a tall glass of water on a hot day.

"I'm sorry, but I was hoping to get here before it arrived. I saw the delivery kid get on his bike and knew I needed to hurry," he said. I stood to greet him, and he didn't even hesitate to cup my face and capture my mouth in a deep kiss. His superpower had to be making me feel better, because he always managed to do it with a simple touch. "Okay. Now you can open it."

I shook out my hands to steady them from the residual shaking before lifting the lid. My mouth dropped open and tears instantly spilled onto my cheeks as I stared at a perfect replica of the rainbow necklace Jake had given me over a decade ago.

"Do you like it?" he asked. The mixture of worry and excitement on his face was identical to the look he'd given me the first time he'd handed me this necklace.

"Are you kidding? It's perfect. I don't even know what to say."

Jake reached inside the box and lifted out the delicate piece.

"This one is real gold, and I had our initials put on the back along with the date we reconnected. Take your other one off and turn around," he said. Turning around, I undid the old chain and then lifted my hair for Jake to put the new necklace on. As it settled on my skin, something settled inside me.

"You're so beautiful," he whispered into the side of my neck a moment before his lips touched the sensitive skin, and his fingertips lingered making goosebumps rise all over my body.

My hand ran over the stunning pendant as I turned to look up at Jake.

"We have something to talk about, but first...." I picked up his hand and nipped at his finger. "Do you know what I'm thinking?" I asked.

He sucked in a deep breath, eyes widening just enough to tell me exactly what he thought I was thinking.

"I might have an idea."

"This would be a good time for you to go lock the door," I said before backing into the doorway to the kitchen. Giving Jake a teasing wink, I pulled the T-shirt off over my head and threw it at him. It hit him right in the face and slid off, revealing eyes full of lust.

I wanted this moment to be ours, for it to be perfect and untainted by the shit that Richard had brought to my door. There was time for dealing with all of that—I didn't know what to do next, and I knew the second Jake found out, he was going to lose his mind. It was going to get intense.

I wasn't spoiling this simple moment between us. We deserved this. *I* deserved this.

"God damn, I love you," Jake growled as the lock clicked into place.

JAKE

"I bet you never pictured using the storage room quite like this," I pondered as Lexi and I lay on our makeshift bed of pallets and blankets. "Why exactly do you have blankets in your storage room, anyway?"

"An old habit," she said, lifting her head from my chest to look me in the eyes. She shrugged slightly. "It wasn't terrible in the back of the ice cream shop. It was warm and quiet, and I had doors I could lock and a place to study in peace. There was a security camera, so I always knew what was happening outside, and I was allowed to eat as much ice cream as I wanted. Kinda sad that it felt safer than anywhere else I could sleep."

Laying my arm over my eyes, I tried to decide how to react to that. I couldn't look at her face as guilt seeped into my chest.

"I'm so sorry, Lexi. I wanted to find you. I never stopped thinking about you." I tightened my arm around her.

Lexi began to laugh, and I removed the arm from my eyes to see her smiling. How could she laugh about this?

"Jake, what would you have done if you'd found me?" she asked.

"I don't know, but we would've had each other at least."

Lexi pushed herself up into a sitting position and reached out to grab my T-shirt and slip it on over her head. Damn, she looked *hot* in my shirt. I decided then and there that I was going to give her as many of my shirts as she wanted and have her wander around the house looking like that all the time.

"Jake, there is a good chance that we wouldn't be sitting here right now if that had happened. We can't say it would've been a happily ever after at that age. We hadn't lived, hadn't seen the world or dated, or...well, just so many things. We could've grown apart or ended up hating each other." She pulled her knees up to wrap her arms around them, and she suddenly looked so small.

"There is no way to say for certain that anything changing in our past would've kept us together forever," she said, sounding very sure. Her eyes glossed over, gaze fixed on a point over my head like she was seeing something only she could see. "I certainly appreciate what we have so much more now, after everything I've been through." She shuddered just a little, like she was shaking herself out of something, and her eyes found mine. "I realize how special the connection we share is, and I cherish every second that we get to spend together."

I sat up to mirror her position. Some things shouldn't be said lying down.

"I feel the same way. I've longed for you the way one longs to find their soul, and now that I've found you...I'm never taking that for granted," I said, reaching out to cup her face. I loved how she immediately closed her eyes and laid her cheek in my palm.

"Do you remember the first time you proposed?" she asked, mouth curling up.

"Do I remember? Please. I could recite what I said to you word for word."

As I sat on the couch, waiting to put my plan into action, I was so nervous that my palms were sweating. I had to keep wiping them off on my jeans. A few weeks ago, I'd told Mrs. Jones that I wanted to learn how to make chocolate chip cookies, and I was so relieved when she didn't question what my motives were. She was probably just excited that a boy wanted to learn to bake something. She'd followed through, and after a few not-so-great results, I finally had what I needed.

I bided my time, and once everyone else was occupied with the movie they'd decided to watch for the night, I nudged Kat and signaled for her to follow me. She nodded that she understood, and we quietly crawled around the back of the couch and out into the hallway before standing. Kat covered her mouth to keep her giggles from catching everyone's attention. Success.

After I grabbed her hand, we ran down the hall, our socks quiet on the tile floor, until we reached the kitchen. I snuck over to grab the container that held the special batch of cookies I'd helped to make earlier, and as quietly as we could, we stuffed our feet into our sneakers and snuck out the back door to go to our spot.

The treehouse had become our own special world—the one spot the other kids were too young to get into and Mr. and Mrs. Jones never went. They hated the climb. We could study there in privacy and spend nights staring out the open door at the stars. It was the perfect spot for what I had planned. Reaching the top of the ladder, I held out my hand to help Kat with the final stretch of the steep climb. I almost dropped the container in the process.

"You're crazy," she said, laughing.

"You're right, I am. I really, really am," I said, and we burst out into a fit of laughter.

After we settled down, I yanked the lid off the container and laid it down, making sure that Kat and I were facing each other as I pulled out the top cookie. Kat's face scrunched up in confusion as she stared at the cookie and the hole cut in the middle of it.

"What did you do to the cookie?" she asked as she grabbed for it. I pulled it out of reach.

"Wait. I have something to say first," I said. Sighing, she crossed her arms and lifted her eyebrow—it was the look she gave me whenever she thought I was being weird. I cleared my throat. "Kat, you're my best friend, but you're also...you're like the best friend I never want to lose."

She tilted her head.

"I don't want to lose you either."

"We know that anything could happen. The Joneses may hate us and send us off next week—we don't know."

"Why are you saying that? Did they say something?" Kat asked,

face suddenly worried. Her blue eyes looked like they were going to fill with tears.

"No, no. They didn't say anything. I'm just sayin' that it could happen."

"Okay," she said, obviously relieved.

Darn it. This wasn't going the way I'd planned in my head.

"I like you, Kat, like...." I rubbed the back of my neck. "Like a lot."

"I like you a lot too, Jake, but I don't get what you're trying to say."

Sighing, I sucked in my bottom lip and decided just to throw it all out there. She'd either be fine with it or push me out of the tree house.

"I'm saying that I want you to marry me." Kat's eyes widened as I picked up her hand and slipped the cookie onto her ring finger. "Kat, you're like my tomorrow," I said, sitting up straighter when she didn't pull her hand away. "I want us to promise to keep it that way. Will you be my tomorrow forever?" I could only hope that the lines I'd wrote and rewrote for weeks didn't sound cheesy and that she'd accept.

As I finished repeating those words from so long ago, Lexi smiled.

"And I said, 'Of course, don't be stupid,' and then ate the cookie," she said with a laugh. Her smile lit up the small room, but it could have lit up the world. "Not a very eloquent response, but in my defense, you made me so nervous. You always made me all jittery." She wiggled around and shivered, making me laugh.

I slowly rocked forward from sitting and onto all fours. My arms flexed with the movement, and Lexi's eyes darted down to follow the play of muscle. I relished every second she ogled me.

"Are these jitters you speak of a good thing?" I asked, grinning.

She licked her lips and laid her hand on my chest as I moved closer and closer like a predator getting ready to snatch its prey—and dear god, I intended to eat each and every bite.

"As much as I want to go for round two, I need to get some baking done so I'll have something to sell tomorrow," she said as she slowly backed away.

"I'm hungry too," I said as she bumped up against the wall, allowing me to cage her in with my arms. "And I know what *I* want to eat." Unable to resist, I dropped my head and sucked on her bottom lip, dragging a moan from her. My hands slid up her legs, pushing the T-shirt out of the way. All I could think about was tasting her on my lips and burying myself deep inside her.

"But...I...need. Oh, Jake," she moaned as I pushed her legs wide open and released her lip only to duck down and replace it with her pussy lips. "I...to...ohhh, yes." She buried her fingers in my hair and pulled my head closer as my tongue dipped deep inside of her.

I'd paid attention to her body, and with every little gasp and moan or clench of her walls around me, I'd learned what she liked. I'd learned what buttons to push to drag the pleasure out and what would drive a screaming orgasm from her body. Tongue swirling around her clit, I slowly slipped a pair of fingers inside of her and pushed up in just the right spot to find the coveted G-spot. In response, Lexi sucked in a sharp inhale of breath as her fingers tightened in my hair.

"Yes, Jake. Just...like...that...ahh," she yelled as she came hard. I licked as fast as I could so as not to waste a single delectable drop.

As I sat back, I wished I could take a picture of this moment. Lexi was still wearing my T-shirt, but it was pooled around her stomach and her legs were spread wide, exposing her to me. While it was incredibly, incredibly sexy, it was the look of relaxed satisfaction playing on her lips that made me smile. I licked my lips clean while stroking my needy cock, which had a one-track mind.

"Come here." I held out my hand to her, and her eyes found mine before dropping lower to watch me stroke myself. I groaned loudly at the intense look on her face as she followed every movement —it almost felt like she was touching me. Sitting back and stretching my legs out straight, I continued to hold my hand out to her. "Come on, Angel."

She did me one better.

"Oh *fuck* yes," I said as she pulled the T-shirt over her head, tossing it on the pile of discarded clothes before moving closer to straddle my legs. She looked like a carved piece of art come to life, and I pulled her ass closer to fight the temptation to dine on the pussy in front of my face once more. If she hadn't squatted down so she was hovering right over my very interested cock, I would've done just that.

I grunted as every muscle flexed at the incredible feeling of her lowering down onto my aching cock. As she bottomed out, we stared at each other eye-to-eye, and even though we didn't say a word, I knew what she was saying to me. It was the same thing I was saying to her.

The way her arms wrapped around my neck and held on tight as she began to move allowed me to peer into her soul. The look of lust mingled with love in her eyes gave me a window into her heart. As she screamed my name and let herself go to enjoy this moment between us, I knew what was in her thoughts.

"Yes, Angel. Yes, that's it. Ride me the way you like," I shouted. Gripping her hips, I helped her keep pace as she neared another orgasm. Arching back, she pressed her breasts into my face, and as soon as I sucked a hardened nipple into my mouth, we came together in a rush.

With each wave of release, I growled into the soft flesh of her breast and sucked harder on the pebbled nipple, making her scream louder. Reluctantly, I released the small, hardened nub and let her collapse against my body as I wrapped her up tight in my arms. We clung to one another as sweat trickled off our skin.

I'd always known that there were different levels of pleasure for doing all manner of things in life, but when it came to Lexi, I realized there was no greater pleasure than pleasing her. Every nerve ending and synapse in my body felt like it was singing. The closest I'd ever come to feeling this in the past was when I just strummed out a tune for the moon and stars, singing for no one but myself.

I hadn't picked up my guitar since I'd moved home as just the sight of it had reminded me of the life I'd been living, but I wanted to sing now. I wanted to write songs about her, about *us*, and sing them from the top of a mountain. *That* was how she made me feel.

"What did you want to tell me before I decided to distract you?" I asked as she rested her head on my shoulder.

"Someone vandalized my store, broke in, and destroyed all the prepared food, and Richard's lawyer stopped by with divorce papers. But he'll only divorce me if I sign off that I'm emotionally and clinically depressed and suicidal and also write him and his family an apology letter for humiliating them so publicly. Oh, and my house is flooded."

I waited to see if there was a punch line to her seemingly blasé admission. Leaning back, I looked at her face, but she just sighed as she lifted her head from my shoulder.

"Angel, what the fuck?"

BEST
FRIENDS

KAT

MY EYES FOLLOWED Jake as he paced across the floor while he argued with whoever was on the other end of the phone. It was probably entirely wrong to think he looked adorable and sexy as hell when he was angrier than a viper with a stepped-on tail. I didn't *want* him to be angry, but hot *damn*.

He'd insisted on having me tell him everything that had happened three times, and then he'd called the Sheriff—who, of course, had already been called by Olly. Jake knew this. According to Jake, the Sheriff was taking too long, and as he apparently knew him, Jake had insisted on putting a fire under his ass. It was kind of adorable.

I turned my head as movement outside caught my eye and saw the Sheriff's car pull up to the curb. Getting up from the chair I'd been occupying to stay out of Jake's path, I made my way to the door and unlocked it before the man could knock.

"Hi there. I'm Sheriff Carr, but you can call me Karl," he said, taking off his hat and holding out his hand for me to shake.

"Lexi Dupree. It's nice to meet you," I said, taking his hand.

"Karl. It's about time you got here," Jake called out before continuing to argue with whoever was on the phone. I'd caught the name 'Miles' at one point, but he was so animated and talking so fast that it had been impossible for me to keep up.

"I told you the guy is useless, there hasn't been a single word since I hired him," Jake growled. I had no idea what he was talking about.

"Don't mind him. He's in grumpy, protective bear mode," I whispered as I led Karl inside.

"I'm used to that. Jake has always been known to be an overprotective grizzly at times."

Karl smiled, and I was immediately put at ease. He was a handsome man with a kind face and an easy-going smile, but it was his intelligent eyes that really reassured me. I'd tried talking to the police about Richard a day after the car accident. They'd wanted to know what had led up to the crash, but when I told them, they acted like I was an overly dramatic housewife trying to cause trouble for my rich in-laws. The officers took my statement, but the investigation into my assault, if it even happened, didn't go anywhere.

"Would you like a coffee?" I asked as he sat down at one of the tables.

"Don't go to any trouble," Karl replied as he took off his hat and carefully laid it on the seat beside him.

"Oh, it's no trouble. I just made a pot. I'll be right back." I slipped past Jake as he turned and marched off in the other direction. After pouring two coffees, I made my way back to the table and sat down as Karl pulled out his notepad.

"Where would you like me to start?" I asked.

"How long have you been in town?"

"I moved here around three months ago," I said before taking a sip of coffee to cover my surprise at the number. I couldn't believe that much time had passed already. It felt like a blink.

"And how long have you had this business location?" Karl asked, looking around the small space.

"Not very long. About six weeks now."

"Have you had any trouble with anyone in the neighborhood?"

"No. Everyone that I've met has been amazing. Well...there was one person, but I wouldn't call it 'trouble,' not like this."

"Let me be the judge of what is important. Tell me everything, and I'll sift through the details," Karl pressed.

Nodding, I sat back in my chair and looked outside, eyes focusing on the Sheriff symbol on the side of Karl's car as I gathered my thoughts.

"Xayne is his first name. I don't know his last name—you'd have to ask his employer. He works for Restaurant Emporium Supplies. He was delivering supplies and asked me out on a date. He was not exactly the best date companion and I started to feel uncomfortable, so I called a friend and left. Apparently, he wasn't too happy about it, and I'm not sure exactly what happened, but Jake hit him, and now he refuses to deliver here."

Karl paused in his writing and flipped back through his notepad.

"This wouldn't happen to have been a few weeks ago on a Friday at a motorcycle bar called Rubin's?" he asked.

"Um...yes?"

Karl shook his head and mumbled something under his breath.

"I know the guy you're talking about. So you think he might have been angry enough to do this?"

I shrugged.

"I don't know. What I *do* know is that he did a short interview for a tabloid where he mentioned me and Jake and went on about how we were playing some sort of sick game with people. It's not true —I didn't even know Jake was there. I didn't even know we were in the same area then."

Karl scribbled down notes that practically looked like they were in another language in the little pad. Without looking, and with a precision that only came with a lot of repetition, he reached out to grab his coffee and take a sip.

"Is there anything else you can tell me that would point me in a particular direction?" he asked as he finally paused and looked up from his notes.

"Yeah. Her ex is an asshole, and the social media magazine I'm on hold with is just as likely to pull this kind of shit," Jake said, cutting in suddenly. "She's being targeted because of a stupid post that went out about how she's an adulterer and—."

"I saw the post," Karl said, cutting Jake off. "Tell me more about your ex."

I fidgeted in my seat nervously and clasped my hands together on the table.

"Jake doesn't agree with me, but I don't think anything to do with the store being vandalized has anything to do with my ex. I mean, maybe—he is capable of anything. But Richard likes mental games. Things that will make you think you're going crazy," I said.

"Maybe not, but I like to know all the players I'm dealing with." Karl sat back and waited for me to speak.

I really didn't want to, but in reality, it was all out there now anyway—the cat was truly out of the bag. My face was on social media, and Richard had already sent a lawyer to see me. I mean, did it really make a difference at this point if I told this man who I really was?

"Before I moved here, my name was Katelin Baldwin, but I had it legally changed. My ex, Richard, is not a nice man. I could try and explain to you everything that he's done to me over the years, but there's no point, so I will sum it up." I took a deep breath to center myself.

"He emotionally and mentally abused me until I tried to run and ended up in a car accident. I was paralyzed for months, and during that time, it became a game of psychological warfare. He would...he would." I took another deep breath and squeezed my hands tighter together.

"He would bring women into the room and have sex with them so I was forced to watch." Karl stopped writing and lifted his head to look at me, but I couldn't tell what he was thinking. "When that wasn't enough, he began sexually assaulting me." I bit my lip hard to keep the tears in check as Karl's eyes hardened very much like how Jake's did.

"Since I ran, he has sent people to break into my friend's house to find information on where I might be, and he did the same with my lawyer's place."

"Did they catch him in the act?" Karl asked.

"No. The person was wearing a full mask and gloves, and I don't think Richard would go himself, anyway. He's more of a 'pay for it to happen while I'm at a fancy public event so I have an alibi' type."

"Well, I might be inclined to agree with Jake on this one. If he'd pay for that, he could pay for this to be done, but I still like to look at all the angles, not just the ones that seem the most obvious." I liked that Karl said that—it meant he was willing to look into all avenues, even the ones other people might dismiss, and that made me feel better.

"Shit," Jake swore as he stomped over. "They hung up on me."

"I can't even imagine why when you asked so nicely," Karl said, smirking widely.

Jake's eyes narrowed as he flopped down into the chair next to mine and immediately put his arm along the back of my chair. The heat of his proximity was reassuring.

"This is all her ex. I just have this feeling. I mean, her store gets vandalized, and then his lawyer shows up with divorce papers that want her to declare that she is crazy? I don't believe in coincidences," Jake said.

Karl crossed his arms as he turned his attention to Jake.

"Maybe. He certainly sounds like he's capable. And you said his lawyer showed up here?" he asked, once more focusing on me.

"Yeah, a few hours ago now. He wanted me to sign divorce papers, but they said that I needed to agree that I'm clinically depressed, suicidal, and a bunch of other stuff. I couldn't do it. Stupid, maybe, but I don't trust him not to use that against me at some point, and I'm not going to be forced into signing something that is a false statement after what he did to me."

Karl nodded.

"I see. I think that was smart, at least until a lawyer can read it over. You never know what might be hidden among the words. As for the spray paint and sneaking in to trash your food, that really feels more like teens out causing trouble, or maybe an enraged fan who didn't like that Jake wouldn't accept their advances, and this is the result."

"I agree with Karl," I said, and Jake huffed sulkily as he crossed his arms over his chest to mirror Karl. As I looked between the two men, I could picture this kind of standoff being something they'd done many times before.

"Fine. We can agree to disagree. What are the chances of finding these jerks?" Jake asked.

"I've already spoken with all the other store owners nearby, and none of them have cameras, and no one who may have been driving by has come forward either. I'll certainly take fingerprints, but those results could take weeks or months," Karl said as he flipped his notebook closed.

"Weeks or months? What the hell? Can't you put a rush on that and get it back in a couple of days or something?" Jake asked. I put my hand on his arm to calm him—he looked like he was getting ready to jump over the table and tackle Karl to the ground. That would be the opposite of helpful.

"Jake, for just a moment, can you remember that you're no longer in Hollywood and that this kind of thing takes time in the real world?" Karl swung his eyes back to me. "Tell me honestly. Do you feel your ex would do this? Are you scared that this is him?"

I sighed as I thought it through because I wasn't sure. I honestly wasn't.

"Capable, sure. He's capable of doing anything. He has the money and resources and is a vindictive, sadistic narcissist who hates to lose and is highly controlling. I mean, the things he did to keep me feeling trapped and scared are despicable, but vandalizing my store...is not really something I'd picture him doing, at least not that fast," I said, trying to put words to all the thoughts in my head.

"I mean, the post just went up. Even for him, that would be impressive to arrange. The lawyer is different—that paperwork must have already been ready, and Richard just sent the guy to get a rise out of me and put me on notice that he now knows where I am. That's just my personal opinion, though. I could be way off base."

Karl tapped his pen on the table.

"Alright, I'm going to give it to you straight. Unless we get a hit off the prints, I don't think we'll find who did this. It's shitty, but without an eyewitness or a camera to pull from, it will be next to impossible to figure out who broke in. I *do* feel it was teens, but it's better to be safe than sorry, so I'd suggest getting a few cameras installed just in case they decide to come back, and I'd get the back door fixed," he said.

"This is ridiculous," Jake fumed. "Someone in this town has to know something or have seen something that could help. You can't walk down the street as a newcomer and not get pegged as someone here to make trouble."

"Although that's true, don't forget we have Crab Fest starting tomorrow one town over, as well as the Blueberry Jubilee, which is already going on just outside of town, and a weeklong concert at the football stadium. Plus, I've been dealing with a local motorcycle group that has arranged a fundraiser for a fallen member's family. Over five hundred bikers have been slowly rolling in to set up camp on a farm until the ride next week. Trust me—there are a ton of new people around right now."

"Don't give me that. Mrs. Wellesley down the street sits smoking in her window at night like a freaky mannequin, and Mr. Harold in the other direction is the resident vampire. He's up all night pacing the floors. You can't tell me they didn't see one suspicious thing. Even if it was a biker, or teens, or a rich man in a suit, they would've seen something." Jake smacked his hand down on the table and then stood and strode off as his phone rang.

"I'm really sorry about him," I said to Karl. I could clearly remember what Jake was like when he got riled up, and until he managed to solve all the issues, he'd continue to escalate things.

It hit me then that I wasn't scared.

Normally, an outburst like that by a man would set off all sorts of tremors and fears, but oddly, Jake's outburst was calming. Although I'd proven to myself that I could stand on my own without a man, there was something comforting about knowing he had my back. I felt positive that he would run into a burning building to pull me out if I needed him to, and my heart warmed as I looked over my shoulder at his glowering expression and flexing forearms.

Karl smiled widely.

"Don't be sorry. I'm used to Jake. You know, when Jake first came to town, he didn't speak to anyone. He was the guy who sat in the corner of the lunchroom and glared at the rest of the kids like they might try and bite," Karl said, obviously delighted to share a little dirt.

"I wasn't exactly the cool kid back then, and he saw me being bullied one day in the hall—that look he's got now is calm compared to the look that came over his face then. He bloodied a few noses and left a couple of other kids with black eyes. The kid who initiated it was lucky to walk away with only a broken arm." Karl suddenly stopped and snickered.

"My mom, rest her soul, was a lawyer, and she more than once ended up having to get Jake out of a cell before he finally turned eighteen. I'd get to sit outside of it while she worked, and we'd play cards through the bars until they released him."

My mouth dropped open.

"Oh my god. I'm so sorry that happened to you," I said, barely able to suppress a smirk of my own.

"Again, don't be. We were tight all through school, and he saved my ass more than once from someone who thought I should be beaten up because I was skinny with glasses and good at school."

"I can picture him doing that."

"Did you know he played football?"

"No, I didn't."

"Him and his brother, Tripp, both did, and for three years, they were on the same team at the same time," Karl said. I leaned on the table, completely captivated by these stories of Jake's past. They were little windows into understanding the man he was now, and they helped bridge the gap from who I'd known Jake to be.

"Jake and Tripp beat the ever-loving snot out of the entire football team one day because they were teasing Jayce. They made the mistake of calling Jayce a faggot because he liked to dance and has always been into fashion. Those two brothers together were a deadly combo. They didn't care if their brother was gay or not, but they weren't letting that group talk shit about him like it was derogatory to *be* gay." Karl smirked like he was rewatching the memory in his head.

"Jake has an unusual compass when it comes to right and wrong. I've tried to tell him more than once that 'an eye for an eye' is not the way, but as you can see, he's a bit stubborn. Whoever did this should be worried, and so should I," he said, suddenly much more serious.

I bit my lip and lowered my voice.

"You don't think he'd do something really crazy, like try to, you know…kill them?"

Karl laughed hard and waved me off.

"No, I don't think he'd go that far, but he does need some time to fume, or he'll combust from his anger and worry over what could've happened." He downed the rest of the coffee and stood from the table. "Tell me, was anything stolen?"

"No money. I don't keep any here—but now that you mention it, they didn't touch the cash register at all. Everything else was dumped on the floor," I said, trying to really think about it. I'd been so focused on cleaning up that I hadn't really focused on *what* I was cleaning.

"Fine. I'll go live, then, if you won't help me," Jake shouted, getting our attention.

Karl opened his mouth as if he were going to argue with Jake, but it was too late. Jake was already live streaming, and I could only hope he wouldn't try to pull me into the video with him. Just because my cover was blown, it didn't mean I wanted my face out there more than it already was.

"Hello, my Beasts. First, I'm sorry that I haven't been on lately. I've been dealing with some personal stuff—but today, I need your help." He stopped talking and looked down as he sighed. It was very dramatic.

"Someone is trash-talking me, setting me up, and purposely trying to make me look bad. Now, I'm not going to stand here and pretend I'm Mr. Innocent. You all know that I've done my fair share of sketchy things, but I always own them." He smirked and let out a little laugh that the audience was definitely eating up. *I* certainly was, and I knew how much Jake was playing up the charm.

"The thing is, this is affecting someone I love. Yes, you heard it here first: Jake Russell admits that he's in love. And this woman who has kidnapped my heart doesn't deserve this kind of humiliation just for knowing me."

He walked around the small shop to show off the banner with the store name on it and then held up one of the lone surviving brownies to take a big bite for the camera. He groaned, and it sounded so sexual that I blushed as my body flushed with heat.

"This *amazing* little bakery is owned by the love of my life. It has the best sweets you'll ever find, but it breaks my heart to have to tell you that it was just vandalized. They destroyed all her lovingly hand-made merchandise. Almost every last piece of it was trashed, and they even had the nerve to spray paint the word 'whore' on the front of her establishment," Jake said, shaking his head.

"When did we become so flagrantly mean? Have you ever known me to cut one of you up for no reason?" He licked his fingers for the camera and gave it a hard stare.

"You've all been there for me for a long time, and I think we've shared a lot over the years. I need to ask all of you for a favor. I'm going to offer an amazing reward for this." He smiled like he was a rockstar playing it up at a concert. It was amazing to watch him switch it on like that.

This was the first time I'd seen him do anything live, and it suddenly hit me that he truly was a global face. How had I ever thought that we could keep our relationship quiet and stay hidden from the world? To be with him meant that I was also tied to all those fans who followed and loved him.

The thought was terrifying. Did that mean we'd never have a semblance of normal? What might our future look like even with us tucked away in this small town, far away from all the lights and action? Most importantly, could I live with however that happened to look?

Yeah. Yeah, I could. I'd follow Jake into hell and back, and I knew he'd do the same for me. That was love. That was what truly being with someone looked like, and I was never letting go.

"I want to know who hired Social Smut to do the hack job on me—and trust me, it's a hack job. Y'all know I love my brother way too much to do something like that to him. How many times have I talked about my family, about how I hold them in reverence and wouldn't be here today if not for them? No matter what other shit I've done in my life, sleeping with my brother's wife? Not. A. F-ing. Chance," Jake spit out.

"Also, the woman they're trashing is not, and I repeat, *not* an adulterer. She is in the middle of an unfriendly divorce from a man who all of you would castrate if you knew the things he'd done to her. All of you who have had a bad relationship come to an end, and I know there's a ton of you out there, can relate to this. I've even sung songs to those of you in similar situations who have reached out to say how much my stories, photos, and songs have made you feel better," he said, his delivery now distinctly softer.

He was telling the truth—I'd seen those videos, as well as the positive messages that always came pouring in for the person who was struggling. In some of my darkest hours, they'd given me hope that people who cared were out there. That he was out there.

"Now we get to the part of this live where I offer you the reward and explain how to win it. I'll write a song and sing it just for you.

That's a one hundred percent dedication and the file sent to you for your own personal use if you can tell me who gave Social Smut the info they needed for the hack job." Jake paused and gave the camera a slow smile. I knew that smile. Something big was coming.

"But...if you can tell me who vandalized her store, then I'll also be giving out a reward of a hundred thousand dollars for the capture of the individual or individuals involved."

I almost fell off my chair at the amount of the reward—that was *far* too generous. My heart pounded hard as it swelled with love. This was *way* over the top, yet it practically screamed how far Jake was willing to go to help and support me.

Tears filled my eyes. I'd gotten so lucky just getting away from Richard, and now that I'd been blessed with a second chance at life with such a wonderful man, I was feeling overwhelmed, but in a good way. In the *best* way.

"And for all of you out there who thought about writing something terrible about the woman I love, maybe because you thought it would be fun or make you feel good to attack her? Please don't." Jake looked over at me, and my lower lip trembled at the look in his eyes.

"She is my end of the rainbow. She is what I hope all of you are lucky enough to find in your lives. If you have any information, please contact the Sheriff's department that I've listed in my bio—there is a number to call. Check ya later, Beasts, and keep rockin'."

"Son of a bitch," Karl swore as his phone began to ring almost instantly. "I'm gonna kill him," he muttered as he answered the phone while he stood up and made his way out the door. I had a feeling Karl was about to get a lot busier.

Jake wandered over as he put his phone away and gave me an uncertain grin.

"I hope that was okay?" he asked.

"I think Karl is planning on stringing you up by your toes. He didn't look too happy when he stepped outside." Glancing out the window, I watched Karl as he paced the sidewalk while talking to whoever had called. He looked decidedly stoic.

"Pfft. Most action he's had in this sleepy area in years. It will do him good. I was talking about if you were okay with it," he said, actually looking a little nervous the longer I didn't answer.

"It's a little late to ask now, don't you think?" I asked as I arched a brow. He blushed and stuffed his hands into his pockets. The stern expression I'd been putting on turned into a smile. "But yeah, I'm more than fine with it. I think it's over the top—like *way* over the top —but I love that you think enough of me, of *us*, to do something like that." Standing, I wrapped my hands around his neck. "I love being your end of the rainbow."

"You always have been, but now the whole world also knows just how much you mean to me," he whispered right before his lips found mine.

Holding him tight as he kissed me, I definitely felt like I was his sweet dessert. I knew for certain that despite it all, this really was our fairytale beginning.

BEST
FRIENDS

KAT

THE WEEKEND HAD BEEN a blur and I'd never thought I'd say thank goodness for Tuesday, but there it was. My official couple days off and Jake and I had plans to spend the day together. After all the turmoil and stress we felt that we deserved some time to ourselves and relax. I had no idea what he had planned. Jake refused to tell me.

It felt completely strange to hear the sound of someone knocking at my door and be excited instead of terrified. Giving myself one last look in the full-length mirror, I almost skipped to the door. Was it possible to feel like a teen again at thirty? I hadn't thought so, but the sound of that motorcycle rumble coming up the street created all sorts of excited butterflies fluttering through my body.

I yanked the door open wide, and it felt like another victory that I didn't look to see who it was first. Smiling, I didn't say anything. Honestly, I wasn't sure my mouth would work if I tried. As usual, Jake didn't waste time. He wrapped an arm around my waist and kissed me like it had been days rather than a few hours since we'd seen one another.

"I missed you," he whispered against my lips.

I was tempted to tell him to forget the date and simply stay in today. Our last date had been...challenging. Jake ended up being photographed multiple times, and I had a panic attack because of it. A repeat didn't seem like a great idea.

"I missed you more," I said and felt my face flush immediately.

God, I sounded like a teenager.

Clearing my throat, I looked away from his eyes.

"Angel, that is not possible. Nothing in this world compares to you, and I miss you every second that we're not together. I worry you'll decide to toss me out on my undeserving ass."

I laughed, but his eyes were serious.

"Jake...I...I feel the same," I admitted.

We stood there staring at one another like we expected each other to disappear. Wrapping my arms around his waist, I hugged him hard and savored how real this moment was. There was no telling how long it would take before the shock of him actually being back in my life would wear off, but I never wanted this feeling to go away.

"I got you something," Jake said. Grudgingly, I pulled away enough so I could look up at him. He held up his other arm to show off the black bag he was carrying. "I got you a few things that I felt were essential for you to ride with me."

"Jake, you didn't have to do that." I stepped back so he could walk inside.

"No complaining. You wouldn't need any of this if it weren't for me and my motorcycle, so it's my treat, no arguments." His eyes were shining, and there was no way I'd ever be able to resist that look, and he knew it.

"Okay. Fine, you win. What did you get me?" I said, the excitement bubbling up as he sat the large bag down.

"First, I got you these." He held out a box. Grinning, I lifted the lid as I stared at the black boots that looked identical to the ones he was wearing, just a whole lot smaller.

"Really? These are for me?"

"Keep looking at me like that, and we're never leaving this house again," he said, and I wasn't entirely sure that he was joking by the look on his face.

Sitting on the couch, I pulled them out of the box and stared at the new addition to my wardrobe. These were total badass status. As I stared at the black boots, I'd never felt more like me than I did right now. I quickly slipped my feet into them, and Jake knelt before me to tie them up. I couldn't help staring at him as his fingers worked the long laces.

"There. All tied up." As he looked up, I cupped his face and kissed him hard, which seemed to take him by surprise.

"Thank you," I said, breaking the kiss.

"Wow, I got that for boots? I can't wait to see what I get for what's next," he teased and gave me his signature cocky grin.

"Give it to me and find out," I said as sensually as possible without laughing. But the fact that Jake had to adjust himself as he mumbled under his breath gave me a shot of confidence like nothing else could.

"Okay, stand up." Jake held out another box, and this time as I opened it, I did giggle. Pulling out my very own helmet, I laughed harder as I noticed the small rainbow that had been professionally painted on the side. "You like it?"

"Are you kidding me? I'm at a loss for words. You do know that you're a complete mush pie, and your followers would never believe you did this and had our symbol custom painted?"

Jake laughed hard. "Tell me about it, but that's because they don't get to see the real me. They don't get to see the Jake that is completely in love with you, and—"

I held my finger against his lips. "No more of that. You're going to make me cry, and then my mascara will run."

Jake smiled, gave my finger a playful nip, but nodded his compliance.

He took the helmet from me and handed me a piece of material. I quickly realized it was supposed to go over my head, so I pulled it into place before he set the helmet on my head. A wave of giddiness washed through me as I stared at the box and was almost positive I knew what it was. Jake lifted the lid, and sure enough, there was my very own black leather jacket. Reaching into the box, I lifted out the beautifully designed leather and hugged it to my chest. I'd lost count of how many nights I'd stared at pictures of him on his motorcycle and pictured myself on the back with him.

"I love it, thank you, Jake."

"Angel, you deserve this and so much more. Come on. Let's get this on you and hit the road. I have a full day planned for us." Doing as he asked, I slipped my arms into the jacket and zipped it up. "Damn girl, you're making me think some very naughty thoughts." Jake's voice came out rough as his eyes looked me up and down.

Stepping in close to him, I smiled wide and stared into eyes that had always held the world for me. "You amaze me, and I love you. I can never say that enough."

"I love you too." He kissed my nose. "Now let's get out of here because I'm really fucking close to doing a repeat of the first night I arrived and pushing you up that wall." His eyes stared at the spot where he'd done exactly what he said, and my body couldn't have gotten any hotter than if I was standing in the middle of a fire.

He led the way out to the bike, and we were flying down the highway that headed out of town within a few seconds. Watching the stunning scenery go by, I realized this was on my bucket list. When you don't know what new torture the next day will bring, you start making a list of things you want to do when you get out or if you get away.

With the wind in my face blowing my hair around, and the feel of holding onto Jake as we traveled down the roads, it was enough to make me want to laugh and cheer but also cry. This was me. This right now, he and I together had always been me, and I held his waist a little tighter.

It took close to an hour to get where we were heading, and I was curious to see what Jake had in store. We slowed and turned into a driveway with a name of a restaurant on the sign, but as we pulled up to park, there wasn't a single vehicle in the lot.

Hopping off, I undid the helmet and looked around. "I don't think they're open, Jake."

"Oh, they're open, but they will only be serving us for lunch," he said, and my mouth fell open.

"You rented the entire restaurant for lunch?"

"Sure did. I'm sick of the flash mobs and photo requests. I want you to feel comfortable and...I haven't even shown you the best part yet." Holding out his hand, I put mine into his as he guided us along a path toward the back of the fancy-looking spot.

This was not the kind of place that sold burgers and fries, and I cringed at the thought of what this would cost. Not even sure why, but an image of Richard sneering at me came to mind. He would hate a spot like this, which helped me push the thought of him away. There was no space in my heart or mind for him anymore.

The further we walked, the more I could see the glittering ocean. I stopped dead as I spotted the large gazebo at the end of the wide dock. One man was standing inside, dressed in a white chef's uniform and I suddenly felt like we should have been in ballgowns instead of the jeans and leather we were wearing.

"Jake, this is...." I couldn't find the right words to express how beautiful it was. A sailboat was on the horizon and made a romantic and soothing backdrop as it slowly floated along. "Just wow."

When he smiled at me, it felt like the world was perfect and that Richard was a distant memory and not a pressing issue. How did he do that? How did he always make me feel okay, happy, and secure? Jake gave my hand a little tug which got my feet moving again.

We greeted the man standing inside the gazebo, who introduced himself as Chef Michaels, the owner and head chef. This area had to be used for parties. It could easily fit fifty people.

"I will go start the meal. Relax and enjoy yourself. There is a path over there to go down to the beach if you'd like," Chef Michaels said. He smiled and slipped out, giving Jake and me some privacy.

Jake pulled out a chair for me and then sat down beside me so we could both stare out at the water.

"Do you remember when we would talk about moving to some-place just like this?" Jake reached for my hand resting on top of the table. "I've never forgotten, and every place I've traveled, I envisioned you sitting with me just like this."

Leaning into him, I laid my head on his shoulder. "I remember everything. Every conversation, every laugh, and smile. I think I've spent more time going over those memories and wondering how to go back in time more than I've thought about anything else in my life."

It terrified me to love him so much. Would I survive losing him again if he decided I wasn't who he wanted? Would the fairy tale we'd dreamed about as kids end up being nothing more than that—a tale?

"Is that pathetic," I asked.

"If it is, then I'm just as pathetic because I did the same thing. I begged Joy and Mark to adopt you too, even when they said they couldn't I didn't give up. I tried to run away so many times I don't know why they kept me around. I was a real handful." Jake wrapped his arm around my shoulders, and I cuddled into him. "God, I prayed every night that you were in a good situation, that you'd found an amazing family as I had. It breaks my heart that it didn't work out that way for you."

"You know the thing is, Jake, everything from the smell of flowers to the breeze on my face...even sitting here right now with you staring at the water. It's all perfection to me. The memories we made are what kept me going when things had gotten really bad and the thought that one day I may see you again is what helped keep me strong."

I lifted my head from Jake's shoulder and admired the way the sun reflected in his green eyes. "You're incredible. You know that?" Jake said and laid his lips on mine.

"Mr. Russell, I apologize for the interruption, but the food is on its way, and I've brought in the wine you mentioned." Chef Michaels sat the bottle down, and I couldn't help smiling wide as I stared at Olly's logo.

I lifted my gaze to Jake, and I knew by the look on his face he'd done it on purpose. My heart soared at his thoughtfulness. It made his gesture even more meaningful. My eyes went wide as server after server arrived with a different dish covered with a cloche on the table. Who did Jake expect to be feeding? There was way too much here. Chef Michaels left with the servers, and I was left staring at twenty or more cloche-covered plates.

"I think you may have gone overboard."

Jake laughed hard as he began pulling off the covers and sitting them aside.

"Yeah, most likely, but I couldn't decide, and I didn't really want to choose for you or possibly choose something you didn't like, so I told him to make me one of everything on the menu."

I smiled wide and grabbed one of the empty plates to begin loading it up. This was incredible. Everything from lobster to steak was laid out like a buffet. By the time we were done eating, I was pretty sure Jake was going to need to roll me out to the motorcycle. I was so full.

However, we continued to reconnect. We talked about everything but stayed away from all sad topics. We'd agreed on that right from the start. This was for us to get to know one another again, not about rehashing our difficult pasts.

Getting up for a walk, we wandered down the path that wound its way down to the sandy beach and left our boots by the edge. This was the first time I'd been able to enjoy the water or the beach since moving here. I loved to feel the soft, warm sand between my toes as we casually strolled along. We never saw another soul, and it truly felt like, for a short while, we were the only two people left on the planet.

"Thank you, Jake," I said.

We stood staring out at the water that seemed magical, like rolling diamonds, as each wave tumbled into the shore. Jake was standing behind me as I leaned into him, and I savored the solid wall and warmth that was him. Even his arms were wrapped protectively around me. Every time I turned around, I thought that no other moment could feel as perfect as the one we were in right now, and somehow he managed to make the next feel just as amazing.

"You don't need to thank me," he said, his tone soft as he moved my hair out of the way to kiss the side of my neck. "I want a million more days just like this one."

"I don't mean just for today, although I'm very thankful for what you did to create this time and space for us. I mean for everything. You've transformed my life seemingly overnight. Aside from the craziness that has happened with the tabloid this is the most alive I've felt in years. And..." I looked down trying to find the words for the nagging guilt in my heart. "And you waited for me, I wish I'd done the same. I know I can't go back in time and change the course of my life and as I've mentioned maybe we weren't supposed to happen back then. The thing is, you waited. You didn't marry or give up hope and..." Tears filled my eyes.

"Angel, stop." Jake softly kissed my lips. "Don't make me out to be some pinnacle of greatness. I was a straight up dick. I did an assortment of things that I cannot take back and...just no. I waited because I was too busy partying and getting drunk and was content to make money and not have any attachments. That doesn't make me great or wonderful. The point is, I'm just happy that you're willing to give me a chance. I want you to know the asshole version of me is gone. He jumped off the last yacht trip I was on and is still swimming in the ocean, and I'm determined not to be that asshole anymore."

Wrapping my arms around his neck, I pulled Jake down so I could kiss his lips. Breaking the kiss, I gave him the best teasing smile I could.

"I wouldn't change too much," I said. "I'm kinda in love with this protective badass version of you."

"Is that so?"

Biting my lip, I looked around and then slowly pulled him down to the sand. "Yeah, I really, really like it."

"Fuck, I love you." He captured my lips, and I held onto him a little harder.

BEST
FRIENDS

KAT

WHAT A DIFFERENCE one live and a couple weeks make. I stepped outside the bakery door and waved at the very long line of people who cheered like I was some sort of celebrity. Jake's impromptu live seemed to be bringing an entire town to my door every weekend, and I was going to have to hire someone to help me make more food.

This whole situation felt absolutely crazy.

I'd never been the type to dream about being famous or popular. So when people began flooding the store and gushing over me, I wasn't sure what to do. Luckily, Jake decided to spend the next few days in the store with me when he began to hear that his followers were going to come to town. I think he was wanting to help just as much as he wanted to run interference. He knew exactly what to say and how to act, which helped me to find my groove. I would've been lost without him helping all day. The customers also seemed to love seeing him in the sexy black apron I got for him. They were filming and taking so many pictures of us and the place that it felt like we should be on a reality television show. That may not be a bad idea.

I was riding a whirlwind. Time sped up so much that I couldn't do anything else other than bake and sell items.

"Hi there, everyone! Thank you so much for coming out to support me, but I've run out of sweets. Because of that, you'll get a fifteen percent discount if you give me your name and come back anytime in the next week."

The first person in line gave me her name, and I jotted it down on a notepad and did the same with the next person and the next. To be honest, I wasn't a hundred percent sure they were entirely here to see me or if they were hoping to get a sighting of Jake.

The sun started to set when the last person gave me their name. As I was locking the door, a delivery van pulled up out front. The young guy made his way toward me, so I let him inside.

"I have a delivery," he said and held out a small bag from the same jeweler that Jake had gotten the pendant from.

"Thanks. Did you need me to sign anything?" I called after the guy, but he'd already rounded the front of the van and was getting behind the wheel.

Untying the ribbon on top of the bag, I reached inside to grab the contents, and my fingers brushed against something brittle. Pulling out the box, I looked into the bottom of the bag. There sat dried petals of a flower. I dumped them out on the table and stared at what was left of rose petals, their edges crisp but their fragrance still strong.

Jake got ripped off if he paid extra to have it delivered with petals. Opening the lid of the jewelry box, I stared at the thin tennis bracelet coated in small diamonds. I ran my fingers over the delicate-looking piece before lifting it up and staring at it in the light. It seemed strange for a 'Jake gift,' but I snagged up the folded piece of paper lying next to the petals on the counter.

To my Rainbow.

Had to be Jake. He was the only one that called me that. It was certainly a pretty piece. I slipped it on and admired it as I twisted my wrist from left to right, watching it sparkle.

Packing up, I shot Jake a text.

L: Heading home. Hope all is going well with the builder. I can't wait to see theplans. I'm looking forward to giving you a very special thank you for all the giftsyou keep giving me. XO

J: LOL! I can't wait to find out what my special gift is. I'm almost wrapped uphere. See you at your place soon. Mom wants us to come over for dinner.

L: Sounds perfect. I can't wait.

J: Love you, Angel. I'm so happy that Olly is able to see you home. Be safe and

I'll be there as soon as I can. See you soon.

L: Love you too.

I didn't have the heart to tell him that Olly had to leave for a meeting that she needed to be away for the night so I had to walk home alone. He would've insisted that he leave the meeting with the builder and that I lock the door and stay put until he arrived. But, I hated the thought of him having to do that or for me to continue living like I needed a twenty-four hour bodyguard.

Putting the phone away, I headed home to finish cleaning up the last of the mess left over from the flood. The guys that had come to fix the pipe managed to get it stopped before everything was ruined but then had the task of pumping out the rest of the water. Now the trick was trying to get the moisture out of all the stuff touched by the water, and the baseboards and parts of the carpet had been very stubborn. It didn't seem to matter how many fans I ran all day, the place still felt damp.

The walk was brisk tonight, and I pulled my coat around me tighter as the dark clouds threatened that snow was just around the corner. I paused outside of Olly's Bookstore and waved to the girl working inside. It felt weird and lonely not having Olly around.

Jake's birthday was in two days, and Christmas was only four weeks away. For the life of me, I couldn't decide what to get a man that didn't need anything. I wanted to find a way to show him how much having him in my life meant to me. Romantic gestures had never been my thing. It was always Jake that was coming up with sweet and considerate ideas.

A headache started forming as I pushed my way into my small house. I was going to be sad to leave this place, but I wanted to move in with Jake. Sure, this wee spot felt like home, and it was great having Olly next door. However, it was time to move. Jake was at a meeting about building permits on a piece of property he'd owned for a few years and promised to show it to me soon.

I groaned, my head pounding harder as I tossed my phone and purse down on the kitchen island and took my coat off.

I needed a shower.

Flicking on the water, I quickly grabbed a change of clothes and then stripped out of my outfit. Taking off the fancy new bracelet and necklace, I left them on the bathroom counter before hopping under the hot spray. The water seemed to help the headache. It had receded to a dull thump by the time I was done. Drying off, I reached for the jewelry in the little tray, and when my fingers only came back with the bracelet, I looked around the small bathroom.

"What the heck?" I dropped to my knees, making sure to search the floor for the necklace, and then stood and stared in horror at the drain in the sink.

"No, no, no."

Leaning over the dark hole, I couldn't see anything, but my heart was pounding like a rabbit in my chest. Why had I left the little tray so close to the edge? I should've been paying more attention. I quickly put on the bracelet again and pinched the bridge of my nose to stop the headache from coming back. Hopefully, the necklace wasn't lost completely.

Jogging out to the kitchen, I grabbed my phone and tried to open the lock screen, but it remained black. I tapped the screen a few more times, but it still didn't turn on. I pressed the on-button, and nothing happened. Oh my god, my phone couldn't be dead. I thought I'd charged it at work.

I began moving to the other side of the island to get my charger when something shiny caught my eye, and I turned my head to stare at the back of a large silver photo frame that sat upright on the coffee table.

I looked around the small space and swallowed hard, the sound loud in my ears, which wasn't helping the headache that was back with a vengeance. Stepping toward the frame, I wracked my brain to remember if it was there when I walked inside. I couldn't remember if I even looked in this direction. It seemed familiar even from the backside, and the hair stood up on the back of my neck as I stared at the curly, ornate edges.

Like I saw my hand through the lens of a movie, I reached for the frame. My fingertips brushed the cool metal, and a shiver broke out all over my body. Swallowing down the fear, I gripped the frame, picked it up, and turned it around in one quick motion. The world narrowed in as I stared at my wedding photo with Richard. My brain screamed that this wasn't possible, but the voice that sounded behind me was all too real.

"Hello, Wife," Richard said, his voice making me spin. I clutched the frame to my chest like a shield. "I thought I'd bring the photo by and remind you who you are."

"How did you get in here?"

"I used a key. One that I had someone steal while you were busy with customers, of course. You were so distracted that you never even noticed my helper slip from the bathroom into the kitchen and return it as well. But alas, you never were that bright." He held up the key on a keychain and twirled it around on his finger. "Quaint spot," he sneered as he looked around.

"What the hell do you want, Richard? Just sign the divorce papers, and you never have to see me again. It's not like you ever loved me. What do you have to gain by dragging this on?"

"Why would I do that when you belong to me," he said and took a small step out from the hallway.

I looked over his shoulder to the bedroom and realized he very well could've been in the house more than once. I swallowed hard at that thought.

"I don't belong to you. I never did," I stood up straighter.

As Richard took another step into the living room area, I had to decide between the front door or the knives by the island. I was closer to the island.

The images of him grabbing me and throwing me as he had

before as I reached for the door handle crossed my mind. When I couldn't reach the handle, I made my decision and stepped toward the island.

Terror clawed at my throat as my muscles began to tremble, but I wasn't giving him the satisfaction of seeing me scared ever again.

"Did you really think I was going to let you go that easy? Oh, don't frown at me. You must have known that as soon as I found you, I'd come to collect what is mine."

Taking another step into the kitchen, I put the island between us. There was no telling what he'd do anymore. The last six months I was forced to be in the house with this man were like living in prison with inmates who all wanted to kill me if I looked at them the wrong way.

"I don't understand. Why do you want to keep me? All I was, was some glorified pet to you. Nothing more than something you could entertain yourself with by abusing me like some would a dog."

The smile that crossed his face was one that spoke of cruelty and what was to come if he got his hands on me. "I'd never kick a dog. They're useful, unlike you."

The fear clenched me like a fist in my gut, the feeling spreading throughout my body, and yet there was a sense of comfort in knowing that the day I'd been regretting was finally here. I'd been so terrified that this man would find me, and now that he had, I was kind of relieved about it. No more running, no more wondering when his disgustingly perfect face would show up at my door.

"Your insults and threats don't bother me anymore, Richard, so go ahead and call me whatever names you want. Call me stupid and weak and a simpleton. Call me terrible in bed and a whore that embarrassed you. Go ahead and call me the worthless bitch you wished you'd never married because none of it bothers me, not a single word," I said, taking another step toward the knives, but I never took my eyes off him.

"Yes, I see that, but where you're going, it won't matter anymore."

"What the hell does that mean?"

"It means that I've made arrangements for you to be hospitalized for the extreme depression that has led you to try and take your life. The depression that has made you strike out at me as well as your poor lawyer who was only trying to help you."

My brow furrowed, and my mouth opened, but I wasn't sure what to ask. The headache took another bite, and I had to suck in a deep breath and squint my eyes as they watered from the extreme pain that felt like something sharp was stabbing me.

"Does your head hurt?"

Richard took a step toward the island, and I held up my phone, my finger hovering over the dark screen, and hoped the bluff would work. "Not another step."

"Or what? Are you going to call your boy-toy? That thing you decided to fuck while you're still my wife," he snarled. "You made me look like a fool in front of my colleagues, and no one does that to me, Kate, so unfortunately for him, I don't think he'll be coming to help you anytime soon."

Fear of a different kind lanced my heart at Richard's words. "What the hell have you done to Jake?"

Richard held up his hand, and my necklace fell from his palm to hang around his finger. I watched it sway back and forth like he was trying to hypnotize me and knew for certain he'd been in the house while I was showering. The thought made me want to vomit. I'd spent years in a home with this man torturing me, and yet I never felt so violated as I did at that moment. Why hadn't I locked the bathroom door? I always locked the door.

"Were you looking for this by chance?"

His eyes cut through me, and I knew he was going to make sure he could torture me forever or kill me. Lust filled his eyes, and violence and the promise of pain burned behind it.

"Answer me, what the hell did you do to Jake," I asked and then stumbled slightly.

"Go ahead and call him," Richard said. "Oh wait, you'll need this." He slid the battery and little key for my phone across the island toward me.

He knew I couldn't call for help. He'd taken my battery. Oh, fuck, what had he done? Hands shaking, I opened the battery area and put the thing back together. I kept my eyes trained on Richard while I turned it back on and then opened it to Jake's number.

It rang four times and went to voicemail which only amped up the shaking that was taking over my body.

"Jake." My voice cracked with emotion as the answering machine came on. "Jake, Richard is here. He's found me, and you need to be careful, please, please be okay. I love you."

I pretended to end the call and put the phone in my pocket. I didn't know how long his answering machine would record, but even if it caught some of whatever Richard said or did was better than none.

"Aw, that was so heartwarming." Richard's lip curled up as he clutched the necklace Jake had given me in his hand.

I watched in horror as he squeezed his hand into a fist and then tossed the gold chain at me. I barely caught the necklace as it hit me in the chest. Tears welled in my eyes as I stared at the little rainbow that was now bent in half.

"Such a cheap piece of crap. You'd think that someone with as much money as he has would at least get you something nice. Then again, it is a cheap fitting piece that suits the cheap whore wearing it." He smiled as I glared. "Now that bracelet, mind you, that is quite lovely."

My eyes flicked up to his and then down to the bracelet.

"I see you are putting it together now. Yes, I got you the bracelet which happens to have something a little special on it to make sure you don't cause too much trouble when I take you out of here. Plus, seeing you in pain as it takes effect is an added bonus. Jake doesn't seem any smarter than you are, throwing your pet name around on social media like that...pretty stupid if you ask me."

That was why he hadn't been quick to grab me and why he'd been standing here talking and gloating. Gripping the bracelet with my other hand, I yanked it off and whipped it at Richard, which only made him laugh.

"Sorry, Wife, but you've had it on too long now, and you were nice enough not to take it into the shower with you. That would've made my plans a little more difficult if you had. I sent you flowers, too, with your favorites and added a black widow spider inside, but you didn't seem to get bit. Pity. That would've been funny. Killed by something that terrified you so much added a sweet appeal I just couldn't resist."

"You? Those were from you?"

I remembered texting Jake and thanking him, but as I replayed the conversation over, I realized I never thanked him directly. I didn't say, 'thank you for getting me the flowers.'

"Yes, and so was the photo of him kissing that pathetic blonde woman who was all over me. I dangled some money in front of her nose, and you don't want to know what she promised to do for me. I really did think you'd leave him after that photo came out. You surprised me, Kate."

All this time, he'd been in town. All this time, he'd watched Jake and me together and had been close enough to know my schedule and routine. My hand went to my stomach as I swallowed the bile threatening to come up. Stumbling backward into the sink, I felt my ass hit the counter as the room began to blur. No. No, I couldn't pass out.

"I have to admit, I've had a lot of fun fucking with you, though. This town, mind you, is annoying. I had to constantly talk to people and apologize, saying 'I was just passing through' and 'looking for directions.' Ugh, so nosy, but it was worth every annoying second. The dejected look on your face when you saw your shop had been broken into was divine, and I was kind of hoping the water would get high enough in the house that you electrocuted yourself. That would've been a fun way to watch you die. But seeing you in a padded cell, tied down to a bed for the rest of your life, seems just as satisfying."

Of course, he'd create a cover. Of course, he'd been prepping everyone for weeks. All this time, I thought he was still in Vegas, but no, he was right under my nose—watching every move I made. This couldn't be happening, my brain wanted to refute everything to protect itself, but I couldn't melt down. That was what he wanted. My phone began to ring in my pocket, which meant it had clicked off from Jake at some point.

"You better get that. It may be important," Richard said and smiled wide.

Pulling out the phone, it showed Eve's number. "You bastard, what have you done?"

He gave a noncommittal shrug, but his face was smug and practically glowing at his own sick amusement.

"Hello, Eve?"

"Oh my god, Kat. You have to get out of town. You need to run. Richard knows where you are." My eyes lifted to Richard. "Mr. Laverty, the lawyer I hired for you, he's dead, and Kat, there's a note that says he was fearful for his life. He named you as the person he was scared of, so now the police are looking for you as a suspect, and Kat, he...he burned down my home. I barely got out alive. He is completely unraveling. I never thought he'd go this far."

My heart hammered in my chest, and with each word Eve said, I became more determined not to let this man take me.

"Kat, do you hear me?" she yelled into the phone as the sound of a siren passed her.

"I hear you, Eve, but you're too late. Richard is here."

"What? Get out, get out now and fight Kat."

The phone clattered to the floor as Richard made his move. He rounded the corner, and in the hazed state my mind and body were in, I was barely able to avoid the initial grab. But with a scream, I brought my elbow across his face and caught him squarely in the nose.

"Bitch," he snarled as he staggered back. Spinning, I gripped the largest knife I had from the block on the counter and turned, swinging it like the unhinged person he claimed me to be.

"Get away from me," I screamed, hoping it would draw some

attention. Richard jumped back from the blade as it narrowly missed his face. "I'm not going with you. I'm never going with you anywhere ever again."

I took another swipe at him, and even though my arm felt like it weighed a ton and my actions seemed slow, I managed to nick the tip of his chin. A bright red line formed. I wanted to ruin more of that pretty face and swung again. Richard jumped back and grabbed his chin as a look of horror crossed his face as a second line joined the first.

"Didn't expect me to fight back?" I jabbed at him and narrowly missed hitting him in the stomach.

I never thought I could kill someone. Violence just wasn't in my blood, yet at that moment, I'd been reduced to a rabid animal that wanted to rip his throat out. He'd taken everything I thought was good about me away, and I thought that part of me was dead and gone forever until Jake found me. If he'd hurt Jake, or if he'd hurt Eve...

"I hate you!" The kitchen swam as my hand grabbed the counter to steady myself.Richard jumped at me. He slammed into me with the force of a bull and drove me back into the fridge with a bang so hard that it lifted off its front feet and slammed back down to the ground. Pain lanced through my back with the sudden abuse. I sucked in a sharp breath as fear danced before my eyes. I knew it was unlikely, but that was a fear I had to live with always now.

"Get off of me," I screamed, pushing at him with my free arm. God, it felt like rubber.

Richard slammed my arm against the fridge over and over.

"Drop the knife, you bitch. I can't wait to see you locked up in a ward you'll never get out of." His hand dug painfully hard into my wrist, and with a yell, the knife clattered to the floor.

"Never," I bit out, and even though I could feel my limbs weakening, I lunged forward and brought my knee up into his crotch.

The look on his face as my knee connected was something I'd cherish forever. He didn't let go, but his hands loosened, and I managed to wiggle away. Making a fist, I slammed it across his face and fell against the counter with my arm's momentum.

"Fuck!" he yelled and grabbed for his nose.

'Get away, just get away,' my brain screamed.

I pulled myself around from the trapped area of the fridge, but my movements were slow and just to take a single step was a struggle. Whatever he'd put on the bracelet was kicking in hard, and it was like staring through a wavering fog to see where to put my next foot. In the brief moment of quiet, other than Richard's groans, I could hear Eve screaming to let her go. I'd forgotten she was even on the phone when I dropped it.

"Eve, call nine-one-one. Call the Sheriff, call for help," I yelled as I pushed away from the island and could hear him coming for me.

I'd thought I'd known fear, but nothing prepared me for the sound of his footsteps as they closed in behind me. I grabbed the large frame off the coffee table, didn't even look to see where he was, and just turned to swing widely at him. The metal connected with the side of his face, and he yelled and then swore as the blood that already coated his skin smeared like abstract art with the impact.

I took three steps toward the door, with the sound of Richard swearing behind me. I screamed as his hand grabbed my hair, and the next thing I knew, I was flying over the coffee table. I hit the ground hard, but he seemed to move fast and was right there picking me up, tossing me like I weighed nothing over the island. I landed with a hard thump on the tile floor.

"You want to know why I married you?" Richard stomped around the island and reached down, hauling me to my feet. My back screamed as loudly as the screech that came out of my mouth. He shook me like I was a rag doll in his hands. "Do you?"

"Because you're a fucking piece of shit," I mumbled, my lips and tongue feeling thick.

I cried out as he used his forehead like he was in a soccer match and cracked me in the nose. It was like an explosion of searing pain erupted behind my eyes that would've brought me to my knees if he wasn't holding me up. The distinct feel of blood was running from my nose and dripping over my lips to run into my mouth.

"No, I married you because you were pathetic, and you still are. You were so easy to control and so naive." He tapped the side of my head hard. "Simple Kate, poor simple Kate that lived like a rat. I couldn't believe how easy it was to convince you that I loved you. You were nothing more than a joke that I decided to keep around because marrying one of those other girls, the ones my parents wanted me to marry. I'd have to pretend to love. They had powerful families that would've been pissed if their little girl had been damaged. You... I could treat you however I wanted and who was going to come to your aid? No one. Not then and not now," he snarled.

He held me away from him by the neck, and even though I couldn't see his face anymore, I could picture the evil look in his eyes and the vicious curl on his lips. It was his prideful look of victory burning in his blue eyes.

"Face it, Kate, it's time to put you back on your leash and lock you up in a pound like the rabid little dog you are."

The smack across the face hit me like a boulder, and Richard let me drop to the floor. Tears streamed from my eyes and joined the blood running from my nose, creating a small puddle. I could feel it hitting the back of my hands. I didn't even know if my eyes were open or closed anymore, and I didn't care. This was it. This was the way I was always meant to die. I'd just managed to hold it off for a little while.

Jake had let me see what it was like to be really happy, but it may have cost Jake his life. If it had, I would be happy to join him and end this because I couldn't go back, and I didn't want to live without Jake.

JAKE

TWO HOURS EARLIER

I LOOKED DOWN at the preliminary blueprints for the house I was planning to build for Lexi and me. The prints had been in the works for a long time, but there hadn't been any rush since it was originally going to be a house just for me. It seemed kind of pointless to rush building a nice home when I had no one to share it with, and I was home so little.

I'm sure I could've found someone to share it with, but the idea of living with anyone other than Kat, or I guess now Lexi, didn't hold any appeal to me.

"So, how long do you think it will take to complete," I asked Joe. The man flipped through a calendar and made some notes before looking up at me.

"It's too late in the year to break ground now, so you have until the end of January to make any final tweaks, and then as soon as the ground is thawed, I can start. That will also give me time to get the final permits in place. Complete and able to move, I'd say this time next year."

I nodded and then smiled as I stared at the rooms and the one labeled nursery. Kids wasn't a conversation that had come up, but I really wanted to have a few with Lexi.

"Thanks, Joe. I'll be sure to have the final version of what we want for that date."

Folding up the large paper, I shook the man's hand and headed to my motorcycle. Looking up at the sky, I groaned and knew that my girl was going to have to be put away for the season. I'd pushed riding my bike as long as possible, but the snow was ready to fly. Stuffing the map in a side pouch, I revved the motorcycle.

The world was full of twists and turns like one of the mountain roads I'd ventured. The next curve could bring you to the most beautiful place you'd ever laid eyes on, or it could be a steep drop. I'd been living my life hanging onto the edge of that steep cliff, and every breath could've been the last one I took as my fingers slipped. That was until the strange fortunes of fate placed her in my path once more.

My phone vibrated. It had to be Lexi.

Pulling out my cell, I opened the attachment. It was from an unknown number, and I growled under my breath as I hit the play button. If this was another defaming job, I was going to be pissed. As the video started to play, what was before my eyes made me long for another defaming scenario.

The video started inside Lexi's bakery, and whoever it was moved around in the darkened space, touching everything. But more importantly, I realized they were installing cameras.

"What the fuck?"

The video changed, and there was a series of still photographs that had obviously been taken from a distance, but they were clear enough to make out that they were all of Lexi alone or of Lexi and me together. That dangerous level of anger brewed in my gut and twisted everything inside of me. My hand tightened on the phone.

This was Richard's doing.

I knew it even if I couldn't see a face. My body shook, craving the taste of Richard's pain. But when the video changed again, a fear that felt like sub-zero temperatures ripped down my spine.

The video was taken at Lexi's place, showing me holding my Angel sound asleep while the predator was in our room. The message, 'It's time for Kate to come home,' scrolled across the screen.

"Oh, hell no." I tapped my wireless earpiece. "Call Lexi."

The phone just rang and rang. Glancing at the time, she should still be at the bakery. Hanging up, I tried a few more times until it became clear she wasn't going to answer. I revved the bike into gear, and stones flew in all directions as the wheels spun on the rocky driveway. As soon as the tires touched the pavement, I floored the bike until the trees were nothing more than a blur. Tapping my wireless earpiece again, I tried a different number.

"Call Karl."

"You have reached Sheriff Carr's voicemail. Leave a brief message with your name and number."

"Damn you, Karl, call me. This is urgent," I yelled into the speaker. "I mean nine-one-one urgent. Please, man...I need you."

As luck would have it, a police car pulled out behind me from a hiding spot by a big old sign surrounded by overgrown bushes. This was perfect. Whoever it was could reach Karl. I pulled over and slammed on the brakes sending more stones flying as the motorcycle fishtailed. It took a minute for the car to catch up, and I was already off the bike and walking in the car's direction but froze as the deputy got out with his gun drawn.

My eyes went wide as I put my hands up. "Whoa, hold on there. I need your help to reach Sheriff Karl."

"Get on the ground face first and put your hands behind your back," the deputy said.

"Didn't you hear me? I need you to radio Karl. I'm a...."

"Get down on the ground now."

"I don't have time for this." Turning, I marched back to my bike and ducked as a bang sounded. I spun around to see the deputy holding his gun, pointing it up.

"That was a warning shot, now do as I said and get down on the ground before I put one in you for real."

I looked at the bike and the ground, tempted to jump on it anyway and take off, but if I was dead, I couldn't help Lexi. I got down on my knees and tried to reason with the guy again. "This is a life and death situation. I need you to radio Sheriff Karl."

A second police car pulled up, and I prayed it was Karl, but it was a female officer. "Isn't that Jake Russell," she asked the first deputy.

"I don't know, but this is the bike from the BOLO."

"BOLO? Look, I don't know what's going on, but yes, I'm Jake Russell. I need one of you actually to listen to me and radio your sheriff, or I'm going to have you fired."

The deputy took an aggressive step forward. "Get face down on the ground now."

"Holy fuck are you hard of hearing or something? Am I speaking another fucking language? Did you not hear what I've been saying?"

"Get down now!" the guy yelled. My nostrils flared, and my jaw cracked as I tried to keep my cool. Getting shot wasn't going to help Lexi. Lowering myself to the ground, I stared at their boots.

"Check the bags," the guy said to the second deputy.

"Shouldn't we do as he asked? I mean, the Russell family has been here for years, and Jake is a local," she said.

"Thank god one of you has a brain," I bit out sarcastically.

"Shut up and stay still, or I'll shoot you. I don't care who you are." I wanted to bang my head off the pavement because, at this point, that action would probably get me further. "Now go check his bags."

"What are you looking for anyway," I asked.

"Like you don't know," the first deputy said.

How did someone so obviously stupid get hired on as a cop? Was the dumb, asswipe-meter not working the day this guy applied? I could hear the second deputy rummaging around in my bags, letting out a low whistle. I looked over my shoulder at her as she pulled out what had to be at least half a kilo of blow.

"That's not mine," I said.

"I'm sure. Cuff him."

"Call your boss, call him now," I yelled as the second deputy kneeled on my back and clicked handcuffs into place. I'd been arrested multiple times over the years, and how fucking ironic was it that I was being arrested now when I'd done nothing wrong.

The guy continued to ignore me as he clicked on his radio. "You can cancel the BOLO. I have the suspect in custody. The tip was good."

"Richard," I snarled as the confusion transformed into under-standing.

He'd set this up, knowing I'd try to stop him. Looking over my shoulder at the second deputy, that seemed to have some sense, I begged with my eyes. "Please, I'm begging you. A life is in danger. Call Sheriff Karl and tell him you have me in custody. That's not a huge ask. It's just doing your job, right?"

"Get him in my car. I'll take him back."

"I really think we should radio the sheriff," she said as she helped pull me to my feet.

"You've been on the job six months, and you think you know better than me? I said get him in the car, or I'm having you written up."

"Wow, dude, you really are a dick, or maybe just dirty. Either way, Karl is going to fire your ass," I said and was tempted to spit on him as the second deputy guided me to the car.

"I'm sick of rich dicks like you coming to this town thinking that they own the place and stirring up trouble. We don't want you or your immoral ways here, and with this much weight on you, you're going away for a long time."

I stopped moving as we started to pass the fucking dick. "You have a big ego and a tiny dick to go with it, which is why you act like a piece of shit to people. But let me make you a promise, deputy. If the love of my life is injured or dies because you wouldn't listen to me...." I leaned in as close as I could. "I really will need to go to jail for what I'll do to you."

"Are you threatening a police officer? Keep it up, Russell, and you'll never see the light of day."

And neither will you.

ONE HOUR AND THIRTY-THREE MINUTES, EARLIER

"Fuck you," I growled and I spit out blood on the floor. The blow had been solid and caught me across the jaw. Asshole had decided I was being too disruptive and thought hitting me would shut me up. All hc did was add to the charges I was going to bring against him.

By the time they had me fingerprinted and then trapped in a cell, I was past the point of no return with my blind rage and it took three of them to get me in the six by six. The fear for Lexi had taken on a life of its own in my mind, and every horrible scenario of what Richard could be doing to her was on repeat. Standing back from the bars, I lifted my leg and slammed my boot into the metal. The whole thing vibrated loudly with the impact.

"Let me out of here," I yelled, and my boot found the bars again. "You fucking idiots, I'll have your job, I'll have all your jobs. Lexi's life is in danger, for fucks sake!"

Slam, slam, slam, slam...

"Knock it off in there," the deputy yelled down the hall.

"Fuck you! If she dies, I'm coming for you, you piece of shit!"

Slam!

Each time my boot found the bars, I found a new obscenity to spew until I was sweating and had to stop to catch my breath. As soon as I could, I started all over again. If the deputy or any of the others in the cells said anything, it couldn't be heard over the commotion I was creating.

The door opened at the far end of the hall again, and I thought that it was the idiot deputy coming to give me shit. I was tempted to grab him and slam his face off the bars, but Karl walked into view.

"Jesus, Mary mother of God, what the fuck is going on down here," he yelled, his eyes narrowed and hands balled into fists. "Jake? What the...?"

"Finally," I gasped and gripped the bars, panting hard. "Didn't they tell you I was in here? Did you not get my voicemail?"

"No, what's going on," he asked as he pulled the keys from his belt.

As quickly as I could spit the story out, I told him what had happened from the time I got the video. The metal bars swung open, and the two of us took off at a jog down the hall and burst through the door into the common area for the officers. The three people that had been sitting there jumped to their feet.

"Grab your stuff," Karl said.

I pulled my leather jacket on and stuffed the loose shit into my pockets. Pointing at Deputy Dickhead I shot him a hard glare.

"Him, he's the one," I said, and if I weren't so terrified for Lexi, I would've been happy to see the smug look slip from his face. Karl's authority filled the room, and the deputy's eyes grew wide.

"Tom, when we get back, we're having a discussion. You better have a good fucking reason for not calling me and ordering the other deputies not to call me either." He held up his hand to cut off the man as he opened his mouth. "Shut it, not now, but if you did take money to do this...I'll find out, and you better start running and pray that his fiancé isn't dead, or I'm pretty sure he'll find a way to bury you."

Tom's eyes flicked to mine, and I let my 'I will kill you' expression speak for me.

"All of you, let's go!"

We ran for the cars, and I slid across the hood of the parked cruiser that was too close to the wall for me to easily run around. I quickly used the wall for leverage, and then jumped in the passenger side window.

"Really? You couldn't just run around the back like a normal person," Karl complained as he floored the car, and it shot backward out of the parking spot. Lights and sirens flicked on, and the tires squealed as we peeled out of the police parking lot.

As I glanced into the rearview mirror, the rest of the cars were just starting to catch up, but it didn't help settle my nerves. The highway took us straight down the main street, and as we crested the hill that led to Lexi's bakery and the road that would take us to her home, a silver sedan pulled out from where we turned. Karl put on the brakes to turn, but I grabbed his arm as I stared at the license plate.

"That's him. I know it. That's the car that was parked outside her house, and that's the plate number I'd given you."

Karl grabbed the radio. "Sylvie, head to twenty-nine Edgewood. Kick in the door if you have to, but tell me what the state of the house is."

"Ten-four."

The car directly behind us veered off as Karl took off after the sedan that was just passing all the stores. As soon as the driver realized we were heading their way, the car took off.

"Son of a bitch," Karl snarled. "Put on your seatbelt."

"What?"

"Now."

Grabbing the belt, I clicked it into place as the car ascended to faster and faster speeds. The radio crackled.

"Sheriff, there's been a struggle here. We have fresh blood, but I can't find anyone."

A crazy mix of relief and clarity that she wasn't dead in the house rushed through me but was quickly replaced with the fear that she was in the car with this man. He had her, but we were going to stop him. There was no other option.

"I'm going to kill him, Karl. I need you to know that he's a dead man. I don't care if you have to shoot me, but he's dying." I looked over at Karl, and he nodded.

I had no idea where our friendship would end after this or if I would even live, but I meant every word. My muscles were vibrating with tension and adrenaline as I pictured wrapping my hands around Richard's throat.

"Did you see that?" Karl said, pulling me out of my thoughts of blood and death. "There." He pointed, and just as he said it, I saw something strike out at the driver. In the dark, it was hard to tell if it was an arm or a leg, but it was definitely a person. The sedan weaved into the empty lane available for oncoming traffic before pulling back over.

"Oh shit. No Lexi, don't fight him," I said under my breath as I pictured the car wrapping around a tree. Every little swerve and jerk the car made felt like a miniature heart attack.

The car jerked again. A snarl of a sound left my mouth as the driver, who I knew had to be Richard, hit Lexi. The car picked up speed again, which I hated but was better than the swerving.

"Sheriff Carr from Sommerville County, requesting backup. I need a blockade on route fifty-two south. Can anyone assist?"

"Sheriff Carr, this is car L-180 and L-182. We are en route to intercept."

"Do you think he'll stop?" I said.

"He'll have to at some point. He'll run out of fuel, and with each mile we go, more cruisers will join in. Once we get near the city, I can request helicopter support."

A wave of relief washed through my body. He wasn't going to get away. We started up the hill that led to the bridge, and I could only watch in horror as Lexi came into view, her arms obviously hitting Richard. The car jerked wildly. Like a car performing a stunt in a movie, it swerved hard to the right, and I yelled as it suddenly disappeared through the guard rail into the water below.

My mind was caught between full-on panic and ice-cold fear as I tried to comprehend what had just happened. Karl slammed on the brakes as we reached the twisted metal of the guard rail, and I jumped out of the car. Without hesitation, I tore off my leather jacket, and ran full tilt toward the spot the vehicle had disappeared and was quickly sinking into the dark ocean water. By the time I dove in, the taillights were almost covered in the inky darkness.

"Jake," Karl yelled, but nothing was stopping me from reaching her.

The water swallowed me up into its black depths, the sudden shock of the cold a jolt to my already panicked system.

I swam for the car that was steadily sinking. Reaching out, I grabbed the handle of the car's passenger side, but it was locked. The roof was almost completely submerged when her face came into view. Our terrified expressions mirrored each other.

No, no, no. This was not happening.

I jerked hard on the door again as Lexi's hand hit the glass from the inside, her eyes silently begging me to help her. Terror like I'd never experienced before filled me.

"Jake! I love you," she yelled and then spat out water.

I kept a hold of the handle as the car began to pull me lower. Stuffing my hand into my pocket, I groped for the key to my bike. Gripping it like a set of brass knuckles, I pulled it out of my pocket and began to punch blindly and as hard as possible at the corner of the window where her hand was still lying. I pulled in a deep breath as my head was submerged below the water, and I could no longer see any movement inside the car.

I didn't try to fight being dragged deeper. If Lexi died, I was going with her.

Please, don't let her die.

That was all I could think of as my fist hit the glass again. The burning in my chest grew because I needed air. My fist hit once more on the glass, and by some miracle, it cracked. I could hear it clearly, so I hit it again and again until it shattered.

Pushing myself into the window, I could feel Lexi on my left, but she wasn't moving as I fumbled with the seatbelt. I couldn't tell if Richard was in the car or not. It was now too dark, and I only cared about getting Lexi out of there. The buckle finally snapped free, and it was tricky trying to pull her out of the car as it plummeted down, but I finally got her free, and we began the long journey to the surface.

Only the bright light of the full moon penetrating the surface told me I was heading in the right direction. It was unbearably quiet, with only my pulse filling my ears and my internal voice screaming for her to live and keep going.

Breaking through the surface with a gasp, my lungs filled with air. Pulling Lexi upright so her head was above the water, I leaned back and began kicking for shore. Another wave of panic hit as I realized we'd moved away from where the car had initially gone in the water.Every second counted.

With each stroke, we made it closer to shore, and my heart was pounding out of my chest. Lights and people were running toward the shoreline, but I could barely see the side of Lexi's face. She hadn't coughed or moved, and it was killing me. Hot tears ran down my cold cheeks as I tried to rein in the terror of losing her for good. There was a splash, and Karl was suddenly beside me.

"Give her to me. You get out and get dried off," Karl said as he gently tugged Lexi away from my weak arms as we moved toward the shore.

He carried her out to those that were waiting. She looked like a dripping wet rag doll as she hung between their arms and then was laid down on the ground. I knelt in the water, frozen in place by the cold and my shaking muscles now that she was on land. Karl grabbed my arm and pulled me out as he asked me questions, but I could only focus on Lexi's still form and those performing CPR on her. Coughing and shaking from the cold, I crawled across the rough surface and gripped her hand in my own.

"Please," I begged, my voice breaking with the emotion crushing me, threatening to destroy me. "Please don't take her," I said through the gasping sobs.

Turning my eyes to her still face, I willed her to breathe. Gripping her hand as tight as I could, I kept begging for her to take a breath and open her eyes. All I could see was how she smiled at me and how her eyes would light up when I looked her way. Someone was squeezing my shoulder, but nothing was going to fix this feeling in my chest.

"Please," I whispered and brought her cold hand to my lips as I closed my eyes and prayed. "Please."

"I've got a pulse," someone yelled.

My eyes snapped open, not sure that I heard correctly. I stared on as the officer I didn't recognize leaned over and breathed air into Lexi's lungs, and her chest rose. Her body convulsed once, and water flew from her mouth as she coughed.

"Roll her on her side slowly. We don't know what other injuries she has," the same man said, and thankfully they rolled her toward me.

Our eyes met, and I was unable to stay away. I crawled the rest of the way to her head and laid down so our foreheads could touch.

"I was—" She coughed, and more water came from her mouth. I immediately cupped her swollen cheek. "So scared...he hurt you," she said, her voice barely a whisper.

"Shhh, it's okay, don't try to talk."

"He...he..." She sniffed, and I realized she was crying. I ran my thumb across her cheek. "Kept saying he'd dealt with you." She closed her eyes tight, and a small whimper escaped her lips that broke me all over again. "I couldn't. I just couldn't if he took you...." Her eyes fluttered open, and her big blue eyes filled with more tears.

Laying my thumb gently over her lips, I tried my best to calm her as her body convulsed with the emotions forcing their way out.

"Shh, it's okay, you're okay, I'm okay. Look at me. I'm right here."

"Jake, the paramedics need to put her on a backboard and get her to the hospital," Karl said, and I looked up to see a dozen pairs of eyes looking at us.

"I'm not leaving her." My hand tightened on hers.

"You're not. You're going to go to the hospital with her. You both need to be checked out, and I've already called your family. They're going to meet you there."

I nodded and let go of her hand so the paramedics could do their job and roll her onto a bright yellow board. Karl helped me to my feet and wrapped a blanket around my shoulders.

"I need you to call her friend Olly. She lives next door. Jayce will have her number." As soon as Lexi was carried away, out of earshot, I grabbed Karl's arm as I locked eyes with my friend. "I need to know if he's dead."

"The divers will be out at first light. Now come on before you go into hypothermic shock or some other shit, and I have that on my conscience too. You gave me a fucking heart attack jumping off that bridge. Do you know how long of a drop that is? You could've broken your neck."

My strides slowed, and I looked back at the water. "Lexi living was more important than whether I lived or died, and if she'd died, it would be my body you'd be pulling up at first light," I said and turned back to face my friend.

This moment passed between us that couldn't have been put into words, but I knew he understood what I meant and what I still would do if Richard wasn't already a floating corpse. And in that brief look, I knew that no matter what I chose to do, he'd understand and turn the other cheek.

JAKE

I COULDN'T SLEEP no matter how long I lay here beside Lexi. I couldn't allow myself to relax. Visiting hours had ended long ago, and the nurses put up a good argument for me to leave, but finally, Karl had stepped in and told them that I should stay. He was camped out in the hall somewhere and refused to go home just in case Richard was alive.

The thought of that man possibly getting away unscathed...no, it just couldn't happen. He either needed to be dead, or I needed to make sure he received the punishment he deserved. I'd underestimated how much of a threat he'd been. Richard was the type that had gotten away with whatever he'd wanted for years, and it had made him bold and stupid.

Softly I ran my fingers through the loose strands of hair around Lexi's face. The monitor, although turned down, still showed a perfectly steady heartbeat. The doctor said she was lucky, and none of the previous back surgery had been damaged. Still, she had swelling and inflammation around her spinal cord and needed to remain quiet and on medication until they got it under control.

Her long eyelashes, which always reminded me of butterflies, fluttered open.

"Hey there, Angel, don't try to move. You need to lay still," I said, shifting as close to her as possible without bumping her body.

"Hey back," she smiled and tilted her head in my direction.

If it was possible, she looked even more beautiful. As soon as my eyes locked with hers, I could feel the emotion I'd bottled up and pressed down, clawing its way to the surface.

"Don't cry," she whispered.

I closed my eyes as she slipped her hand under my cheek. She was finally warm to the touch, and my body shook with the image of her being pulled from the water.

"I thought I lost you. When the car went over the bridge, my heart stopped beating." I kissed the palm of her hand.

"I couldn't leave with him, and he said he'd taken care of you. I thought he killed you, and...."

"Shh, it's okay, I'm okay, and you're going to be okay. The doctor says you just need to rest for a few weeks, and they'll keep you here under observation, but I'm not leaving your side." Leaning in, I gave her lips a soft kiss.

"Thank you for saving me—the car filled with water so fast after Richard put the window down. I tried to follow him out the window, but he drugged me, and with all the junk in my system, I couldn't seem to get the buckle undone. It was so cold and dark, and I started to panic and...." The monitor began to jump as her heart rate increased.

"Angel, look at me. You're not there; you're here in the hospital and safe. Please never thank me for saving you. If anything, I failed to protect you. I promised he'd never get to you, but he'd been playing both of us for weeks. I..." I closed my eyes and pushed the anger down for now. "I'm just so sorry." Pushing myself up, I grabbed the twin chocolate chip cookies the nurses left and tore the package open.

"Don't say that. I feel blessed. After everything I've been through, to even be alive right now is a miracle, and you did that."

My hands paused as I stared into Lexi's eyes. She didn't even understand just how amazing she was. She was an angel sent from heaven to save my heart before it became dark and jaded with a world that could be so cruel. She'd lived through so much pain, loss, and betrayal, yet she was still as sweet and strong as the day she first walked into the Jones' home. I remembered it so clearly. How I looked over from the video game, I'd been playing as the social worker brought her into the house and how instantly my world changed forever.

"What are you doing," she asked as I continued to stare at her in wonder.

"I'm making you something," I said, and she chuckled as I made a hole in the middle of the first cookie. Making a hole in the second cookie, I lifted her hand and held the cookie to slip onto her finger.

"I know I've proposed a couple of times already, but...the first time we did this, we were kids, and I meant it then, but at the time, I was a boy with promises I couldn't keep. Today I'm the man who has loved you since the day we met, and I intend to keep that promise if you'll still have me. The second time wasn't done right, so I'm going to try this again. Lexi, you're my twin flame, a soul that swirls and mixes with my own in a way that could never be put into words, but I feel to the core of my being. It felt like my heart stopped beating the day we were separated and only began to beat again the day I walked into your bakery."

Lexi was smiling wide, with little crinkles at the sides of her eyes, making her look like the angel she was. Clearing my throat of the clogged emotion, I continued.

"The moment you're out of this hospital and feeling well enough, I want to marry you. I want us to get married in front of my family and our friends, and then I want to take you to a few of my favorite spots around the world that never felt right to see without you. Will you marry me for real this time Lexi?"

She giggled as she smirked, her eyes shining in the dim light. "Of course, don't be stupid, now give me the cookie," she said, and I burst out laughing so hard that Karl came rushing into the room to see if we were alright.

"We're good," I said, still laughing. Karl wiped his sleepy eyes and left, closing the door.

I slipped the makeshift ring on her finger and placed the other on my own. Lexi held out her hand like she was admiring the most beautiful diamond in the world and then took a bite out of the side.

"I love you forever," I said.

"And I love you forever," she said as I laid down beside her once more.

41

JAKE

ONE MONTH LATER

LEXI WAS STILL RECOVERING SLOWLY. Walking and sitting up were the hardest parts for her, and her movements were jerky when she was worn out. But she was walking, breathing, and smiling, and I couldn't ask for more.

She'd had a few setbacks and would need another back operation, but she'd handled the news with a smile and grace like she handled everything else. She'd said, 'having someone with her who truly loved her made her want to live and get better as quickly as possible.' The fact that she knew I wasn't going anywhere and trusted me to help her meant everything to me.

However, I couldn't let her see it, but my heart broke when the doctor said he didn't think Lexi should carry a child. Her back had weak areas that may or may not ever be fully healed, and the weight of a child pulling on her spine was a real concern.

"Jake, I'm sad too, but we have options. We can use a surrogate to have our child but look at you and your family. You three boys are as close as any blood brothers, and you love Joy and Mark as if they were your birth parents. We could adopt and help change someone else's life. Heck, we can do both. I always wanted a big family, and it feels right to have that with you."

I had no idea how she managed to be amazing about everything. I certainly wasn't as understanding, but then again, her experiences over the last seventeen years had given her a different level of understanding when it came to the meaning of pain and setbacks.

My new favorite pastime was getting Olly to bring over the cheesiest romance novel she could find and reading Lexi chapters while I pretended to be both the main characters. I thought I was pretty good at pretending to be the sweet heroine, but she'd laugh until tears ran down her cheeks. There was nothing in this life I was taking for granted ever again. Every laugh or smile we got to share— every touch and whispered word of love was treated like the first and the last.

Of course, my family had made pests of themselves the entire time Lexi was recovering, but she seemed to love their hovering. When Olly and her mother, Marie, arrived at the hospital, Olly shocked me as she proceeded to hug me in a pint-sized bear hug.

"I'm so sorry I wasn't here, and I'm sorry I judged you so harshly," she said as she bawled like a baby.

I had no idea what to do, so I just hugged her back until she finally let go. Luckily, that seemed to have broken all the remaining tension between us.

My mom was still fighting her own battle, and even though she'd lost most of her hair and a ton of weight, you'd never know that she was ill when you talked to her. She refused to be treated like a patient and insisted on helping look after Lexi. No matter how many times Lexi and I told her not to, she'd do it anyway. If it weren't for knowing she wasn't my biological mother, I'd almost say she was because of how equally stubborn we both were.

Lexi's friend Eve arrived in town two days ago, which was good because I had some work that needed to be finished. I knew that while I was gone, Lexi would be cared for by four women who would fuss over her more than I ever could. They were like a pack of lionesses protecting her. Karl was the only one who knew where I was really going 'for work,' but to the rest of the world, I was doing a photoshoot in Dubai.

Leaning back in the plush chair of the hotel room, I stared outside at the setting sun and the bright colors of the beautiful landscape. Sure it was hot this close to the equator, but it truly was exquisite here. I hated that Richard had made it out of the car and worse that he callously left Lexi to drown, but I was also confused about how he managed to escape all the authorities looking for him. He'd managed to get to shore, run away and then flee the country. The man was a snake that had slithered away in the dark, murky water, but that was why I was here.

It hadn't taken very long at all for Richard's whereabouts to become known once the news got out of what had happened. People finally saw how sick he really was. I'd sat and watched a press conference of his mother speaking. Crocodile tears slid down her cheeks as she professed not to know a thing about her son's abusive ways. Not to mention, he was the lead suspect in the murder of Lexi's lawyer. I had no doubt in my mind that Richard had the man killed. Richard was too fucking spineless to do it himself, but I pinned him for the type that would hire someone to do his dirty work, and I was taking a page out of his book.

Thankfully, Lexi had avoided all news relating to Richard or the crash and simply wanted to leave her past where it was. We moved into the farm until our house was built and we not only had gates installed, but guards sat on the property to keep the disrespectful people with no boundaries at bay.

On the plus side, my followers set out on a mission to find 'the man' who almost killed Lexi and me. Some people made videos of their visits to the bridge I'd leaped off of to save Lexi, and I'd been contacted to make a movie about it, which boggled my brain. There was no way I was doing anything like that unless Lexi wanted it to happen.

Millions of people had banded together to find Richard, and it was then that I realized that the followers and posting content schedule had never been my problem. It was the lifestyle I'd chosen to live that was the issue. That fake persona I masked myself with was solely to impress people, and I grew to hate that life and myself. That had been a version of Jake Russell that didn't truly exist. Now I knew I could be an inspiration without living that lie, and so far, things were on a much better track.

As I heard the keycard slip into the door lock, a click sounded throughout the now-dark hotel room. The man of the hour stumbled in, his silhouette the only thing visible. He flicked on the light, and the spacious area instantly filled with fear. Richard stank of alcohol and depression—what a pathetic waste of space. His hair was a mess, his tropical shirt was half untucked, and the tail of it stuck out between the zipper in his pants like a colorful cock. The stench of his sweat slapped me in the face. Uhhh, he smelled horrible.

Richard reminded me of a stoned frog, with his eyes wide as they kept doing this strange erratic blinking. I half expected him to stick his tongue out and catch an insect.

"Hello Thomas, or should I say, Richard, which would you prefer?" He looked like a statue because his breathing seemed to have stopped. "I can see you're shocked to find me here, but you really shouldn't be that surprised. I mean, you did try to kill the one woman I've loved my entire life. You must've known I'd hunt you down." I forced out a hard smile, knowing the look would be cold because all I was focused on was killing him. "What, cat got your tongue?"

"H-How..." was the only word Richard managed to stutter out, his voice laced with the slow drawl that accompanied too many late nights that were fueled by alcohol.

"How doesn't really matter, does it? What's important is that I made a promise to a woman that I'd keep her safe and never let you near her again. You made me break that promise, and you almost killed her."

My hand clenched into a fist as I tried to control the building anger.

"How very manly of you. First, you try to crush the soul of an angel, and then you leave her in a car submerging into the deep, dark depths of the ocean. I'm not even sure how you live with yourself, but I also don't care."

"What are you going to do?" Richard licked his burned, cracked lips that screamed his lily-white ass wasn't made to handle long doses of this climate.

Placing my hands on my chest, I smiled innocently. "Me? I'm not going to do anything, but I may have arranged for something to be done."

Richard bolted for the door like the cowardly creature he was. The door whipped open with a bang, and then there was dead silence. The whole scene made me smirk because I knew my special hired friends were waiting to bring the sniveling snotbag back into the room.

"You know what is really great about you choosing to hide out," I asked as the men herded Richard into the center of the room. "More than enough people in this world will gladly do a job for money even if that job is not so scrupulous. Normally I'd say that's a bad thing, but when it comes to this particular situation, I couldn't be happier. As it turns out, the fact that you're off the radar makes my plans for you easier. So, thanks for that."

"Help, help me," Richard called out and then collapsed to the floor as one man's fist connected with the side of Richard's head. Blood dripped from the corner of his pretty boy face. For a man that boasted about how dangerous he was, he certainly didn't seem that way now. It amazed me how some men could act so tough when it came to hurting someone that was smaller or weaker than themselves but put them up against a greater foe, and they always tucked-tail and showed their true nature.

Picking up the thick envelope, I pulled out the divorce papers that my lawyers had drawn up for Lexi. The terms were very generous in all areas, and of course, there was no appendix forcing her to sign off on being suicidal. However, I added a spot that detailed everything he'd done and how he tried to kill her. That way, if she wanted, she could always look at it and know that it was official and she'd fought back and won.

Walking over, I squatted down, handed him the pen, and dropped the clipped papers onto the floor. "Sign it. Don't argue, and I will let you live. You give me any reason at all, and I'll simply have you killed right now." Richard stared at me and then reached for the pen. "Smart choice."

As soon as the last page was initialed and signed, I put the pages back into the envelope for safekeeping. "Alright, boys, do your worst," I said.

"What? You said you wouldn't kill me," Richard complained.

"Who said anything about killing you," I smirked as I reached out, closed the blinds, pulled the heavy drape into place to block out the world outside, and turned to watch the show. Fists and boots found their mark until Richard was a bloodied mess.

They hauled Richard to his feet, his body slack in their hold. Walking forward, I gripped his chin in my hand and stared into the eyes of the man that almost cost me my everything. "You'll never see the outside of where you're going ever again. Also, I've ensured that you'll be treated fairly and with as much care as you treated Kate."

"Please, don't do this," he mumbled through his split lip while blood dripped to the floor.

"I need to make sure you can never hurt her again, and as much as I'd love to slit your throat and watch you bleed out on this floor in front of me, I can't take the risk of being separated from what's mine. Killing you, although however unlikely, might land me in prison, and I can't have that happen. I'm sure you understand."

Taking a step back, I looked at my hand and the large silver rings I wore. With all the fury of a man possessed, I let my fist fly. Richard's head snapped to the side, sending blood and teeth flying before he went completely lax. I gripped his chin and lifted his head again, but he was out cold. Fuck! I wanted at least a second shot.

Letting his head drop, I sought out the man in charge of the small group. "You'll see that he never escapes," I asked as I walked into the bathroom to grab a towel. I emerged, wiping Richard's blood off my hand, but I took a moment to memorize the stain on my knuckles. He deserved so much worse, and that was exactly what he would get.

"Yes, he'll be given our very worst accommodations and our full attention, and he may find himself in the rough areas that do not treat ignorant Americans very well."

I handed over the thick envelope that held the large sum of cash I was paying to make sure Richard was given the extra special treatment.

"I'll send more next month. Be sure to let me know if he happens to have an unfortunate accident. There is always extra for unfortunate accidents that he manages to live through so he can have another."

The four men smiled and nodded as I left the room to let them take care of the man and the cleanup. I didn't know the specifics of what they'd do to him, but it really didn't matter because no one messed with my family. Ever.

BEST
FRIENDS

# Epilogue

KAT

JULY 4TH, 8:00PM

I COULDN'T BELIEVE how much my life had changed in the last ten months. It was like I'd escaped from hell and managed to find this paradise that I didn't think could exist. Eve decided to stay. She didn't have a home to return to, and her job allowed her to work remotely, so now I had two of the best friends a girl could ask for, and I'd inherited an entire family.

"Thanks for staying open and doing this for us, man," Jake said.

"No problem, the money you're spending is worth it. So you two were just married," the tattoo artist asked, never looking up from his work. Now that the buzz of the gun was no longer on my arm, it was kind of hypnotic.

"No, we're on our way to be married," Jake answered as the large burly man worked on his arm.

"Isn't it some bad luck or something to see the bride before the wedding?"

"To us, we've been married since we were kids. This is just making it official," Jake said and got a raised eyebrow from the tattoo artist, but he didn't say anything further.

"Well, in that case, there you go, you're all done," the guy said and stood to clean his tools.

Jake smiled as he looked at me, and I couldn't have kept the grin off my face if I'd tried.

"Are you ready to get married," Jake asked as he stood from the chair, looking every ounce of sexy as I knew he would. His black jeans and dress shirt made him look dangerous and set my blood on fire. He was the boy that captured my heart and held it, but as a man, he stole it for good, and I never wanted him to give it back.

"More ready than I have been for anything in my life," I said, smiling back.

Jake flipped his arm over and held it out for me to see. Lifting my own, I flipped my arm over and put it next to his. Tears of joy pricked my eyes as I stared at the song lyrics we'd decided on for our tattoos.

Once I was Lost.

But now I am Found.

BROOKLYN

If you like it dark and edgy then look no further. Brooklyn Cross has always had a deep passion for writing that stemmed from a wild imagination. When she is not busy typing away about the next character you will fall in love with, you can find her walking with her dogs on the farm and sipping a hot cup of coffee.

In addition to getting her degree in business she was highly competitive in the equestrian sport of dressage, with aspirations of an Olympic dream. She is an entrepreneur at heart and has coached and trained many of a riding enthusiast or their wonderful mounts, but always found herself drawn to writing full-time.

"Writing is what I love. I just want to be authentic with my characters. To tell a story that others can immerse themselves in and enjoy, but also relate too. If I can make you smile, laugh, cry, or your heart pound then I have done my job. To drop people into my worlds and for a short time have you live alongside my characters, is what I have always wanted."

CROSS

Below are the links that you can use to find me if you'd like to follow me on my social media platforms.

Book Bub: <u>Brooklyn Cross Books - BookBub</u>
Goodreads: <u>Brooklyn Cross (Author of Dark Side of the Cloth) | Goodreads</u>
TikTok: <u>Author Brooklyn Cross (@authorbrooklyncross) TikTok | Watch Author Brooklyn Cross's Newest TikTok Videos</u>
IG: <u>Brooklyn Cross (@author_brooklyncross) • Instagram photos and videos</u>
FB Group: <u>Crossfire - A Brooklyn Cross Reader Group | Facebook</u>